Praise for Patrick Redmond

'A dark and bloody tale which keeps the tension going right until the last page ... A superb, intelligent read – I can't wait for the next one' Joanne Harris

'The setting is genuinely chilling, and the atmosphere of menace and sterility riveting' *Daily Express*

'A skin-prickling page-turner' *Daily Mail*

'Redmond shows himself to be a scrupulously fair writer who refuses to stereotype his characters and views human behaviour with a high degree of compassion' *Financial Times*

'The lurking tension and twisting cruelty in Redmond's writing and plotting make for a hypnotic, compelling read' *The Bookseller*

'The ghastliness of the English class system lies at the heart of Redmond's creepy psychological thriller ... Du Maurier meets Patrick Hamilton' *Guardian*

'Powerfully evokes the terrible effects of cruelty and bullying, and the unravelling nightmare is sustained with suspense and pace' *Sunday Mirror*

By the same author

The Wishing Game
The Puppet Show
Apple of My Eye

About the author

Born in 1966, Patrick Redmond was educated in England and the Channel Islands, and studied law at Leicester University and the University of British Columbia in Vancouver. For eight years he worked as a solicitor at various firms in the City, specialising in international law. He now writes full-time. *All She Ever Wanted* is his fourth novel.

You are welcome to visit his website at
www.patrickredmond.co.uk

All She
Ever Wanted

Patrick Redmond

POCKET
BOOKS

LONDON · SYDNEY · NEW YORK · TORONTO

First published in Great Britain by Simon & Schuster UK Ltd, 2006
This edition first published by Pocket Books, 2007
An imprint of Simon & Schuster UK
A CBS COMPANY

1 3 5 7 9 10 8 6 4 2

Simon & Schuster UK Ltd
Africa House
64–78 Kingsway
London WC2B 6AH

www.simonsays.co.uk

Simon & Schuster Australia
Sydney

A CIP catalogue record for this book is available from
the British Library

ISBN–10: 0-7434-3029-8
ISBN–13: 978-0-7434-3029-6

Printed and bound in Great Britain by
Cox & Wyman Ltd, Reading, Berks

To Beti and David

Acknowledgements

Firstly, thanks go to my mother Mary Redmond, and to my cousins: Julia Davy, Elizabeth Skingley, Anthony Webb and Michael Webb for all their love and support.

Secondly, thanks to my friends: Michael Codner, Paula Hardgrave, Gerard Hopkins, Simon Howitt, Iandra MacCallum, Rebecca Owen, Lesley Sims, Theo Theodoulou and Russell Vallance for their constant encouragement throughout the writing process.

Thirdly, thanks to my editor, Kate Lyall Grant, and to all at Simon & Schuster.

Fourthly, thanks to my agent, Sheila Crowley, as well as to Linda Shaughnessy and all at AP Watt.

Finally, a special thank you to Gillian Sproul, simply for being Gillian Sproul.

Prologue

London, October 2004

It had been a long day. Remarkable too, in its dark, disturbing way. And for the two policemen heading this particular investigation it was still far from over.

'Do you believe it?' asked Tony Webb.

Nigel Bullen, tired but knowing that bed was hours away, gave a noncommittal shrug.

'This is twisted. I mean seriously sick.'

'Tell me something I don't know.'

They faced each other in the corridor, both clutching plastic cups of lukewarm coffee. Tony was smoking while Nigel, who had recently quit and was suffering appalling cravings tried to ignore the smell of tobacco. 'What about you?' he asked. 'Do you believe it.'

Tony blew smoke into the air. 'I'm reserving judgement. For now at least.'

'I bet the media won't. Two more hacks have been on the phone trying to ferret out information.

They're going to turn this mess into a bloody circus.'

'Can't blame them though, can you? It's a big story and they've got their jobs to do.'

'Just as we have.' Nigel gestured towards the room at the end of the corridor. 'Better get back in there. I'll keep leading. You jump in as and when.'

Tony stubbed out his cigarette. 'OK.'

They entered the interview room. It was spartan: white walls, a harsh overhead light and a table with recording equipment. Nigel had always found it a depressing place. 'Like a cell in a loony bin with the padding taken out,' he had once observed to a colleague. Now, as he considered the darkness of the story unfolding before him, the comparison seemed chillingly apt.

The suspect and a lawyer sat behind the table. They had been whispering to each other but now fell silent. A sign of guilt, perhaps, though Nigel had been in his profession long enough to know that simply being in the presence of a policeman could make even the most innocent of people feel they had something to hide. It was just one of the pitfalls of the job.

But it *was* his job. And he meant to do it.

Five minutes later and the interview was underway. 'It wasn't like that,' the suspect said for the third time. 'I swear it wasn't.'

'Wasn't it? That's how it looks to me and that's how it'll look to a jury. You see that, don't you?'

Silence. The suspect stared at the ground, looking pale, frightened and suddenly much younger. More like a child than an adult. The way suspects so often did when confronted with the enormity of what faced them. For a moment Nigel felt sympathy. Then he remembered the details of the case and the feeling vanished as quickly as it had come.

'Let's start again. Go right back to the beginning. And remember, I want to know everything . . .'

But he never would. Just as he would never know the true beginning of it all. A crime is like a carpet of emotion. A thousand different feelings weaved by a thousand different hands on a thousand different days.

And this one had been started many years earlier, involving people who, in the first acts of creation, could have had no clue as to the monster their crude handiwork would finally produce.

Part 1

Reinvention

Havelock: Essex Coast

September 1987

'Here comes another one, Tina. Are you ready?'

The little girl in the life jacket felt the dinghy rock as the wave rushed towards them. When it hit she let out a scream of excitement as cold water sprayed her face and filled her mouth with salt.

'Were you scared?' her father asked.

She shook her head. Nothing could scare her when she was with him. He would always keep her safe.

He grinned at her while around them other boats turned back into the shelter of the estuary. The wind was building and the water growing turbulent but she didn't mind. She wished they could sail out further into the North Sea towards Denmark and Russia and all the other places in the world her father had sailed to when he was younger. One day they would sail to them together just as he had promised her they would.

The sky was filling with clouds. He stared up at

them, looking completely happy. In the perfect world she had created inside her head that was how he always looked. Though only eight she already knew that things were rarely perfect. But if there were enough moments like this then she would be happy too.

A man on a nearby boat called out for them to turn back. 'Shall we do what he says?' her father asked.

She shook her head, watching as another wave raced towards them. Even bigger than the last and threatening to drench them completely. Not that it mattered. The waves could have been as big as houses and she wouldn't have cared.

But her father was steering the dinghy around. 'Suppose we should,' he said. 'You know what your Uncle Neil's like about his precious boat. The slightest breeze and he starts to panic.' Momentarily his face darkened, then it broke into a smile. 'Not to worry. We'll come out again soon. On a better day than this.'

She masked her disappointment with a smile as bright as his. 'Yes, Dad.'

'That's my girl.'

An hour later they walked along the harbour path. Boats bobbed on the river beside them but soon the tide would be turning, sucking all the water away and leaving them marooned on the mud flats beneath.

They passed Hodgsons Boat Yard where her father had once worked and the Sailors' Rest pub on the corner where he liked to drink. An elderly man sat at an outside table eating an early supper of fish and chips and watching her father with disapproving eyes. Having him beside her made her feel brave so she stuck out her tongue, causing the man to look away. She looked up at him, wanting approval but finding his attention focused on the water they had just left. She tugged his hand and he turned and gazed down at her. A tall, heavyset man with unruly dark hair and strong, hard features. Once she had heard a neighbour describe him as looking like a ruffian, but with her he was always gentle.

'Was I getting the evil eye?' he asked.

'Yes. But I gave it back for you.'

He bent down and kissed the top of her head. 'That's my girl.'

They followed the path as it turned and led into the town. One long, shabby central street dotted with shops and dozens of smaller roads running off it. They walked up the right hand side, passing Kendall Street, where her Uncle Neil and Aunty Karen lived, before turning into Ansell Street: two rows of drab red brick terraces built in the nineteen-thirties. Cars lined each side, occasionally double parked. The neighbours were always complaining about the lack of parking space.

They lived at number 19: a small house with a living room, kitchen and cloakroom downstairs and a bathroom and two bedrooms above. Her mother, a slim, pretty woman with dark blonde hair and a good figure was waiting for them in the living room.

'Hi, Mum,' she called out cheerfully.

'You're soaking, Tina. I told you not to get wet.'

'Don't be angry with her, Liz,' said her father. 'It's my fault, not hers.'

'Supper's probably burnt. You said you'd be back earlier.'

'Well, we're here now. We're not that late and we like burnt food, don't we, Tina?'

'Yes!'

Her mother looked tense. 'Tina, go and get changed. Quickly!'

Leaving her parents together she headed for her bedroom. It was at the front of the house with walls covered in posters of pop stars. A tiny desk stood by the window. Above it were two maps; one of the world, the other of Ireland. Her father had been born in a village in Connemara where he said the country-side was full of shades of green the like of which she had never seen. But she would see them one day. When she was older he was going to take her there, just as he was going to take her to all the other places he had ever visited.

In the centre of the desk was the diary Aunty Karen had given her for her birthday back in February. 'I used to keep a diary when I was your age,' Aunty Karen had told her. 'I wrote in it all the time. Things that had happened, poems and stories and anything else I felt like. I found my old diaries recently and had fun remembering what I'd done and felt when I was your age. Perhaps, when you're my age you'll look back and do the same.'

The diary was blue with her name, Christina Ryan, painted on it in white letters. Impulsively she picked up her pen and began to write.

I'm going to be a sailor when I grow up. I'll have a boat of my own and I'll paint it red and call it Firehorse and Dad and I will sail in it wherever we want and never turn back, not even if there are the worst storms in the world.

Someone was shouting outside. Old Mr Jones from across the road was angry because his car was blocked in. As he waited for the offending vehicle to be moved he saw her in the window and waved.

Her mother was calling. Closing her diary she began to change her clothes.

Dinner was burnt, just as her mother had feared. Charred sausages, rock hard potatoes and blackened peas. She covered them in ketchup to improve the taste.

'Don't use so much,' her mother told her.

'Leave her alone,' said her father while doing the same.

'I'm just saying . . .'

'Well don't. It's only ketchup' He went to fetch a beer from the fridge.

'A bit early for that,' her mother observed.

'It's just one for Christ's sake.' As he spoke Tina heard the Irish lilt in his voice. He had come to England when only ten but traces of the accent still remained. As he sat down again he took a swig of beer while staring at her mother as if defying her to say something. Instead she pushed food round her plate, her expression thoughtful.

'I saw Irene Clark today,' she said eventually.

He nodded.

'She works in the supermarket and was saying they're looking for more people.' A pause. 'So I was thinking . . .'

'I can guess.'

'It's a job, Pete.'

'Sure it is. Putting tins on shelves. Who wouldn't want to do that all day?'

'We need the money. I've asked Mr Rennie if I can work more but it's not possible at the moment.'

Mr Rennie was a local solicitor for whom her mother did part-time secretarial work. He wore shiny black suits and walked with his toes pointing outwards. Her father used to do impressions of him, likening him to a penguin. They made her laugh, though sometimes she felt guilty because the previous year, when her father had been in trouble, Mr Rennie had been the one to sort things out.

'Irene's boss will be in the shop tomorrow morning. You could go and talk to him.'

He gulped down more beer. 'Excited about school, Tina?'

'No. I wish the holidays weren't over.'

'You have to go to school,' said her mother.

'But it's boring.'

'You still have to do it. Sometimes we all have to do things we don't want to do.' As she spoke her mother watched her father continue to sip beer while a motorcycle raced past the house, the rider revving the engine and whooping with excitement.

'Will you see him, Pete?'

'Maybe.'

'Please. We really need . . .'

'I said maybe. Don't nag.'

'I don't mean to.' Her mother reached across the table and touched her father's arm. 'I'll get pudding. Ice cream and peaches.' A nervous laugh. 'Even I can't burn that.'

As her mother stood at the sink Tina caught her father's eye. 'Don't argue,' she mouthed. 'Please, Dad.'

He picked up a ketchup-covered potato and tapped her on the nose with it. 'Don't worry,' he mouthed back. 'Everything's fine.'

Her mother returned to the table. 'Tina, what have you got on your nose?'

'Ketchup.'

'Well, wipe it off.'

'Yes, funny face,' joined in her father. 'Wipe it off this instant.' He winked at her. She winked back and did as she was told.

*

The following morning she walked to school with her cousins, Adam and Sue.

All three attended the primary school at the top of the high street. Ten-year-old Adam was two classes ahead of her and seven-year-old Sue was one class behind. Both were small and dark and resembled their mother, Aunty Karen, who was going to the Post Office and walking part of the way with them.

They were making slow progress. Sue was trying to avoid stepping on a single crack in the pavement. 'Can't you walk a bit faster?' Aunty Karen asked.

'No, Mum. It's bad luck. Everyone knows that.'

Adam pointed to a sweet shop across the road. 'Mark Fletcher nicks stuff from there.'

'No, he doesn't, Adam. He's just trying to impress you.'

'He does. He nicks loads of stuff. Last week he nicked two singles from Rocking Sounds. He says it's easy 'cos the punk girl who works there is too stoned to notice.'

'Adam!'

'Well, she is. He also nicks condoms from Boots to make water balloons.'

'What are condoms, Mum?'

'Nothing, Sue. Just keep avoiding the cracks.' Aunty Karen looked at the traffic. 'There was an accident on the Melchott road first thing,' she told Tina. 'Uncle Neil heard about it on the radio. I hope he's not held up. He's got a meeting at ten.'

Uncle Neil was Tina's mother's brother. He worked in a bank in Melchott; the nearest town of any size and home to the comprehensive school all three of them would one day attend. He had recently been promoted and talked about it all the time. Her father told her that if Uncle Neil's head grew any bigger it would explode. He did wonderful impressions of Uncle Neil, though she had never told anyone else in the family for fear they would be upset.

'You're quiet this morning,' observed Aunty Karen. 'Not looking forward to school?'

'Not really.'

'Mrs Abbott, your new form teacher, is very nice. You liked her, didn't you, Adam?'

'No. She was a real bitch.'

'What's a bitch, Mum?'

'Watch out, Sue. There's a crack.' Aunty Karen glared at Adam. 'And a certain person will get a crack himself if he doesn't watch his language.'

They approached the supermarket. 'Dad's going to work there,' Tina told them.

Aunty Karen looked surprised. 'Really?'

'He's going to see them about a job today. Well, Mum said he should see them.' As they passed by she looked through the windows at the staff in their dreary blue uniforms. She tried to picture her father wearing one but couldn't. Perhaps Aunty Karen couldn't either.

But if he didn't get a job there would be arguments. Bad ones.

Suddenly she felt scared; remembering what had happened the last time the arguments had been bad. She didn't want that to ever happen again.

Aunty Karen smiled reassuringly. 'I'm sure he will see them, Tina. It's just a job, after all. If he doesn't like it he'll find one he does soon enough.'

'And if he does work there,' added Adam, 'we can nick stuff.'

'Adam!'

Sue stepped on a crack and howled. 'Now I'm going to have bad luck.'

'You certainly are. I'm about to beat your brother to death.'

'That's good luck, Mum.'

Aunty Karen burst out laughing. The sound was infectious and soon Tina was laughing too and telling herself that everything would be all right.

And it was.

Her father saw the people at the supermarket and got a job starting the following Monday. He told them about it at supper that evening. Her mother was pleased, talking about how useful the money would be. She was pleased too but when she tried to describe her day her mother didn't seem interested. She told herself it didn't matter. Her father's job was the important thing. New timetables and seating arrangements were nothing compared to that.

The week passed quickly. She settled back into the

school routine and decided that she liked her new teacher. Philippa Hanson, the prettiest girl in the class, had modelled dresses for a catalogue and brought in a copy to show them. 'I'm going to be a proper model when I grow up,' she boasted. 'The photographer said I was a real stunner.' Tina said she'd like to be a model and Philippa said that ugly people with red hair couldn't be models. One of the boys told her she was pretty and then asked to copy her answers in the maths test which she let him do in return for some sweets.

She spent Friday night at Uncle Neil's who was away on a course so Aunty Karen let them stay up late and watch a ghost story on television. 'On condition you don't have nightmares,' Aunty Karen told them before watching the whole thing through her fingers. 'You're a real wimp, Mum,' observed Adam. 'I've seen much scarier stuff than this at Mark Fletcher's. We saw one film where a man had knives instead of arms and went round killing people snogging in cars.' He was just describing a particularly gory scene when the ghost burst onto the screen making Aunty Karen scream and the rest of them shriek with laughter.

On Sunday afternoon, after reading a book in her bedroom, she came downstairs to find her mother cleaning in the living room.

'Where's Dad?'

'Gone for a walk.'

'Why didn't he take me?'

'Probably didn't want to.' Her mother was dusting a set of china figurines that stood on the mantelpiece. They had been a wedding present from her father. Her mother was very proud of them and cleaned them constantly.

'Why not?'

'I don't know. I'm not a mind-reader.' Her mother's tone was irritable, just as it always seemed to be.

'I've finished my book. Mrs Abbott thought it would be too difficult for me 'cos it's meant for eleven year olds but I read it all.'

Silence. She was hoping for praise but her mother kept dusting.

'Mrs Abbott says my English is really good. We had to write stories and she said mine was the best. Do you want to read it?'

'Later.'

'I could read it to you.'

'Not now, Tina.'

'It's not very long. Only two pages. It's about . . .'

'Tina, I'm busy and the last thing I need is you under my feet.'

'Sorry, Mum.'

She left the house and made for the waterfront, hoping to find her father. It wasn't difficult. He was sitting in his favourite place; the bench at the end of the harbour path, smoking a cigarette and staring down the estuary towards the sea.

'Hi, Dad.'

18

He didn't answer. Seemingly too wrapped up in thought to notice her. She tapped his arm. He turned, saw her and smiled.

'Hi, you.'

She sat down beside him. 'Mum's cross with me.'

'Why?'

'She was cleaning and didn't want to hear my story.'

'You know what she's like about cleaning. Woe betide the person who disturbs her when she's holding a duster.' He took a drag on his cigarette and blew smoke into the air. His hands were big and powerful. Sometimes he got into fights and his knuckles would be bruised but he always gave better than he received.

'Dad?'

'What is it, funny face?'

'Are you cross with me?'

'Why should I be?'

'Because when you went for a walk you didn't take me.'

He put his arm around her. 'That doesn't mean I'm cross with you. Sometimes grown-ups like to be on their own. That's all.'

'Do you want to be on your own now?'

'No, not now.'

She leant against him, feeling the warmth of his chest. A wind blew off the water. It was growing colder and though the tide was in there were few boats on the estuary. The sailing season was coming to an end. But there would be other summers to enjoy.

She thought back to the previous summer. The arguments had been bad then. So bad that one evening her father had stormed out of the house and stayed away for a week without a single phone call. She had begun to believe that he would never come back until one day he had met her at the school gates with a smile on his face and presents in his arms. That had been a good day. The best of days.

But she didn't want to live through another like it again.

'Are you scared about your job?' she asked him.

'Why should I be scared?'

'Because it's new. I was scared last week about being in a new class and having a new teacher but now I like it. And we can walk there together 'cos it's on the way to school. Maybe Mum will let me wait for you so we can walk home together too.'

He stroked her hair. It was cut short, like a boy. 'You want to look after me, do you?'

'Of course. I love you, Dad.'

For a moment a troubled look came into his eyes. Then it was gone and his smile was as bright as ever. 'I love you too, funny face.'

'I've got an ugly face and horrid hair. Monkey face ginger nut. That's what the girls at school say.'

'They're just jealous.'

'No they're not.'

'They will be one day. Your hair's auburn like my mother's was. You've got her face and her green eyes

20

too. When she was your age people told her she was ugly but when she grew up she left broken hearts wherever she went.' He kissed the top of her head. 'Just like you will.'

She remained pressed against him, listening to his heartbeat and the soft rustle of chest hair against the fabric of his shirt. He smelled of tobacco, strength and the sea. Her Dad. The person who loved her best in the world. The only one who could banish all her fears and make her feel totally safe.

'Everything's all right, isn't it, Dad? It is, isn't it?'

'Everything's fine, funny face. Don't worry anymore. Everything's fine, I promise.'

They stayed like that for some time, him stroking her hair as they watched the last boats of summer bobbing in the breeze.

The next morning she woke to see the sun creeping through the curtains and filling her room with light. Stretching, she turned to look at the clock on the bedside table. She had to be up at half past seven and hoped it was earlier so she could carry on lying there, preparing herself for the day ahead.

But it was ten to eight.

She felt confused. Her mother always knocked on her door to check she was up. Why hadn't that happened today? What was going on?

Rising from her bed she walked out onto the landing. 'Mum? Dad?'

Silence. The house was still. Perhaps her parents had had to go out. Perhaps her mother was expecting her to prepare herself for school and would be angry if she hadn't done so on their return.

She washed her face and hands and put on her school uniform. Then she made her way downstairs, only to realize that the house wasn't silent after all. From the living room came the sound of sobbing.

Alarmed, she hurried in. Her mother was sitting on the sofa, wrapped in a dressing gown, her hair uncombed and her eyes red from crying.

'Mum, what's wrong?'

No answer. Her mother just carried on crying as if she were not there.

'Mum!'

Still nothing. Her eyes scanned the room and came to rest on the coffee table. A note lay in the centre. She picked it up and recognized her father's handwriting.

Three short lines. That was all he had left them.

I've tried but it's no good.
I'm suffocating here and I can't stay.
I'm sorry.

She read them once then tried to read them again. But suddenly she was unable to make sense of their meaning; her brain refusing to process the information they contained.

'He's gone, Tina.' Her mother's voice. Thick with tears and raw emotion.

She shook her head.

'You've read it. You see what he says.'

'It's just words.'

'It's goodbye.'

'He'll come back.'

'No, he won't.'

'He will. He did last time.' She swallowed. 'He has to.'

Her mother wiped her eyes. 'Go to school.'

'But he will come back. He will, Mum. I know he will.'

'Go to school.'

'But Mum . . .'

'Go to school! I don't want you here! Get out and leave me alone!'

As she hurried up the street she told herself that everything would be all right. That he would be waiting for her at the end of the day with a smile on his face and presents in his arms, just as he had the last time.

But he wasn't.

The days that followed passed in a blur. She sat through her lessons, trying to concentrate but hearing nothing. Her evenings were spent at Uncle Neil's. Aunty Karen made a fuss of her, cooking all her favourite meals. Uncle Neil was rarely there. 'He's keeping your Mum company,' Aunty Karen explained. She tried to argue that she could do that but Aunty Karen said it wasn't necessary. 'Sometimes grown-ups need to be with other grown-ups, Tina. It's only for a little while and then you can go home again.'

'Will Dad be back by then?'

'I don't know.'

'He will.' She spoke decisively, then looked to Aunty Karen for reassurance.

But none came. Just a gentle smile. 'Eat your tea, Tina. Don't let it get cold.'

The week ended. She returned to her mother but her father stayed away. She tried not to be afraid. He had gone away before but he had returned, just as he would this time. All she had to do was be patient.

And so time passed; days growing into weeks and on into months. Still she waited and still he did not come.

A wet evening in November. She sat with her mother in the kitchen, eating stew that had been reheated from the previous day. She didn't like stew but ate it anyway, wanting to make her mother happy.

Not that her mother seemed to like it either. She just picked at it, looking tired and drawn. She was working full time for Mr Rennie now they no longer had her father's earnings to rely on. But they would do soon. When he came back to them.

Tina tried to make conversation; talking about a school project on the history of sailing. 'We have to make ships. There's going to be an exhibition at the end of term and I'm making a Viking longboat.'

Her mother lit a cigarette. 'That sounds fun,' she said half-heartedly.

'It is. I told Mrs Abbott how Dad likes the Vikings and that it's going to be a present for him when he comes back.'

'Tina . . .'

'He *is* coming back.'

'How do you know that?'

'I know he wouldn't go away and not come back.'

'Then you don't know him at all.'

'He promised me . . .'

'What did he promise?' Her mother's tone was harsh. 'That everything would be all right? That there was no need to worry? I've heard those promises too, more times than I can remember, and the one thing they taught me is that his promises don't mean anything.'

'They do! He wouldn't just say them. Not to me.'

'You think you know him better than me, do you? Even though you're just a child and I'm an adult who knew him long before you were even born?'

Her mother's voice was growing shrill. She didn't want to be shouted at. Not when she was starting to feel scared. 'No, Mum. Sorry.'

'Have you finished your food?'

'Yes.'

As her mother gathered up the plates she remained at the table, staring into the living room and the window that looked out onto the street. The curtains were drawn but she could hear the footsteps of people passing by outside. At school she had learned that no one in the world had the same fingerprints. The same was true of footsteps. She could have identified her father's in a crowd of thousands. She listened now but could not hear them.

But she would do soon. She was sure of it.

Or at least she wanted to be. But the fear wouldn't go away.

Her mother washed dishes at the sink. She walked towards her. 'Can I help?'

'I'm fine.'

'I could dry.'

'They can drain. Haven't you got homework?'

'Yes.'

'Then go and do it.'

She knew she should. She didn't want to make her mother angry. But she didn't want to be alone either. Not when fear clung to her like a leech, trying to suck away all her hope.

Impulsively she put her arms around her mother's waist, hugging her. Aching to be hugged back. To feel loved. To feel safe.

For a moment her mother responded. Then she felt herself being pushed away.

'Go and do your homework, Tina.' The tone of voice did not allow for protest.

'Yes, Mum.' Meekly she did as she was told.

'I know where your dad is,' said Philippa Hanson.

'Where?'

'In jail.'

It was a cold, dark December afternoon. She sat with the rest of her class, working on their ships for the school project. Mrs Abbott had left them alone after making them promise to work in silence.

'He's not! You shut up.'

'Or what? Going to hit me with your ugly stick?'

'I'm not ugly.'

'Yes you are.' Philippa began to laugh. 'Look everyone. She's going to cry.'

'I'm not!'

'Crybaby. Just because your dad's in jail.'

'He's not!'

'Where is he then?' asked someone else.

'He's . . .' She struggled to think. 'He's on his ship.'

'They don't have ships in jail,' sneered Philippa, 'and that's where he is. Best place for him, that's what my mum says. She says he's a waste of space. So does my dad. They both hate him. Everyone hates him just like everyone hates you.'

'They don't. Shut up!'

'My dad says he's a thug,' added Stuart Scott. 'He hopes he never comes back.'

'Well he will and then you'll be sorry.'

'No he won't. They're not going to let him out of jail just because you start crying.' Philippa began to clap her hands. 'Cry! Cry! Cry!'

27

She shook her head, sticking out her chin, trying to be brave. But others joined in the chant and her lip was starting to tremble.

The classroom door burst open. Mrs Abbott marched in, looking angry. 'What's all this noise? I told you to keep quiet.'

Silence descended like a blanket. Mrs Abbott folded her arms. 'Well?'

Still silence, except for a nervous giggle from someone at the back. Mrs Abbott continued to look angry. 'Philippa, have you been picking on Tina again?'

'No, Mrs Abbott.'

'No she hasn't, Mrs Abbott,' chorused two of Philippa's friends.

'Has she, Tina?'

Tina stared down at her desk, not trusting herself to speak.

'Tina?'

She looked up. Everyone was watching her. Philippa's gaze was challenging, as if to say 'tell tales on me and see what happens.'

'No, Mrs Abbott.'

'Carry on with your work, all of you. In silence!'

She focused her attention on the longboat she was building. It was going to be good. The best in the class. Her dad would be proud of her when he saw it. When he came back.

A tear trickled down her cheek. Sensing others still

watching she wiped it away and smothered those that threatened to follow.

Christmas Day. She sat with her mother in the living room of Uncle Neil's house, watching Adam and Sue open their presents.

The floor was covered in brightly coloured paper. Aunty Karen was gathering it up, checking for tears. 'Don't rip it off like that,' she told Adam.

'Why not? It's just paper.'

'Expensive paper that could be used again.'

'It's not expensive, Mum. You got it from the market where it's only a quid for twenty sheets. Mark Fletcher says you have to go to the posh card shops to buy expensive stuff.'

'Or steal it in his case, no doubt. Who wants more Christmas cake?'

'I do,' Adam told her.

'Please would help,' said Uncle Neil who was sitting in a chair by the corner, reading the autobiography of an eminent businessman and wearing a blue sweater, both of which had been presents from Aunty Karen. He was slim like his sister and had the same dark blond hair that was now starting to recede.

'I'd like some, *please* Mum,' said Sue smugly while examining the contents of a 'Glamorous Miss Make-Up Kit'.

'What about you, Tina?' asked Aunty Karen. 'Go on. I made it myself.'

'OK. Thanks.'

Aunty Karen went to the kitchen. Tina looked at the small pile of her own presents that lay on the floor beneath her feet. A skirt from Aunty Karen and Uncle Neil, a game from Adam and Sue and a book of fairy tales from her mother. It was a book she had already read but she hadn't liked to tell her mother that.

'Look, Tina,' cried Sue, holding out a bright pink purse. 'This was in my stocking.'

She nodded, trying to look pleased. There had been no stocking for her this year. Her mother had been too busy to prepare one. She told herself it didn't matter. That there were more important things than presents to think about.

Her eyes kept darting towards the hallway, waiting for the knock that would signal her father's return. She knew he would come. He would not miss Christmas. Not when she was waiting for him.

What if he goes to our house instead? What if he doesn't think to come here? What if he doesn't come at all?

But she wouldn't allow herself to consider that even for a moment. Not when she had a present wrapped and waiting for him. Not when she had a million things to tell him. Not when she thought about him every second of every day.

Does he think about me? Does he miss me like I miss him?

Aunty Karen reappeared with the cake. Adam

examined an electronic game and complained because it didn't contain batteries. 'How am I supposed to play it without them?'

'They told me the batteries were in there,' Aunty Karen told him.

'Well they're not. What a waste of time.'

'A bit more gratitude young man,' said Uncle Neil sternly. 'When I was your age I didn't get half as many presents but still managed to be twice as grateful.'

'You did, Dad. You told me you got your train set the same year you got a new bike and they must have cost at least twice as much as this lot.'

Aunty Karen burst out laughing. Uncle Neil frowned. 'Whose side are you on?'

'Yours, and stop fussing, Adam. I'll get you batteries next week. Try opening the present with red paper. You won't need batteries for what's in there.' She turned to Tina. 'You're not eating your cake. Is it too dry?'

'No, it's lovely.' She took a bite to show willing. The icing was sweet and the filling moist. It was a good cake. A very good cake. But she didn't want cake. She wanted her Dad. She tried to swallow but couldn't. A lump had formed in her throat. Choking, she dropped her plate, spraying cake everywhere.

'Tina!' shouted her mother. 'What are you doing?'

She rose to her feet, ready to tidy up.

'Stay where you are. Leave things alone. You'll just make a mess like you always do.'

She sat down again. Aunty Karen came to sit beside

31

her. 'It doesn't matter,' she said soothingly. 'If you can't make a mess at Christmas then when can you?'

'I'm sorry.'

'It doesn't matter, Tina. Really it doesn't.' Aunty Karen gave her a hug. She tried to respond but she didn't want a hug from Aunty Karen. She wanted one from her mother.

Or her father. She wanted a hug from him more than all the presents in the world.

Sue was showing Uncle Neil the different colours of eye shadow in her make-up set while Adam continued to tear open presents and leave paper scattered across the floor. Both of them looked happy, as did Uncle Neil and Aunty Karen, while her mother sat beside her on the sofa acting as if she would rather be somewhere else.

She hates it here. She hates being here without Dad. And she hates me too.

She picked up the book of fairy tales and pretended to read, hoping her mother would notice and be pleased. But her mother just stared into space and noticed nothing.

Don't let her see you're upset. Don't make her angry. Not today.

She swallowed a mouthful of cake and prepared to eat another, smiling as brightly as the others, masking all the darker emotions that raged beneath.

Come back, Dad. Please come back. I'm trying to be brave but it's hard and I can't wait much longer.

*

32

January 1988.

'I'm worried about Tina,' Karen told her husband.

'She's all right. She's got her mother.'

'Has she?'

Neil put down his newspaper. The two of them were in the same living room where three weeks earlier they had celebrated Christmas. 'What do you mean?' he asked.

'You know what I mean.'

'If Tina's upset it's not Liz's fault. She's not the one who walked out on a child.'

'Not physically, no.'

'She's having a bad enough time without you making digs.'

'Tina's having a bad time too, or haven't you noticed?'

'Of course I have but Tina's a child. Children are resilient, they get over things quicker than grown-ups do.'

'A lost toy, perhaps. Not a lost father.'

'Some father.'

'I'm just saying . . .'

'He's no loss. He should have stayed at sea where he belonged. Getting drunk, having fights and not messing up other people's lives.'

'And just how did he mess up Liz's life?'

'He was the one that got her pregnant.'

'Oh, wake up, Neil!' Karen's exasperation boiled over. 'She wanted him to get her pregnant. He was the love of her life and she knew he didn't want to stick around. Getting pregnant was her last throw of the dice. Get a bun in the oven and hope the man feels guilty enough to walk you up the aisle. It's the oldest trick in the book.'

'My sister doesn't play tricks.'

'Yes she does. Only this one backfired. Pete may have stuck around but it was Tina he was close to, not her. And she hated that. She still does.'

'That's rubbish.'

'She's jealous of her own daughter. Always has been.'

Neil's face darkened. 'What do you know about it?'

'More than you think.'

He picked up his paper again. 'You don't know anything.'

'I know what it's like to feel jealous of my own child.'

Slowly he put it down again. 'Do you?'

She managed a smile. A small, shamefaced gesture. 'Yes. I'm human after all. When Sue was born I remember you coming to hospital to see her. I remember the way you fussed over her, going on and on about how beautiful she was. How perfect. Your perfect little girl. I was jealous then. For years I'd been the most important female in your life and suddenly I wasn't anymore. She was.'

His own expression softened. 'But you can't think I love her more than you. You must know that I don't.'

She held up her hand. 'You don't have to say that.'

34

'But it's true.'

'But even if it wasn't it wouldn't matter. Sue is our child. Our responsibility, just as Adam is. If we did love them more than we love each other that would be fine because they need us more than we need each other. Being a parent is the most important role either of us will ever play. More important even . . .' she hesitated, then decided to risk a joke, 'than being projects manager at the bank.'

It was his turn to smile. 'Nothing could be that important.'

They both laughed. The tension eased. But only for a moment.

'That's what I'm trying to say, Neil. I was jealous but I threw the feeling in the rubbish where it belonged. Liz never has.'

The anger returned to his face. 'She's a good mother.'

'Do you really believe that?'

'Yes.' His tone was firm. 'And I don't want to talk about this anymore.'

'But . . .'

'Subject closed. Talk about something else or keep quiet. I don't care which.'

For the second time he picked up his paper. This time she let him read.

February. In the crowded playground, Tina pushed through a group of younger children, trying to escape the older group who were chasing her.

'People get killed in prison,' shouted Philippa Hanson. 'I reckon your dad's dead.'

'He's not. He's not!'

'Yes he is. Your dad's dead!'

She kept trying to escape but reached the far wall of the playground and had nowhere else to go. She kept her back to them, trying to keep her head up and her back straight while they surrounded her and began to chant.

'Dead Daddy! Dead Daddy! Dead Daddy!'

The bell rang, signalling the end of playtime. For a moment they still surrounded her. One of them kicked her leg. Another punched her arm. Then they ran back inside.

She remained where she was, staring at the wall, breathing slowly, trying to compose herself. Not wanting them to see they'd upset her. Not wanting them to have something else to hate her for.

Her Dad wasn't dead. He couldn't be. If he was she would know it in her heart. She would. She was sure of it. They were wrong. They didn't know anything. He was alive and well and would soon be coming back to her. That weekend to be precise. Her birthday. He had let her down at Christmas but she had forgiven him that. Christmas was special for everyone but her birthday was only special for her. And he wouldn't let her down again.

He wouldn't. Not again. Oh please, God, don't let him let me down again.

She took a deep breath, rubbing her arm, waiting for the pain to subside. Her leg hurt too but they wouldn't know that. Not if she kept her head up. Not if she kept being brave.

Not much longer. Only until the weekend. Then he'll be home again.

So the week passed. Her birthday came and went. But still he stayed away.

A Friday afternoon in May. The last lesson before the half-term holiday. Mrs Abbott, knowing the class would be restless, had decided to let them pass the time drawing pictures.

The bell rang. A cheer echoed around the room. 'Off you go then,' she told them. 'But quietly!'

'Yes, Mrs Abbott. 'Bye, Mrs Abbott.' With all the stealth of rampaging elephants they charged for the door.

All except one. Tina Ryan walked slowly towards her desk, a picture clutched in her hand and a thoughtful expression on her face.

She smiled. 'And what can I do for you, Tina?'

Tina handed her the picture. A boat on the water with a man and a girl sitting together at the tiller. The boat was red and had the name *Firehorse* painted on the side. It was a drawing full of colour and joy but still the sight of it made her sad.

'That's lovely,' she said softly.

'Would you like it?'

She was taken aback. 'Me? But what about your mother?'

'She won't want it.'

'Yes she will. You give it to her and I'll bet she'll be thrilled.'

Tina shook her head.

'But it's ever so good. Your pictures are the best in the class. You take it home and tell her that.'

'It won't make any difference. She'll still throw it in the bin.'

'Your mother throws your pictures in the bin?'

The thoughtful expression became troubled. 'It's only because they'd make a mess if we put them on the wall. Mum has to work hard in her job and she has to clean too and it would just make more mess. That's what she says.' A pause. 'And she's right.'

Mrs Abbott sat back in her chair and studied the girl who faced her; taking in the close cropped hair, the hunched shoulders and wary eyes. The girl whom the others had made their scapegoat. The girl who waited faithfully for a father who was never going to come back.

And as she did so she felt an ache in her heart.

This isn't right. It shouldn't be like this. Not for her. Not for any child.

But she wasn't a social worker. Just a teacher. Her responsibility was to teach young minds the three Rs and that was all. She couldn't wave a magic wand and transform young lives, much as she often wished that she could.

'It's a lovely picture, Tina. I'll have it gladly.'

At last a smile. 'Thank you.'

She rose to her feet. 'No. Thank *you*. It'll brighten my kitchen no end.' Impulsively she bent down and kissed Tina's cheek.

And Tina hugged her back. Hard. Urgently. As if her life depended on it.

Then she stepped away. The troubled look back again. ''Bye, Mrs Abbott. See you in a week.' Quickly she turned and was gone from the room.

Seven o'clock on a Saturday morning in June. Tina dusted the mantelpiece in the living room.

She had been up for an hour, determined to clean the house from top to bottom. Her mother always spent Saturday mornings cleaning and she wanted to save her a job. When she had finished downstairs she would take her breakfast in bed. Tea with a slice of lemon, cereal with creamy milk and toast with raspberry jam. All her favourite things. Anything to please her. Anything to make her happy.

She reached for one of the china figurines. A milk-maid with buckets hanging from her shoulders: her mother's favourite because her father had said that it reminded him of her. As she dusted it she heard the sound of a motorcycle engine being revved. Colin Hart from down the street was up early too. The sound set her teeth on edge. He had removed the silencer and the neighbours were always complaining about the noise. She hoped it wouldn't wake her mother. She didn't want her surprise to be spoiled.

The bike came roaring down the road. As it passed the house the engine spluttered and let out a small explosion. It made her jump.

And she dropped the figurine. It fell to the ground, smashing into a dozen pieces.

She stared down at it, feeling sick.

'What have you done?'

Again she jumped. Her mother stood in the doorway, wrapped in a dressing gown. She swallowed, her throat suddenly dry. 'Mum . . .' she began.

'What have you done!'

'I'm sorry, Mum. I was just cleaning.'

Her mother moved across the room, crouching down beside the broken figurine, trying to push the pieces together.

'I'm sorry!' She burst into tears. 'I didn't mean to! I was just trying to help.'

'It's ruined.'

'No it's not. We can stick it back together again. I'll get the glue. We can . . .'

'It's ruined!' Her mother stood up, her eyes blazing. 'And it's your fault.'

'Mum . . .'

'It was all I had. All he left me. Now you've ruined it like you ruin everything.'

She wiped her eyes, trying to control her tears. 'I'm sorry . . .'

'It was all I had! Now I have nothing. Nothing!'

'You've got me.'

'You?' Her mother's expression became savage. 'You?'

'I love you, Mum. I didn't mean to do it. I promise I didn't. I'll get you another. I'll get you anything you want just please don't be angry with me. Please!'

Her mother grabbed her by the arm and dragged her across the room. She cried out in pain but her mother ignored her, marching her up the stairs, into the bathroom and thrusting her face up against the mirror.

'Look at yourself, Tina. Just look at yourself! Stupid, ugly and useless. That's all you are and all you'll ever be. No wonder your father left you. No wonder he couldn't wait to get away and leave you behind!'

'He didn't leave me! He loved me!'

'So where is he then if he loved you so much? Where?' Her mother began to shake her. 'He didn't love you. He was embarrassed by you just like I am. We were doing fine until you came along and ruined it. He'd still be here now if it wasn't for you. It's your fault. Everything is your fault! I wish you'd never been born!'

By now she was howling. Unable to bear it any more. She tried to wrap her arms around her mother, desperate to be held. To feel loved and wanted. But her mother just pushed her away and marched from the room.

She sat on the floor, still sobbing.

He did love me. He did! He did!

And it was true. It had to be true. Because to think anything else was unbearable.

Then why did he go? Why did he leave you if he loved you so much? If he really loved you how could he hurt you like this?

Slowly she rose to her feet. Again she stood in front of the mirror; staring at her face. As ugly as her mother had said. She was everything her mother said. Stupid, ugly and useless. She hated her face. She hated herself.

Did Dad hate me too? Is that why he went? Is that why he stays away?

She wiped her eyes, then wrapped her arms around herself, searching for the comfort that no one else was there to provide.

Sunday morning. One week later. Alan Jones, enjoying a brief easing of his arthritis, walked his dog, Spider, along the harbour path.

It was early. Not yet eight. He always liked to walk when there were few other people about. The tide was out and the estuary was nothing but a mudflat, dotted with marooned boats and a tiny central canal where half a dozen swans swam in circles, honking at each other. The air was heavy with the smell of mud, oil and salt. A dank, depressing smell that the returning water would soon smother.

He walked on down the path, watching Spider sniff at a discarded crisp packet. To his right was the old playground: a set of swings, a slide and a roundabout, all in need of a lick of paint. His eyesight was good and he could see the cigarette butts that littered the ground. He shook his head, disapprovingly. So many of the local kids were smoking by the time they reached their teens. But it could have been worse. At least they weren't taking those terrible drugs the papers were always banging on about.

In the distance he could see the bench at the end of the path. A small figure sat alone, staring out across the mud towards the sea. Tina Ryan. Watching for her father, perhaps. Poor kid. Pete Ryan was gone forever. Good riddance too.

But not for her. He was her dad, after all. Your dad's your dad and you're always going to love him. Even if he's not around to know it.

He had never liked Pete Ryan. Had always found him threatening. A heavy drinker with a fondness for using his fists. A big man with an imposing physical presence. The sort who had only to walk into a crowded room for everyone to turn and look. 'Too big for this place,' Alan's wife Nora had always said. 'He won't stay, you mark my words. One day he'll up and leave and that'll be the last we'll see of him.'

Tina was nothing like her father. A quiet, mousy little kid who wouldn't say boo to a goose. A kid who kept to herself and seemed to have no friends. No, nothing like her father. The apple had fallen far from the tree in that particular case. But as Alan watched her sitting alone he found himself hoping that Nora was wrong. That Pete did come back.

Because she needs him. Even if this town doesn't.

He felt a twinge in his hand. The arthritis was returning. He whistled for Spider. 'Come on boy. Let's go home.' Spider gave the crisp bag a final sniff then trotted towards him. Together they made their way back to town, leaving Tina to watch alone.

Tina's Diary. September 1988.

Today was the first day of school. I didn't want to go. I had bad dreams about it all last night. This morning I tried to make myself sick by putting my fingers down my throat but it didn't work. I told Mum I felt sick but she didn't believe me. Even if I was really sick she'd make me go. She knows I hate it. I think she's glad.

At break someone put a drawing in my desk of a grave with Dad's name on it. I didn't want to cry but did and everyone laughed. I hate crying. I hate them too.

I had tea at Aunty Karen's. She made chicken and chips and Uncle Neil brought us choc ices. Adam looks really grown up in his comprehensive uniform. He says it's much better there than at primary school. I wish he was still at our school. If he saw people hitting me he'd stop them. Now he can't any more.

I wish I could stop them myself. I wish I was like Dad. People were scared of him. I bet when he was my age no one ever made him cry. But I'm just a stupid crybaby like they say and no one's ever going to be scared of me.

Sue likes school. She has lots of friends and no one ever picks on her. I wish I was like her. I wish I was her. I wish Aunty Karen and Uncle Neil were my parents. I wish that more than anything.

But I don't. Not really.

I just wish Mum loved me. A bit. That's all. That would be enough.

Star light. Star bright. First star I see tonight. Up on high, bright in the sky, grant me this wish I wish tonight.

Star light. Star bright. First star I see tonight. This wish I wish with all my might. Dad comes back and makes everything right.'

November. She sat in class, trying to read a book while listening to Philippa Hanson boast about her cousin, Lee, being in a pop group. 'They're called Midnight Angel.'

'Must be crap with a name like that,' observed Stuart Scott.

'No they're not,' snapped Philippa. 'They're really good.'

'That's right,' agreed Bianca Craig, one of Philippa's friends. 'I've heard their record.'

'And they've got their picture in *Smash Hits*.' Philippa produced a copy and people crowded round to look. 'That's Lee. He's the lead guitarist. That's Brett. He's the singer.'

'They look like poofs,' said Stuart, provoking laughter from the boys and a chorus of protests from the girls. 'They look gorgeous!' 'I really fancy Brett.' 'I fancy them all!' 'You're so lucky, having a cousin who's famous.' 'I wish my cousin was famous too.'

Tina remained at her own desk. Outside the rain was coming down in sheets so they were confined to the classroom for their mid-morning break. Mrs Fleming, their form teacher, was supposed to be sitting with them but had gone to make a phone call. Tina hoped she came back soon. She didn't like it when there was no teacher around.

'They're making a video next week,' continued Philippa. 'There's going to be models in it. Lee says when I'm older I can be in their videos 'cos I'll be a model too.'

'Assuming they're still famous then,' said Scott.

'Shut up! What do you know?'

'Yes, what do you know?' echoed Bianca. 'Philippa knows more than you. She's been in catalogues!'

'I'm doing another one this weekend,' said Philippa smugly. 'Mum's taking me up to London. A famous photographer is taking my picture.'

'What's his name?' asked Stuart.

'I don't know but he's really famous. Lee says so and he should know. He knows tons of famous people and so does his girlfriend. She's famous too. She's an actress.'

'What's *her* name then?' asked Stuart. 'Kim Basinger?'

'Her name's Cheryl if you must know and she's done loads of stuff on TV.'

'Like what?'

'A commercial for shampoo. And she was on *Casualty* once.'

'Wow,' said Stuart sarcastically.

'Everyone watches *Casualty*.'

'So what part did she play? A burns victim?' More laughter from the boys.

'Of course not. She's really pretty. Only ugly people play burns victims.'

Tina tensed, sensing what was coming.

'Ever thought about being on *Casualty*, Tina?' asked Bianca. Yet more laughter. Male as well as female. She kept her eyes focused on the page, trying to show no reaction.

'You should send your picture in,' said Philippa. 'They'd see you wouldn't need any make-up and sign you up on the spot!'

The laughter continued. She looked up. They were all staring at her, waiting for a reaction. Hoping for one.

But she was learning how to deal with it. How to survive. The most important thing was to be inconspicuous. To keep silent. Do nothing to remind them you were there. And if they did remember and said things the trick was to look like it didn't matter. That it wasn't important. That it didn't hurt.

No matter how much it did.

'Maybe I will,' she said quietly, then looked back down at her book.

'Stupid crybaby,' sneered Philippa. 'No wonder your dad pissed off. If you did send in your picture they'd just write 'Too ugly' on it and send it back.'

The laughter continued. But not for as long as it once would have done.

Because I'm not crying. And I won't. Even though I want to.

I'm never going to let them see me cry again.

The conversation resumed. Philippa boasting, Stuart sniping, others speculating on how wonderful it must be to be famous while Tina stared down at her book, masking the emotions that churned inside her, so silent and still that she might as well not have been there at all.

January 1989.

She sat on the sofa at Uncle Neil's with Aunty Karen and Sue. Uncle Neil was at a work dinner and Adam was upstairs doing his homework.

The television was on, showing a programme about

the fashion industry. Models paraded up and down a catwalk while classical music played in the background. 'Music is essential in the presentation of fashion,' droned the voiceover. 'No designer ever puts on a show without giving careful consideration to the accompanying music.'

'It'll take more than a nice tune to sell this crap,' observed Aunty Karen.

'It's not crap, Mum. You don't know anything about fashion.'

'I know more than these designers. Look at that one. It's like a shroud with chicken wings all over it!'

'You don't know more than the designers, Mum. You're not rich like they are.'

'The only reason they're rich is because they flog their tat to gullible women with more money than sense. Mrs Harper from Church Close is the perfect example. Every time I see her she's wearing an expensive new designer frock and she looks awful in all of them. Last week she was wearing . . .'

Suddenly Aunty Karen's voice was drowned out by the sound of an electric guitar playing overhead. Rising to her feet she marched into the hall. 'Adam!' she shouted up the stairs. 'You're supposed to be doing your homework!' Receiving no answer except the whine of a poorly executed riff she charged upstairs.

'I like the gold dress best,' said Sue. 'Which one do you like, Tina?'

'That's my favourite too,' Tina told her. But she

didn't care about the clothes. Her interest was in the models who wore them.

It was the way they moved that fascinated her: gliding down the catwalk with heads held high, shoulders back and hips swaying, radiating confidence with every step. They reminded her of the swans she saw on the water. They were like swans, all of them. Each one beautiful, confident and strong and everything she longed to be but wasn't.

One in particular held her attention. Saffron Ellis, a labourer's daughter from the East End of London who was one of the most successful models in the country. She had read all about Saffron in one of the gossipy magazines Aunty Karen was always buying. 'I was really geeky when I was a kid,' Saffron had told the article writer. 'I had long, lanky limbs and all the other kids said I was a freak. They used to call me scarecrow. At first it used to upset me but then I thought sod you! I'm going to be someone one day. You just wait and see.'

And now she was. She was a model. Famous and loved by everyone. She had shown them all, just as she had said she would. But she was beautiful. And everything was easy when you were beautiful. When you were beautiful you could dream your dreams because one day they would surely all come true.

The guitar stopped playing. Aunty Karen re-entered the room. 'Right, that's Jimi Hendrix taken care of. Who wants a cup of tea?'

'I do, Mum.'

'What about you, Tina?'

'Yes, please.'

'Why don't you come and help me make it?'

They stood together in the kitchen, waiting for the kettle to boil. She positioned herself in line with the doorway so she could still see the television. Aunty Karen told her that Adam and his friends wanted to start a band. 'Fortunately Mark Fletcher's mother has said they can practise in her house.' A laugh. 'Can you imagine what your uncle would say if they tried to practise here?'

She could, and laughed too.

'Do you like music, Tina?'

'Yes.'

'Maybe you'll form a band with your friends one day.'

What friends?

Aunty Karen was smiling at her. She smiled back, wondering how much Adam and Sue had told her of what happened at school.

Perhaps they've told her nothing. I hope so.

Because I don't want her to know.

'Your mum and I were in a band once? Did you know that?'

She nodded.

'I'm glad you never saw us. We were terrible! We used to sing cover versions of sixties songs in the local pubs. One evening your dad was in the audience. That was how he and your mum met.'

Another nod. Models continued to glide down the

catwalk. She longed to be like them but even if she wished on every star in the sky that particular wish would never come true.

'How are things with your mum, Tina?'

'Fine. She gets tired sometimes, working for Mr Rennie but he's still a good boss.'

'I meant how are things with you and her?'

'They're fine too.'

'Really?'

'Yes.'

'You know you can tell me if they aren't. You can tell me anything. I'll keep it a secret. Nobody has to know except me.'

She turned away from the screen. Aunty Karen was staring at her. A kind, warm-hearted woman who drove Adam and Sue mad with her fussing but would never dream of telling either of them that they were stupid, ugly and useless. She ached to open up but knew she never would. Though she loved Aunty Karen she would never tell her anything. Secrets never stayed secret. One day her mother would know and the knowledge would only make things worse between them. And she couldn't have borne that.

'Everything's fine,' she said softly. 'Really it is.'

Aunty Karen was still staring. Feeling embarrassed she turned back to the screen. The show was over and Saffron Ellis was being interviewed. Her face filled the screen, bigger than in all the magazine pictures Tina had ever seen. A mane of jet black hair and piercing blue eyes. She stared at it longingly, dreaming of how perfect her life would be if only such a face belonged to her.

'What are you looking at?' Aunty Karen asked.

'Her. On the TV. She's really beautiful.'

Aunty Karen came to look. 'No, she's not.'

'She is.'

'No. She's got great colouring but her face isn't even pretty. It's quite ordinary.'

'I think she's beautiful.'

'And so does she. That's the point. That's what makes her beautiful. The fact that she believes she is.'

'But . . .'

The sound of the guitar started up again. Aunty Karen's face darkened. 'Bloody hell! Tina, switch the kettle off when it's boiled. I'll be back in a minute.'

Again Aunty Karen raced upstairs. Tina remained where she was, staring at Saffron's face on the screen. The face that Aunty Karen thought was ordinary. Perhaps Aunty Karen was right. She was a grown-up, after all, and grown-ups were always right.

But in her eyes it was still the most perfect face in the world.

How does she do it? What magic does she have inside her to do it?

And could I, one day, have it too?

March. Rosemary Fleming looked up from her marking to study the class that sat before her.

The room was silent except for the scratching of

pencils on paper as they all struggled with the maths test she had set. Stuart Scott stared out of the window, watching the local butcher deliver meat for future school lunches. 'You won't find the answers blowing in the wind, Stuart,' she said sharply.

'You never know, Miss,' Stuart told her. A few boys giggled.

'And don't be cheeky. Keep your eyes on your work.'

She continued with her marking. Stories the children had written under the heading of 'A Perfect Summer's Day'. She finished Philip Clark's description of riding his bike over a local common and turned to Jane Bridge's tale of meeting her favourite pop star and having him go down on one knee – not an easy feat as he was riding a Harley Davidson at the time – and proposing before whisking her off to Hollywood for a star-studded wedding. She rolled her eyes, marvelling at how different ten-year-old girls were now from her day. But as her day had been over forty years ago perhaps it wasn't that surprising.

She heard whispering. Philippa Hanson was mouthing something to Bianca Craig. 'Your own work, Bianca,' she said forcefully. Bianca nodded but Philippa kept mouthing. 'And if you carry on trying to help her, Philippa, you'll end up standing in the corridor.'

'Yes, Mrs Fleming,' said Philippa archly, then, like Stuart before her, turned her attention back to her work.

Jane Bridge's story now marked – 'Imaginative, if a

little implausible, and just for the record Gretna Green is in Scotland, not California,' – she started on Tina Ryan's effort. A three page account of sailing on the estuary. A good effort too that evoked a real sense of being on the water. She gave it a good mark and was pleased to do so. Tina was a bright, hard-working girl who always did her best.

She looked up, towards the desk near the back where Tina sat. The head was bent low over the exercise book but it was still easy to spot. The only red in a sea of black, brown and blond. Close-cropped, which was a shame yet understandable. One of the reasons she liked Tina was that she never tried to show off or stand out from the crowd. In fact she generally vanished into it; never speaking unless she was asked a direct question, and then only answering reluctantly and in a voice so soft that one had to strain to hear. The sort of child whose body language signalled a desire to be ignored, which she generally was what with so many more forceful children clamouring for attention. Not a good thing for a teacher to do, but as Tina did well in her lessons it probably didn't matter.

Putting Tina's work to one side she started to read the next story.

Tina wrote her answer to the penultimate question and looked up. Mrs Fleming was marking the essays they had written the previous day. Her perfect summer day would be spent sailing with Uncle Neil and her cousins.

That, at least, was what she had described. But it wasn't true. To be perfect her only companion would be her father.

But she couldn't write stories like that. Not any more. Mrs Fleming liked making people read their work aloud and she had learnt the hard way that to commit such dreams to paper was only to invite more ridicule from her classmates. It hurt having to erase him like that but that was just how it was. He wasn't there and she had to survive.

Mrs Fleming was very old. Nearly sixty, according to Aunty Karen. A plump, kindly-looking woman with a well meaning manner who missed things that her former teacher, Mrs Abbott, never would. Like the teasing and the whispering. It wasn't as bad as it had once been but it still occured. When Mrs Abbott had seen it happening she had tried to stop it but now Mrs Abbott was gone and she was on her own.

I wish I could stop it myself. I wish I could make them scared of me.

I wish . . . I wish . . . I wish . . .

Beside her exercise book lay a set of coloured pens. A present from Sue for her tenth birthday the previous month. A landmark occasion that she had convinced herself her father would return to celebrate. She had waited for his return. Prayed for it. But now the day was long gone and she was still waiting.

And she hated him for that. She didn't want to but she did.

But it didn't matter. She would forgive him everything if he would just come back.

Would you? Would you really?

The thought upset her. She scanned the room, looking for distraction. Once again Philippa was mouthing
to Bianca. This time Mrs Fleming hadn't noticed, just
as she didn't notice so many things.

Philippa turned, clearly bored and searching for distraction herself. Quickly Tina looked back down at her
page.

*Don't be noticed. Don't stand out. Don't remind
them you exist.*

*Don't let them see you're afraid and that you hate
them for it.*

Just like you hate Dad.

Her pencil moved across the page, drawing circles in
the margin. Suddenly the hatred was like a fire burning
her heart. The circles grew bigger as the feeling became
so intense that she wanted to scream.

The pencil nib snapped. Picking up her sharpener
she made herself another and finished her test.

May. On nights when she couldn't sleep she would rise
from bed and play the game she kept as secret as the
grave.

Taking up her position in the corner of her room
and placing a book upon her head she imagined she
was standing on a catwalk. Shutting her eyes she would
picture it running out in front of her with crowds sitting

on either side, waiting for her to appear. In her mind the music would swell and slowly she would begin to walk, swaying her hips, keeping her head high and her shoulders back, trying to move just like the models she watched on television.

She had been playing the game for months now; getting better every time. More often than not she would make it across the room with the book still in place on her head. But on occasion it would fall to the floor, just as it did this time; the thud causing the music to stop and the crowds to disappear.

She stood in the darkness, listening for movement. Had her mother heard? She crossed her fingers, waiting for a raised voice and the sound of footsteps but hearing nothing except the pounding of her own heart.

Slowly she bent down and picked up the book. As she stood up again she felt suddenly ridiculous. It was a ridiculous game. The sort that only someone stupid, ugly and useless would ever want to play. The sort that would make her classmates despise her even more if they were here to see her play it.

But they're not here. I'm alone and I can be who I want to be.

She thought of Saffron. Of a face that was ordinary yet could still appear stunning. Of the magic that could bring about such a transformation.

Where does it come from? How do I find it?

Because I want to find it. More than anything I want to find it.

It was there. She was sure of it. It *had* to be there. Sometimes she would reach out her hand as if to seize it yet it always remained out of reach.

Returning to the corner she put the book back on her head, closed her eyes and resummoned the music and the crowds. This time the book stayed on her head all the way across the room. All part of a game she played alone in her room and which no one would ever be allowed to see.

But in her head they all saw it. Aunty Karen and Uncle Neil. Adam and Sue. Her classmates and teachers. Her mother, looking happy and proud. Her father, looking just as he had on the day before he had vanished from her life. All of them sitting in the audience, cheering and applauding.

Because she was special. She was a star. She had the magic and it would protect her from ever having to feel stupid, ugly and useless again.

When she moved she was someone. When she moved everyone turned to look.

November 1991. Two and a half years later.

A dreary Monday morning. Tina stood with Adam, Sue and half a dozen others on Havelock High Street, holding her school bag and waiting for the Melchott bus.

It came around the corner at eight-fifteen, just as it did every weekday. As it approached, she scanned the lower level, looking for free seats. She hated sitting upstairs but as the bus was almost full by the time it reached them that was usually what she had to do.

The bus pulled up at the stop. They piled on, waving their passes at the driver. Most of the downstairs seats were occupied by adults who preferred its quiet atmosphere to the rowdier one above. Only two remained available. An older boy, grabbed the first. Sue, who had only started at Melchott Comprehensive two months earlier took the second beside a girl in her class.

Following Adam and the others Tina made her way to the upper level. It was crowded there too. All the seats at the front were taken. Adam headed for the back row where Mark Fletcher and his other friends were waiting. Tina saw an empty double seat, about two thirds of the way back and made her way towards it, passing Philippa Hanson and Bianca Craig who were poring over the latest edition of *The Face*. Saffron Ellis was on the cover. Tina had bought a copy herself, just as she bought everything she could about Saffron. Philippa now wore a small stud in her right ear. Jewellery was forbidden at school and Philippa was always being told to take it out but would always put it back in again the moment the teacher or prefect's back was turned.

She sat down in her seat, close up against the window. In the double seat opposite Stuart Scott copied homework from another boy whose name she didn't know. Melchott Comprehensive had two thousand pupils and the bus stopped at two other small towns before reaching the High Street, as well as the stop on the west side that was closer to the homes of people like Philippa.

Opening her bag she searched for her book. A Patrick O'Brien novel with pages that dripped with the smell of the sea. She loved reading sailing stories. Across the aisle Stuart complained about his companion's handwriting. He was no longer in her class which was a blessing, but Philippa still was. As they drove out of Havelock she tried to read but the motion of the bus made it difficult. Closing the book she rested her head against the glass and began to study the people around her.

Mark Fletcher was talking about his band, speaking more loudly than was necessary to attract the attention of a sulky looking girl called Natalie who sat two rows ahead. Mark fancied Natalie. Tina had told Adam this once but he had told her she was talking rubbish. Not wanting to make an issue of it she had backed down, but now, watching Mark cast fleeting glances in Natalie's direction she was more sure than ever that she was right.

Not that Mark had much chance there. Natalie had eyes for no one but an older boy called Dean who livened up the journey by flicking matches at the heads of two smaller boys who sat in front. Recently the elder brother of one had taken exception and a fight had broken out, necessitating the driver to stop the bus and come upstairs to calm things down.

Mark knew Natalie liked Dean. Tina was sure of that. Once, a couple of weeks ago, Mark had deliberately slammed into Dean, but when Dean had reacted angrily he had quickly apologized and moved on. Mark was jealous of Dean but was also scared of him. She was sure of that too.

Fifteen minutes passed and they entered the suburbs of Melchott. On the street below boys walked in a group, all wearing the green and gold uniform of Abbeycroft: a small private school in the town. Dean and others hammered on the windows, shouting abuse and receiving numerous V signs in return. Stuart joined in. Early the previous year his parents had divorced and his father now lived alone in a Melchott flat. Stuart gave the impression that it was of no importance, but in those quiet moments when he didn't realize he was being observed, she would see him look downcast and knew that it was all an act.

Philippa and Bianca continued to read their magazine. Three years earlier, Philippa had boasted of her cousin Lee's success in a band called Midnight Angel, but after one minor hit they had faded from sight and Lee now worked in a London pub. She had felt a deep sense of satisfaction when she had heard, though she had never given any indication of this to Philippa.

Others had though. Some had laughed about it. Philippa had acted as if it didn't matter though Tina was sure that it did. Especially as Philippa didn't seem to be doing much modelling work anymore. It was a good six months since a catalogue had been brought into class and thrust in all their faces. No doubt, if someone were to laugh about that, Philippa would act as if that didn't matter either. That it didn't hurt.

But it did. She was sure of that too.

They were in the centre of Melchott now; waiting at traffic lights. Another group of Abbeycroft boys walked by, provoking the same jeers. She pretended to read her book, keeping her eyes downcast, raising them only occasionally. Noticing everything while no one noticed her.

Half past four that afternoon. She let herself into the house; it was empty, just as it always was on her return from school. Her mother was still at work. A note on the kitchen table told her to take a casserole from the freezer and leave it to thaw. Having done so, and after making a cup of tea, she headed upstairs.

Her room was much as it had been on the day her father left. Only the posters had changed. Images of Wham! had been replaced by those of Depeche Mode and The Cure, but the desk still stood by the window and maps of Ireland and the world still hung above it.

On the bed a pile of clothes lay folded and ready to put away in her drawer. Amongst them was the swimming costume she would need for her class's fortnightly swimming lesson the following day. She hated swimming. Having always been small for her age she had started to grow and the tightness of the costume only served to emphasize her lanky limbs and general ungainliness. In the changing room all the girls stared at her, just as they stared at each other, competitively examining changes as puberty took hold and the journey towards womanhood began.

She sat down at her desk, rubbing her abdomen, longing to feel the dull ache that signalled the start of her period and an excuse to avoid exercise. But her sports teacher never accepted such an excuse unless accompanied by a parental note and she knew better than to ask her mother for one when she was not due for at least a week.

Opening her school bag she took out a pile of books in readiness for the evening's homework. An hour apiece for Maths and Geography as well as a list of vocabulary to learn for an impending French test. Not that she minded. She was in the top stream for most subjects and took pride in doing well. She wished her mother would take pride in it too, but when she talked about her academic successes she received nothing but half-hearted praise followed by a reminder of some unrelated failing.

She checked her watch. Quarter to five. After putting on a tape she took her diary from her desk drawer and began to write.

Another crap day. We spent History in the
library, working on our projects. I was working
on my own but then the new girl, Jennifer, came

to talk to me. It was the first time I'd spoken to her and she seemed nice. She likes sailing and told me about her uncle who lives in Suffolk and has a dinghy. We were getting on well until Philippa came over and asked Jennifer if she was talking to me because she was a dyke too. Everyone laughed and Jennifer turned bright red and went to sit somewhere else.

At lunchtime I listened to Adam's band rehearse. They're really terrible. I bet even Philippa's cousin's band weren't as bad. Brian, the drummer, said I couldn't come in as they didn't want stupid kids hanging around but Adam said it was OK as long as I was quiet.

Mark Fletcher kept making jokes about the ginger geek in the corner but he said them in a nice way so I didn't mind. I like Mark. He's funny and not as full of himself as Adam's other friends. If Natalie prefers that idiot Dean to him then she's even more stupid than she looks.

As we went to get the bus home I tried to talk to Jennifer again but she just ignored me. I hated her for that.

But I don't really blame her. If I were her I'd probably do the same.

I just wish . . .

She put down her pen, remembering Oscar Wilde's comment on diaries that 'One should always have something sensational to read on the train'. But there was nothing sensational about hers. Just taunts and hurt feelings and wishes that would never come true. The sort of entries to make most train travellers hurl themselves onto the tracks. Maybe that was why she hardly ever wrote in it any more.

Her copy of *The Face* lay on the window ledge. She skimmed through its pages, looking at the models in the fashion spreads. One of them had long red hair. Her own was still short. Aunty Karen was always telling her to grow it, saying it was lovely and that people who said otherwise were either jealous or stupid. But Aunty Karen always said nice things and even if she grew it twice as long as the model in the photograph it wouldn't look half as good.

She stared at Saffron Ellis on the cover. Deep blue eyes set in a face touched by magic. She still believed in the magic. Sensed that it existed somewhere. But in spite of all her prayers and silent games alone in the dark its source remained as big a mystery as ever.

The map of the world was old and battered. She kept meaning to take it down yet never did. Often, while doing her homework, she would stop and stare at it, tracing its surface with her fingers, wondering where her father was, what he was doing and whether he ever thought of her. One of her desk drawers was crammed with presents she had bought him for all the birthdays and Christmases they had missed. She still bought him presents, knowing it was a waste of money but unable to stop. The hope of his return, once as thick and strong as Navy rope, had been worn away to the thinnest of threads. A mere flick of the wrist could have severed it completely, but in spite of all the promptings of reason, her heart would not permit it.

Five o'clock. Half an hour before her mother returned. Picking up her pen again she made a start on her homework.

Seven o'clock. She ate supper with her mother in the kitchen.

It was a rare occurrence. Generally they ate separately. The fact that they were eating together suggested that her mother had news to tell.

'Mrs Blake loved my story,' she said between mouthfuls. 'The one about the gladiator falling in love with the slave girl and having to fight lions in the Colosseum to save her.'

'Where did you get an idea like that?'

'From *Spartacus*.' She had watched the film at Aunty Karen's the previous Sunday afternoon. Her mother had been out, doing overtime for Mr Rennie at his office. At least that was what she had been told. Six months earlier Mr Rennie had divorced his wife, who now lived in Kent with their two children. Since then her mother had changed her hairstyle and was taking increasing care with her appearance. She was sure the two developments were related but her mother had never yet said anything to confirm it.

'And *Quo Vadis*,' she added. 'I saw that at Aunty Karen's too. Anyway, Mrs Blake says that one of the local papers is holding a story-writing competition and she wants to send mine in. If I win I get twenty pounds and they'll print the story.'

'I expect there'll be a lot of entries.'

'But Mrs Blake thinks I've got a real chance. She said it was the best story she'd seen in ages.' She paused, hoping her mother would ask to read it, yet conditioned by experience not to feel disappointed when the request never came.

'Are you pleased?' she asked.

'Of course. Well done.'

'Thanks.'

Silence. They continued to eat.

'Must you slouch like that?' said her mother suddenly. 'It looks awful.'

'Sorry.' She straightened her back.

Her mother put down her fork. 'I meant to tell you something. I won't be here tomorrow evening. You'll be having supper at Uncle Neil's.'

'Are you doing more overtime?'

'No. Colin Rennie's taking me out to dinner.'

'Oh.'

Her mother lit a cigarette. 'You'll be staying the night too. It's the most sensible thing. I'm not sure what time I'll be back and you need to be in bed early for school.'

'Where's he taking you?'

'Some Italian place in Melchott. I can't remember the name.'

'It might be Orsinis. That's in Praed Street near the Arcade. It looks really nice.' And it did from the outside. Ornate decorations and candles on the tables. The perfect place for a romantic dinner.

'Perhaps. Like I said, I can't remember.'

She picked at her food, feeling her mother's gaze upon her and sensing that more reaction was expected.

'How do you feel about that?' her mother asked.

'I don't mind staying at Uncle Neil's.'

'That's not what I meant.'

She looked up. Her mother's eyes were questioning. 'Well?'

'Well what?'

'Are you pleased for me?'

'Yes.'

'Good.' A quick smile. 'I thought I'd invite Colin here for dinner next week. I—'

'But what about Dad?'

The smile faded. 'What does he have to do with it?'

'Nothing, I suppose.'

'Exactly. I was thinking Wednesday night. That's good for Colin. I know—'

'What if he comes back?'

'He's never coming back. We both know that.'

'We don't.'

'Grow up, Tina.'

'But we don't. Not for sure. We don't know *anything*

about him for sure. We don't know where he is or what he's doing.' She swallowed. 'We don't even know if he's alive.'

'Good riddance if he's not.'

'Mum!'

Her mother stubbed out her cigarette. 'I might have known you'd be like this.'

'Like what?'

'The first nice thing that happens to me in ages and you try and spoil it.'

'I'm not.'

'Why can't you be happy for me? Is that too much to ask?'

'I am, Mum. Really. I'm just saying—'

'I bet if Aunty Karen was in the same situation Adam and Sue would be pleased for her but not you. You have to try and spoil it the way you spoil things for everyone.'

'I don't.'

An angry exhalation.

'It wasn't my fault Dad left.'

'Then whose fault was it because it certainly wasn't mine.'

'Wasn't it?' she said, before she could stop herself.

Her mother reached across the table and slapped her face.

They stared at each other. She rubbed her cheek. It wasn't the blow that hurt. It was the look on her mother's face. The eyes narrowed into slits; projecting hate like electric rays.

'Listen to me, Tina, because I'm only going to say this once. Colin will have dinner with us next week. I expect you to be on your best behaviour. You will not mention your father or do anything else to embarrass me. You've ruined enough things for me in the past. You will not ruin this. Do you understand?'

She continued to rub her face.

'Do you understand?'

'Yes.'

'Now go to your room. I don't want to see you for the rest of the evening.'

She rose and walked into the living room. The china figurines still stood on the mantelpiece. All except the one she had broken. As she stared at them a rage flared up in her so powerful that it made her whole body shake. For a moment she had the urge to smash them all into a million pieces.

But it wouldn't do any good. It wouldn't change anything. It wouldn't make her mother love her. It wouldn't bring her father back.

Breathing slowly, choking down her emotions, she made her way upstairs.

That night she dreamed of sailing down the estuary and out to sea. She was eight years old again and both her parents were with her. They had their arms around each other and were smiling. She was smiling too, feeling the wind against her face and tasting salt in her mouth. It was a good day. The best of days. Everything in her life was perfect and nothing was ever going to change.

Then the wind began to build; the waves growing turbulent, making the boat rock harder and harder until her parents lost their balance and fell into the water. Screaming with fear she leaned overboard, stretching out her hands to reach them. Her fingers tangled in their hair. The hold was good. Secure enough to pull them both to safety.

But when she tried to do so her body would not obey her. Instead her hands pushed downwards, keeping their heads underwater, trying to drown them both.

The following afternoon. She left the female changing room at Melchott Sports Centre and headed for the exit, relieved her swimming lesson was over for another fortnight.

'Tina!'

She turned. An athletic-looking woman in T-shirt and shorts was striding towards her. She waited, wondering what she had done wrong.

The woman held out her hand. 'Hello, I'm Meg Sullivan.'

'Hello.'

'Your teacher told me your name. My husband and I run Aquabats. It's a swimming club for local kids. Have you heard of us?'

'No.' A drop of water trickled down the back of her neck. The consequence of having dried herself too quickly. She wiped it away, then added a polite 'Sorry.'

'Don't apologise. We only started it a couple of months ago. We meet here three afternoons a week after school and I wondered if you'd like to join. I've watched you swim and think you have real potential.'

'Me? But I'm terrible.'

'What's terrible is your technique. If we improved it you could be very good. Have you ever tried swimming butterfly?'

'No. I know what it is though. It looks really difficult.'

'Not once you've mastered the basics. You've got the right build. Slim with broad shoulders. Like I said, you could be a very good swimmer if you worked at it.'

Another drop of water ran down her neck. A group of girls from her class walked past, staring curiously at Meg. Philippa was amongst them. She heard the whispered word 'dyke', followed by muffled giggles and felt herself blush.

But Meg was smiling at her. She had a nice face and a wonderful figure. The sort of figure Tina would have given anything to possess.

'The other club members are a fun group. There're a few from your school and others from Abbeycroft. Next month we're competing against a club from Romford. Perhaps you could take part. Apparently their female butterfly swimmers are very good and I need someone to match them.'

She smiled herself. 'Better not ask me, then.'

'Don't put yourself down. You've got the raw material. You just need to learn how to use it. We're meeting tomorrow. Why not come along? We usually all go for a burger afterwards.' A laugh. 'If you beat the girls from Romford, I'll even pay for yours.'

She risked a joke. 'And fries too?'

'Even onion rings. So, what do you think?'

'I don't know. I have a lot of schoolwork.'

'All the more reason for coming. Isn't a healthy body supposed to make a healthy mind? Anyway, think about it.' Meg gave her a piece of paper. 'That's my number. Call me if you decide to come. I hope you do. It's fun, it keeps you fit and it's great for the figure.'

Her ears pricked up. 'Really?'

'Have you ever seen a competitive swimmer with a bad one?' Meg looked at her watch. 'I have to go. Do come, Tina. I think you'll enjoy it.'

Meg walked away. She gazed at the piece of paper. The handwriting looked strong and confident. Like Meg herself.

But it was a stupid idea. Meg was just being nice.

It's great for the figure.

Perhaps it was. But it was still stupid. Totally stupid.

Putting the number in her pocket she went to catch her bus.

January 1992.

Saturday evening. She ate dinner at home with her mother and Colin Rennie.

It was the second time he had been their guest. Her mother was pulling out all the stops, just as she had on his first visit. The living room furniture had been pushed against the walls and the kitchen table moved into the centre and covered with a new tablecloth. After a starter of home-made soup they now ate steak cooked very rare. She preferred her meat well done but she was not the one her mother was trying to impress.

Colin swallowed a huge mouthful and gave a contented sigh. 'Just the way I like it.' She felt relieved, knowing who would be blamed if the evening was not a success.

A bottle of wine stood at the centre of the table. Colin refilled his glass, then did the same for her mother. 'What about you, Tina? Just a drop?' She wanted to say yes but could feel her mother's eyes upon her. Politely she shook her head.

Colin continued to eat, shovelling down food like a high-power vacuum cleaner. Drops of blood hung above his lips. He wiped them away with his napkin, his gold cufflinks catching the light. His casual blue suit was as shiny as his work ones. She remembered the way her father had likened him to a penguin and felt a sudden need to laugh.

As he ate, Colin told them about the villa his friends had bought in Spain. 'A lovely place outside Malaga.

Five bedrooms, half an acre and a pool for only quarter of a mill. Friends of mine have a similar place near Melchott and it cost twice as much. But that's the great thing about Spain. You get so much more for your money.'

He talked a lot about money. She had already learned that his new sports car had cost twenty thousand pounds, and that his watch was a Rolex. No doubt he would have told her the price too, had she seen fit to ask.

'So how are you getting on at school, Tina?' he enquired.

'Very well, thank you.'

'What's your favourite subject?'

'English.'

'Why's that then?'

'I like writing stories.' Though her tale about the gladiator and the slave girl had not won the newspaper competition she had made the final five and received an honourable mention. However, as she was under strict instructions from her mother not to talk about herself she kept this information quiet.

'My son, Charlie, likes English too. He wants to be a journalist but I've told him to become a merchant banker in the City. That's where the big money is.'

'Isn't your friend, Doug, a banker?' asked her mother.

'And making a packet. Not that I have any grounds to complain. The legal profession has been very good to me.'

Her mother nodded. Tina did the same, half expecting Colin to tell them his annual salary. He was a small, unprepossessing man and it struck her that there was something rather pathetic about his boasting. As if he were more concerned with trying to bolster himself than impress the two of them.

Not that he impressed her. Instead she found him creepy. Her mother was wearing a new dress that showed more than a hint of cleavage and he kept sneaking peaks at it. Her mother didn't seem to realize, but she did. That was her skill. The one advantage of spending one's life trying not to be noticed. It gave you all the time in the world to notice the behaviour of others.

They finished their steak. Her mother went to fetch dessert. 'Chocolate cheesecake,' she told Colin. 'I know it's one of your favourites.'

'It certainly is. What about you, Tina?'

'Yes. Particularly Mum's.'

Her mother moved into the kitchen. The dress was tight and showed off the curve of her buttocks. Colin stared at them, his expression momentarily lecherous. She wondered if the two of them had slept together. When Adam had asked her the same question she had become indignant and told him that the answer was a definite no. But even if she was right it was only a matter of time. Because that was what Colin wanted. It was written all over his face.

And that's all he wants. Mum can't see it. But I can.

Colin asked her more questions about school. As before she answered politely but concisely, keeping her achievements and her observations to herself.

A dreary February afternoon, two days after her thirteenth birthday.

School was over and she walked through Melchott Town Centre, heading for the bookshop in the Arcade. A book token was in her pocket; a present from Uncle Neil and Aunty Karen with which she planned to buy a biography of Mary, Queen of Scots. They were studying the Tudors in History and the story of the ill-fated Scottish Queen had captured her imagination. She had already searched the school library but found insufficient material to satisfy her curiosity.

A girl of about twenty was busking outside the Arcade, singing a folk song in a strong, clear voice. A crowd had gathered to listen. As she stopped to do the same the door of a nearby newsagents opened and a man emerged.

And at that moment her world stopped dead.

It was her father.

He paused outside the shop, opening a packet of cigarettes and lighting one before turning and walking away in the opposite direction.

She tried to run after him but found herself frozen to the spot. Shock had turned her to stone. Opening her mouth she attempted to call out but her lungs were paralyzed. All she could do was stand and watch, as still as a statue while inside she was screaming.

A woman pushed past her, heading into the Arcade. The jolt released her from the spell, setting both her body and her tongue free.

'Dad!'

He didn't hear her. Just kept on walking. She charged after him, pushing through the crowd, almost flattening someone without even realizing they were there. She was blind to everything except her father. Dropping her school bag she ran as fast as her legs could carry her, convinced that if she didn't reach him quickly he would vanish into thin air, just as he had done on that terrible autumn morning four-and-a-half years earlier.

'Dad! It's me! Wait for me! Please!'

Still he didn't hear her. But it didn't matter as at last she caught up with him, stretching out her hand to seize the end of his coat. As he turned she flung herself at him, wrapping her arms around his neck, bursting into sobs of uncontrollable joy.

Only to hear him say, 'Who are you? What the hell are you doing?' in a voice that had not the slightest trace of an Irish lilt.

He pushed her away. Clutching onto his hands she looked up into his face. But it wasn't his face. Just that of a man who looked like him.

'You nearly flattened me. What the bloody hell do you think you're doing?'

She opened her mouth but again paralysis took hold. All she could do was stare. He stared back, his expression a mixture of anger and concern. 'Are you all right?'

She managed to nod.

'Well don't do that again. You could cause someone an injury.' Then he pulled his hands free, turned and walked away.

She remained where she was, watching him go, feeling the emotions churn inside her so violently that she thought she might be sick.

And she felt something else too. Eyes crawling all over her. Everyone was staring. Even the busker. A woman walked towards her, holding out her school bag. 'You dropped this, love. Are you OK? You look like you've seen a ghost.' The words were kind but she could see through them. See that she was being laughed at. They were all laughing. They were all glad.

Because it's just me. Tina Ryan. Stupid, ugly, useless Tina Ryan. Only good to be laughed at and despised. The girl whose father couldn't wait to get away from her. The girl whose mother hates her just like everyone hates her.

The woman looked anxious. 'You're crying. You're not all right at all. Why not come and sit down for a bit.' More kind words but it was all lies. A trick to make her reveal more of her own weakness for general amusement.

She took the bag. 'I'm fine,' she whispered. 'Nothing's the matter at all.'

Then it was her turn to walk away.

Ten minutes later. She sat on a bench in a small park, staring down at the ground.

The park was empty. On summer afternoons it was full of teenagers who used its concrete slopes to skateboard but now it was growing dark and there was no one else there. She was crying. Despising herself for her weakness but unable to stop. The longing for her father, previously just a manageable ache, was now so raw she thought her heart would burst. She wished she had not gone out that afternoon. She wished she had not made such a show of herself. She wished . . .

Wishing. Always wishing. Her whole life was one long wish. But wishes needed magic and there was none strong enough to make even the tiniest of hers come true.

A sound penetrated her brain. The whizzing of wheels on concrete. A skateboard slid along the path towards her. Looking up she saw the rider was Stuart Scott.

He stopped, picked up his board and stared down at her. 'Why are you blubbing?'

'I'm not.'

'Yes you are. You're such a baby. No wonder everyone hates you.'

She wiped her eyes. 'They don't.'

'Yes they do. Why are you crying, little baby? Upset 'cos you've got no friends?'

'Leave me alone.'

'Or what? Going to cry some more and drown me?

You're such a fucking baby. No wonder your dad left.'

'It wasn't my fault.'

'Yes it was. Wait 'till I tell everyone about this.'

'Don't tell anyone. Please.'

'What's it worth? How much money have you got?'

'Twenty pounds.' She reached inside her pocket for the book token and held it out to him. 'You can have it. Just don't tell them.' The tears started again. 'Please.'

'I don't want some stupid token.' He tore it into pieces and threw them on the ground. 'I want real money.'

'But I don't have any.'

'Tough shit then.' He turned to go.

She rose to her feet, grabbing hold of his arm. 'Please, Stuart . . .'

'Fuck off.' He shoved her hard, pushing her down onto a piece of earth where flowers grew in the summer. Then he started laughing. Looking down at her and laughing.

And suddenly it happened. The rage that had been building inside her for so many years exploded out like molten lava, possessing her as completely as a malign spirit. Letting out a scream of pure fury she jumped to her feet and slammed her fist into his mouth, knocking the smirk straight off his face.

'You tell them then! But if you do I'll tell them the reason your parents divorced was because your mum found out your dad's queer! She left him because he was always hanging around toilets trying to pick up men and suck their cocks! He loves sucking cocks! He can't get enough of them. Even yours!'

He stumbled, dropping the skateboard, wiping a lip that was starting to bleed. 'That's crap!'

'No it's not. Not the way I'll tell it. I'll make it sound really good. You think I can't? I'm much brighter than you. I'm not the one in the remedial classes. I'm not the moron. I've got ten times more imagination too and I'll make them believe it. Every word!'

He paled. She saw him swallow. And it felt good. Unbelievably good.

'They won't believe it. They bloody won't!'

'Yes they will. They'll believe it because they'll want to. People always want to believe bad stuff. Poor little Stuey. Imagine people believing you let your dad suck you off for ten quid a go. That's the only way he'll give you money. But you don't care. Secretly you like it because you're queer too. That's why you tried to rape me just now. That's why I had to fight you off because you're so desperate to prove that you're more of a man than your filthy queer father.'

'You shut your fucking mouth!'

The skateboard lay between them. Picking it up she swung it at him, missing his head by millimetres. 'Or what? What are you going to do, Stuey? Hit me again? You just try it, you filthy bum boy! You try it and I'll kill you! I'll beat your useless brain out and tell them it was self defence because you're a pathetic, bum boy rapist.' She took a step towards him. 'In fact I'm going to do that anyway because I hate you and right now the only thing I really want is to see you dead!'

Again she swung. This time the board hit his arm. He was backing away and it was only a glancing blow. But it felt wonderful. Like every joyous occasion in her life condensed into a single moment of total euphoria.

He turned and ran. She threw the board after him, hitting him on the back. He snatched it up and carried on running. She stood and watched him go, laughing as loudly as she could, consumed by a belief that she could take on the whole world and win.

Then the belief vanished and she was herself again.

Slowly she sat back down on the bench, feeling cold, alone and terribly afraid.

Because she *could* have killed him. The rage had been so great that had he stayed she wasn't sure if she could have stopped herself.

She began to tremble, breathing deeply, expelling every drop of air from her lungs as if it would take the fury with it. That was what she had to do. Banish it. Cast it out for ever.

Use it.

The voice came from nowhere. As seductive as a siren's lullaby.

Use it. It's a weapon. A weapon gives strength. A weapon gives power.

She shook her head, as if there was someone else with her. In a way there was. The thoughts in her head were so alien that it was like listening to a stranger.

A stone lay on the bench beside her. As hard as the rage itself. She picked it up and squeezed it as tightly as she could, as if it were a living thing she had to destroy.

You scared him. Something you thought you could never do. You can scare others too. Use it, Tina. That's what it's for.

'I can't,' she whispered. 'It's too strong.'

Yes you can. This time it controlled you. Next time you must control it. You can do it if you try. Focus it. Train it. Use it every chance you get. It will give you all the strength you'll ever need and save you from ever having to feel frightened again.

Time passed. She remained on the bench while in the sky above the last drops of light were swallowed by oncoming night.

Nine o'clock. She let herself into the house.

Her mother emerged from the living room, looking angry. Aunty Karen followed, looking relieved.

'Where the hell have you been?'

'Sorry, Mum.'

'Is that it?' Her mother's face was crimson. 'What were you doing all this time?'

'Thinking.'

'*Thinking?* Well that's just you all over, isn't it? Why not try thinking about me for a change? Do you know how worried I've been?'

'Why would you be worried?'

'Because I'm your mother!'

Liar. You're upset because Aunty Karen expects it. And because you were supposed to be having dinner with Colin tonight.

'It's all right, Liz,' said Aunty Karen soothingly. 'She's here now. That's all that matters.' She touched Tina's arm. 'We were worried something had happened to you.'

Something had. But she kept that to herself.

'I'm sorry,' she said again.

'Just call next time,' Aunty Karen told her, 'and let us know where you are.'

'That's not too much to ask is it?' added her mother. 'Even of you.'

'No, Mum.'

'Have you eaten?' Aunty Karen asked. 'Do you want some food?'

'No. I'm tired. I want to go to bed.'

Without waiting to be dismissed she walked upstairs, carrying her schoolbag and with the stone still clasped in her hand.

The following morning she sat upstairs on the bus.

Mark Fletcher was trying to impress Natalie who kept making eyes at Dean. Philippa and Bianca giggled and gossiped while others shouted abuse at Abbeycroft boys on the street below. It was a typical school day. The same as any other. Except that there was nothing typical about it at all.

Stuart sat two rows ahead of her, his mouth bruised

and swollen. She had hit him even harder than she had realized. But nobody knew that. He was telling a story about fighting off a couple of older boys who had tried to steal his skateboard.

'Who were they?' asked someone.

'I think they were some of the gypo kids from out near Epley. My mum said she'd heard they'd been causing trouble and that's why the police are moving them on.'

People kept asking questions. Stuart answered them all, making himself out to be a hero. It was a good story. Better than she would have expected from him.

But not as good as the ones she could tell.

She kept expecting him to turn and stare but his eyes remained focused in front.

Because he's scared, Tina. You scared him.

And you still do.

The journey continued. She sat alone, watching the others and keeping her strange new thoughts to herself.

One week later. She studied her reflection in the bathroom mirror.

Her skin was pale. Prone to freckles and unable to tan. Her forehead was too prominent, her nose too large and her jaw too heavy. She knew all her faults. Could recite them by rote like a multiplication table.

But not this time.

She reached out a hand, stroking her reflected eyes. Two drops of dark green that clashed with the whiteness of her skin and the redness of her hair. She had always hated her colouring. Longed to be blonde and blue-eyed. Longed to be what people told her was right.

Maria Callas had hated her looks too. She had read that in an article in one of Aunty Karen's magazines. But she never let that hold her back. Instead she used it as a spur to drive herself on to become who and what she wanted to be. In the end she had become what was considered beautiful through sheer force of will.

Embrace what you have. That was what the article had said. Be proud of what you can't change.

Because it's not what you've got. It's how you use it.

Aunty Karen kept telling her to grow her hair. That it was striking, as were her eyes. Perhaps they were. Perhaps all she needed was to learn how to use them.

She stared at her face, remembering all the times she had been told she was ugly. Feeling the fury like a dragon curled in the pit of her stomach, breathing out smoke that warmed her insides and brought her spirit to life.

Her eyes came to life too. Suddenly they blazed. Sparkled. Shone.

And they were lovely.

Believe it, Tina. Believe it.

Her colouring was striking, her forehead proud. Her nose was roman, her jaw strong. People couldn't see that now but one day they would. She would make them see it.

On the sink beside her was the eyeliner she had bought

three days earlier. Each morning she had steeled herself to put it on but had always found an excuse not to do so. She reached out her hand towards it, then pulled it back. Again her nerve failed. It was ridiculous. The whole thing was ridiculous. She was just Tina Ryan, stupid, ugly and useless. To imagine she could ever be anything else only proved just how stupid she really was.

But you tried, Tina. And you're going to keep on trying.

Sighing, feeling frustrated, yet strangely excited, she went to prepare for school.

Two days later. She boarded the bus for school.

Downstairs was virtually full. Sue grabbed the last available seat. She followed the others upstairs towards her usual double seat near the back. Normally she kept her head lowered to avoid being noticed. This time she held it high, wanting to be seen.

And she was. Philippa noticed and nudged Bianca, both of them turning to stare.

She sat down. The bus began to move. In a moment it would start just as she had planned. The stone from the bench was clasped in her hand. She squeezed it hard and told herself that she was ready.

'Look, everyone. Tina's wearing eyeliner!'

People turned. Philippa and Bianca were laughing. Others did the same, but not Stuart who studiously avoided her gaze. Which was just as well for him.

It is, Tina. Believe that, and believe you can win.

'Stupid cow,' jeered Philippa. 'Do you really think make-up's going to make you any less ugly?'

The laughter continued. Adam, from his seat at the back, called out for people to leave her alone. She was grateful but didn't want his help. This was her fight and she had to win it on her own.

'Take it off,' Philippa told her. 'The only way you could be less ugly is if you wore a bag over your head.'

She kept squeezing the stone, conjuring up the memories she needed. The taunts and the insults. The years spent waiting for her father. Her mother hitting her. Feeling the rage stir. Sensing its power. Focusing it. Controlling it. Preparing herself for battle. Until at last she was ready.

'You're right,' she said calmly. 'I will take it off.'

'Good thing too,' laughed Philippa. 'What a waste of make-up!'

'When you get another catalogue job.'

Philippa stopped laughing.

She raised her voice so that everyone could hear. 'Or when hell freezes over, which will probably be sooner.'

Philippa's eyes widened. Tina continued to squeeze the stone, feeling her confidence increase. She had hit the nerve dead centre. Now all she had to do was keep on hitting.

'It's such a shame. You were going to be the next Cindy Crawford. That doesn't seem so likely any more, does it? Not if even second-rate catalogues won't hire you.'

Philippa opened her mouth, then closed it again. She looked flustered as well she might. That was the wonderful thing about knowing how not to be noticed. When you did decide to enter the fray no one saw you coming in time to martial their defences.

'Shut up!' Bianca told her. 'You don't know what you're talking about.'

'Don't I? Come on, Philippa, tell us? When are you doing a cover shoot for *Vogue*?'

'I don't have to tell an ugly cow like you anything.'

'Poor Philippa. Don't they want you anymore? What a surprise. Don't you remember that photographer telling you that you were a real stunner. I do. It was all you talked about for weeks. Mind you, what would he know? Most photographers are queer anyway.'

Out of the corner of her eye she saw Stuart flinch. The sense of power increased.

'You shut your mouth!' Philippa told her.

'Never mind. At least you had your moment of glory and I'm sure your pop star cousin will find you a bar job if you ask him very nicely.'

'Shut up!'

'Washed up at thirteen. We'll have to start calling you Has-been Hanson.'

Someone laughed.

Bullseye.

'Or Past-it Pippa. I prefer that one. It's got a better ring to it, don't you think?'

The laughter swelled. Soon it seemed as if everyone

was laughing. Philippa's expression was half fury, half bewilderment. Once the fury would have frightened her but now she had fury of her own, a million times more powerful than Philippa could ever imagine. At the moment she was in control of it, letting it out drop by drop like corrosive acid. But if she did let it explode it wouldn't just be Philippa's dignity that was threatened. It would be her life.

And that felt good.

She began to laugh herself. Keeping her head high and matching Philippa's stare while all the time squeezing the stone that grew hot in the palm of her hand.

Mid-morning break. Philippa and Bianca cornered her in an alcove off one of the corridors, just as she had known they would. Like most self-satisfied people they were highly predictable.

Philippa's eyes were blazing. All the confusion was gone. Clearly she had used the intervening time to regain her composure and was now ready for battle. But Philippa wasn't the only one. And Tina had had far longer to prepare.

'So you think you're a comedian, do you?' Philippa snarled.

'Maybe. I'll certainly never make it as a model which makes two of us, doesn't it?'

'You're an ugly, pathetic little cow. You think your life is bad? It's paradise compared to how it's going to be from now on.'

Tina gestured to Bianca. 'If I'm so pathetic then why do you need reinforcements?'

'I don't.'

'That's right,' agreed Bianca. 'Not against a loser like you.'

'God, it can speak. I thought it was just for decoration. And I also think that someone, in spite of all her big talk, is too scared to take me on alone.'

'I'm not scared of a freak like you!'

Smiling, she began to make clucking noises.

'Do her, Phil,' urged Bianca.

She folded her arms. 'Yes, go on Past-it. Do me.'

The anger was still in Philippa's eyes. But the confusion was back. Understandably. This wasn't the way Tina Ryan was supposed to behave. Tina Ryan was supposed to back away and beg for mercy, not look excited as if this was what she wanted.

Which it was. More than anything it was.

Control it, Tina. You don't need violence. You can destroy her with words alone.

She gave Bianca a wave. ''Bye, Bianca. We don't need you. This is between Past-it and me. That's right, isn't it, Past-it?' Again she made the clucking sound. Philippa flushed.

'I'm staying,' said Bianca.

'No, you're not,' Philippa told her. 'I can do this loser on my own.'

'Well done, Past-it. You've got more guts than I thought.'

93

Bianca hesitated. She gave her another wave. Reluctantly Bianca slid away.

They faced each other. She continued to smile. 'Well?'

'You've made a big mistake, fucking with me.'

'You didn't make a mistake about my dad though.'

The look of confusion intensified. 'What do you mean?'

'He *is* in jail, just like you always said. I had a letter from him last week. He was done for assault. Half killed a man in a fight in some shitty pub in London. Maybe the same one your loser cousin works in.'

'You don't know anything about my cousin.'

'But my dad knows all about you. I've written and told him everything and he hates you as much as I do. He gets out in a few months and is going abroad but he's offered to pay a visit here first and do a job on your face. It would be a good job, too. Don't you remember how useful he was with his fists? After he'd finished with you no one would ever want to look at you again.'

Philippa paled.

'Oh don't worry, Past-it. I'm not planning to ask him. After all, what's the point? It wouldn't hurt you. Not when no photographer is ever going to want to take pictures of your face again.'

'Shut up!'

'Anyway, I don't hate you any more. I feel sorry for you actually. It must be horrible having to come to terms with the fact that you're not as special as you used to be.' A pause. 'And never will be again.'

'I told you to shut up!'

'Don't take it so hard. All the boys still think you're pretty. Well, sort of. And I'm sure they'll go on thinking it too. For a few more months anyway.'

They continued to stare at each other. Philippa looked half ready to strike, half ready to run. Tina kept her arms folded, breathing slowly, focusing on the rage. Feeling its power. Knowing, just as Philippa might be starting to sense, that any fight could be to the death.

She took a step forward. 'So if you want to do me then go ahead. Any time any place. I'm looking forward to it.'

'You're a fucking freak,' Philippa told her. Then turned and walked away.

She remained where she was. The battle was over. She had won.

And suddenly she felt terrified. Alone, vulnerable and helpless. An urge swept over her to run after Philippa and beg forgiveness.

This isn't me. I can't do this. I can't!

Her legs started to shake. She wanted to cry. She wanted her father.

But he's not here, Tina. And you don't need him. All you need is the rage. It will protect you. It will give you strength. It can let you be whoever you want to be.

The shaking began to subside. She breathed slowly, listening to the pounding of her heart until that too began to slow.

She left the alcove, keeping her pace steady and her head high.

March. She ate breakfast in the kitchen while watching her mother make coffee.

'I'm going to be late tonight,' her mother told her. 'I'm having a drink with Colin. There's the rest of the quiche in the fridge. You can have that for supper.'

'Thanks, but I won't need it. I'm having a burger in town.'

The coffee made, her mother sat down at the table. 'Who with?'

'A swimming club. Meg, who runs it, says they usually go for a burger afterwards.'

'You're joining a swimming club?'

'Yes.'

'Why? You've never shown much enthusiasm for sport before.'

'Meg's seen me swim. She says I could be really good if I worked at it.'

'I doubt that.'

'Why?'

Her mother waved her hand dismissively.

'Why? How would you know? You've never seen me swim.'

'You're not exactly the athletic type, are you?'

'And you're not exactly an expert, are you?'

Her mother's face darkened. 'I beg your pardon?'

'I said you're not exactly an expert. When was the

last time you did any exercise? And anyway, as you've never bothered to come and see me swim I'd say Meg was better qualified to judge my ability than you.'

The look of anger remained. Together with more than a trace of surprise.

'I should be back by half-past-seven and I'll call if I'm going to be any later.' A pause. 'Which I won't be,' she added placatingly.

'What about your schoolwork?'

'It won't affect it, and if it does I'll stop going. I know how important it is.' Another pause. 'And how proud you are when I do well.'

Her mother didn't answer. The look of surprise increased.

She took her plate to the sink and rinsed it through. 'See you later, Mum,' she said brightly, then went to brush her teeth and apply her eyeliner.

Half past four. She walked into Melchott Sports Centre.

Meg stood by the reception desk with half a dozen boys and girls, all Tina's age or slightly older. One girl she recognized from the school bus. Someone who boarded before her and always sat downstairs. All of them looked athletic, strong and confident. A sense of panic consumed her. What was she doing here? She didn't belong. It was a stupid mistake. Suddenly she wanted to turn and run.

Meg strode over to greet her. Again she was struck by how wonderful Meg's figure was. And remembered why she had come.

'Tina! I was so pleased to get your call. I'd assumed you weren't interested.'

'I'm sorry. I've had a lot of schoolwork. But I'm here now.'

'Which is great. I thought that we'd try working on your front crawl and see if we can improve that technique.'

She smiled. 'Miracles do happen.'

'It won't take a miracle. Stop putting yourself down.' Meg smiled too. 'Going to come for a burger afterwards?'

'Yes. And I'll pay for it too. After all, I haven't won any competitions yet.'

'But you will. I'm sure of it. Come on. Let's go and get changed.'

Together they headed for the changing rooms.

April. She sat in class, completing a French test. The teacher read out a French word or phrase then gave them a short period of time to write down the English translation. Too short, judging by the amount of head scratching that was going on around her. Fortunately she was well prepared and was so far looking at a perfect score.

She stretched in her chair, feeling an ache in her back. Now that she was swimming regularly undiscovered muscles were making their presence felt. At the previous session Meg had shown her how to do the butterfly stroke. It was just as hard as it looked. But she would master it. However long it took.

Sucking on her pen she fiddled with a lock of hair behind her ear. She had decided to let it grow, as Aunty Karen had always urged her to. She was wearing eye-liner, even though make-up was forbidden at school and teachers were always telling her to remove it. Obediently she would do as she was told, only to re-apply it as soon as their backs were turned, just as Philippa did with her ear stud.

Philippa sat two rows ahead of her, looking as baf-fled as most of the others in the class. Subdued too. Word of her new nickname had spread and others were starting to call her Past-it Pippa. Most avoided doing it to her face. But they still did it. And Philippa knew. That was the important thing.

There had been an attempt at retaliation of course. Bianca had christened Tina The Elephant Girl. An effective moniker that should have stuck to her like glue. Only it hadn't. A few people used it but in a very half-hearted way. To be effective a nickname had to be appropriate and perhaps this one didn't seem as if it was.

Perhaps.

And she didn't think it was so appropriate anymore. That was the important thing.

Philippa turned and stared at her with eyes full of the familiar mix of anger and bewilderment. She stared back, feeling the shape of the stone in her pocket, squeezing it gently as if tickling the sleeping dragon inside herself.

They continued to stare at each other. Philippa was the first to look away.

May. She watched a comedy programme with Aunty Karen, Adam and Sue.

It was an improvisation show. A panel of comedians were fed one liners by the host and then required to come up with witty retorts. Each time the host spoke she delivered a retort herself. Aunty Karen laughed at all of them but that was just her way of being kind. But Adam and Sue weren't inclined to be kind and both of them laughed too. The sound was like music to her ears. Wit was a talent she wanted to develop, like a bodybuilder working on a muscle. It was a weapon that could wound and scar. Philippa had already discovered that. If necessary others would too.

The programme continued. Another line was fed. She shot back with a line that prompted more laughter while fiddling with hair that continued to grow.

A warm evening in late July. She sat in the playground by the harbour path with Adam and his friends. The tide was out and the air was full of the dank, dark smell of mud and circling seagulls wailing at the temporary retreat of the sea.

Someone had brought a CD player. Nirvana blasted from its speakers. Adam and his band wanted to be like Nirvana though they had more chance of walking on water. Once she would have kept these thoughts to herself. But not now.

They were all smoking, sharing a packet of cigarettes Mark Fletcher had lifted from the local supermarket. Meg was a smoker too. 'I know I shouldn't,' she had told Tina over a burger. 'But bad habits die hard. Anyway, two of my friends are personal trainers and they both smoke like chimneys, though that's not an invitation for you to start.'

She had though. Just the occasional one, enjoying the soft, warm feel of the filter between her lips. If it threatened to affect her performance in the pool she would stop but it hadn't yet and she continued to make progress. Having mastered the butterfly she was now improving her speed at every attempt. Though the summer holidays had started the club remained active and she never missed a meeting, enjoying the exercise and the camaraderie with her fellow swimmers whom she was now growing to know and like.

Mark passed round a bottle of beer, lifted from the same supermarket as the cigarettes. When it reached her she put it to her lips but didn't swallow. Alcohol dulled the senses and she wanted hers finely attuned at all times.

The current song ended and another one started. Brian, the drummer, took a swig of beer and wiped his mouth. 'It must be so cool touring America. Imagine playing stadiums and shagging all those groupies.' He grabbed his groin and howled.

'Better hurry up and get famous then,' she told him. 'Unlike normal girls groupies don't care how much of a jerk someone is.'

The others laughed. Brian glared at her. 'Just 'cos no guy would want to do you.'

'Does that mean you wouldn't? Phew.' She wiped her brow. 'But just to be on the safe side can I have that in writing.'

More laughter. Brian continued to glare. She returned his stare, remembering all the taunts he had thrown her way in the past and how they had hurt. He was still throwing them but now they just bounced off her like rubber balls. Unlike hers did on him. She kept up the duel of eyes until eventually he looked away.

Her cigarette was finished. She stubbed it out and accepted Mark's offer of another. Karl, the lead singer, exceptionally good-looking and totally narcissistic sat with his arm around a pretty but stupid looking girl called Zoe. 'Look at her trying to act grown up,' Zoe jeered. 'I bet she thinks she's really cool.'

'How could I think that when I'm hanging around with someone like you?'

More laughter. Karl included, much to Zoe's chagrin. She sensed that Karl was confused by her. Girls generally fell at his feet and she was clearly expected to do the same. Not that there was any chance of that. Brian wasn't the only one who had thrown taunts at her with no thought to the pain they might cause. But she could throw them too and with far more skill. Just as her swimming was growing stronger her wit was growing sharper. Too sharp sometimes. Playing with fire, though she knew that if she needed him Adam would defend her.

And if he didn't Mark would. Increasingly she caught him staring at her. Just as he was doing now.

'What?' she asked him.

'It's quarter past eight. Shouldn't little girls like you be in bed?'

'Why? Are you offering to tuck me in?'

'Don't be stupid,' Zoe told her. 'He's well out of your league.'

'Absolutely,' agreed Mark. 'I'm an international playboy.'

'Even though the only person you've ever played with is yourself.'

Yet more laughter. Mark smiled at her. She blew smoke at him and smiled back.

August. Karen walked to the supermarket with Sue and Tina, who was spending the weekend with them while her mother was away.

The high street was crowded. Karen, irritable from the heat, wiped sweat from her forehead. 'Must you slouch like that?' she asked Sue.

'Don't nag, Mum.'

'It looks terrible.'

'Nag nag nag.'

'Well it does. And it's bad for your spine.'

'Give it a rest, Mum. If your tongue flaps any more you'll take off.'

'Don't be cheeky!' snapped Karen before starting to laugh. Sue did too, slouching as badly as before while Tina walked beside them, staring into space, lost in thought. In spite of the heat there was a breeze that lifted the hair that now hung just below her shoulders. Karen was glad she had decided to let it grow. It really suited her.

Once Tina had slouched even worse than Sue. Now she kept her head high and shoulders back. She was growing tall just as her father had been, and her developing figure promised to be a good one like her mother's. Her stride, formerly quick and nervous, was now slower and more confident. There was even a faint sway in her hips. Though adolescent gawkiness was clearly evident it could not hide an underlying grace. It reminded Karen of the models she saw on television. Girls who were learning to control their bodies and carry themselves like thoroughbreds.

Yet Tina seemed unaware of this. She remained lost in thought, moving instinctively as if guided by a programme in her brain that after years of dormancy had suddenly become active.

It was a wonderful change.

Magical even.

There was a commotion up ahead. Two teenage boys chased each other down the street, whooping and laughing. One of them barged between Tina and Sue, almost knocking them to the ground.

Tina turned on her heel. 'Wanker!' she shouted after him. People stopped to stare at her while she glared at his fast retreating back, her eyes blazing while her body radiated strength and the threat of violence. Just as her father had done when his blood had been up.

In spite of the heat Karen felt a sudden chill. As if she had just seen a ghost.

Then the anger faded. Tina flushed. 'Sorry, Aunty Karen.'

'Don't worry, sweetheart. Are you OK?'

'Fine.' Tina touched Sue's arm. 'What about you?'

Sue nodded, then turned and shouted 'Wanker!' as loudly as Tina had done, but with none of the underlying sense of threat.

'Sue!'

'Well he asked for it. Don't nag, Mum.'

'I'm not.'

'Nag nag nag.'

Together the three of them continued on towards the supermarket.

September. The start of the new term. Tina was half way out of the house before realizing she'd left her Maths book in the living room. Turning back she went to fetch it.

Her mother sat on the sofa, having a cup of coffee and a cigarette before leaving for work at an accountants office in town. Colin had found her the job, arguing that if they were seeing each other romantically it was better not to work together too. Perhaps he was right, though the previous week Mark had seen him leaving a Melchott pub with a pretty young woman. 'Arm in arm and very cosy,' was how Mark had described it. But Colin was a tactile person and the woman could just be one of these rich friends he was always talking about.

Could be.

The book was on the coffee table. She picked it up. 'See you tonight, Mum.'

'You're wearing make-up.'

'Only a bit.'

'Why?'

'Why not? Loads of girls in my year do. Anyway, it looks good.'

A snort. 'Who told you that?'

'Some boy I had sex with. Can't remember his name.'

Her mother's jaw dropped. She laughed. 'Relax, Mum. I'm only joking.'

'Jokes like that aren't funny.'

'Neither are digs about my looks, but hey, no one's perfect.'

Her mother frowned. 'What's got into you?'

'Nothing. Are you seeing Colin tonight?'

'What if I am?'

'Just asking. Are you?'

'No. He's got to work late.'

'Was he working late last Thursday too?'

'Yes.' A pause. 'Why?'

She didn't answer.

'Well?'

'You like him a lot, don't you?'

'He likes me a lot too,' said her mother, just a little too emphatically.

She knows about the other woman. Or at least she suspects.

'He's a jerk, Mum. You could do much better.'

'I don't need advice on my love life from you.'

'At least I care about you. That's more than he does.'

Her mother rose to her feet. 'Here we go again.'

'What?'

'You trying to spoil things for me, just like you always do.'

She felt the anger stirring inside her. Taking a deep breath she swallowed it down. 'No I'm not. I'm just . . .'

'Yes you are. Go and take that make-up off. You look like a tart.'

'Well you should know. After all, you're letting Colin treat you like one.'

Her mother slapped her face.

She walked away, not trusting herself to speak. On reaching the door she turned back. 'Mum.'

'What?'

'Don't *ever* hit me again.'

Then she left the house, her make-up still in place.

*

A wet evening in October. Her swimming session finished and a burger devoured she rode the bus home.

A girl called Kim sat beside her. The same girl she had spotted when she first joined the club. Kim was a year above her at school. The two of them had become friends and always sat together on bus journeys.

'You should cut your hair,' Kim told her.

'No way. I like it.'

'Even though you can barely fit it under your swimming cap. I don't blame you though. If I had hair like yours I'd grow it too.'

'Thanks.'

'Do you think Rick's good-looking?'

She laughed. Kim had had crushes on almost all the boys in the club. 'Don't tell me you fancy *him* now.'

Kim blushed. 'Do you think he fancies me?'

'Yes, but not half as much as he fancies himself.'

'He's not that bad.'

'He is. Trust me, Rick will never love any girl as much as a mirror.'

More laughter. 'Who do you fancy then?' asked Kim.

'No one. Boys are idiots.'

And it was true. They were. All except Mark.

He was still taking sly looks at her. Just as she took them at him. Nothing had developed between them. Not yet. But it would.

The journey continued. She continued to laugh and gossip with Kim.

*

November. Eight o'clock on a Wednesday morning. Shaun Barrett, the Australian lifeguard at the Melchott pool, watched the early morning swimmers go through their paces. It was always the same people. Office workers generally, grabbing a quick half hour's exercise before a day at their desk. Them and the teenage girl with the red swimming hat who had recently joined their number.

He watched her plough up and down the fast lane, alternating crawl and butterfly. Most British people were lousy swimmers but her technique was good and growing better with every visit. As she finished her current length an overweight man jumped into the lane and began to breaststroke his way towards the other end, forcing her to stop and wait until he was a reasonable distance ahead. Shaun watched her tread water. Though her eyes were obscured by goggles he could tell by her mouth that she was angry. He found himself wondering why she came here day after day, pushing her body to the limit, and what she thought about as she did.

She looked in his direction. He gave her a wave. Her frown became a smile. Then she moved off again, propelling her body through the water with all the strength she possessed, kicking her legs so ferociously that it was as if she were trying to dislodge a demon attached to her heel.

Half past eight. Her swim over, Tina stood in front of the mirror in the women's changing room staring at her reflection. Her shoulders were growing powerful, her limbs lean and strong. Meg had been right. Swimming was good for the figure. Very good. She could almost feel it changing on every visit.

Pulling off her swimming cap she let her hair fall free. It framed her head like fire, accentuating her eyes that shone like two emeralds at the centre of her face. A blaze of colour that could extinguish lesser lights as easily as fingers snuffing out a candle.

Two women were changing behind her. She could see them out of the corner of her eye casting glances in her direction. Studying her. Envying her, perhaps, just as she had once envied others. One whispered something to the other. Both of them giggled.

Suddenly she felt exposed. Vulnerable. Ridiculous. A frightened, ugly little girl trying hard to be something she was not and never could be.

Ignore them, Tina. They're just jealous. They wish they had what you have. The power to be whoever you want to be.

The feeling went as quickly as it had come. She continued to stare into the mirror, studying the way her costume clung to her body like a second skin while stroking her belly as if soothing the dragon back to sleep.

Mid-morning break. As she walked down the corridor she saw Philippa approaching, carrying a pile of books under her arm. The two of them were no longer in the same class. Philippa had been moved to a less academic one at the end of the previous year. Just as she had slipped from the modelling heights now she was sliding from the intellectual ones too.

As they passed each other Tina thrust out her shoulder, slamming into her one-time nemesis and knocking her to the floor.

'You bitch! You did that on purpose!'

'Damn right. Want to make something of it?'

A woman teacher hurried over. 'What's going on here? Philippa? Tina?'

'Just an accident, Miss,' she answered sweetly. 'Isn't that right, Pippa?'

Philippa flushed. Tina stared down at her with eyes that said 'tell tales on me and see what happens'. Just as Philippa had so often done to her in the past.

'Yes, Miss,' said Philippa quietly. 'It was an accident.'

'Well pick these books up before someone falls over them. And Tina, go to wherever you're going.'

'Yes, Miss. Of course, Miss.' She headed off down the corridor, passing Mark who stood talking with a group of friends. Briefly their eyes locked. His were as curious as ever, if slightly wary. She wondered if he had seen what had just happened. Whether he disapproved.

But it was none of his business. Philippa deserved it, just as everyone who had ever hurt her deserved it. When something developed between them she would explain that to him and make him see it the way she did. And that would be soon. She was sure of it. Absolutely sure.

Smiling she strode on.

February 1993.

A Sunday lunchtime. She walked through Melchott town centre, carrying her swimming stuff in a bag. In two weeks time the club was competing against a club from Basildon. 'Just do your best,' Meg had told her. 'No one expects you to win. At this stage it's all about practice and experience.'

But she wanted to win. To be the best. To shine and be special. Another one in the eye for everyone who had ever tried to put her down.

As she made her way along the High Street she saw Mark standing outside the Arcade. Calling out his name she headed over.

'Swimming again,' he said. 'You'll be growing gills soon.'

'Of course. They're all the rage now and I have to keep up with fashion.'

He laughed. She felt pleased. In recent weeks she had sensed a distance growing between them. Natalie had moved and no longer caught their bus. She had hoped he would come and sit with her, but instead he remained at the back with Adam and the gang.

But that was just what boys did. It didn't mean anything. He still looked pleased to see her and he still laughed at her jokes. He was still her friend. If nothing else.

'We've got a competition coming up,' she told him. 'The opposition are really good so I need to practise as much as possible.'

'I wouldn't worry. No one'll beat you.' Another laugh. 'They wouldn't dare!'

She laughed too. A strange thought entered her head.

He's scared of me. He likes me but he's scared of me.

But that was stupid. He had no reason to be scared. He was her friend and soon, hopefully, would be more. She would never hurt him or even want to.

Unless he hurts you, Tina. Then you'd make him wish he'd never been born.

She shook her head, as if trying to dislodge the idea. 'Do you want to go for a coffee?' she asked. 'My treat to make up for all the fags I've scrounged.'

He looked sheepish. 'I'd like to but I'm meeting someone.'

'Who? One of the band? They can come too and I can be your groupie and tell everyone how cool you are.' She rolled her eyes. 'Unless it's Brian of course.'

'No, it's not him. Actually it's . . .'

He stopped, his face lighting up. She turned, following his gaze.

And saw Natalie approaching, smiling as broadly as him.

The sight was like a blow. It left her winded.

'You don't mind not coming, do you, Tina?'

She didn't answer.

'Tina?'

'I didn't know you were seeing her.'

'I won't be for long.' A nervous laugh. 'Not when she finds out what a jerk I am.'

'If she thinks that she's even more of an idiot than she looks.'

She turned back. He was watching her, his eyes anxious.

Scared?

She forced a smile. 'Don't worry about it. Have a nice time, OK?'

His face relaxed. 'Thanks. See you soon.'

'Hope so. Who else am I going to scrounge fags off?' She walked away quickly before Natalie joined them. When she reached the end of the street she turned back. The two of them were standing together talking animatedly. Natalie said something and Mark laughed, loudly and enthusiastically. Just as he did with her. Then, arm in arm, they headed off in the other direction.

Suddenly time went into reverse. It was a year ago and she was standing on the same street, watching the man she thought was her father walk away from her. A lump came into her throat. She swallowed it down, feeling stupid, vulnerable and weak. Most of all weak.

You are weak, Tina. He's made you weak. You've let him make you weak.

She shook her head.

It's true. You let your guard down. Do that and you give your power away. Do that and you give others the power to hurt you just like your father did.

The lump returned. 'But he was my dad,' she whispered to the air.

And look what he did to you. Look what they all do when you give them power. You're better than this, Tina. Stronger. You don't need any of them. All you need is the rage.

Confused, still shaking her head, she made her way to the bus.

Half an hour later she arrived home.

Her mother was out, spending the day with Colin. The relationship continued to drag on despite more sightings of him with other women. Tina wasn't happy about it but there was nothing she could do. Her mother was more likely to grow wings than take any advice she had to offer.

Besides, it didn't matter. Not when she had more important things to think about.

She entered the living room, heading for the kitchen, and found her mother sitting on the sofa, nursing a glass of red wine.

'Mum, what are you doing here?'

Her mother didn't answer. Just stared down at the wine in the glass. An almost empty bottle stood on the coffee table.

'Mum?'

'We didn't go out. He called and said it's over.' A pause. 'That he doesn't want to see me any more.'

A wave of pity swept over her. 'Oh, Mum.'

'He said he's seeing someone else now. Someone he likes better.' A bitter laugh. 'He said I shouldn't feel bad though. That it was fun while it lasted.'

She cursed him under her breath. 'I'm so sorry. Really I am.' Stretching out a hand she stroked her mother's arm.

'Don't touch me!'

Her mother turned towards her. Her eyes, though dulled with alcohol, still managed to look savage. She felt a lurch in the pit of her stomach.

'You must be loving this. This is just what you wanted. From the moment I started seeing him this is what you wanted. Well I hope you're happy now!'

'I didn't want this! I'll admit I didn't like him. I thought he was a jerk. But I didn't want him to hurt you. I'd never want anyone to do that. You're my mother!'

'God help me!'

'Mum!'

Her mother rose to her feet. 'You had to spoil it, didn't you? Just like you spoiled it between your father and me. Just like you spoil everything you touch!'

'That's not true. Mum . . .'

'Look at you. Long hair and make up and thinking you're something special all of a sudden. Well you're not. You're the same stupid little brat you always were. No wonder Colin wanted to end it. Who in their right mind would want to be stepfather to you?'

The anger was stirring. The dragon starting to breathe fire. She began to panic. 'Mum, I don't want to hear this now.'

'No wonder your father left! No wonder he couldn't wait to get away!'

She shook her head, feeling the rage surging through her veins. Knowing she had to get away before it consumed her completely.

'It wasn't my fault.'

'Of course it was! Everything is your fault!'

'Fuck you!'

Her mother slapped her face. Hard.

And the rage took control.

She punched her mother in the mouth, just as she had once punched Stuart. Her mother staggered back, the look of fury replaced by one of shock and fear.

And it felt good. Even better than with Stuart. A million times better.

She grabbed her mother by the hair, shaking her like a rag doll before throwing her to the floor to cower behind the sofa. Seizing a figurine from the mantelpiece she hurled it at her. Then a second, then a third, while all the time she could hear herself screaming the same words over and over again.

'It wasn't my fault! It wasn't my fault! It wasn't my fault!'

She threw another figurine. It hit the wall, inches above her mother's head, breaking into a hundred pieces. She heard her mother scream. She was still screaming herself.

'It wasn't my fault! All you do is blame me for everything that ever goes wrong in your life and I'm sick to death of it! You do it again and this will be nothing. Do you understand me? You do it again and I swear to God that I'll kill you!'

One last figurine remained on the mantelpiece. She knocked it onto the floor where it smashed like all the others. Leaving her mother cowering she ran from the house.

Two hours later. She sat on the bench at the end of the harbour path, staring out across the mud and the marooned boats that littered its surface. There was hardly anyone about. Just a few people walking dogs. It was cold and the wind sharp. She should have been shivering but anger and adrenalin kept her warm.

She was smoking. Breathing out fire just like the dragon. Consuming a packet of cigarettes Mark had given her the previous week. He had never given her a whole packet before. At the time she had thought it was because he fancied her. Now she knew it was only guilt.

Someone sat down on the bench beside her. Turning, she saw Aunty Karen.

'So, Mum came bleating to you, did she?'

'Oh, Tina . . .'

'I don't need this now. I want to be left alone.'

'No you don't.'

'Don't tell me what I need. You're a housewife, not a psychiatrist. It takes more than watching *Oprah* to become one of those.'

'Do you want to tell me what happened?'

'I've told you what I want.'

'Your mother's in a terrible state. You really frightened her.'

'Good.'

'You don't mean that.'

'A psychic as well as a psychiatrist. Is there no end to your talents?'

Silence, except for the wailing of seagulls overhead. She expected Aunty Karen to leave but the bench remained occupied.

'She wanted to call the police. Thank God your uncle's out for the day, otherwise he might have let her.'

'I don't care if she does. It'll be her story against mine and mine'll be better. I'm much cleverer than her. I'll run rings round the stupid bitch before we even start.'

Another silence. She waited for a reprimand but none came. The absence of one suddenly made her want to explain.

'She said it was my fault.'

'What? Colin?'

'Dad. Always Dad. That's what I can't stand. I don't

care what else she says. I can deal with anything else. I just can't deal with that.'

'She's hurt, Tina. Your father hurt her very badly.' A sigh. 'Not that that's an excuse. He hurt you far worse I'd say.'

She shook her head. 'I'm all right.'

'It wasn't your fault, Tina. None of it. Your father just didn't belong here. I always knew that. Even before you were born I knew that. But he *did* love you. You were the reason he stayed as long as he did.'

'He didn't love me. How could he leave me if he loved me? He must have known how much it was going to hurt me. How can you do that to someone you love? I hate him for that. I hate him but I still miss him. I don't want to but I do. Every time someone knocks on our door I think it could be him. I hope and pray it's him. It's stupid but I can't stop myself. I want him back! I want my Dad!'

She burst into tears. Aunty Karen moved closer, cradling her as if she were a small child, stroking her hair, whispering soothing words while waiting for the storm of emotion to blow itself out.

'I'm so sorry, Tina. For what your dad did to you. For the way your mother treats you. I know how much pain you've been through. No one should have to go through that, least of all a child. I wish I could make it go away. I'd give anything to be able to do that.'

She wiped her eyes. 'I'm sorry too,' she whispered.

'What for, sweetheart?'

'For what I said just now. Those horrible things. I didn't mean them. You're the closest thing to a real mother I've got and I don't want to hurt you.'

'You didn't hurt me.' Aunty Karen continued to stroke her hair. 'But Tina, listen to me. You're angry and God knows you have a right to be but lashing out won't make the pain go away. I know your mother treats you badly but I also know that deep down she loves you and she needs you. You need each other. You may not realize it but you do.'

'She doesn't love me.'

'Yes she does. You're her child. Who else in the world does she have but you?'

'She hates me.'

'She hates herself. Blaming you is her defence. It's not right but it's the only way she knows how to cope. You're stronger than her. Much stronger. Strong enough to forgive. That's what you have to do, Tina. For your own sake let the anger go. Don't keep hold of it. Don't let it grow because it'll only turn round and destroy you if you do.'

She stared into Aunty Karen's eyes. They were soft and warm, just as once years ago her father's had been. She wanted to jump into them. Escape back to that time when everything had been safe and there had been no pain.

That's right, Tina. Escape back to the person you were. The girl who sat in a classroom, praying not to be noticed. The girl who cried for her father's return and

121

her mother's love. The pathetic girl everyone despised. That's what it means, Tina.

Because if you lose the rage you lose everything.

She pulled away. 'You're wrong. I don't need her. I don't love her and I certainly don't need her. I don't need you either. I'm sorry, Aunty Karen. I love you more than anyone in the world, but I don't need you. I don't need anyone and I never will.'

A look of great sadness came into Aunty Karen's face. 'Oh, Tina . . .'

'Tell Mum to do what she wants. I don't care. Thanks for coming to find me. I'm grateful but now I want to be on my own.'

'Are you sure?'

'Yes. You don't have to worry about me. I can look after myself.'

'I love you too, Tina. Like you were my own child. Don't ever forget that.'

Aunty Karen kissed her on the cheek then walked away. She remained where she was, lighting another cigarette and staring out across the mud.

Half an hour passed. She remained on the bench, watching the returning tide creep across the mud plane, burying the dank smell of oil with the freshness of salt.

Footsteps approached. Sue sat down in the space her mother had vacated. She blew smoke into the air. 'Fuck off.'

'Charming.'

'Sorry. Fuck off, please.'

'Is that what you're going to do? Fuck off. Run away like your dad did.'

'I'm not my dad.'

'But you're like him. That's what Mr Jones from your street says. The old man with the dog called Spider. I heard him tell mum that when you were younger you were nothing like your dad but now you remind him of your dad more each day.'

'What does he know?'

'At least he remembers your dad. I don't. Not really. Only bits.'

She took a drag on her cigarette. 'Like what?'

'Like one time when you, me and Adam were really small and playing at your house. Your dad came in and we ran towards him and he picked all three of us up at the same time. I remember thinking how strong he was. Much stronger than my dad. He even smelled strong. I can't describe it but sometimes a man walks past me and he has the same smell and it always makes me think of your dad.'

The tide continued its progress, liberating the becalmed boats that rose up to bob on its surface. She watched the wind catch in their sails and relived her own memories.

'Can I have a cig?' asked Sue.

'You don't smoke. It'll just make you cough.'

'No it won't. I smoke all the time. What sort are you smoking?'

'Marlboro Lights.'

'I like Silk Cut.'

'Sure you do.'

'I do. Where did you get those? Did you steal them?'

'No. Mark Fletcher did.'

'Why did he give them to you?'

'Because I gave him a blow job.'

'You didn't!'

She lit one and held it out. 'Go on then. Impress me with how grown-up you are.'

Sue inhaled deeply, then began to choke.

She laughed. 'See?'

'It's only because they're not Silk Cut. If they were Silk Cut I'd be fine.' A pause. 'Your mum was crying. You made her cry.'

'I don't care.'

'She's your mum.'

'She's a bitch. She got what she deserved.'

'But she's still your mum.'

'I don't need her or dad. I don't need anyone.'

'I wish I was like you.'

The comment took her by surprise. 'Why?'

'Cos you're tough. And you're gorgeous. That's what the boys in my class think.' A sigh. 'I wish they thought that about me.'

'It's easy. Just learn how to hate. You can be whoever you want if you do that.'

'What do you mean?'

She watched the cold, red winter sun sink towards

the horizon. 'Nothing,' she said quietly. 'Forget it.'

'Don't go away, Tina. I'd hate it if you did.'

She took the cigarette from Sue's mouth. 'Don't smoke any more. It's a stupid habit and I know you don't like it.' A smile. 'Don't worry. I won't tell anyone.'

'I'll smoke a thousand a day unless you promise to stay.'

'How will *you* get a thousand cigarettes a day?'

'Easy. You're not the only one who can give blow jobs.'

Again she laughed. Sue stared at her. 'Do you promise?'

The boats continued to bob on the water. She wondered if her father was on a boat somewhere, riding the waves with the wind in his face and the taste of salt on his lips. Was he thinking about her? Did he ever think about her anymore or had he forgotten her completely?

Not that it mattered. She had forgotten him too. Or at least she didn't need him.

Which was almost the same thing.

'I promise. Don't worry any more. You look cold. Why don't you go home?'

'You come too.'

'Not yet. I want to sit here a bit longer. After all, it's a shame to waste your cigarette.'

'Love you, Tina.'

'Love you too. Even though you can't smoke.'

Sue walked away, just as Aunty Karen had done.

She remained where she was, staring out across the newly returned water.

It was late by the time she arrived home. There was no sign of her mother. Perhaps she was still at Uncle Neil's. Perhaps she was at the police station telling tales about her psychopathic daughter. Perhaps she was hiding in her bedroom. Tina didn't care which: her mother's life was her own. She had no interest in it. Not any more.

She went to the kitchen, drank a glass of water, then made her way to bed.

The next morning she sat in the kitchen, eating breakfast. Her mother sat with her, sipping coffee. The radio was playing, the DJ's prattle failing to fill the vast gulf of silence between them. Her mother's mouth was swollen, just as Stuart's had once been, and her blonde hair looked as if it had been attacked with shears. It was remarkable how destructive the fury could be.

But only when she lost control of it. She had done so the previous day but she would never do so again. From now on she would always be in control.

Her mother kept staring at her. The same look of bewilderment she had seen in the faces of so many others over the past year.

She's waiting for me to grovel. To beg for forgiveness.

But I'm not sorry. And hell will freeze over before I'll tell her that I am.

She finished her toast. Rising to her feet she headed for the living room.

'I could leave too,' her mother said softly. 'Just like your father did.'

She turned back. 'Is that the best you can do?'

'Do you think I'm joking?'

'Do you think I care? Threats are supposed to make people afraid of you, not despise you even more than they do already. If you want to leave then go ahead. I'll help you pack. I'll even let you take my suitcase. It's bigger than yours.'

'I'm not joking, Tina.'

'Let's pack then. I've got time. The bus doesn't go for half an hour.'

'You can't treat me like this! I'm your mother!'

'God help me.'

Her mother swallowed.

'Dad hated you. He told me that when we were on the boat together. He hated how clingy and possessive you were. I hate you too, just like I hate him. You're both weak. You're both losers. Go ahead and leave but do it because you want to and not to hurt me because, believe me, I won't even notice that you've gone.'

She took a step forward, putting her hands on the table, staring into her mother's face.

'But if you stay then know how it's going to be from now on. I'll work hard and do well at school. I won't stay out late or get into trouble. I'll be the sort of daughter any decent mother would be proud of. But outside of that my life is my business. It has nothing to do with you any more and it never will.'

Then she walked back into the living room, leaving her mother at the table.

Half past seven that evening. Swimming practise over she walked down the street towards the house. The living room light was on, just as she had expected. Her mother wasn't strong enough to cope without Uncle Neil and Aunty Karen to lean on. Too weak and too frightened. Just as she had been before the rage.

She entered to the smell of paella. Her favourite dish. A peace offering from her mother, as if a plate of food could cure what was wrong between them.

Her mother appeared from the kitchen. 'Are you hungry?'

'Yes.'

'Good. Supper will be ready in ten minutes.' The eyes still looked bewildered, as if to say 'I don't know who you are'. But then, her mother had never taken the trouble to find out who she really was. Once that had hurt more than all the blows; now it was nothing. As trivial as rain.

'I'll get changed,' she said, then went upstairs.

May. Three months later.

The school bus arrived at quarter-past-eight, just as it always did. She boarded with the others, waving her pass at the conductor. Though there were numerous spaces downstairs she made her way to the upper level. Once she had hated the way her shoes clattered on the stairs. Now she relished the sound. It was like a declaration. 'Watch out everyone. Here I come.'

Her usual double seat was part occupied. Kim was waiting for her. She headed down the aisle, striding where once she would have scurried, passing Philippa, Bianca and Stuart, all of whom watched her warily out of the corners of their eyes. Due to her early morning swimming sessions she was not the regular passenger she had once been. She suspected they were glad about that. As well they might be.

The usual group of boys occupied the back row. Adam went to join them. She watched them laugh and joke together. Once she had found them intimidating. Now they reminded her of a row of sitting ducks on a fairground stall while her tongue was a rifle with which she could knock any or all of them from their perches whenever she chose.

She sat down next to Kim. 'Didn't think you'd be joining us today, Tina. Not with the competition against Romford next week.'

'Thought I'd have a day off. Don't want to wear myself out before the main event. Do you remember how smug the Romford girls were when they beat us last time. This time I'm going to wipe the grins off their faces.'

And she would. She was growing faster and stronger all the time, her skill developing just as her figure did.

Recently she had joined a dance club. Dancing was good exercise, as well as wonderful for poise and posture. She loved the way dancers carried themselves. As confidently and gracefully as the models she had once watched so wistfully on television.

Kim began to talk about her latest crush. The two girls in front joined the conversation. Both were in Kim's year and had also become friends. She started to tease Kim, telling her that all boys were idiots. 'I don't know why God gave them brains. The only organ they know how to think with is the one between their legs and even when they're thinking as hard as they can it still isn't much to write home about.'

Kim and the others laughed. She continued to make jokes while sensing others watching her. Philippa glanced furtively in her direction, wondering, perhaps, if she was the cause of their mirth. She glared back and Philippa quickly turned away.

Mark was watching her too. She could feel his eyes like two small points of heat on the back of her neck. Mark was no longer seeing Natalie. After months of lusting over an ideal it had only taken him a couple of weeks to become bored with the tedious reality. She was glad of that, though had never let him see it. When they sat with Adam and the gang in the playground by the harbour wall she treated him just as she always had, tossing barbs in his direction and catching his in return. Sometimes hers were cutting but she would usually follow a particularly lacerating one with a kinder remark. It was just fun, after all. Just a game. There was no need for him to be hurt, and if he was then it just meant that he was weak and not deserving of her attention.

Besides, someone else had that now. A boy who went to Abbeycroft and was one of her fellow stars on the swimming club. 'He fancies you rotten,' Kim and the other girls kept telling her. She fancied him too but gave little indication of this, mixing occasional flirtatiousness with bored indifference, increasing his interest while retaining complete control of the situation.

The bus rumbled on. She continued to make jokes, keeping her friends in constant fits of laughter like a comedian with an audience in the palm of her hand. It made her feel good. The sense of belonging. The sense of power. The knowledge of being in control.

Lunchtime. Caroline Derry, who taught a third year class at Melchott Comprehensive, sat, thinking in her classroom. A new girl would be joining the class after the half term break. A shy, anxious girl who was clearly frightened at the prospect of starting at a new school and could easily become the target of bullies were she left unprotected.

To guard against that, Caroline planned to ask Tina Ryan to keep an eye on her. Take her under her wing so to speak. Tina was a tough girl whom the others seemed to hold in awe. A girl who marched down corridors and into classrooms as if she owned them and was as likely to be bullied as she was to grow another head.

The previous weekend, Caroline had met an elderly teacher from Havelock called Rosemary Fleming and the two of them had compared notes on some of the children they had both taught. Rosemary claimed to remember Tina, though she clearly didn't. The girl she described had been little more than a shadow. A timid, mousy child whom the others had laughed at and despised on those rare occasions when they bothered to notice her at all.

But it was easy to make mistakes. After teaching for decades it was inevitable that sometimes one child could be confused with another who bore no relation to them whatsoever.

Yes, she would ask Tina to look after the new girl. That would be best.

Smiling to herself, pleased at solving a problem, she went to have lunch.

Saturday. Four days later. As she left the supermarket, weighed down with shopping, Karen saw Tina walking on the other side of the street.

She stopped to watch her, feeling a strange mixture of pride and worry. The ugly duckling of two years earlier had vanished, replaced by a tall, elegant swan who carried herself superbly, gliding down the street as if it were a catwalk, oblivious to the admiring glances that came her way. Going about her business with an aura of total self sufficiency. Needing nothing from anyone. Supremely confident in who and what she was.

But Karen knew better.

Tina's hair hung down her back. A glorious mass of auburn that caught the rays of the early summer sun. It was like plumage. The plumage of an angry, damaged swan who used it both to entice and to hide the scars that lay beneath.

Tina passed a group of boys. Most turned to stare. One began to whistle. She ignored them all, continuing on her way. Again, Karen felt proud. But the worry remained.

Sunday evening. Eight days later.

Tina sat at her bedroom desk, staring at the trophies she had won in the swimming competition that afternoon. One for butterfly, one for crawl. She had won each event comfortably, wiping the grins from the faces of the Romford girls, just as she told Kim and the others that she would.

Aunty Karen had come to watch her compete. Her mother had stayed away. Not that it mattered. She didn't want her mother's support. She would never want anything from her mother again. Or her father.

The desk drawer where she had kept the presents she had bought him was now empty. She had thrown them away, just as she had done the maps of Ireland and the world. All of them were remnants of a life that someone else had lived, assuming you could dignify it with the word 'life' at all.

Reaching into her top drawer she pulled out a diary. The one this other person had kept. The baby girl. The spineless, pathetic little nothing whose entries had been pitiful pleas for love and dreams of magic. The weakling who had never understood that the magic came from within. That it was made of rage and the strength to never need anyone ever again. She hated that girl. More than Stuart. More than Philippa. More even than her parents.

She hated that girl more than anyone else in the world.

But times changed. Eras ended. The Queen is dead, long live the Queen.

Picking up her pen she began to write:

One day I am going to be somebody. One day I will be famous and everyone will know my name. Newspapers will write about me and everyone who's ever hurt or despised me will read them and boast that they once knew THE Christina Ryan. My father, wherever he is, will read them and wish that he'd never left me. He'll come crawling back on his hands and knees, begging me to forgive him, and when he does I'll laugh in his face and send him crawling away again.

Because I'll have other men to love me. Men

who will never leave me. Men who will do anything I ask. Men who would kill if need be, just to stay in my life.

One day it will happen. I'm going to make it happen.

Whatever it takes.
Whatever it takes!

Whatever it takes.

Part 2
Subjugation

London: October 2004

It was nearly midnight and the police station was busy processing the evening's business. The usual batch of drunk and disorderlies. A man who had beaten up a prostitute. Another who had knifed someone during a mugging. That and the constant phone calls from journalists asking about the case the whole country was talking about.

Nigel Bullen stood in the corridor with psychiatrist Clive Lovell who had just finished speaking with the suspect.

'So, what do you think?' Nigel asked.

'The desire was there, unquestionably. But desiring an act isn't the same as bringing it about. You won't get an admission. I'd put money on that.'

'But is there an admission to be made? Could it all be circumstantial?'

'I can't say yet. The denials were very plausible but

that's hardly surprising when you think what's at stake.'

'You were in there for hours. You must have an opinion.'

Clive gave a sad smile. 'Oh I do. On one thing at least.'

'And what's that?'

'That Philip Larkin was right. They fuck you up, your mum and dad. They may not mean to but they do . . .'

Central London: June 2004

Four Months Earlier

A hot Friday night and the club was packed. While those high on drink, drugs or adrenalin filled the dance floor, others gathered on its fringes, alone or in groups, watching them and each other. All striving to be noticed or waiting to be impressed.

For Dan Hedges: rich, good-looking and deeply self satisfied, the wait was over. As his friends ogled a blonde nearby he stared at the girl who stood on the other side of the dance floor, talking with two others. Dan liked tall, elegant girls with luxuriant long hair and this one ticked all the boxes. He took a drag on his cigarette and prepared to make his move.

But there was no need. Turning, she registered his gaze. He winked at her. Briefly she looked disdainful. Playing hard to get. He breathed out smoke and winked again. She smiled, said something to her friends and made her way over, striding through the dancers who made a path for her progress. He drank in her appearance. Her figure was superb and she moved like a goddess.

'Hi,' he said when she reached him.

'Hi yourself.' Her voice was low and throaty. Another turn on.

'Enjoying your evening?'

'Not excessively.'

Aware of his friends listening he began to perform. 'Then allow me to improve it.'

'Do you think you can?'

'I'm sure of it.'

'How wonderful.' She gestured to his cigarette. 'May I?'

He offered her one. She seized the packet, turned and strode back to her friends. His own started laughing. He laughed himself to mask embarrassment.

Two minutes passed. To his surprise she returned with a somewhat depleted pack.

'So you couldn't keep away.'

She looked amused. 'If you say so. Thanks. My friends were very grateful.'

'I'm Dan. I'm a broker.'

'How nice for you.'

'It is. I earn a fortune.' He wanted her to be impressed but the look of amusement remained. Though her eyes were lovely her features were unremarkable. Not that it mattered. She projected the illusion of beauty as effortlessly as breathing.

'What's your name?' he asked.

'Chrissie.'

'A beautiful name. It suits you. Tell me, Chrissie, why is someone as gorgeous as you on her own?'

'Tell me, Dan, do you moonlight as a cook?'

'Why do you ask that?'

'Because you reek of corn.'

His friends laughed. Again he felt embarrassed. 'Not corn. Curiosity.'

'I'm not on my own. I'm with friends.'

'You know what I mean.'

'Boyfriend?'

He nodded.

'Working late.'

'At what?'

'Why do you ask? Worried he might earn more than you?'

His embarrassment increased. 'Of course not,' he said, trying not to sound defensive.

'Of course not. I must get back. 'Bye, Dan. Enjoy your evening.'

She turned to go. Not wanting to admit defeat he caught her arm. Her eyes narrowed and quickly he released his grip. She had a presence about her. Strength, self-possession and a hint of danger. He began to feel out of his depth. Acutely aware of his friends he tried to make up ground. 'Why not stay? I feel like champagne and hate drinking it on my own.'

'Poor old rich old you.'

'If you don't like champagne I could get something better.'

'And what's that?'

He put a finger to his nostril and made a sniffing sound.

'Snuff? How suave. Are your pipes colour co-ordinated with your slippers?'

Again his friends laughed. 'You know what I mean,' he said irritably.

'Coke? Sorry, I should have guessed when I saw your nose bleeding.'

Panicking, he put his hand to his face but felt nothing. 'You got me there.'

'You sound impressed.'

'Shouldn't I be?'

'Not when you make it so easy.'

He began to feel angry. 'You think I'm obvious?'

'Aren't you?'

'You don't know anything about me.'

'A pretty face, a big wallet and an ego for a personality. What else is there to know?'

His anger increased. 'So what do you do that's so special?'

'A lot of things, though snorting drugs in club toilets isn't one of them. But don't take it to heart. With your money and special brand of charm I'm sure you won't be alone for long.'

This time he let her go. 'Nice going, Casanova,' jeered his friends. 'Another broken heart to add to the collection.'

'Fuck her.'

'You wish.'

'Fuck you. I'm getting another drink.'

As he stood at the bar he noticed a pretty dark-haired girl staring at him. He winked at her. She giggled and he beckoned her over. 'Hi, I'm Dan. I'm a broker.'

'I'm Natalie.'

'A beautiful name. It really suits you. Tell me, Natalie, why is someone as gorgeous as you on her own?'

More giggling. He made a joke. She laughed, the sound soothing his bruised ego. Yet as they spoke he kept gazing over her shoulder at the tall girl with the long hair who stood talking with her friends, as oblivious to him as if they had never met.

Monday morning. Three days later. Chrissie sat in the living room of her flat.

Her flatmate, Tara, appeared in a dressing gown. 'Hi,' she said. 'There's coffee made if you want some.'

'Thanks.' Tara, a recently qualified accountant yawned. 'God, I hate Mondays.'

'I know the feeling.'

'No, you don't. You love your job. This week we're doing the books for a sewage company. I wish you'd taken that jerk up on his offer of drugs. I could do with something to dull the pain.'

'I'm meeting Mel tonight if you want to come.'

'Not Kev? Is everything OK between you two?'

'Why do you ask?'

'You don't seem to be seeing much of each other.'

'We're just busy, that's all.' She rose to her feet. 'Want to come?'

'Sure, unless I've slashed my wrists in the meantime.'

'Well if you do then please don't leave me your clothes. I have an image to maintain.'

Tara laughed. 'Bitch!'

'Have a bearable day. See you tonight.'

The two of them shared a third floor flat in a new development in Islington. As the morning was warm and the sky clear she decided to walk to work. Heading south, she made her way through Clerkenwell and Farringdon before turning west towards Tottenham Court Road and down into Soho. Though still early it was already full of people heading for offices or drinking coffee in alfresco cafes while breathing in the smell of a dozen different cuisines already starting to emanate from restaurant kitchens.

Magwitch Productions, an independent film company, was located between a sandwich bar and a health shop. The front door was already open. Bob Monk sat at his desk, talking hard on the telephone. 'But Jan, you've seen our casting suggestions. Chrissie e-mailed them to you last week.' A pause. 'Well she said she had so yes.' He looked up and saw her. 'Did you?' he mouthed.

'Twice,' she mouthed back.

Rolling his eyes he continued talking.

Her office was next to his. While waiting for her computer to warm up she listened to her telephone messages. One was from an anxious sounding Kevin. 'Hi, it's me. Guess you didn't get my message yesterday. Hope everything's OK. I'm in the office. Call me, yeah? Miss you.' She considered doing so, then decided it could wait.

E-mails arrived in a flood. One was from a literary agent friend called Anna, telling her about a new book. 'Would make brilliant film. Am sending a copy. Read quickly! Bidding war developing as I type.' She laughed, recognizing Anna speak for 'We're desperate to sell. For God's sake make an offer!'

Bob appeared in her doorway. 'What's so funny?'

'Just one of Anna's hyper sales pitches. Did Jan find his list?'

'Not before my eardrums took a pounding.'

'You're too nice. Next time put him through to me. I'll set him straight.'

'We need him, remember.'

'Not that much. You said yourself there are other sources if he bailed. Anyway, he obviously wants in and why not? It's a great project. Trust me, he's not going anywhere.'

Bob smiled. He was a small, stocky man in his late forties with a bald head and kind face. She had worked as his assistant for a year and enjoyed doing so.

Though passionate about his work he was hopelessly non-confrontational and had a dread of using the word 'no'. But that was where she came in. She could browbeat and stonewall with the best of them.

'Free for lunch, Ballsy?' he asked, using his nickname for her.

'Why's that, Brains?' she replied, using hers for him.

'I'm taking that new casting agent out.'

'I'm supposed to be meeting my cousin. I could cancel if it's important.'

'Don't worry. Is this your rock star cousin?'

'Yes. The family free spirit. Compared to him I'm tragically conservative.'

Laughing, he headed back to his office. An e-mail arrived from Kevin, reading much as the message he had left on her phone. Quickly she typed a reply.

'Am fine, just frantic. Will call tonight.'

She was about to press send, then guilt got the better of her.

'Miss you too,' she added.

The message despatched she focused on the day ahead.

Lunchtime. She sat in a bistro on Fleet Street with Adam and his fiancée, Rachel.

Adam wore an expensive suit that had once hung loose but now looked tight. He worked for an Insurance company in the City and client lunches were taking their toll. 'Tell me,' she asked him, 'is it true or just a vicious rumour that you were once actually interesting?'

Adam looked indignant.

'It's true?'

'No, it's a lie. Who spreads these things?'

'I don't know. Just twisted people.'

Rachel looked confused. She had never got their humour, but then unless it involved wedding plans Rachel didn't get much of anything.

'How's the project going?' Adam asked.

'Great. Bob's all fired up about it. He thinks it could really be something.'

'What project?' asked Rachel.

'Chrissie's got Bob to option a book she read. She's already identified a potential screenwriter and worked out possible casting and locations.'

'Now all we have to do is raise about three mill in finance.'

'Ouch.'

'Sounds like a wedding,' Rachel told her. 'You wouldn't believe how expensive one can be.'

'Really, Rachel? Is that a fact?'

Adam kicked her under the table. Smiling sweetly she kicked him back. As Rachel complained about the cost of floral decorations a waiter arrived with their drinks. Knowing she shouldn't she lit a cigarette. Rachel hated smoking. But that was part of the appeal.

'There's so much to do,' droned Rachel while trying

to avoid the smoke being blown in her direction. 'I don't know how we'll get it all done.'

'I can imagine. You've only got a year to buy a dress, book a church, hire a caterer and write some invitations. A workload like that would kill me.'

'There's more to it than that.'

'No there's not. It's a wedding, not the Olympics. The important thing is tying the knot with the man you love, not making sure the bridesmaids' orchids match the napkins.'

Rachel looked hurt. 'I'm sorry if I'm boring you.'

'You're not,' said Adam quickly.

'Of course you're not. I feel like I could listen to your wedding plans for hours but maybe that's because I already have.'

A bewildered Rachel sought refuge in the ladies. 'Stop winding her up,' said Adam once they were alone.

'Oh piss off, Ad. You're as bored with it as I am.'

'No I'm not.'

'Liar, liar, Calvin Klein boxer shorts on fire.'

'All right I am. But it's her big day. I want her to enjoy it.'

'So do I, amazingly enough. I just don't want to hear about it every time we meet.'

'That's what Mum said. When we went out for dinner Rach talked about seating plans non stop for an hour. Mum almost nodded off!'

She laughed. Though smiling he began to look wistful.

'Thinking about your Dad?' she asked.

He nodded. Uncle Neil had died of a heart attack the previous year. Though she had never been close to him she missed him now he was gone. But not as much as Adam who had lost a father. That was something they now had in common.

Except that she never missed hers. Not even for a second.

Reaching across the table she squeezed his hand. 'When she comes back I promise to be nice.'

'Even if she talks seating plans?'

'Don't push your luck, buddy. Blood ties only count for so much.'

He laughed. Rachel returned and their food arrived. She stubbed out her cigarette. 'Don't take any notice of me. I've just had a shitty morning.'

'It's all right,' Rachel told her. 'I know what a joker you are.'

'That's me. Maybe I should do a stand-up routine at your reception. You needn't worry about cost. I'd do it for free.'

'We're going to Havelock this weekend,' said Adam, hastily changing the subject. 'Why don't you come? You could see your mum.'

'No thanks. I can wait until Christmas.'

Rachel looked shocked. 'You're not seeing your mother until Christmas?'

'So?'

'I'd hate not seeing my mother for so long.'

'Why? Not enough people to talk weddings with?'

How's Kev?' asked Adam, again changing the subject.

'Working flat out.'

'I really like him,' said Rachel. 'Do you think he'd mind wearing a morning suit for the wedding?'

'I'm sure he wouldn't. After all, we all want your big day to be as perfect as possible.'

Yet again Adam kicked her. Trying not to laugh she kicked him back.

That evening she met her friend Melanie. It was just the two of them. A depressed sounding Tara had phoned to say that she had to work late.

Melanie, a publishing assistant, lived in a large flat in Maida Vale owned by her parents. After coffee there they walked through wide streets lined with elegant white stone houses. 'I love this part of town,' she told Melanie.

'Me too. It's really peaceful but only five minutes from the buzz of the Edgware Road. There's a great Burmese restaurant there. We'll have to go next time you're here.'

'Definitely. Where's this pub you were telling me about?'

Melanie led her down a sidestreet. The Wayfarer was on the left, just yards from the Little Venice canal and the narrow boats moored on its banks. Inside it was small and cosy; more like someone's living room than a public place. Subdued lighting, oil paintings on the wall and The Byrds playing softly in the background.

While Melanie bought the drinks she sat down at a table in the corner. Nearby a group of middle-aged men in jumpers drank beer and talked about sport. They reminded her of the locals who had frequented the Havelock pubs, putting the world to rights over a pint. One of them raised his glass to her.

'Do you think he's cute?' asked Melanie as she returned with two glasses of wine.

'Do me a favour. He's old enough to be my grandfather.'

'Not him. The barman.'

She looked over. A man of about thirty with dark hair and a goatee was talking to an elderly woman sitting on a stool. 'Why? Do you?'

'Yes.' Melanie giggled. 'So don't tell Rick. You know what he's like.'

She did. Recently Melanie's boyfriend, Rick, had made a pass at her at a party, only backing off when she had threatened to kick his balls into orbit. Rick was a nasty piece of work but Melanie was besotted and would never believe it if she were told.

But that was Melanie. Naive, trusting and provoking in her the same sense of protectiveness she felt towards her cousin, Sue. That and relief that she would never need anyone to feel protective towards her.

Something nudged her leg. A white Staffordshire

Bull Terrier with black fur around one eye stared hopefully up at her. Patting its head she finished her drink then went to buy another round. 'Great choice of music,' she told the barman.

'You like this stuff?'

'Love it.'

'My parents raised me on it. They always said sixties music was the best.'

'My aunt said the same.'

He poured the wine. 'Who else do you like?'

'Donovan. And Joni Mitchell. I love her voice.'

'What's your favourite Joni Mitchell song?'

'"Woodstock".'

'Mine too. Is Bullseye bothering you by the way? I can put him behind the bar if he is. The landlord lets me bring him in on condition he doesn't bother anyone.'

'He's not bothering me. Does he like crisps?'

'Loves them, but not as much as pizza. We don't serve food so people bring them in from the Italian place next door. Once he swiped a whole one and nearly got me the sack.'

'So what flavour crisps does he like?'

'Ready salted. Don't be fooled by the designer collar. He's a simple mutt at heart.'

Laughing she paid for the round and returned to Melanie.

'What were you talking to Jack about?'

'Who?'

'The barman.'

She fed Bullseye a crisp. 'Music and mutts.'

Melanie began to describe a proposed trip to Portugal. As she listened she thought about Kevin. She had called him that afternoon and arranged dinner for the following evening. He had said he had a surprise for her. She had one for him too but had kept quiet about that.

Joni Mitchell began to sing 'Woodstock'. She looked up, caught Jack's eye and mouthed a thank you. He gave her a grin then continued talking to the elderly woman.

The following evening she had dinner with Kevin at a Thai restaurant in the West End.

A waiter brought a bottle of wine. 'Did you have a good swim?' Kevin asked as he filled her glass.

She nibbled a prawn cracker. 'Not really. I kept having to negotiate breaststrokers. I don't know why they call it the fast lane. It takes them forever just to do a length.'

'Well, you look great. You always do after exercise.'

'Are you saying I look crap the rest of the time?'

'No! Anything but.'

'Relax. I'm only teasing. You look great too. New shirt?'

'Yes. Do you like it?'

'Very much.'

'I hoped you would.'

'Well I do.'

Silence. She longed for a cigarette but resisted temptation. He would only insist on lighting it for her, just as he tried to do everything for her.

She thought back six months to their first date. It had been in a restaurant similar to the one they sat in now. He had arrived late, full of stories of how busy a stockbroker's life was, making out that he was hugely important and doing her a favour by fitting her into his packed schedule. Other girls might have been intimidated but she had realized he was just trying to make an impression. Puffing himself up. Playing a game.

But she could play too. Countering his affected indifference with affected boredom. Tapping into his insecurities just as he was trying to tap into hers. Their early dates had all been like that. Emotional poker matches with each guarding their hands until eventually he had folded and shown her his. Told her that he thought she was special and that being with her made him happy. The revelation had been a welcome one because being with him made her happy too.

And it had. For a time. He was always trying to please her: constantly buying her presents, always wanting to do what she wanted to do. At first she had enjoyed his devotion. Then it had grown irritating. Stifling. Something she would be happier without.

Their food arrived. She began to eat. 'Is it OK?' he asked. She nodded, wishing he would stop worrying.

Show some of the backbone that had attracted her in the first place.

He handed her a brochure for a luxurious hotel in Cornwall. 'This is the surprise I told you about. It used to be a stately home. They've even got a resident ghost. It's near the coast too. Only a couple of miles from the best scenery in the county. I thought we could go this weekend. You've always said it's a part of the world you'd like to see.'

She gazed at him. A handsome man in his late twenties whose eyes had once radiated confidence but now seemed as soft and pleading as those of the dog she had fed crisps to in the pub. Steeling herself, she prepared to break the news.

'I don't think it's a good idea, Kev.'

'Don't worry about money. It's my treat. If this weekend's no good we could pick another. Just let me know which one's best for you.'

'It's not the money.'

'Then what?'

She put down the leaflet. 'I don't think we should see each other any more.'

He swallowed.

'I'm sorry.'

'Is it the hours? I told you it won't be for long. It's—'

'It's not the hours. It's . . .'

You

'Me. I just don't feel ready for a serious relationship.'

'Who says it's serious? I thought we were just having fun. That's what we always said, that it was just fun.'

'But it's not just fun, is it? Not to you. You want more from me than I can give and that's why I think we should call it a day.'

Another silence, while on a nearby table people laughed loudly at a shared joke. He was still staring at her, the puppy-like eyes full of unspoken reproach, making her feel like a bully persecuting someone weaker than herself.

But he shouldn't be weak. If he wasn't weak this wouldn't be happening.

'It doesn't have to be the end. We can still be friends.'

'That's easy for you to say. You're not the one being dumped.'

'We all get dumped.'

'You told me it had never happened to you.'

'I lied. I was trying to impress you. That's what people do on first dates, isn't it?'

He looked close to tears. The sense of guilt increased. She didn't want to hurt him. Though she didn't respect him she didn't want to hurt him.

'I'm sorry, Kev.'

'Are you?'

'Of course. What do you take me for?'

'Everything my sister said you were.'

'What do you mean?'

'She always said you didn't care about anyone except yourself.'

'That's not true.'

'The first time she met you she said you were dangerous: damaged goods. That you weren't capable of real feelings and would hurt any guy who cared about you.'

The guilt vanished, replaced by anger. 'And what does your airhead sister know about anything?'

'She knows about you.'

'She knows nothing! What has she done with her life except get married, breed babies and sponge off her husband? She's a spineless cow who's never had the guts to try and have a career and achieve something and hates women who do and if you listen to her crap then you're an even bigger loser than I thought.'

Again he swallowed. The hurt was back. 'I'm not a loser.'

'Whatever. It's over, Kev. Shit happens. Deal with it. Grow a backbone and stop being so fucking weak!'

The people on the next table were staring. 'Something to add?' she demanded. Hastily they resumed their conversation, talking louder than was necessary as if to make the point.

She breathed deeply, furious with herself for losing her temper. For losing control.

'I didn't mean that, Kev. I've never thought you were a loser. You're a really great guy. You're just not right for me.'

She expected him to protest. Instead he said nothing.

Unexpectedly she found his silence wounding, yet she respected him for it.

'You'll find someone else. Everywhere we go I see girls staring at you. A couple of months and you won't even remember my name.'

'Don't,' he said. 'Not now, OK?'

'OK.'

They finished their meal in silence while the people on the next table continued to talk too loud.

The following afternoon she walked through Soho with Bob, the two of them returning to the office after a meeting.

'You're quiet,' he remarked. 'Everything OK?'

'Kev and I split up.'

'How did he take it?'

'Who says I was the one to call time?'

He didn't answer. Just laughed.

'Well?'

'Come on, Ballsy. When did anyone ever finish with you?'

Never

'That doesn't give you the right to assume.'

'So he broke the mould, did he?'

'No.'

'Thought not.' He stopped outside a patisserie. 'I'm famished. Think I'll get a Danish.'

'You just want to drool over the guy behind the counter.'

Feigning indignation he entered the shop. She remained where she was, smiling. Drooling was all Bob would ever do. He lived with a photographer called Malcolm and each was devoted to the other. It was a strong relationship, reminding her of the one that had existed between Uncle Neil and Aunty Karen. She hoped Adam and Rachel's would prove as strong. Everyone needed someone to depend on. To love and be loved by.

Well, almost everyone.

A young gay couple walked past, hand in hand. One of them looked like Kevin. Again she felt guilty. Again she pushed the feeling away. She was only twenty-five and had a career ladder to climb. Goals to achieve. Emotional attachments were distractions she didn't need.

Bob appeared, holding a cream slice. 'Want some?'

'So much for being famished.'

He handed her half. Gorging inelegantly they continued on their way.

Saturday evening. She made her way up the stairs towards Melanie's flat. Melanie stood waiting at the door. 'Why don't you use the lift?'

'Lifts are for slobs.' She handed over a bottle of wine.

While Melanie went to fetch glasses she entered the living room. It was expensively furnished and more than twice the size of her own. One of the perks of having wealthy parents.

Melanie returned with the wine, glasses and crisps on a tray. 'How was last night?'

'Brilliant.' She had been to a dance club near King's Cross. 'The music was great. Seventies disco stuff. You should have come. You'd have loved it.'

'I wish I could have but Rick hates me going out without him.'

'Next month they're having an eighties electro night. You must come to that.'

'Sorry about you and Kev by the way.'

'Don't be. I'm fine.'

'If Rick and I split up I'd be gutted.'

'You'd survive. I'd get you through it. When is he back? Tomorrow?'

'This afternoon. Actually he's coming round soon.'

Her heart sank.

'You don't mind, do you?'

'Not at all,' she said, trying to sound pleased.

Half an hour passed. They finished the wine. Melanie suggested opening another bottle but she declined, never liking to drink more than a couple of glasses. Besides, the prospect of spending time with Rick was growing less appealing by the second. Pleading tiredness she made an early exit.

As she left the building she saw him approaching. He flashed his trademark cocky smile. 'Hello, Chrissie. Not leaving, are you?'

'Looks that way, doesn't it. How was your trip?'

'Very successful. We closed the deal.'

'That's an interesting turn of phrase. Wouldn't a better one be "put the deal to bed"?'

'I don't know what you mean.'

'They have drugs for amnesia.'

'You've got me all wrong.'

'Sure I have. You're a lovely guy; Mel is lucky to have you. When you're not hitting on anything with a pulse, that is.'

'I really care about her.'

'Her, or her parents' money?'

He flushed. 'Her. Not that it's any of your business.'

'She's my friend. That makes it my business.'

'You really think you're something, don't you?'

'Because I turned you down? Don't flatter yourself. That's just being hygienic.'

'Don't mess with me.'

'Is that a threat?'

'What do you think?'

'That featherweights shouldn't try fighting out of their division.'

He glared at her. She stared back, feeling the dragon stir within. It had lain dormant for years but it was still there. Waiting to be summoned. Ready to destroy.

'Hurt Mel and I'll make you sorry for it. Remember that.'

He pushed past her towards Melanie's flat. She continued on towards the tube.

But before she reached it she had a change of heart. Tara was away, visiting her parents. Though she usually enjoyed having the flat to herself, on this particular evening she didn't feel like sitting alone. So, after ordering a pizza at the next door restaurant, she entered the Wayfarer.

It was only half full, just as it had been on her previous visit. She recognized some of the drinkers but not the barman who served her a diet coke. Sitting in the corner she reached into her bag for the book Anna had sent and began to read.

Twenty minutes passed. She received a text from Sue. *'Rachel is driving me mad. Who cares what colour wedding stationery she uses?! Miss you. Come home soon.'* Her pizza arrived. As she started to eat a black nose pushed its way into her lap.

Startled, she looked up. Jack hurried over. 'I'm really sorry . . .' Recognition dawned on his face. 'Hi. How are you?'

'Fine. Here to start your shift?'

'I'm not working tonight. We're off to a party.' He tugged Bullseye's ear. 'Bullseye likes a good party.'

'As much as he likes a good pizza?'

'No way. Give him a slice and he'll be your friend for ever. Want a drink?'

'Thanks. Just a mineral water.'

He made his way to the bar. Bullseye climbed onto the seat beside her and swallowed the offered pizza slice whole. 'Nice manners,' she observed as Jack returned with the drinks.

'I know. He was a star pupil at canine charm school.'

'Bullseye was the name of Bill Sykes's dog. Wasn't he a Staff?'

'Actually he was an English Bull Terrier. I think that was the breed they used in the David Lean film but in the musical they used a Staff.'

'Don't take this the wrong way, Bullseye, but I thought the David Lean film was better.'

Jack covered Bullseye's ears with his hands. 'So did I.'

She laughed. He did too. It was a nice laugh. He had a nice face: not good-looking but attractive with lively dark eyes and an impish grin.

'I was only a kid when I saw it,' he told her. 'My parents made me watch it. I was expecting to be bored but it gripped me right from the opening scene of Oliver's mother walking through the rain to the workhouse.'

'I first saw it with my aunt. I was only a kid too but not as young as my cousin, Sue. Do you remember when Bill murders Nancy? My aunt decided that bit was too scary for Sue and sent her out of the room until it was over. Big mistake. Sue began imagining a Victorian *Texas Chain Saw Massacre* and had nightmares for weeks afterwards!'

Again he laughed. She gave Bullseye another slice of pizza that vanished as fast as the first. 'Good choice of name. It suits him.'

'I didn't choose it. He used to belong to an old man who lived on the boat next to mine. Last year the man went to live with relatives who don't like dogs so I inherited him.'

'You live on a narrow boat?'

'Yes.'

'What's it called?'

'*Persephone.*'

'Good name. How many berths?'

'Technical language. You know about boats?'

'A bit. I grew up on the Essex coast.'

'So you're an Essex girl.'

'Yes and I've heard all the jokes.'

'I grew up in a place called Sheeps Wallop. Imagine the jokes I used to get about that.'

'That sounds very West Country.'

'Devon to be precise.'

'So you like cream teas, hate outsiders and believe in crop circles.'

'Absolutely. And when you have an orgasm you drop your kebab.'

More laughter. She shared the rest of the pizza with Bullseye and accepted Jack's offer of another drink while around them Saturday night drinkers radiated weekend bonhomie.

'I'd better go,' she said eventually.

'Do you want a coffee?'

'Do they serve it here?'

'I meant on the boat.'

'What about your party?'

'I'm not in the mood any more.'

'So I see.'

'No offence taken if you don't want to come. I've

enjoyed your company almost as much as Bullseye enjoyed your pizza.'

She stared at him, considering. It wasn't a development she had envisaged, though perhaps it would just be a coffee.

Yeah, right. He's a man. Does a bear shit in the woods?

But she was single, he was cute and there were worse ways to end an evening.

'Why not,' she said, stroking Bullseye's head. 'At least I'll have a chaperone.'

Together they left the pub.

They walked along the canal path surrounded by elegant town houses until they reached a green narrow boat with *Persephone* emblazoned on its side in gold letters. As he opened it up she watched another cruise past, making the other boats rock gently. Through its windows she saw men in dinner jackets and women in evening dresses dance self consciously to the latest pop tunes.

Persephone's main cabin was rectangular with a sofa, TV and stereo at one end, a cooker and sink at the other and posters of The Kinks on the walls. She walked through it, passing a shower on one side and a toilet on the other before coming to a tiny bedroom with a double bunk. 'Cosy,' she observed.

'Well it suits me. How do you like your coffee?'

'Strong and black with no sugar.' She sat down on

the sofa. Bullseye jumped up beside her and climbed onto her knee.

'Shove him off if he's being a pest.'

'He's not.'

'You're an animal lover.'

'And you love The Kinks.'

'Best group ever.' Reaching under the sofa he pulled out half a dozen old 45s. 'This is my pride and joy. Each cover signed by each member of the group. My dad met them in the sixties. These used to belong to him.'

'Used to?'

'He died a few years ago.'

'I'm sorry.'

'Thanks. He was a good bloke. I still miss him.' Jack returned to the stove. As she flicked through the records a memory rose unbidden to the surface of her mind. Sitting with her father on Uncle Neil's boat, listening to him sing 'Waterloo Sunset'. He had had a good voice: deep and resonant. She had always loved listening to him sing.

Suddenly she could hear it in her head, as clear as if he were in the room. But remembering wasn't the same as missing.

'Chrissie?'

She turned. Jack grinned. 'You were miles away.'

'Sorry. Just thinking about what I've got to do tomorrow.'

'I was asking if you want an ashtray.'

'Please.'

He handed her one then continued to make coffee. 'How about a joint?' he asked.

'No, but don't let me stop you.' She noticed a yellow cotton apron decorated with flowers hanging on a peg. 'Very fetching.'

'It belonged to my ex-girlfriend. I keep meaning to throw it out.'

'Why did you break up? If you don't mind me asking.'

'It's no big deal. We just drifted apart.' He sat down beside her. 'Do you have a boyfriend?'

'Not any more.'

'That sounds recent.'

'Same story as you. We drifted apart and it was no big deal. Are you still friends?'

'Yeah. Well, sort of. Are you?'

'Yeah. Well, sort of.'

They both laughed.

'Are you a dancer?' he asked.

'No. Why?'

'The way you move, I guess. It's very . . .' he stopped, clearly searching for the right word, '. . . expressive. Graceful but purposeful. Like you're making a statement.'

'What statement?'

'Look but don't touch. At least not without an invitation.'

'Well interpreted.'

'I went out with a trainee psychiatrist once. She was big on body language.'

'And what did she say about yours?'

'Touch but don't look. It's less unpleasant that way.'

She laughed. Bullseye, asleep on her knee, began to snore.

He took a drag on his joint. 'So what *do* you do?'

'I work for a film production company.'

'Do you have any films in production now?'

'One. A ghost story set in Norfolk. It starts shooting in a couple of weeks.'

'Will you have to go there?'

'Yes but my boss will do most of it. He's better at dealing with actors' egos.'

'You don't like actors?'

'No, which is ironic as I went to drama college. Only for a year though. Long enough to realize it wasn't for me. Who wants to sleep with some scuzzy casting director just for the privilege of getting over-excited in a soap commercial.' She sipped her coffee. Strong and black just as requested. 'Have you heard of Emma Sothern?'

'No.'

'I was at college with her. She's in Hollywood now. The only person from our year who's done well.' A pause. 'I wouldn't want to be her though.'

'But you're driven, aren't you?'

'Is that another of my subliminal statements?'

'No. Just a hunch.'

'A correct one. You need drive to get somewhere.'

'Why do you want to get somewhere?'

'Why not? It's better than staying still. Don't you have ambitions?'

'Sure. Earn enough to keep me in drink and dope and Bullseye in Pedigree Chum.'

Bullseye woke, sneezed, climbed down from the sofa and trotted towards the bedroom. 'Our chaperone has deserted us,' she said.

'Are you pleased?'

'That depends on whether you're going to make a move on me.'

'Should I take that as an invitation?'

'What do you think?'

'That it's what you think that counts.'

'I think we fancy each other. I also think we're both single and like it that way.' A smile. 'And I think it would be fun.'

'So do I.' He moved towards her, then stopped. 'Just promise me something.'

'What?'

'That however good it is you don't drop your kebab.'

More laughter. It felt nice. And when he kissed her it felt even better.

The following morning she sat in the main cabin, eating the breakfast he had prepared. Burnt bacon and an egg with a broken yolk. 'I'm not much of a cook,' he said apologetically.

'Don't worry. It's lovely.' She checked her watch. Almost eleven. She had planned to be gone by ten but they had slept late, only rising when Bullseye had barked to be let out. He was sitting by her now, looking as wistful as he always did when there was food around. She wondered if this was something all dogs learned as puppies. Canine survival 101. She gave him her final piece of bacon which, like everything else, he seemed to swallow whole.

'Don't give him bacon. It makes him fart.'

'And pizza doesn't?'

'No comparison. In ten minutes we'll need gas masks.'

'Not me. I must go. Thanks, Jack. I had a lovely time.'

'You don't have to rush off. I'm not doing anything.' He gave her one of his impish grins. 'You could help wash up.'

'Not in that apron. I'm sure your ex was great but she had no taste in kitchen wear.'

'Stay and chat while I do it.'

She was tempted but knew that goodbyes should always be brief. 'I've got things to do. I'm sorry.'

'It's OK. Thanks for coming. I had a lovely time too.'

Her bag was on the floor. She picked it up, searching for her tube pass.

'We could do it again if you like,' he said.

She continued fiddling with her bag, keeping her face lowered to hide her smile.

'What do you think?'

'Maybe. Why not give me your number.'

He wrote it down. 'What's the fastest way to the tube?' she asked.

'Turn right at the bottom of the canal path. I'll walk you there.'

'No need. I'm a big girl. Besides, you need to find your gas mask.' She kissed his cheek. ''Bye, Jack. Take care.'

'You too, Chrissie.'

Six hours later. After a swim and a workout she had returned home to give the flat its weekly clean and finish the book Anna had sent.

Her mobile bleeped. Another text from Sue, ranting about Rachel. She had hoped it might be from Kevin. She wanted them to stay friends. He was a nice man. The sort Aunty Karen would love her to marry unless Rachel had put Aunty Karen off weddings forever.

The radio was on; the DJ taking requests for favourite songs. Someone asked for 'Jennifer Juniper'. She remembered telling Jack that she liked Donovan and wondered if he was listening too.

A key turned in the front door. She went to welcome Tara back.

Tuesday. She sat at her desk, reading a memo from Francis Chester, the director of the Norfolk film. At only twenty-seven, Francis had a host of documentaries and low budget films under his belt, together with a reputation for being difficult. Having previously praised the screenplay he had now decided to rewrite it. Clearly there would be problems on the set.

Not that she would have much chance to resolve them. The American studio putting up the bulk of the finance was trying to control the decision-making process. 'But that's just the way it is,' Bob had told her. 'When we've got more films behind us we'll be the ones calling the shots.'

But she wanted to call them now. To do more. To be more. Francis was only two years older than her yet already had real clout in the industry. Everyone knew him: his opinions mattered. That was what she yearned for: to be someone people talked about. Admired. Envied.

Like they did Emma Sothern.

She thought back to the girl she had known at college. Quiet, serious and with nothing to mark her out from the crowd. A girl she had barely noticed. Until that fateful final afternoon.

Sod it. I'm just biding my time. One day I'll be ten times as famous as her. One day she'll be telling everyone that she was at college with me.

And it would happen. She would make it happen. Even if she didn't know how.

An e-mail arrived from Melanie. '*Sorry about Saturday. Let me make it up to you. We've got a table at the National Book Awards next week and there are a couple of spare seats. Think I can wangle you one. It's being filmed for TV. A chance to network AND pose!'*

Instantly she felt better. Let Emma Sothern swan around in Hollywood. She had her own eggs to fry and, unlike Jack, she would not break a single yolk.

She wondered what he was doing. Lounging around on the boat, probably, doing more dope. Poor Bullseye would soon be taken into care for being a passive canine pothead.

Shaking her head, she typed a reply to Melanie.

She phoned Jack on Wednesday.

She was sitting in a cafe. His number rang then went to voicemail. She left a message saying she was around on Saturday if he wanted to meet. Her tone was friendly but casual. It wasn't a big deal. She could easily find something else to do.

Putting down the phone she sipped her coffee. A man stared at her from a nearby table. Plump, homely and old enough to be her father. But at least he was straight. In Soho that was something of a rarity.

She blew a kiss at him. Blushing, he looked away.

Thursday afternoon. Jack sent a text saying he was free on Saturday night.

Sadly she no longer was. Tara had invited some college friends for dinner and made her promise to attend. There was no way she could pull out. Unless she pretended they'd had a definite arrangement.

It was tempting. Tara's college friends were very dull. An evening with them was about as exciting as watching paint dry.

Only she couldn't. A promise was a promise and Tara was a friend.

So she'd understand. And besides I'd never inflict Rachel's wedding plans on her.

She sent a text back, agreeing to meet.

Saturday evening. They sat in a Lebanese cafe on the Edgware Road, drinking industrial strength coffee while all around them Arab men breathed clouds of sweet smelling smoke into the air from bubbling houka pipes.

'Have you ever smoked one of those?' he asked.

'No, but I bet you have.'

'Naturally.'

'Do any of your recreational activities not involve illegal substances?'

'It's not illegal. Just scented tobacco. It's the inhaling that makes you light headed.'

'Yeah, right,' she said, starting to laugh.

'Yeah, right!' he replied, doing the same.

Later they returned to the boat to drink wine and listen to Joni Mitchell. 'I used to have loads of CDs,' he told her, 'but someone broke in and stole most of them. That's the problem with living on a boat. The security isn't great.' He stroked Bullseye's head. 'And sadly my security guard wasn't on board to scare them off.'

'At least they didn't take your Kinks records.'

'Yeah, that would have really hurt.'

The evening was warm and the cabin door open, letting in a breeze and the sound of voices from neighbouring boats. 'When I was a kid,' she told him, 'I wanted to live on a boat and sail around the world.'

'I wanted to be a rock star.'

'So did my cousin. He used to play guitar in his bedroom so loud the ceiling shook. It drove my aunt mad.' She smiled at the memory.

'It must have been tough growing up without parents?'

'Who said I didn't have parents?'

'You did.' He hesitated. 'Well you've never mentioned them. I assumed you'd grown up with your aunt and uncle.'

She shook her head.

'So where are they?'

'My mother lives in Essex. My father's dead.'

'When did he die?'

'I don't know.'

He look confused.

'He walked out one day. We never heard from him again. He might as well be dead.'

Confusion became sympathy. 'That happened to a friend of mine. It took him years to get over it. In fact I don't think he ever has. Not completely.'

Firehorse

A voice inside her head whispered the name. The

boat she was going to paint red and sail around the world in with her father. Just the two of them for ever.

But that had been someone else's dream.

'It wasn't like that for me. I was very young when he left. I barely remember him. Certainly not well enough to miss him.'

'You can still miss having a dad though.'

'Not one like mine. He was a loser: never worked; drank too much; got into fights. Who needs someone like that screwing up their life?'

The sympathetic look remained. 'At least you had your mother.'

'Are you kidding? From the day he left all she did was play the victim. As I see it, when bad stuff happens you deal with it and move on but all she knew how to do was wallow. She's an even bigger loser than him and that's saying something.'

She stopped, feeling suddenly exposed. Her glass was empty, and not for the first time. Silently she chastised herself. Drink loosened the tongue: made you reveal more than anyone, let alone a virtual stranger, needed to know.

'So there you have it,' she continued, making her tone light. 'Christina Ryan, this is your life. Thank you Michael Aspel for having me on your show.'

'It doesn't have to be the end of the show.'

'Yes it does. Who cares about the past? It's the present that's important.'

'Doesn't one affect the other?'

'Not for me.'

Silence, while in the background Joni Mitchell sang 'Chinese Cafe'. It was one of Aunty Karen's favourite songs. She missed Aunty Karen but not enough to return home.

As if reading her mind he asked 'How often do you see your mother?'

'Christmas.'

'What about her birthday?'

'Mothers don't have birthdays. They're twenty-one for ever. Didn't yours teach you anything?'

'Certainly not how to roll a decent joint. I worked that one out all by myself.'

'And how proud she must be.'

'I bet your mother's proud of you.'

'Perhaps. It's not something I waste time worrying about.'

He nodded.

'Do you think I'm hard?'

'Not hard. Tough.'

'Isn't that the same thing?'

'I don't think so. Hard means heartless. Tough means knowing how to take care of yourself. It's not inherent; it's something that's learned.'

She remembered what Kevin's sister had said about her. 'Then you're right because I do have a heart. I do care about people. But I know how to take care of myself too and the sad thing is that most people don't.

Like my friend Mel who you saw me with in the pub. If someone tried to hurt her she'd have no idea how to stop them. I can't think of anything worse than being as helpless as that.'

Another silence. Her eyes roamed over the cabin, coming to rest on the apron on the peg. 'Was your ex-girlfriend tough?'

A look came into his eyes. One she couldn't read. 'No. Not really.'

'What was her name?'

'Alison. Ali. That's what everyone calls her.'

'It's a nice name.'

'Christina's a strong name. It suits you.'

'Thanks.' She continued to look about the cabin. The kitchen area was untidy. Pans lay in the sink and mugs covered the surrounding surface. Her own kitchen was immaculate: she hated mess. In her home, just as in her office, everything had to be tidy.

A strange thought crept into her head.

This will have to change

Then crept out again.

He went to roll another joint. 'Want to share it?'

'No. Dope doesn't have any effect on me.'

He returned to sit beside her. She wondered why she had felt the need to justify her refusal. It was uncharacteristic behaviour. As if she were trying to impress.

Maybe that's because he isn't.

She realized it suddenly. All the time they had spent

together he had been friendly and funny but never tried to impress. A refreshing change from other men she had dated.

But this wasn't a date. Just an extended one night stand. A bit of fun. That was all she wanted; all either of them wanted.

She watched him breathe smoke into the air. He was smaller than her. Five foot eight at most. Stocky and with similar colouring to her father, though his features were more boyish.

'What would happen,' he asked, 'if your dad came back?'

'He won't.'

'But what if he did?'

'Then he'd sit me on his knee and tell me never to get involved with a sailor.'

'But every girl loves a sailor.'

'And a sailor loves every girl. That's the point.'

They both laughed. But when the conversation resumed she made sure her parents were not discussed again.

When she woke it was still dark. For a moment she felt disorientated. Uncertain where she was. Then she felt a warm body beside her and remembered.

He was lying on his back, snoring. Momentarily she was tempted to wake him but then thought better of it. It was his bed after all.

She pressed closer to him, feeling the tickle of his

chest hair against her skin. Kevin's body had been as smooth as her own. Well toned too. Something she could never say of Jack. In a body beautiful contest his would barely make it through the first heat.

But it still felt nice.

Her eyes adjusted to the darkness. In the ceiling above the bunk was a small porthole. Through it she watched clouds drift across the face of the moon. It was raining, drops tapping on the glass like weak fingers. Another boat passed by on the canal. She wondered where its occupants were going and felt glad to be safe and warm inside.

Jack turned in his sleep. His face was inches from hers. She stroked his goatee. It tickled, just like the rug on his chest. Normally she hated facial hair but on him it looked good.

Impulsively she kissed his cheek then closed her eyes and went back to sleep.

The following morning. Again he had prepared breakfast: fruit, bread and cheese. 'I didn't want to risk cooking,' he told her. 'Not after last time.'

'Your cooking's good.'

'And your nose is growing.'

'No, seriously. Next time I'll have to cook for you.'

'Next time?'

She realized what she'd said and felt annoyed with herself. It made her look eager.

'That would be nice,' he said.

She repressed a smile. Bullseye appeared, sniffed her plate then wandered off in disgust.

'Maybe one night next week,' she suggested.

'Which one?'

'Wednesday? If you're not working, that is.'

'If I am I can change shifts.'

'Wednesday it is then.' She stopped herself from adding, 'It's a date.'

The boat began to rock. A middle-aged man put his head round the cabin door. 'Jack, do you want . . . Oh, sorry. I didn't realize you had company.'

'It's fine. This is my friend, Chrissie. Chrissie, this is my neighbour Stephen.'

Smiling, she held out her hand. Stephen shook it. 'Pleased to meet you, Chrissie. Jack, we're taking the boat down to Camden at lunchtime. Want to come?'

'Can I let you know?'

'Sure.' Stephen bent down to pet Bullseye. 'How are you, handsome?'

'Pissed off because we haven't given him bacon.'

'Oh well, his loss is the ozone layer's gain. Sorry again for interrupting.'

'Stephen seems nice,' she said, when he had gone.

'So is Camden on a day like this. Want to go?'

She did but had already made plans with Tara and couldn't cancel again. Besides, she would be seeing him again on Wednesday. Not that it was a big deal.

'Sorry. I told my flatmate I'd go to the cinema with her.'

'What's the film?'

'A Greta Garbo silent at the NFT.'

'Do you like silent films?'

'Yes. I like watching the actors. It's true what Norma Desmond said in *Sunset Boulevard*. They really did have faces then.'

'You have a great face. Strong, like your name.'

'And the cheese.'

He laughed. His own face was unshaven and his sweatshirt had a hole. Unlike most of the men she knew he seemed totally unconcerned with his appearance.

'Do you like silent films?' she asked.

'Those I've seen.'

'Next month they're showing *Phantom of the Opera*. It's brilliant, apparently.'

'Maybe we should go.'

Again she hid her smile. 'I must go now.'

As she walked along the canal path she watched a solitary swan glide along the water. It reminded her of the ones a frightened child had watched back in Havelock, sitting on a bench at the end of the harbour path, waiting for a father who was never going to come.

But that was in the past. She didn't wait for any man; they waited for her. That was how it was and how it was going to stay.

Lunchtime. While waiting for Tara she killed time window shopping on Oxford Street.

She passed a menswear shop. The dummy in the window wore a red sweatshirt. It looked good on the dummy but would look even better on Jack.

Buy it for him. He needs to smarten up if he's going to be with you.

But he wasn't. She'd only just escaped one relationship. The last thing she needed was to run headlong into another.

Especially not with a doper. That will have to stop too.

Only it was none of her concern. Just as her relationship with her parents was none of his.

She moved on, searching for distraction from another window.

Two hours later. She sat with Tara in a darkened auditorium, watching the Garbo film.

It was called *Love.* A version of *Anna Karenina*, with Garbo and John Gilbert in the lead roles. Tara, hungover from her dinner party, guzzled sweets and ogled John Gilbert. 'Is that man beautiful or what? I could stare at that face all day.'

She nodded though the face that fascinated her was Garbo's. The masklike face with eyes that said whatever the viewer wanted them to.

When she was fifteen she had read a book about Garbo that had talked about the impact of her film debut. Of how cinema audiences across the world had gasped when that inscrutable face first appeared on the screen. She remembered reading that in her bedroom in Havelock and vowing that one day audiences would react to her own face in the same way.

But that was never going to happen. Not now.

Tara continued to prattle on about John Gilbert. She found the noise distracting. Wished that she had come to see the film alone. Or with Jack.

She imagined him sitting beside her, telling her that she had a face like Garbo. That she could be up there on the screen making an audience gasp, just as Garbo had.

Make my dad gasp. Make him see what he left behind. Make him sorry.

Make him proud.

Make him feel something about me. Wherever he is.

Only it didn't matter where he was. Just as it didn't matter if she never saw Jack again.

The story reached its conclusion. Tara began to cry while still gorging on sweets. Though hungry Chrissie declined the bag whenever it was offered, keeping her attention focused on the screen and her appetite, like her emotions, under control.

That evening Liz Ryan stood alone in what had once been her daughter's bedroom.

It looked just as it had on the day Chrissie had left for college. Posters still hung on the wall. The desk still stood in the window with books piled upon it. To others she blamed her failure to change it on laziness. Only to herself would she admit that it was hope.

There had been times in those last years before Chrissie left that she had tried to reach out to her. To rekindle the relationship between them. But in her heart she had known it was futile. There had never been a relationship between them. Since the day Chrissie had been born all they had done was co-exist. It was her own fault, no one else's. Pinning all her hopes on a man who had never wanted to love her while pushing away a child who wanted nothing more.

Now that child was a woman. One who was achieving success, so Karen said. That was the hardest part: her sister-in-law knowing more about Chrissie's life than she did.

'Give it time,' Karen told her. 'You're her mother and she loves you. She'll always love you, just as she'll always love her father. One day she'll make peace with you. I'm sure of it.' The words, kindly spoken, were meant to comfort yet never did.

A poster hung above the bed, bigger than the others, dwarfing them all. On it was a human heart pierced by a knife. At the bottom, written in blood, were three words: LOVE IS WAR.

Turning off the light she left the room undisturbed.

Tuesday lunchtime. As Chrissie walked back to the office she was caught in a summer storm. Needing shelter she entered a record shop.

Browsing through the CDs she found a compilation containing the only ever hit of the long defunct

Midnight Angel. She remembered Philippa Hanson boasting about her cousin's impending superstardom and wondered if he was still working in an East End pub. She decided to buy it so she could show Adam the next time they met.

On her way to the checkout she passed a display of Kinks albums and wondered how many of them had been stolen from Jack's boat.

Suddenly she had an impulse to buy them for him. She pushed it to one side. They'd only get stolen again.

She wondered what he was doing. The previous afternoon she had sent him a text but had yet to receive a reply. He was probably too busy. Or too stoned. She assumed that was the reason. Hoped it was the reason.

The shower ended. As she left the shop she noticed calendars in a rack by the door. One had a picture of narrowboats. Perhaps *Persephone* was one of them.

As she moved closer to look a song began to play in her head.

There is always something there to remind me.

Changing her mind she left the shop. But the song continued to play.

On Wednesday afternoon she heard from him.

It was nearly five when a text came through on her mobile. She recognized his number and felt relieved. A small part of her had wondered if she would hear from him at all. Not that it mattered.

Smiling, she opened it up.

'Can't make tonight. Something's come up. Will call. J.'

The words felt like a slap. Momentarily she felt upset. Then furious. What was he playing at? Cancelling at the last minute. Jerking her around. Something's come up indeed.

Or did something mean someone? Was he spending the evening with someone else? A girl he'd picked up in the pub just as he had picked her up.

But what if he was? As lays went he'd been good but not outstanding. And that was all he was. A lay. If a rather forgettable one. Just as she had been to him.

Except that she hadn't been. He had liked her. Thought she was special. Every instinct she had told her that and on the subject of men her instincts were never wrong.

Were they?

Oh, Chrissie, get a grip! Stop bleating like a baby. If he's hurt you then hurt him back. Make him sorry.

But he hadn't hurt her. Only her pride, not her emotions.

And with the metaphorical shaking administered, she continued her work.

Two hours later. She stood in a crowded wine bar with Tara. Young people in suits stood in groups while pop music played in the background. As she sipped her drink she swayed to the beat feeling male eyes crawling over her. It made her feel good. Over Tara's shoulder she saw a woman studying her enviously – that made her feel even better.

A man approached, offering to buy them both drinks. He reminded her of the one who had offered her drugs in the nightclub a few weeks earlier. The same arrogant good looks and air of self satisfaction. But he was hers for the taking, as was any man if she wanted him enough. As was Jack if she wanted him enough.

When hell froze over.

She spoke with the man, deflating his posturing with flirtatious putdowns, while all the time swaying to the music, feeling eyes upon her and revelling in the sense of power it gave.

Thursday evening. The night of the Book Awards.

They were being held at an exclusive hotel in Mayfair. She walked with Melanie along a red carpet lined with photographers calling out to a loutish TV presenter posing ahead of them. 'What's he doing here?' she whispered to Melanie. 'I didn't think he could read.'

'Presenting an award.'

'Let's hope the autocue has phonetic spelling.' She continued up the carpet, moving slowly, imagining it was a catwalk and that the photographers were there for her.

Once inside, they entered a huge dining room with dozens of tables in front of a stage with giant video screens on either side. Their table was near the back.

She sat next to a middle-aged historian of whom she had never heard. Melanie introduced her to the rest of the table. Mostly sales executives and publicity staff. 'The really big cheeses are on the next table,' Melanie explained. 'Including our very own guest celebrity couple.'

'Who are they?'

'Evelyne Cauldwell and Alexander Gallen,' said another girl. 'Evelyne's parents are friends of the MD. They were supposed to be here tonight but had to pull out so Evelyne and Alexander agreed to come instead. Assuming they turn up. People like that often don't.'

'Speak of the devil,' hissed Melanie. The publicity girl fell silent. A tall, attractive and beautifully dressed young couple made their way towards the next table. Lady Evelyne Cauldwell, successful fashion model, the face of an exclusive cosmetics range and daughter of an Earl accompanied Alexander Gallen, great grandson of American steel tycoon Joseph Gallen and recent heir to one of the largest private fortunes in the country. The MD hurried to greet them.

'What a fantastic dress,' said Melanie, once they were out of earshot.

'Isn't it,' she agreed. 'And if she didn't walk like she had a tiara stuck up her arse she'd look great in it.'

Most of the table burst out laughing. Melanie looked alarmed. 'Sorry,' she mouthed, trying in vain to look apologetic.

The lights dimmed and the ceremony began. As the meal wasn't being served until after it was over everyone began to get drunk. A man with a camera appeared and thrust it in the face of the historian. 'They need it for my reaction shot,' he told Chrissie. 'I'm nominated in the biography category for my life of Emily Wickford.'

'Who?'

'Exactly. I don't have a prayer. Jason Fox will win for his life of Hemingway. He's the smug git in the smoking jacket three tables away. He can't write to save his life but at least people have heard about the people he split infinitives about.'

'So who was Emily Wickford?'

'A Victorian missionary who travelled the South Sea Islands, married a local chief and ended up being murdered by headhunters.'

'That sounds much more interesting than Hemingway. There's no mystery to him. His whole life was one big act of overcompensation for having a tiny dick.'

'Keep feeding me lines like that. They'll help when I need to muster my loser's smile.'

The ceremony continued. The loutish presenter took to the stage, delivered a couple of ill-judged jokes and muffed the names of the nominees for best biography, having to be corrected by the host. As expected, Jason Fox won. 'What's his book called?' Chrissie whispered to the historian. 'The Old Man and the Tiddler?' He burst out laughing just as his face was captured on camera, thus appearing a magnanimous loser. An elderly philosopher won an award and was so drunk that he bumped into the podium and then spent two minutes thanking everyone who had ever lived except his ex-wives who were reviled as greedy harpies. The host thanked them all for attending, the cameramen vanished and the dinner began.

Before they started eating the MD rearranged the seating. He, Evelyne and Alexander moved onto their table, replacing the sales executives. 'You look like more of a fun crowd,' he explained.

The food arrived. Foie gras followed by venison. Evelyne picked at it, complaining about her work schedule. She was a patrician looking blonde in her early twenties with good but inexpressive features; one of the current crop of celebrity models whose success had as much to do with connections as ability. Alexander, also blond, was in his mid- to late-twenties and handsome in a *GQ* sort of way. He was talking to the MD and one of the publicity girls, both of whom listened with the rapt attention only money and position can inspire. An attention Chrissie could not command. At least not yet.

The historian asked about her work. She told him about the book she had persuaded Bob to option. 'It's about a girl who loses her identical twin and tries to find a replacement. A bit like *Single White Female* but with more emphasis on the psychology.'

'Sounds good. I'm sure you'll have no trouble raising the funding.'

'If only. The first thing any potential backer wants to know is which star is attached. It's all about names in the film business.'

'But you need a name to sell a film, don't you?'

'Yes, but you shouldn't. A good story's a good story. Stars usually demand all sorts of changes and it ends up as their vehicle rather than your project. There's an actress who'd be brilliant but she's hardly known so we'll end up with some talentless bimbo icon of the lads mags who thinks the way to portray inner turmoil is to get her tits out at every opportunity.'

He laughed. She realized that the rest of the table were listening to their conversation. 'You sound very cynical,' remarked the MD.

'Not cynical. Realistic. Ideals are all very well but if you want to operate within the system you have to play by the rules.'

'Or try to change them,' said Alexander.

'Easier said than done.'

'It's worth trying though. If you don't fight for your project then who else will?'

She found his comments irritating. Biting her tongue she played with her wine glass. He watched her; his eyes curious. Above his right eyebrow was a faint scar like a tiny V. She wondered what had caused it.

'I don't like films that are too psychological,' said Evelyne dismissively. 'All that emotional scars stuff. I find it boring.'

Her irritation increased. 'Boring,' she replied sweetly, 'or just too difficult to follow?'

Evelyne's eyes widened, her face registering expression for the first time. Maybe she wasn't such a bad model after all.

'I'm sure yours wouldn't be difficult to follow,' said Alexander, smiling at the rest of the table. 'We'll see all of your heroine's scars the first time she decides to strip.'

Everyone laughed, currying favour at her expense with someone whose only claim to fame was to have been born rich. And she wasn't having that.

'And how did you get *your* scar I wonder? Fall off your polo pony and cut yourself on your silver spoon?'

Alexander looked startled as did everyone else. She turned her attention back to the historian. After a brief silence the rest of the table continued their own conversations.

An hour later. She stood in a hallway outside the dining room, checking her mobile for messages. But there were none. At least not from Jack.

What is he doing? Why isn't he contacting me? And why am I so bothered?

'Christina?'

Alexander stood beside her. The sight of him made her feel awkward. 'What can I do for you?' she asked, defensiveness making her curt

'Let me apologize. I'm sorry if I sounded patronizing. I didn't mean to. In my own rather clumsy way I was trying to be encouraging. Anyone can tell how much your project means to you and I really hope it comes out the way you want it to.'

Flustered, she just nodded.

'I can see you're busy. Once again my apologies.' He turned to leave.

'Wait. I'm the one who should apologize. I was very rude. I get oversensitive about my work sometimes. Not that that's any excuse.'

'Yes it is.' He smiled. 'Thanks.'

'No problem.' She risked a joke. 'Besides, I'm sure you're far too good at polo ever to take a tumble.'

'Actually I've never played it.'

'But you must, Alexander. If the rich don't play exclusive games the whole fabric of society collapses. You must see that.'

His smile broadened. He was one of the country's most eligible bachelors according to the media, combining looks, youth and fabulous wealth with membership of the glamorous Gallen clan. She would have expected him to be arrogant but there was no trace of that in his face which was warm and kind.

'Alexander sounds too formal. Call me Alec.'

'So does Christina. Call me bitch.'

He laughed. She noticed the MD hovering nearby, watching them anxiously. There was no sign of Evelyne. 'Where's your girlfriend?' she asked.

'She's not my girlfriend.'

'The glossies think she is.'

'My grandmother was friends with her parents. We've dated a few times, but basically we're just friends too.'

'Except in public.'

'Well, Evelyne likes the attention.'

'And two famous faces are better than one.'

'I guess so.'

'Don't you like the spotlight?'

'No. I haven't earned it. Evelyne's the celebrity. I'm just well connected.'

'That's all she is. Do you think she'd have got anywhere near as far in her career if she hadn't been a distant cousin of the Queen? Her only achievement is to have been born with a title and that's no achievement at all.'

'You don't like her, do you?'

'It's not that. It's just that she's hardly another Saffron Ellis.'

'Who?'

'A childhood idol.' She softened her tone. 'I don't dislike her, personally. I dislike what she represents: this notion that children of the rich and famous have, that fame is their birthright; that they can try anything, regardless of whether they have talent, and success will just fall into their lap. And the awful thing is that it so often does. It's not like that for the rest of us. If we want recognition we have to work for it and even then the chances of achieving it are pretty remote.'

'Not for you. I bet you could achieve anything you wanted if you put your mind to it.'

She was touched. 'Thanks, Alexander. I appreciate that.'

'Alec,' he corrected her.

'Alec.'

The MD came to join them with a popular woman author of historical romances. A photographer appeared followed by Evelyne who slid between Alexander and Chrissie to rest a proprietary hand on his shoulder. Once the picture was taken she went to find Melanie.

Jack called on Saturday morning.

He sounded cheerful, telling her that he had spent the last few days taking the boat down the canal with a friend from Devon who had paid him an unexpected visit, which necessitated his cancelling their so-called date.

'Sounds fun,' she said. 'You certainly had the weather for it.'

'Absolutely. You should see Bullseye. He's got an amazing tan.'

She didn't want to laugh. She was angry with him. But to give any clue of this would only make him think he was important so she laughed anyway.

'I'm around this weekend,' he said, 'if you want to meet.'

'I can't. I'm busy.' That evening she was going out with the man she had met in the winebar. A lawyer called Ben. At least she thought his name was Ben.

'That's a shame. Another time?'

'Sure. I'll call you sometime.' She prepared to hang up.

But didn't.

Sunday evening. She prepared supper for the two of them at her flat while he inspected her CDs in the living room. 'Put one on if you want,' she called out.

'You're a traitor. Some of these are by modern groups.'

Turning down the gas she went to join him. He was crouched on the floor, flicking through the titles. 'What are Linkin Park like?'

'Too loud for an oldie like you.'

'I'm only thirty.'

'Go on then, granddad. Make your eardrums bleed.' As he put on the CD she poured the cheap and cheerful wine he had bought. She had spent the previous evening drinking overpriced cocktails with Ben in an exclusive wine bar in Knightsbridge. Ben was short for Benedict, in honour of a grandfather who had been a QC. Or was it Benjamin in honour of a great uncle? The information had been as memorable as the date itself.

Jack inspected the photographs on the mantelpiece. 'Most belong to my flatmate,' she explained. 'Though the two on the end are of my aunt and cousins.'

'You don't look like them. Who do you look like?'

'My dad's mother, apparently.'

'Your parents weren't redheads?'

'No. My mother's blonde. Dad was dark like you, and also like you he and the comb were never formally introduced.'

'I do comb mine. It just has a life of its own.'

'So did dad's. He had great hair. He used to let me pull it. He loved having it pulled.'

'I thought you didn't remember him.'

'I don't. Just the odd memory. Who do you look like?'

'My dad. That's what everyone says even though he was bald at my age.'

'Then you mother was a lucky woman. Isn't baldness a sign of virility?'

'Perhaps, but it's not a way I'd choose to display mine.' He laughed but she sensed a note of anxiety. Perhaps he was worried about losing his hair. Not that there was much chance of that. But she found the fear endearing.

He looked as scruffy as ever: crumpled sweatshirt and battered trainers; a tuft of hair stood up behind his ear. She restrained an impulse to smooth it down. 'I wouldn't worry,' she told him. 'You'll still have birds nesting in yours when you're a pensioner.'

'You have great hair. A girl at my school had hair your colour. She didn't like it and always kept it short. I thought she was mad but there was no telling her.'

'I've always liked mine. I'd never cut it short.'

A text came through on her mobile: Ben, asking if he could see her again. For a moment she was tempted to tell Jack, wanting to make him jealous. Except that she didn't want that at all.

Later they sat together in the kitchen, eating the thai curry she had prepared.

'This is delicious,' he said. 'You shouldn't have gone to so much trouble.'

'I didn't. It's an easy dish.' It was also her best, but she kept that to herself.

'Where's your flatmate?'

'At her father's retirement party. Where's yours?'

'Being dogsat by my neighbours.'

'Is that Stephen? The guy you went to Camden with?' He nodded. 'Him and his partner, Tim.'

'Does it bother you they're gay?'

'Should it?'

'No. I was just curious. My ex-boyfriend would have freaked if his neighbours had batted for the other side.'

'So Kev was homophobic.'

'Not him. A guy called Angus I dated last year.'

'Why did you break up?'

'He got clingy. I hate that sort of thing.'

He swallowed a huge mouthful of food. 'Me too.'

'Was Ali clingy?'

A strange look came into his eyes, just as it had the last time his ex-girlfriend had been mentioned. It bothered her. It shouldn't have done but it did.

'No. She wasn't like that.'

'What was she like?'

'Nice.'

'Just nice?'

'Pretty. Sweet.'

Boring?

'Do you miss her?'

'Sometimes. You get used to having someone around, don't you?'

She nodded. Sometimes she missed Kevin. Not him personally, just his presence. So it wasn't really missing. Just as Jack didn't really miss Ali.

His plate was empty. She gave him a second helping. 'Sorry I couldn't come to Camden.'

'We can go another time.'

'When?'

He swallowed another mouthful. Silently she scolded herself for sounding eager. It was just the prospect of travelling on a narrow boat. Doing something new.

'Next weekend?' he suggested.

'OK. Just make sure that if you cancel you give me enough time to make other plans.'

He looked sheepish. 'Sorry about Wednesday.'

'Don't be. I wasn't bothered.'

He continued to wolf down his food as if it were the last meal he would ever eat. Her father had been the same. She remembered sitting in the kitchen in Havelock, watching him eat while her mother complained about slaving for hours over a meal only to see it devoured in seconds. According to Aunty Karen her mother had had the kitchen redecorated. It looked good, so Aunty Karen said. She would see for herself at Christmas.

Picking up her mobile she took his picture. 'I'm sending this to my Aunt. She refuses to believe my cooking is edible.'

'I hope you got my good side.'

'You mean there is one?'

'Ha ha.'

'No, it's a nice picture. You don't look too receding.'

'You think I'm receding?'

'I'm teasing.' She gave him the phone. 'You look as bouffant as can be.'

He took a picture of her. 'You photograph well. The camera likes you.'

'Yes, you can have another helping.'

'I'm serious. You'd have done well on the big screen.'

He handed her back the phone and she studied the image. It *was* a good picture. Her drama teachers had always told her that she had the potential for a great career in front of the camera. She had believed them until that afternoon when everything changed. But that was the past and the past didn't matter. Not to her. Not ever.

She deleted her picture. 'Scrub mine too,' he said. 'You don't want your aunt to think you're hanging out with lowlifes, however bouffant.'

'Particularly not lowlifes with bottomless pits as stomachs.'

'While we're on the subject of stomachs, any chance of some more?'

Again she refilled his plate while leaving his picture stored on her phone.

Quarter to eight the next morning. After showering she entered the living room to find Jack sitting on the sofa sipping the coffee she had made him and talking with Tara.

She felt flustered. 'I thought you weren't coming back this morning.'

'I had to pick up some stuff,' Tara explained.

'And found a strange man. I hope you didn't think he was a serial killer.'

'If only. Any excuse to avoid work.'

Jack laughed. The sound annoyed her. It hadn't been that funny.

'Anyway,' added Tara, 'he's assured me he's not.'

'Of course he's not. Murder would be too much like hard work.'

More laughter from Jack. This time she felt pleased. He finished his coffee and she saw him to the door.

'So that's the guy you missed my dinner party for,' observed Tara. 'I don't blame you. He's cute.'

'Oh come on. He's no oil painting. Kev was cute.'

'Kev was good looking. Jack's sexy. I bet he's great in bed.'

'He passes the time.'

'Well if you get bored then point him in my direction. He can help pass my time whenever he wants.'

'I don't think you're his type.'

'He's a man, isn't he? For type read anything with a pulse and tits.'

'Jack's not like that. You don't know him.'

'I was only joking. I wouldn't really make a move on him. Anyone can see by the way you look at him how smitten you are.'

She was taken aback. 'I'm not smitten.'

'And I don't have a pulse and tits.'

'I'm not. I could never get keen on someone like him. He's hardly in Kev's league.'

And that was true enough. Kevin had been handsome, successful and driven. As for Jack, well, he was just . . . Jack.

'So if I came onto him you wouldn't mind?'

'No.'

'Liar.'

'I wouldn't. If you're interested I'll try and fix you up with him.'

And she meant it. Only she didn't think he'd be interested. Just as he was hardly in Kevin's league, Tara was hardly in hers. Tara always complained that men never noticed her when the two of them were out together.

No, Jack wouldn't be interested.

Would he?

'Anyway, I thought you were still lusting after that guy at work.'

'So is everyone else. As the first good-looking man to hit our department in living memory he can have his pick.'

'Then just make sure he picks you. Be assertive. Make it happen.'

'That's easy for you to say. You're gorgeous.'

'Gorgeousness is a state of mind. Believe that and you can have any guy you want.'

Except Jack. Not that I'd care, because I wouldn't. I honestly wouldn't.

One hour later. She arrived at work to be greeted by a beaming Bob. 'Someone's popular this morning,' he told her.

'What do you mean?'

'Check your office.'

A bouquet of flowers lay on her desk. Bob hovered in the doorway with Sian the receptionist. 'They've only just been delivered,' Sian told her. 'Who are they from?'

She searched for the attached card, certain they were from Ben, her date of Saturday night. As she had no intention of seeing him again she found the gesture depressing.

Christina – wishing you all possible luck with your film project. Let me know how it's coming along. Best wishes, Alec.

'Christ!'

'Really? I didn't know they had Interflora in heaven.'

'Very funny. They're from Alexander Gallen.'

Sian's jaw dropped. 'How come?' asked Bob.

'He was on my table at the book awards. We had a quick chat.'

'During which you made a big impression judging by the size of the bouquet.'

'It's not that big.'

'Oh please. You'll need a forklift truck to get it home.'

Alexander's business card was attached to the one from the shop. He worked for a research unit in Whitehall. She remembered the media commenting on this the previous year when he had inherited his fortune; observing that it was refreshing to see someone so privileged doing a normal job and not using his family's wealth in the pursuit of fame, in contrast to his American-based cousins. There had been a lot of interest in him at the time, and his association with Evelyne had helped it to continue.

'He was just curious about the twins project,' she said.

'The project or the person behind it?'

'I thought he was going out with Evelyne Cauldwell,' said Sian.

'No. That's just a stunt to get Evelyne more photo ops in the glossies. Mind you, who can blame her? If it wasn't for her connections no one would notice her at all.'

Bob raised an eyebrow. 'Do I detect a touch of the green-eyed monster?'

'Do you hell. Alec's not . . .'

'Alec?'

'He asked me to call him that.'

'How romantic.'

'Oh shut up. I'm not interested in him.'

'Methinks the lady doth protest too much.'

'I'm not! He's not a patch on Jack. I wouldn't . . .' She stopped, realizing what she'd said.

'Who's Jack?' Bob demanded.

'Nobody.'

'Doesn't sound like nobody. Why haven't you told me about him?'

'Because it's none of your business. Sian, do me a favour and put the flowers in water. I'm not taking them home. They can brighten up this place instead.'

Sian disappeared with the bouquet. Bob remained in the doorway. 'I'm all ears.'

'Thought you looked a bit odd this morning.'

'Tell me about Jack?'

'He's some guy I've seen a couple of times. It's nothing serious. Now let's talk about something else.'

'No. Tell me more. Is he as cute as the guy in the pattisserie?'

She threw a stapeler at him, hitting his shoulder. 'Ouch!'

'Serves you right.'

'For that you can come with me to Norfolk and help supervise the crew setting up.'

She thought of her trip to Camden. 'When exactly?'

'Thursday.'

'But we'll be back by Saturday, won't we?'

'Why? Something planned with Mr Nobody.'

'No.'

'Good because we'll have to stay the weekend.'

She couldn't hide her disappointment. 'Must we?'

'I'm teasing. You can come back early. I won't spoil your romantic rendezvous.'

'It's not romantic.'

'But it is a rendezvous. Thought so. You can't hide anything from me.'

'It's just a bit of fun. The stupid jerk'll probably cancel anyway. Not that I'd care.'

Bob leaned against the doorframe, a knowing smile on his face.

'What?' she demanded.

'Pow! That's what it's like, isn't it? It was when I met Malc. Plodding through the West End one evening, wandered into a bar to avoid the rain, got chatting to some guy and suddenly my whole world was turned on its head.'

'That's because you're a soppy lump. I'm not.'

'But you are human or are you going to deny that too?'

She waved her hand dismissively.

'OK, we'll go out for lunch tomorrow. See how much you eat. The first two months with Malc I hardly ate a thing.'

'Pity you're not in that state now. You could do with losing a few pounds.'

Again he laughed. She did too. She was fond of him but he wasn't half as perceptive as he liked to think.

Even though she had been eating less recently: she seemed to have lost her appetite. But only because she hadn't been doing much exercise. Once she was swimming every evening she'd be eating enough to feed the five thousand.

Just like Jack. If the flowers had been from him she wouldn't have left them in the office. They would have had pride of place in her bedroom. But only because she wouldn't have wanted to hurt his feelings.

Bob continued to smile, his face full of that special warmth it always had when he talked about Malcolm. The light of his life. The person he would be lost without. But she would never depend on anyone like that. She would never allow herself to be that weak.

'Lunch it is,' she told him. 'I'll eat you under the table.' Switching on her computer she focused on the day ahead.

Later that morning Melanie called. 'Guess who's been asking about you?'

'Alexander Gallen. He's just sent me flowers.'

'Wow! What are they like?'

'They've got long stems and coloured heads and grow in gardens.'

'You don't seem very excited.'

'It's hardly the first time some guy's sent me flowers.'

'This isn't some guy. This is Alexander Gallen.'

210

'Who's deigned to notice a humble wretch like me. How honoured I feel.'

'Do you think he'll call you?'

'It won't do him much good if he does.'

'Why not?'

Because of Jack, she was about to say, then stopped herself, remembering that Melanie thought Jack was cute. Not that it mattered, she was already devoted to Rick. Besides, Jack wouldn't be interested in her. She wasn't his type. Even though she was pretty and sweet and nice. Just like Ali.

And nothing like me.

'Having just got out of one relationship the last thing I want is to rush into another. Especially not with someone who thinks he's doing me a favour asking me out.'

'I don't think he's like that.'

Neither did she but as excuses went it was more than adequate.

'Tell me if he phones. Everyone here is dying to know.'

'If you like I'll conference you in on the call. Listen, I'm busy. Talk later, OK?'

Once she had put down the phone she picked up Alexander's card. His e-mail address was at the bottom. She sent him a thank you message, keeping it brief, polite and uneffusive. She didn't want him, or anyone else, thinking she was flattered.

Even though, secretly, she was.

*

Tuesday lunchtime. She sat in a Soho bistro with Bob, ploughing through a big meal just to make the point.

He went to talk to a casting agent on a nearby table. A text came through on her mobile. She felt anxious, just as she did every time one arrived, worried that it would be Jack cancelling the trip.

But only because she was looking forward to the experience.

It *was* from him, telling her that he had spent the morning looking for Bullseye who had gone AWOL from the boat and turned up at a nearby fast food joint, scrounging handouts. As she read it she started to laugh, and realized that her heart was pounding. Suddenly she felt angry: with him and with herself, with the whole situation.

Then cancel the trip. Take control.

But why should she cancel? She wanted to go: it would be fun, it would be different. And that was all.

A half-eaten slice of cheesecake lay on her plate. Though more than full she ate it anyway, making sure that her plate was empty by the time Bob returned.

Tuesday evening. Jane Matthews sat in a crowded city wine bar with her husband Harry and his best friend Adam, drinking a bottle of Pinot Grigio.

'Where's Rachel?' she asked Adam.

'Shopping with her mother. But my cousin Chrissie's joining us. Is that OK?'

'Absolutely,' Harry told him. 'It'll be nice to see her.'

Jane nodded, though her feelings were mixed. Chrissie was friendly and fun and always had loads of gossip about people in the media world. She liked her, she really did. Yet she also found her intimidating.

It was her manner. The supreme confidence. The way she spoke her mind and made no attempt to ingratiate herself with others. The air of purpose and direction.

The fact that she was exactly the sort of person Jane longed to be.

'Here she is,' said Adam, gesturing towards the tall, striking young woman striding through the crowds, drawing the eyes of most men and more than a few women as she did so. It wasn't just her appearance, it was the energy she brought with her. Strength, purpose and danger. Like an exotic jungle cat entering a room of neutered toms.

Chrissie made her way to the bar, returning to their table with another bottle of wine, kissing Adam's cheek and giving Harry and Jane a dazzling smile. 'I haven't seen you two for ages. How's life?'

Harry began to talk about work. He was a barrister, making good strides in his career. Jane was a secretary at his chambers and though she enjoyed her job, being with Chrissie always made her feel that it was lacking; that she should be doing more.

Chrissie offered round a packet of cigarettes, Adam took one. The man on the next table began to give

PATRICK REDMOND

them dirty looks. Registering this, Chrissie blew smoke in his direction before telling them about an awards ceremony she had attended the previous week; describing how a soap actress had preened her way up the red carpet only to realize she had left her mobile in a taxi and been forced to charge back down it again, sending photographers flying.

'Were there any stars on your table?' Stuart asked.

'No.'

'You told me Alexander Gallen and Evelyne thingy were on it,' Adam pointed out.

'They're not stars. Just celebrities.'

'What were they like?' Jane asked, trying not to sound too interested.

'He's nice. She's a bitch and a bore. All she talks about are shoes and eyebrows.'

They all laughed. Chrissie asked Jane about her job. Jane tried to make it sound as challenging as possible, wanting to impress while fearing she had little chance of doing so.

Time passed. Chrissie went to the ladies while Harry went to buy more wine. 'Do you think I'm boring her?' Jane asked Adam once they were alone.

'Why do you think that?'

'My life's pretty humdrum compared to hers.'

'No it's not, and even if it was she wouldn't care. She's not like that.'

'I wish I was like her.'

'Why?'

'Why not? She's gorgeous. Confident. She makes me feel inferior.'

A smile spread across Adam's face. Wry. Nostalgic.

'What's funny?' she asked.

'She wasn't always like this. When we were kids she was really shy. Now she makes me and my sister look like wallflowers but back then we were a million times more confident than her.'

'Oh sure.'

'Sure. For years she had no friends apart from Sue and me. She used to get bullied something rotten. She was one of those kids who seem to have the word 'victim' tattooed on their foreheads. She was odd looking too. Everyone thought she was ugly. And then . . . I don't know. She just changed.'

Chrissie and Harry returned to the table. Harry poured out the new bottle of wine. 'The barman fancies you,' he told Chrissie. 'He kept trying to find out if you were attached.'

Chrissie groaned. 'Jane, if I start snogging your husband then don't take it seriously. I would snog Adam but we're not big on incest in our family.'

'Though you are big on metamorphoses by the sound of it.'

'What do you mean?'

'Well, not your whole family. Just you. Adam was telling me you used to get bullied at school.' She laughed. 'I'd love to see someone try and bully you now.'

Chrissie's eyes narrowed. Jane stopped laughing.

But it was Adam that Chrissie turned to.

'What have you been saying about me?'

'Just what you were like at school.'

'And how *was* I exactly?'

'Well, you know. You got bullied. You didn't have any friends.'

'Rubbish.'

'No it's not. Anyway, who cares? It was ages ago.'

'And it's crap!'

'Why are you getting wound up? We were all different when we were younger.'

'Well you certainly were. God, you used to embarrass me. Always fancying yourself as this cool guy when really you were just a hanger on. Mark Fletcher and his friends used to laugh about you behind your back. They thought you were a joke. None of them wanted you in the gang. Mark told me the only reason they didn't kick you out was because they thought you'd start crying about it.'

Adam flushed. 'That's not true.'

'Yes it is. Anyway, what does it matter? It was ages ago like you said.'

Silence. Jane stared down at her hands, wishing she had never opened her mouth.

Chrissie exhaled; the sound like escaping steam. 'I'm having another cigarette,' she announced. Again the man on the next table seemed indignant but the look Chrissie gave him was so venomous that he quickly turned away. She offered the packet to Adam; he shook his head, looking upset. Suddenly her expression softened. 'Hey, I was only teasing. They didn't really laugh at you, just as I was never that loser you told Jane I was.' She gave Jane another dazzling smile. 'Cousins, eh? Can't live with 'em. Can't kill 'em.'

Then she laughed; the sound as strong and confident as always. She resumed her description of the awards ceremony, coming out with salacious gossip that had Jane and Harry chuckling. As she spoke she put her arm around Adam, stroking his cheek affectionately until eventually he started chuckling too.

The following afternoon Alexander phoned Chrissie.

'I'm looking at the *OK!* spread on the ceremony,' she told him. 'There's a picture of you, me and Evelyne with the MD. They gave the event four pages which is four less than they devoted to a reality show bimbo flaunting the splendours of her gracious drawing room.'

'How shaming.'

'Not to worry. Word has it that she's blown all her money on botox injections, can't pay the mortgage and is about to have her gracious drawing room repossessed.'

He laughed. 'So how goes the project?'

'Slow but these things always are. We'll get there in the end.'

'I don't doubt that.' A pause. 'So you're probably very busy at the moment.'

'As always.'

'Too busy to have a drink sometime? I'd like to hear more about the project. We didn't have enough time to talk about it when we met.'

She smiled to herself.

'Perhaps at the end of the week,' he continued.

'I can't. I'm going on a business trip.'

'May I call you next week?'

Her first instinct was to say no. If he was interested in her then it wasn't fair to pretend that she felt the same.

But though she hated to admit it, she was flattered. So she said yes.

The call over she continued to study the photograph. Her name was given as Christina Bryan. She imagined people she knew sniggering about it and cursed the editors for their carelessness. They wouldn't have misspelt Evelyne's name.

Or Emma Sothern's.

But why would they when both were famous?

Momentarily self doubt consumed her. This wasn't the future she had planned for herself. What was she in the group of smiling faces but a hanger on? A nobody basking in the light of others when she wanted to be the light herself. The one around whom others fluttered. The person whose achievements others read about, envied and admired. Look upon my triumphs, ye reader and despair.

Look upon them, Dad. Look at the frightened little girl you abandoned. Look at the strong woman she's become and hate yourself for leaving her behind.

Because you're still alive. I'd feel it in my heart if you were dead and I'd be glad.

Even though a part of me would die with you.

She rubbed her temples, trying to dislodge the thoughts that swarmed there like parasites. They were stupid. Evidence that she was tired and in need of the break her weekend trip would provide. Assuming that it wasn't cancelled.

But she didn't want to think about that.

Shutting the magazine she left her office, searching for distraction elsewhere.

It wasn't cancelled.

Saturday afternoon was beautiful. The perfect weather for July. She stood with Jack at the helm while Bullseye perched on the roof like a figurehead, barking out greetings to people they passed on the canal bank.

They entered a long tunnel, the front lamp reflecting off cold, stone walls that dripped condensation while birds flew ahead like angels guiding them back into the light. They continued on through Regents Park, past the Zoo and the grand houses on the ridge above the water. Jack allowed her to steer, trying not to look apprehensive as she took them around a tight corner. 'Relax,' she told him. 'My dad taught me how to handle a boat.'

'But you don't remember your dad.'

She let the front drift towards the bank, laughing at his look of panic before guiding them clear, seconds before a collision. 'I'm used to the North Sea. This is like sailing a raft across a swimming pool.'

'Try taking her down the Thames. You won't find that so simple.'

'Is that a dare? Then I accept. What are we waiting for?'

'Not this weekend. It takes a day just to get to Limehouse. We'll do it another time.'

'I'll hold you to that,' she told him, contriving another near collision before effortlessly steering them to safety.

Once in Camden they explored the market. She bought him a T-shirt decorated with a skull and cross-bones, insisting that he put it on there and then. 'It looks good,' she told him. 'Lose the belly and I could quite fancy you.'

He pointed to a hideous bikini top decorated with the words SERVING WENCH in big red letters. 'I could definitely fancy you in that.'

'In your dreams, Blackbeard. I may be a wench but I never serve.'

They spent the evening on a pub crawl. Wherever they went he seemed to end up in conversation with people. She watched him talk to a scruffy young couple, making them laugh as they waited to be served. He was still wearing the T-shirt she had bought him, together with a pair of battered jeans. From behind he looked short and dumpy. More like a garden gnome than the man of her dreams. Not that he was. Not in a million years.

He brought the couple to join them, introducing them as Trevor and Trish who also lived on a narrow boat. She tried to appear welcoming while resenting their presence. Moving closer to Jack she studied their reflection in a mirror on the far wall, noticing how incongruous they looked together. Smart Soho girl meets dishevelled layabout. Yet another confirmation of how ridiculous the whole situation was.

Yet still the realization depressed her.

Trish was staring at her, a curious expression on her face. Did Trish think they looked incongruous together? Or was Trish just attracted to Jack?

Instinctively she draped a proprietorial arm over his leg.

Trevor complained about the rising cost of mooring fees. Bored beyond endurance she steered the conversation onto a more interesting topic. Taking control of the situation while keeping her arm firmly draped around Jack.

Later, after sex, they lay together staring up at the ceiling.

'You were rude to Trevor,' he told her.

'He was boring. They both were.'

'They were OK.'

'Oh please. Even Bullseye is a more stimulating con-versationalist.'

He laughed. From the other end of the boat Bullseye emitted thunderous snores.

'They liked you,' she said. 'For some unknown reason.'

'Don't you?'

'No. I just use you to practise faking orgasms.'

He put his arm around her. She snuggled closer, feeling the boat rock as another slid past in the water.

'They'd have liked you too if you'd let them.'

'I didn't stop them.'

'You intimidated them.'

'Is that a fact, baldy?'

'I'm not going bald.'

'But you are easy to wind up. So what's intimidating about me?'

'You project strength. The way you move. The way you talk. Whatever you do you project it.'

'And that's bad?'

'Not bad. It just makes people feel they can't be weak around you.'

'Then I'm doing them a favour. People shouldn't be weak: the weak get hurt. The most important thing in life is to know how to fight and defend yourself.'

'Is that something else your dad taught you?'

'You Freud, me Jane?'

'I'm just saying.'

'Well don't. My dad's gone. He has nothing to do with anything.'

'Except you being a psycho at the helm.'

She nibbled his ear. 'Wimp.'

'Wanting to keep my boat in one piece is not being a wimp.' He stroked her hair. 'You still think about him, don't you? Even though you pretend you don't.'

'You still think about your dad.'

'But mine's never coming back. Yours could walk in on us now for all you know.'

'And take you to task for corrupting me. Not that you need worry. I'd defend you.'

'Would I need defending?'

'He'd eat you for breakfast.'

'Even now? He must be nudging sixty.'

'Fifty-two. Still young, really.'

'What was he like?'

'Big. Everything about him was big. When he entered a room you felt his presence and when he left it you felt his loss. He filled the space, as they say.'

'Sounds like someone else I know.'

'I'm nothing like him. I'd never walk out on a child.'

He kissed her shoulder. 'Is that what you want? Children? I mean some day.'

'Doesn't everyone? Don't you?'

'I guess. Think I'd make a good father?'

'Sure. They'd roll the best joints in class.' She tangled her fingers in his chest hair. There were a couple of spots below his right nipple. Kevin's skin had been clear and had always smelled of soap, aftershave and everything that signified making an effort. Jack smelled of beer, smoke and the water. Take me as you find me. She admired that.

'Do I intimidate you?' she asked him.

'Do you want to?'

'Of course. Got to keep you on your toes. That way you're nearly as tall as me.'

'I like you like this.'

'Like what?'

'Soft.'

Weak.

But that showed how little he knew her.

'Was Ali soft?'

'Yes.'

'Then I pity her. If you're soft you're vulnerable.'

'You don't have to be soft to be vulnerable. Just human.'

She remembered Bob saying something similar. But Bob didn't know her as well as he thought either.

'If she was as nice as you say then why did you let her go?'

'What does it matter?'

'I'm just curious.'

'Because she deserved better than me.'

And you want her back

The thought came from nowhere. As unwelcome as a cramp. She pushed it aside. 'You're right. What does it matter? The past is done. It's the present that's important. And no, my dad didn't teach me that. I worked it out all by myself.'

She sat up, staring down at him. A sweet, direction-less man with an impish face and chubby body that she wanted to wrap herself around and stay close to for ever. But only because she'd been drinking; alcohol giving shallow emotions a depth that the cold light of day would quickly dispel.

He continued to stroke her hair. 'You've worked a lot of things out by yourself. I guess you've had to. It's not like you had your parents to help.'

'I never needed them.'

'We all need people.'

'I don't. Least of all you.' She tickled his balls. 'Except for one thing, of course.'

'But we've only just finished.'

'I'm sure you can still rise to the occasion.'

'You'll be the death of me, Chrissie Ryan.'

'Then it's your funeral.' She leant over him, her hair covering his face like a shroud.

She woke early, escaping from a dream of sitting on a bus, staring out at an endless row of billboards all emblazoned with the name Emma Sothern while face-less children jeered and threw paper pellets that tangled in her hair like confetti.

Jack lay beside her, sleeping on his side. She had stopped him sleeping on his back, tired of being dis-turbed by incessant snores. But it was for his own good. People always felt more rested if they had slept on their side.

Feeling thirsty, she rose and moved into the main cabin, pouring herself a glass of water. The kitchen area was tidy. Everything washed and put away. Another change she had introduced. It was more hygenic that way. She was only thinking of him.

The air in the cabin felt stale. Putting on his robe she went to sit in the bow. Though only five, dawn was already breaking. Bullseye rose from the sofa and trotted out after her. She lit a cigarette. The canal was silent and still. All the occupants of the other boats were sleeping. She tapped ash into the water and watched it float away.

The yellow cotton apron was in her hand. The one that had belonged to Ali. Holding it up she lit a corner, watching the flames devour the fabric. When it grew too hot she threw it into the water where it drifted away like a tiny Viking longboat on its way to Valhalla. Momentarily she felt guilty. But Jack was always saying that he meant to throw it out. She was saving him a job. Just thinking of him. That was all.

Bullseye clambered onto her lap. She continued to smoke, stroking his head while watching the light spread across the sky.

Chrissie's diary. Sunday July 25th.

I miss Jack. Only two hours since we said goodbye and already I miss him.

It's so stupid. What is there to miss? He's good in the sack but not great. He's no intellectual and wouldn't know culture if it bit him on the arse. His only idea of a good time is getting wasted. He's like a kid. Someone who's never grown up and doesn't know the meaning of the word responsibility. I suppose that's what comes of living on a boat. If things get difficult you up anchor and move on. The whole country is covered in canals. He could go anywhere and no one would be able to find him.

Not that I'd want to. I'd be well rid. If Aunty Karen met him she'd tell me I could do better. Not that she'd need to. I know it already.

But knowing it doesn't stop me missing him.

There was a message from Kev on the phone when I got back. He says he's missing me. I should be pleased but I just felt annoyed. He's setting himself up to get hurt again and only a weakling does that. And he is weak. Like all the men I go out with. I don't know why. I just seem to attract them.

Except Jack. When I'm with him I'm the one who's weak.

But I'll get over it. I'm just feeling tired tonight. Tomorrow will be different. I'll be me again. I'll be strong.

I'll be in control.

On Monday morning Alexander phoned. Again she felt flattered. She didn't want to but she did.

They made small talk for a couple of minutes, then he asked her out. She turned him down as gently as possible, talking about how busy she was. He took it well but she could sense his disappointment. It made her feel guilty and good at the same time.

The conversation over she stared at the phone, willing it to ring again. Wanting to hear Jack's voice telling her that the weekend had been amazing and suggesting dates for the trip down the Thames that he had discussed but never finalized. She could have suggested them herself but pride had held her back.

She wondered what he was doing. Who he was with. Was he telling them about their weekend? How was he describing her? As someone special or just someone.

Five minutes passed. Her eyes remained focused on the phone. Waiting for him to ring. Needing him to ring. Despising her weakness but unable to control it.

But there was a way to feel strong again. Picking up the receiver, she dialled Alexander's number.

Tuesday evening. She sat in a private member's club in a Georgian house off Berkeley Square. A quiet, restful place, all oak panneling, subdued lighting and respectful staff, some of whom looked as old as the building itself.

She sipped her wine. Alexander did the same. He was dressed casually: a jacket and shirt with no tie. It suited him better than the dinner jacket he had worn to the awards.

'Is it OK here?' he asked. 'We could go somewhere livelier if you prefer.'

'I like it.' She looked about her. 'Does Evelyne?'

'No. It's too private. She prefers places where you go to get seen.'

'So her evening's not complete unless she ends up in the next day's papers. Well, that figures.' She laughed. 'Sorry, that was catty.'

'But true.'

'How does she feel about you seeing me?'

'She doesn't know. Not that it's a secret. Like I said, she and I are just friends.'

'And we're just here to talk about my work.'

'Of course.'

'Of course. But what about you? You work in research, don't you?'

He nodded. 'Military history. Research projects for the government and anyone else who wants to employ us.'

'It's not what I'd expect someone in your position to do.'

'What should someone in my position do?'

'Nothing, with all that money. That's very judgmental, isn't it?'

'Would you work if you didn't have to?'

She considered for a moment. 'Yes, I think so.'

'So do I. I think you'd be bored otherwise.'

'So being rich is boring? Don't ever go public with

that: the people who run the lottery would take out a contract on your life.'

Laughing, he made his way to the gents. She turned on her mobile, hoping for a text from Jack. Two came through at once: Melanie and another friend wanting to know how her evening was going. Both excited because of who she was with. It would have been different had she been with Jack. No one would have been excited then. No one but her.

His photograph was still stored in the memory; his cheeks bulging with food like a squirrel hording calories for a long winter. She wondered if they would still know each other when winter arrived. Assuming he still wanted to know her now.

Alexander returned. Hiding her disappointment she continued to drink her wine.

'Where are you from originally?' he asked.

'Havelock. A one horse town on the Essex coast. You're from New York, aren't you?'

'Yes. I lived there until I was six. Then I came here.'

'That must have been traumatic. Or had McDonalds colonized the UK by then?'

Again he laughed. She tried to remember what she knew about him. An only child who had been orphaned at an early age and raised by a grandmother from whom he had inherited his fortune. The papers had made a great deal of that, comparing him to the Onassis heiress. The poor little rich boy whose money couldn't protect him from loss.

'Do you have a big family?' he asked.

'Tiny. Like you. How old were you when your parents died?'

'Six when my father died. He was in a car accident. My mother died in childbirth.'

'With you?'

He nodded.

'I'm sorry.'

'Don't be. It was worse for others than for me. I never knew her so I couldn't miss her. My grandmother always said I should be glad of that.'

'But you knew your dad. You must miss him.'

'A bit, but my memories are sketchy. I need photographs to help picture his face.'

'At least you have photographs.' None existed of her own father. She had burnt them when she was fourteen. Not that it mattered. If she wanted to see his face all she had to do was think of the sea.

Alexander was staring at her. A handsome, softly spoken man with enough money to buy anything he wanted. Except love. Nothing could buy that. Not that she would ever need to. Not that she would ever need it.

'So why did you come to England? Did your grandparents live here?'

'Yes. My grandfather was English.'

'What was he like?'

'Kind. From what I remember. He died a year after I arrived.'

'It must have been hard. Losing so many people when you were young.'

He shook his head. 'When you're young you're better able to adapt and forget your life was ever different.'

She nodded. Not that she had ever forgotten. But she had adapted.

'Your grandmother must have doted on you.'

'She did. My mother was her only child.'

'Just as you were hers.'

'Do you have brothers and sisters?'

'No,' she said, wondering if that was true.

'So we're both only children. Aren't they supposed to be spoiled?'

'If so then I got royally screwed.'

'Were your parents strict?'

'No. Just boring. Unlike your relatives.' She lit a cigarette. 'What's Isabella Neve like?' she asked, referring to a New York *it* girl who rivalled Paris Hilton in the headline grabbing stakes. 'She's your cousin, isn't she?'

He nodded. 'Pretty wild.'

'I'll say. I read about her rap star boyfriend trying to shoot her in a Manhattan club.'

'It wasn't quite as dramatic as that. Apparently the gun wasn't loaded and he was waving it at a bouncer. Mind you, Isabella milked it for all she was worth, doing talk shows and ending up with a record contract. Another of my cousins told me all about it, joking that it's nice to see the entrepreneurial spirit passing down the family line.'

She laughed. 'Told you we were boring in comparison.'

'I'm sure that's not true. It's as you said when we first met. If you've got money and connections it's easy to get attention. It's not right but that's just how it is.'

'Yeah, it's not right.'

'Has that annoyed you?'

'Not unless you're going to tell me that you've just landed a record contract too.'

'No way. Unlike Isabella, I know my limitations.'

Silence. She stared at her handbag, longing to check her mobile again. Knowing she was being rude but unable to stop herself.

'You don't have to stay if you don't want to,' he said gently.

'Sorry. I've had a stressful day and feel a bit distracted. You know what it's like.'

'So what do you do when you're not working?'

'I love swimming. And dancing.'

'What sort of dancing? Classical or modern?'

'Modern. There's a club I go to in King's Cross, it's a dump but the music's great. Sometimes we dance all night.'

'We?'

'Me and my flatmate.'

'So your boyfriend's not a dancer?'

She didn't know. It had never seemed as important as just being together.

Again Alexander was staring. She wondered why he

liked her. She had never given him any encouragement but perhaps that was the appeal. He was probably so used to girls throwing themselves at him that one who didn't must have seemed something of a challenge.

Perhaps.

Whatever the reason she would be a fool to alienate him. Not this early in the game.

'What boyfriend?' she asked.

Wednesday lunchtime. Chrissie met her friend Anna, the literary agent.

They sat in a coffee bar off Ludgate Circus, far away from their usual Soho haunts. Chrissie had insisted on it as a meeting place, based on reports of its lively atmosphere. Sadly the reports had been misleading as the place had all the character of a paper cup. Even the coffee was lousy.

As was the company. Normally Chrissie was full of life but on this occasion she seemed distracted and Anna knew why.

'So what's he like?'

'Who?'

'Alexander Gallen of course. How was last night?'

Chrissie didn't answer. Her eyes drifted towards the counter.

'Well?'

'It was OK. We had a couple of drinks and a chat.'

'And no shag. That's the spirit. Don't let him think you're easy. Keep him gagging.'

Silence. Anna waited for laughter but none came.

'Are you seeing him again?'

'Maybe. Do you think she's more attractive than me?'

'No. She's more conventionally beautiful but my sources tell me she has all the personality of wet cement. A bit like this place, really.'

'I'm not talking about Evelyne.'

'Then who?'

Chrissie gestured to the girl behind the corner. A tall, slim redhead with a pleasant but unremarkable face. Anna was confused. 'Why are you asking?'

'Do you?'

'Get real. She looks like your anaemic twin. Why? Did you come here with Alexander? Did he say he fancied her? He did, didn't he? Oh, Chrissie, wake up. He's just trying to make you jealous. So much for not being excited. You can't fool me.'

'I'm not. Anyway, he's not that sort of person. He's . . .'

'Loaded?'

'Nice. You'd think he'd have a huge ego but he doesn't.' A sigh. 'And he likes me.'

'And that's *bad*?'

'For him, maybe.'

'What are you talking about?'

'I'll end up hurting him. That's what I do, apparently. Hurt any guy who likes me.'

'Who told you that?'

'Kev.'

'That's just sour grapes.'

Again Chrissie turned to stare at the girl behind the counter. 'Is it?'

'Yes. I know what I'm talking about. When it comes to men I wrote the book.'

At last Chrissie smiled. 'No you didn't. You just sold the rights for more than they were worth.'

'That's the spirit. I'm bored here. Let's go somewhere else.'

They made their way to the door, leaving their coffee cups on the table. The girl from the counter went to clear them.

'Thanks, Ali,' said the man at the till. 'You're a star.'

Thursday evening. Energized after a long swim, Chrissie phoned Jack.

She sat in the gym changing room, watching women of all ages inspect themselves in mirrors. A depressing reminder that for many insecurity was a life sentence.

He answered on the third ring. 'I was just going to call you.'

'Then I've saved you a job. I've been thinking about our trip.'

'Trip?'

'Down the Thames. Next week would be good for me. Let's do it then.'

'Next week?'

'You can get someone to cover for you, can't you?

You're always saying how the other barman wants more shifts.'

'Um . . . yes. I suppose. It's just a bit short notice.'

'It's plenty of notice. Where's your will to be wild?' He laughed.

'So it's agreed then,' she said quickly, careful to phrase it as a statement. 'Good. It'll be fun.'

'As long as you don't sink us.'

'Relax. I'm used to the North Sea. Besides, I've done a course in lifesaving and could save your stash in a force ten gale.'

'What about me?'

'You'll be so high you could float to shore. We can finalize the plans this weekend. I'll come over one night. How's Saturday? That's best for me.'

'Saturday it is then.'

As she hung up she noticed a woman watching her with an amused smile and felt like a teenager arranging to meet the boy on whom she had a crush.

But she wasn't a teenager. And she never had crushes.

Rising to her feet she went to shower.

The following morning she told Bob her plans. He looked concerned. 'You're supposed to be coming up to Norfolk with me next week.'

'You told me the week after,' she lied. One of Bob's failings was forgetfulness. Though annoying it had its uses.

He looked depressed.

'Call me if there's an emergency. I'll cut the trip short.' She had no intention of doing so but at least it might make him feel better.

Which it did. His face relaxed. 'You look excited,' he told her. 'It must be the prospect of spending time with the man of your dreams.'

'Don't start that again.'

'So if he cancelled you wouldn't be bothered.'

'No.'

'And what of Alec? Sian tells me he called twice yesterday.'

'Why are you so fascinated by my private life?'

'Because it's a lot more interesting than mine. This weekend Malc and I are shopping for kitchen units. Hours of bliss at IKEA.' A pause. 'Do you like Alec?'

'Yes. As a friend.'

'And how does he like you?'

'That's his business.'

'Have you told him about Jack?'

'No.'

'Well, why should you? It's just a bit of fun. Nothing serious. Nothing you could end up getting hurt by.'

'I don't get hurt.'

'We all get hurt.'

'Only if we let ourselves.'

'Be careful, Ballsy. You're not as tough as you think you are.'

'And you're not as smart as you think you are. Don't worry about me. I know how to look after myself.'

'I hope you're right,' he said gently. 'I really do.'

Tuesday morning. She stood on the boat at Limehouse marina, waiting for the gates to the Thames to open.

It was a beautiful morning. Sunny and mild, just as the previous day had been. They had spent it travelling through the London canals, Jack showing her how to work the locks. It had been hard but she had enjoyed it. Being outside on a boat. She had missed it more than she had realized.

The gates began to open, tidal water pouring in like lava. As Jack guided them out onto the river she sat at the front with Bullseye. The wind was strong and waves slammed the sides of the boat. 'Try not to be sick,' he called out.

'No chance.' She jumped up onto the roof and walked across it, stopping to pirouette and wave to the occupants of another boat before dropping down to stand beside him.

'You're nuts. You could have fallen in.'

'Let me steer.'

'No chance. Hit a wave at the wrong angle and we'll capsize.'

'Go on. Let me.' She seized the helm and began to navigate them through the turbulence, laughing at his look of panic. Not that he had any need to worry. Her father had taught her well. Relaxing, he put his arm around her while Bullseye, excited by the movement, ran barking from one end of the boat to the other.

They continued onwards, through Bermondsey where people waved to them from balconies, passing under Tower Bridge and on towards St Paul's and Whitehall. She gazed around her, taking in all the sights as if seeing them for the first time and pointing them out to him as if he had never seen them either.

'Enjoying yourself?' he asked with a smile.

'It's fantastic! When I was at college we had a Christmas party on the Thames but the boat was a tank, the weather was lousy and we had to spend our whole time in the bar. It was nothing like this.' Impulsively she kissed his cheek. 'Thanks, Jack. I'm really grateful.'

'My pleasure. Is your arm tired? Shall I take over?'

'Absolutely not. I could steer for ever.'

He stroked her hair. 'I bet you could.'

They passed St Paul's. He went below to open a bottle of wine. On Westminster Bridge tourists waited with cameras that caught the rays of the sun. Calling out a greeting she waved up at them. And then it happened.

A seagull swooped low, no more than six foot from them. Bullseye, sensing prey, rose to his feet, lunged for it and fell into the water.

'Jack! Jack!'

He charged out of the cabin.

'What do I do? What do I do?'

'Slow us down!'

'How?'

'Turn the fucking handle!'

She tried, but in her panic only increased their speed. He snatched the controls while she watched Bullseye plough through the water towards them. And the engine. 'Jack, the engine! What if he hits it?'

'He won't. Just lean out!'

'I can't! There's nothing to hold onto!'

He grabbed the waist of her jeans. 'I've got you. Now . . . oh shit!'

The wall of the bridge was feet away. Cursing, he steered as hard as he could. The front of the boat missed the stone by inches. Bullseye continued to fly towards them. With Jack holding her jeans she leant out, grabbed his collar and pulled him to safety. He began to bark, shaking off water and drenching them both.

They re-emerged from the shadow of the bridge to find people leaning over, calling out anxiously. 'Is he all right? Did you get him? Oh thank God!'

She rose to her feet. 'Well, that'll liven up their holiday snaps,' she said nonchalantly.

He burst out laughing. She did the same. Both of them releasing tension after the drama of the moment. Water dripped from his hair into his eyes and down onto his chin. She wiped it away while he gave her a grin so big it threatened to split his face in two.

And at that moment she knew she loved him. Completely. Utterly. It was like a drug rush. A euphoria so powerful that she couldn't even breathe.

He leaned towards her, wanting a kiss.

Suddenly the euphoria vanished, replaced by all consuming fear. She backed away, feeling trapped. Wanting to scream. To turn and run. But there was nowhere to go.

His grin faded. 'What is it?'

'Nothing.'

'You're shivering,'

'I'm just cold.'

'You're upset.'

'I'm not.'

'Don't be. It was only an accident.'

'I'm not!'

'Chrissie, hey.' He tried to put his arm around her. 'He wasn't in any real danger. Everything's OK. I promise you it is.'

She breathed deeply, the smell of oil and mud filling her nostrils just as it had on the harbour wall when her father had promised her everything would be all right. The day before he walked out of her life for ever.

'But he *was* in danger. Look at him. He's just a little dog. As defenceless as a child. He could have been hurt and you should never hurt anyone who's that defenceless. It's the worst, most disgusting thing anyone could ever do!'

Then she burst into tears.

Again he tried to hold her. Pushing him away she sought refuge in the cabin.

Ten minutes later. Jack stood at the helm waiting for Chrissie to reappear.

He called her name but heard nothing. His concern increased while Bullseye, oblivious, lay snoring at his feet.

Then the cabin door opened and she emerged. She had changed her clothes. A clean blouse and shorts. A simple outfit though she wore it as if it were a designer dress. Her hair, newly combed, shone in the light. Everything about her seemed to shine. Even her eyes, though slightly red, had a new glow. A harder glow. As if she were coated in an invisible layer of steel.

'Are you OK?' he asked anxiously.

'Fine. Sorry about before.' Bending down she stroked Bullseye. 'I must be fonder of this little guy than I thought.'

'He's fond of you too. You saved him after all.'

'So much for his not being in danger. Are all your promises as worthless as that?'

'What do you mean?'

'Nothing.' She began to laugh, the wind catching in her hair. She looked beautiful; tall, strong and vibrantly alive. A human force of nature inspiring in him a complicated mixture of desire and trepidation. He wondered why she was here. What it was she saw in him.

Where it was all going to end.

She stood behind him, wrapping her arms around his chest. He stroked her cheek with his free hand. She bit his finger, gently at first then so hard she almost drew blood.

'Ouch!' He pulled his hand away.

'Just reminding you who's in charge.'

'Bully.'

'Poor little Jacky. Better grow some balls or no girl's ever going to love you.'

'There's nothing wrong with my balls.'

'Of course not. You're full of testosterone. I can see that by your bald patch.'

'I'm not going bald!'

Again she laughed, tightening her hold on him as he guided them on down the river.

Extract from a radio interview with Emma Sothern: 19th November 2005

'Do you think acting is a hard profession?'

'Yes. Not the work itself. If you're passionate about something then it's never hard. But it's hard in that so much depends on luck.'

'Do you think you've been lucky?'

'Absolutely. I think I have talent but I was also spotted by the right people who gave me the right breaks and that doesn't happen to everyone.'

'Like your college contemporaries. Christina Ryan was one of them, wasn't she?'

'Yes.'

'Were you friends?'

'Acquaintances but not friends.'

'What was she like?'

'Confident. She always had this air of purpose about her. That's what I remember. You meet people like that sometimes who seem to know exactly where they're going and never waste time worrying about whether they'll make it. They just know they will.'

'But she didn't get there, did she? She left after only one year.'

'Yes.'

'Were you surprised?'

Silence.

'Do you think she had talent?'

'It was strange. When we did plays she'd always be cast as the dominant female. That was how she came across so I suppose it was natural. Playing yourself is always the easiest type of part. But the funny thing was that when she performed those parts she never seemed very natural. You were aware she was acting and that's one thing an audience should never know.'

'Do you think that's why she left? The realization that she didn't have what it took?'

'No. She had what it took. Just not in the way you'd have thought.'

'What do you mean?'

Another silence.

'She might have been better in comedy, perhaps?'

'No.'

'Or perhaps . . .'

'It was on her last day. That's when I saw what she could have done.'

'What happened on that day?'

'We were doing improvisations. Put in pairs, given a situation and told to run with it. Chrissie was with some guy and their scene was a man telling his wife that he's leaving her because he feels trapped in the relationship.'

'Was she good?'

'Not at first. Initially she was quite stilted. But then she began to get into it, really into it. Suddenly she was amazing. It was so real, the way she acted. You could feel the emotion coming off her. The fear and desperation. At one point she actually started crying. The whole class applauded when it was over including our teacher and even Robert De Niro would have found it difficult to get more than a 'not bad' out of him.

'Chrissie and this guy were the last to perform. When it was over she left the room in a hurry. I don't know why but I followed her. She went into the toilet. I waited outside but ten minutes passed and she hadn't come out so I went in to see if she was OK.

'She was standing by the sinks, staring at herself in the mirror. Completely focused on her own reflection. So focused that she didn't notice I was there. I said her name but she didn't answer so I told her how good I thought she'd been.

'And then . . . I don't know. It was weird. She said, 'That wasn't me.' I asked her what she meant but she just kept saying it. Over and over like a mantra. I asked her if I could get her anything and then she turned towards me with this look of fury and she said 'Tina's dead . . .'

'Tina?'

'Yes. That was the name she used. 'Tina's dead. She doesn't exist. I killed her years ago!' She almost screamed it. Then she marched past me out of the toilets.

'That was the last time I saw her. The next day someone told me she'd quit college. I never heard anything about her after that. Not until a year ago when the papers were full of all the terrible things that had happened . . .'

Sunday evening. Chrissie sat in her flat, listening to Aunty Karen on the phone.

'Tell me more about Jack.'

'What's there to say. He's nice.'

'But not special?'

'No.'

'Is Alexander Gallen nice?'

'How do you know about him?'

'I saw your picture in *OK!* Well actually I didn't. That awful woman at the Post Office did and showed it to me when I went in. Why didn't you tell me you'd met him?'

'It's not that exciting.'

'It is for me.'

'Maybe you should get out more.'

'If only. The highlight of my life is gossiping about which member of the flower committee is sleeping with the rector.' A pause. 'I miss you, Chrissie.'

'I miss you too.'

'Then come home.'

'I will.'

'When?'

'Soon.'

'When is soon?'

'Never if you give me grief.'

'I'm your aunt. That's my job.' Another pause. 'I saw your mum today.'

She felt obliged to ask the question. 'How is she?'

'Still cut up about your uncle.'

'Some things never change.'

'What do you mean?'

'Her trying to steal the limelight. Making out her loss is greater than everyone else's.'

'That's not fair.'

'Isn't it?'

'He was her brother. Her only family except you.'

'Don't.'

'What?'

'Try and make me feel guilty. If you want to see me then come to London. We could go shopping, see a show. It would be fun.'

'But not as fun as having you sitting in my living room, stuffing your face with biscuits and telling me all your news like you used to. Come home, Chrissie. Just for a weekend. Bring Jack. I'd love to meet him.'

'You wouldn't be impressed.'

'I don't care. If he makes you happy that's good enough for me.'

'I don't need a man to make me happy.'

'But you're not happy now, are you? Something's bothering you. I can hear it in your voice. What is it?'

She didn't answer.

'Maybe I can help and even if I can't I can at least listen and that might help in itself.'

Suddenly she wanted to tell everything. How she felt about Jack. How it made her feel about herself. How it seemed as if the ground beneath her feet had turned to quicksand ready to pull her under and never let her back up into the light.

Yet again she asked herself how it could have happened. How she could have let it happen. How she could have been so weak.

But she wasn't weak. She was strong. She had to believe that because if the belief crumbled then

249

everything else would crumble too and she would be left with nothing.

Except Tina.

'Chrissie?'

'Don't worry about me. I can look after myself.'

'Are you sure?'

'Yes. I'd better go. I will come home soon, that's a promise.'

After putting down the phone she walked into the kitchen. On the side was a china replica of Windsor Castle that Jack had given her as they had sat together on the river bank beneath the castle walls. 'Something to help you remember the trip,' he had told her. Not that she needed help. The memory would stay with her like a scar.

She picked it up and stared at it. Cheap, sentimental rubbish. The sort of gift she would once have sneered at before love had turned her world on its head.

There was dust on it. As she wiped it away she had a vision of her mother dusting the figurines her father had left and of herself watching, aching for her mother's attention; yearning for her approval; willing to do anything just to make her smile.

And now I am her. Doing what she did. Feeling what she felt. Being as weak as she was.

She threw the ornament onto the floor, smashing it into pieces.

*

The following morning she sat at her desk, phoning potential investors for the twins project. Bob was still in Norfolk. She wished she was there too. Film sets were busy places. The perfect place to be when you didn't want time to think.

But she wasn't and she did.

Sian appeared, wanting to know about her trip. She described the route and places of interest, aware that she sounded like a presenter on a TV travelogue. All facts and no feelings. But that was only right. Her feelings were too complicated to explain.

They had gone as far as Marlowe, spending nights moored by the river and exploring the towns they passed on the way. Jack claimed to have enjoyed the trip but she didn't believe him. Not when she had done so little to make things easy.

She hadn't meant to be unpleasant, had tried to act as if everything was normal. But constantly she had felt the need to make digs, masking them as jokes even though some were too savage to be easily laughed off. References to his lack of direction; comparisons with his brother who was a successful estate agent and whom he felt had been the parental favourite. The need to make him feel inadequate around her. Vulnerable. Grateful.

She hadn't wanted to do it yet had been unable to stop. Words had always been her strongest weapon and suddenly the need for protection had become all consuming. She knew what she should do. Delete his number and picture. Erase all trace of him. Love was just a feeling and even if she couldn't control it she could still control the way she acted on it which was the same thing.

Well, almost.

And she *would* do it. Soon. When she felt ready.

Her mobile rang. Alexander's number came up on the display. She found his persistence reassuring. As comforting as a warm hug on a cold night.

As she prepared to answer him a voice whispered softly in her head.

Don't do it. This isn't right.

But it felt good and that was the same thing.

Well, almost.

So she took the call.

The following evening Alexander showed her his Kensington flat.

It was huge: three double bedrooms, two bathrooms, a gleaming kitchen, grand dining room and vast living room all elegantly furnished and with towering high ceilings.

'Someone has good taste,' she said when the tour was over.

'The interior decorators. I just signed the cheques.'

'When did you move in?'

'When I was twenty-one. My grandmother thought I should have my own place.'

'And where was her place?'

'A house in Notting Hill.'

'Which probably made this flat look like a garrett.'

'It still does. I haven't sold it.'

'Why don't you live there?'

'It's too big. A couple live-in and take care of it. I just use it for parties.'

'Do you throw many?'

'About three a year. For friends and work colleagues.'

'Sounds fun.'

'You'll have to see for yourself when I have my next one.'

They entered the living room. As he opened a bottle of champagne she examined the photographs on display just as Jack had done when he had visited her. 'Are these your parents?' she asked, pointing to an attractive young couple beaming for the camera.

'Yes.'

'You look like your father.' She picked up a wonderfully lit black and white portrait of a beautiful young woman with long, luxuriant hair. 'Who's this?'

'My grandmother.'

'It's a fantastic picture. Who took it?'

'Cecil Beaton.'

'Wow. Were they friends?'

'Just acquaintances. She told me he was too gossipy for her. Apparently his nickname was Malice in Wonderland.'

'I'm not surprised he'd want to photograph her. She has a great face.'

'So have you. Very strong. I guess people tell you that all the time.'

She remembered Jack telling her after their second night together. Only a month ago though it seemed like another era. Before the revolution that had changed everything.

'Not really,' she said, accepting the offered glass.

'How was the boat trip?'

'Exciting. The poor dog fell in the river and we nearly rammed Westminster Bridge trying to save him.' She sipped her drink, staring at a painting hanging on the wall. Close up it was just a mass of colour but from a distance she could make out a Russian church. 'That's clever. Who's it by?'

'Oleg Mazarov. A Ukrainian artist who's exhibited in my cousin's gallery.' A pause. 'Does the dog belong to Jack?'

'Yes.' She took another sip. 'Is the art gallery in New York?'

'Yes. How do you know him? Were you at college?'

'No way. College would be too much like hard work for him. Which cousin is this?'

'Byron Neve. Alexandra's brother.'

'Not the one who's dating . . . what's her name. That actress. Stephanie Shelby?'

'Stephanie Shelley. Yes. So how *do* you know Jack?'

'I met him through a friend. He works in a pub she goes to. Aren't Byron and Stephanie in some reality show about their lives?'

'Yes.'

'Are you going to appear in it?'

'No chance. Byron asked me but I made it very clear I wasn't interested.' He sipped his own drink. 'Is Jack a good friend?'

'You could say that. Are you good friends with your cousins?'

He nodded. She rolled the champagne in her glass waiting for the inevitable question.

'Are you a couple?'

'No. And while we're on the subject of couples, how is Evelyne?'

'Throwing tantrums in Milan. She's doing a show over there.' Another pause. 'Would you like to be?'

'No, I can throw tantrums anywhere.'

'I meant would you like to be a couple with Jack.'

She took out her cigarettes. 'Do you mind?'

'Not at all.' He gestured to an ashtray.

'Would you like one?'

'I don't smoke.'

'Very American. I was in LA with my boss last year and the amount of grief we got when we tried to light up.'

'So are you?'

'Jack would like us to be. I'm not so sure.'

'Why not?'

'He's possessive. Gets uptight if any girl he likes so much as say hello to another bloke. I can't stand that sort of thing.'

'I don't blame you.'

'Don't get me wrong. He's funny and cute and there's a lot to like about him. And I do like him. Just not as much as he likes me.'

The phone rang in another room. A man's voice came through on the answer service. Alexander rose to his feet. 'Would you mind if I took this. My best friend's having trouble at work and I want to check he's OK.'

She was touched. 'Of course not. I'd do the same if it was a friend of mine.'

Once he was gone she blew smoke into the air and watched it hang there, thinking of the lies she had told because she wanted so desperately for them to be true.

What am I doing wrong? Any man is mine if I want him enough. That's how it's been with all the others. Why isn't it true of him?

Needing distraction she picked up the photograph of Alexander's grandmother, marvelling at its elegance and style. A style that her own modern age seemed to have lost. And as she did so she realized that the face was not beautiful. The features were unremarkable yet made lovely through a combination of presentation and sheer force of will. An illusion that a girl called Tina could never master until another called Chrissie had shown her the way.

In the background she could hear Alexander talking. His tone was reassuring, protective and supportive. All indications of someone who knew how to be a good friend. It was an admirable quality, particularly in someone whose position could buy him all the friends he could ever want.

He returned to the room. 'How is he?' she asked.

'Fine, thanks.'

'How do you know him?'

'We were at boarding school together. We started on the same day.'

'How old were you?'

'Nine.'

'That's young. You must have been homesick.'

'We both were. Graham, particularly. He used to cry himself to sleep but don't tell him I told you that.'

'I won't. Bitch's honour.'

'You'd like him. Him and his wife.'

'Were you best man at the wedding?'

'Yes and I made a lousy speech. I was so nervous that I drank to calm myself down and ended up so sloshed that I forgot what I wanted to say.'

'I'm sure I'd have done the same.'

'I doubt it. I can't imagine you being nervous of anything.'

'You don't know me that well.'

'Not yet but I'd like to.'

Again she was touched. He was smiling at her. A decent man whose company she enjoyed. It was just friendship but friendship was good. Friendship was safe. It could never hurt the way love did.

An idea came to her. One that made her smile too. 'Do you like dancing?' she asked.

Friday evening. Chrissie stood with Alexander at her favourite dance club.

It was in a cellar near King's Cross: a dank, cavernous place with walls that dripped moisture and always made her think of the thieves' kitchens she had read about in Dickens. But it was a great place to dance. Music slammed into every alcove and bounced off again like rubber, creating a huge blanket of sound.

They were in the comparative quiet of the bar area, talking to Tara and a gay couple called Scott and Nick who were friends of Bob. Alexander, who had insisted on buying the round, handed her a bottle of water. She wiped her forehead. 'I need this.'

'You're a fantastic dancer.'

'You're not bad yourself.'

'Unlike Scott,' said Nick. 'I think he's a closet straight.'

Scott let out a melodramatic gasp. 'Oh no, I've been inned.'

She laughed. Alexander did too. Tara nudged her arm, gesturing to a muscular man dancing topless in the centre of the dancefloor. 'He's cute.'

'And gay,' Scott told her. 'We've seen him in enough clubs to know. Besides, no one straight dances that well.'

'Except you, Alec,' said Nick teasingly. 'Unless there's something you want to tell us.'

'Well actually . . .' Alexander began. More laughter. She felt pleased she had invited him. He looked pleased too. Clearly he wanted her friends to like him, she liked him for that.

Scott and Nick returned to the dancefloor. Chrissie and Alexander remained by the bar talking with Tara. In the distance Chrissie could see Rick, topless and clearly inebriated, flaunting a gym-pumped body to Melanie and any other female whose eye he could catch. His presence was the sole fly in her evening's ointment.

A record she liked began to play. 'Let's dance,' she told the others.

But before they could do so Rick and Melanie made their way over. Melanie looked exhausted. 'I didn't realize this place would be so hot.'

'Then take your top off,' Rick told her.

'No way.'

'Why not? You've got nice tits.'

Melanie blushed. Chrissie's hackles rose. 'Not as nice as yours though.'

Tara laughed. Chrissie expected Rick to react but instead he slapped Alexander on the arm. 'Are you buying?'

Melanie's blush intensified. 'Rick!'

'What? It's not like he can't afford it.'

'Of course,' said Alexander politely. 'What would you like?'

'Mel'll have a water. I'll have a Becks.'

Chrissie's hackles rose further. 'Please would help.'

'Yes, ma'am.' Again he gave Alexander a supposedly friendly slap. 'Watch your back with this one, mate. She's got more balls than most guys.'

'Yourself being the exception,' she retorted. 'At least until you started on the steroids.'

Alexander bought the drinks. Rick grinned at her. There was a dangerous light in his eyes. Clearly he was looking for trouble. Not that it mattered, she could take him with one hand tied behind her back. But she didn't want Alexander's evening to be spoiled.

'What are you two doing this weekend?' she asked, attempting to ease the tension.

'My parents are in town,' Melanie told her. 'We're seeing *Mamma Mia*.'

'You'll love it. It's brilliant. All those great songs.'

Rick continued to grin. 'Like "Money, money money? Always sunny in the rich man's world". What do you think, Chrissie? Does money buy happiness?'

'Shut up,' Melanie told him.

'Why? Chrissie knows I'm only joking. You know that, don't you, Chrissie?'

Alexander reappeared with the drinks. Melanie went to the toilet. Rick took a swig from his beer. 'You're a brave man,' he told Alexander. 'Being on your own in a place full of predatory girls. Isn't that right, Chrissie?'

'You tell me. As catches go they don't come any

bigger than you, though quite *what* they'll catch is another story.'

Again Tara laughed. Alexander, however began to look uncomfortable. 'Why don't you two dance,' she suggested. 'I'll join you in a minute.'

Once they were gone she turned on Rick. 'Leave him alone. He hasn't come here to listen to your crap.'

'Of course not. He'll be hearing more than enough from you.'

'What's that supposed to mean?'

'What do you think?'

'That you're talking out of your arse.'

'I bet he hasn't been up yours yet. What are you holding out for? A diamond ring? A pad in the South of France?'

'Don't confuse me with you.'

'I've seen the way he is with you. You've got him by the balls. He really thinks you're something. And I've seen the way you are with him too. Falseness and flirty smiles. Teasing his prick in the hope it's going to spurt gold. Kudos to you, Chrissie. From one so-called gold-digger to another, congratulations on hitting the motherlode.' Then he turned and walked away.

She remained where she was, fighting an urge to throw her drink at his head.

Because it was lies. Alexander was a friend. There was no question of her using him.

She felt her mobile buzz inside her pocket. Checking

the screen she saw she had a voice message. Bob, probably, telling her about plans for the following week. Another trip to Norfolk was on the cards. This time she had insisted on going too. She sought out an empty alcove to listen to it.

But it was from Jack. The sound of his voice was like an electric shock, releasing a thousand butterflies in the pit of her stomach.

'Hi. Just phoning to see how you are. Hope work's OK. Take care, yeah.'

And that was it. No suggestion of meeting. His tone warm but casual, as if she were nothing more than a minor league friend. And it hurt. So badly that it made her want to scream.

Someone nudged her arm. Rick stood beside her, his grin broader than ever. In her emotional state the sight of him made her feel exposed. Vulnerable. Like a girl threatened by a bully she was unable to fight.

'Go away,' she told him.

'What are you doing? Booking a private viewing with Versace?'

'Leave me alone.' She tried to sound forceful but her voice was weak. Only it wasn't her voice at all; it belonged to someone she thought no longer existed.

'You're a joke. What do you think Alexander's going to do? Give you a bit of class? Don't kid yourself. Some things can't be bought. Drape yourself in all the jewels you can but you'll still be a trashy Essex girl on the make. You can't change what you are,

Chrissie. There's not enough money in the world to do that.'

Then he began to laugh at her, just as Stuart had done on the day she had thought she had seen her father. The day she had discovered the rage.

Suddenly it descended. A blinding, blood-red mist.

She kneed Rick in the balls. Gasping he began to collapse. Grabbing his hair she dragged him back up and stared into his eyes. And this time when she spoke her voice was hard as steel.

'Listen to me, you little prick. I know all about you. The corners you've cut at work. The client meetings you've attended high on coke. I could smash your career any time I want and if you ever mess with me again then that's exactly what I'll do.'

He rubbed his groin. 'Fucking psycho.'

'That's right. I am a psycho. I can hate like you wouldn't believe but you'd better believe that I hate you and if I want it then Alexander will too. Like you said, I've got him by the balls. He'll do anything I ask and what with all the heavy hitters he knows we can make sure the only job you'll ever get in the City is lavatory attendant. Do you understand?'

He continued to rub his groin. She slammed his head against the wall. 'Do you?'

'Yes.' It came out as a whimper.

'Good. Now keep out of my face and concentrate on making sure Mel enjoys the rest of her evening because if she doesn't I'll have you for that too.'

Another nod. She stared into his eyes and saw fear. And it felt good. Just as it had with Stuart all those years ago.

Leaving him in the alcove she returned to the dance floor. Alexander did a double take when he saw her. 'You look radiant.'

'Of course. I've just remembered who I am.'

'What do you mean?'

'Nothing. Just the buzz of being here.'

They began to dance. In the distance she saw Rick rejoin Melanie, his usual swagger no longer in evidence. The realization made her feel even better. She went into a spin. People began to applaud. She brushed hair back from her face and gave a mock curtsey. Alexander applauded too. 'Darcey Bussell eat your heart out.'

'No chance of that. Ballerinas never eat anything.'

He laughed. Then leant forward to kiss her. She responded eagerly. Wanting to be excited; wanting to be thrilled.

But she wasn't. It was pleasant and that was all.

They continued to dance, surrounded by dozens of others, all lost in the thudding whirlwind of sound.

Saturday evening. Gail Butler sat with her husband Graham and Alexander Gallen on the balcony of their Bermondsey house overlooking the Thames, watching the sun set behind the gothic edifice of Tower Bridge.

'So, how was last night?' she asked Alexander.

'Great.'

'What was great about it?' asked Graham. 'The music or the company?'

'Both.'

'Told you he was smitten,' Graham observed with a smile.

Smiling too, Alexander shook his head.

'Yes you are. It's written all over your face just like it was when you got a crush on our matron at prep school.'

'I did *not* have a crush on her.'

'Yes you did and who can blame you? Nudging fifty and with a figure like a Russian shotputter. No wonder you kept grazing your knees, you just wanted to feel her delicate touch as she doused you with iodine.'

Gail punched Graham on the arm. 'Leave him alone.'

'I'm just teasing. When are we going to meet her, Alec?'

'Never if you insist on revealing all my secrets.'

'Hey, what are friends for? Besides, I still haven't lived down your Best Man revelations about me writing love letters to Sharon Stone. This is payback time.'

A pleasureboat slid past them, sending waves to break against the wall below. 'Why don't you go and make some coffee,' Gail suggested to Graham.

He groaned.

'Go on. I made supper. Now it's your turn to break a leg.'

He headed off to the kitchen. 'It was a great meal,' Alexander told her.

'I was sure I'd overdone the meat. The new oven cooks everything twice as fast as the old one did.'

'No, it was fantastic. You're a brilliant cook.' He patted his stomach. 'As my expanding waistline shows.'

'You're a racing snake compared to Graham. He's put on a stone since we got married.'

'Well you know what they say: the way to a man's heart is through his stomach.'

'Then I'm about to lose Graham's. As of tomorrow I'm putting him on a diet.'

He laughed. She offered him more wine but he declined. She thought of her impending hangover and envied his self control.

'Are you really going to put him on a diet?'

'I don't know. Dare I risk it?'

'Yes. You could feed him salad for the rest of his life and he wouldn't mind. Anyone can see how happy he is. You're the best thing that's ever happened to him.'

She felt a warmth inside her stomach. 'Do you really think so?'

'Definitely.'

'But what about you?'

'What about me?'

'Are you happy?'

'Of course. What do I have to be unhappy about?'

'Your grandmother.'

'That was a year ago.'

'Which isn't long to get over a loss.'

'It's long enough for me.'

She didn't believe him but was reluctant to push the point. 'Tell me about Chrissie. What is it you like about her?'

'Her shotputter physique and dab hand with the iodine.'

'Apart from that.'

'She's very striking. You really notice her when she enters a room.'

'You could say the same about Evelyne.'

He shook his head. 'She's very different to Evelyne.'

'In what way?'

'She has this strength about her. She knows exactly who she is and if people don't like that person then it's their problem, not hers.'

'I envy her that.'

'Why? You have the same quality yourself. I see it at my parties. You draw people to you without even trying. You know who you are and you don't apologize for it. Not that you need to. From where I'm standing that person is someone pretty special.'

Again she felt warmed, just as she often did around him. That was his skill. Making people feel good; telling them what they needed to hear. A skill that often seemed more like a defence mechanism. A means of preventing people from probing into areas he preferred to keep secret.

But her curiosity remained.

'You are smitten, aren't you?'

He nodded.

'Even though you haven't known her very long.'

He didn't answer, instead turning to stare at the water. A narrowboat made its way towards Tower Bridge. He followed it with his eyes while she watched him, wondering, as she so often did, what was going on inside his head. A feeling she knew Graham shared. 'That's the thing with Alec,' he had said to her on more than one occasion. 'I'm probably closer to him than anyone is but often I feel that I don't know him at all.'

'Alec?'

Still he didn't answer.

'Be careful. It *has* only been a year. You're still vulnerable like I was after my dad died.'

'But you were much younger than me when that happened.'

'I was twenty-two. You were twenty-five. We were both young to lose people.'

'You got over it.'

'But it took a long time. For at least two years I wasn't operating on full capacity in any area of my life. It took me that long to put myself together again and I had my mother and brothers to help me. It's harder for you. Your grandmother was your only family or at least the only family that mattered.'

'You don't need to worry about me.'

'But I do. You've been a brilliant friend to us and I care about you. I'm sure Chrissie's great but don't rush into anything. Not when you're still recovering from a loss.'

For a moment his eyes were thoughtful. Then he smiled. 'You're wrong. I still have family that matters. Graham's like a brother to me and now you're like a sister. How could I feel vulnerable when I've got two people as special as you in my life?'

She heard footsteps. Graham returned with the coffee. Alexander joked that they would need a knife and fork to serve it. Graham laughed. She did too, yet again feeling the warmth inside herself. As always he knew exactly what to say to make her feel special.

And to stop her probing at feelings he preferred to keep hidden.

Thursday. Six days later. Back from Norfolk, Chrissie checked her e-mails.

She was feeling optimistic. The trip had been a good one. As well as enjoyable bitching sessions about Francis Chester with his much put upon assistant director she had negotiated a discount with the caterers and interested the visiting American investors in the twins project. Alexander had also expressed an interest in investing. The two of them were meeting that weekend to discuss it further.

As she scanned through her inbox her phone rang. She saw Jack's name on the display and felt a lurch in her stomach. She tried to ignore it but the need to hear what he had to say proved too strong.

'Hi, Jack.'

'Hi! I thought you'd dropped off the face of the earth.'

'I've been in Norfolk for the last few days.' Her tone was warm but distant, mimicking the one he had used in his message.

'Well no chance of you dropping off anywhere then. Very flat, Norfolk, as the great Oscar Wilde once said.'

'Actually it was Noel Coward.'

'Really? I thought he was one of the Beach Boys.'

'Philistine.'

'Smart arse.'

Her lips began to twitch.

'I was worried about you. It's not like you to keep silent for so long.'

'I'm fine. Just busy.'

'Then I won't disturb you. Take care . . .'

'Do you want to meet?' The words were out before she could stop them.

Silence. She realized she was holding her breath.

'That would be nice,' he said.

Nice?

'When's good for you?' he asked.

Now. Any time, day or night. Just tell me and I'll be there.

'Tomorrow evening?' he suggested.

'Why not. I don't have anything better to do.'

*

Friday evening. Warm and clear. She headed towards the boat, bracing herself to tell him that whatever existed between them was over. It would have been easier to do it over the phone but that was the coward's way and she had never been one of those. She hoped he would be upset yet told herself that it didn't matter. The important thing was to end it. Take control. Eradicate a needless distraction and let her life return to normal.

He was tying ropes in the bow, the muscles in his arms flexing with the effort. The T-shirt she had bought him was stained with oil, just as all his clothes seemed to be. It was like his very own fashion label. What made him him.

Bullseye leapt onto the bank and ran barking towards her. Jack looked up, smiled, and all her good intentions flew out of the window.

'Just got to finish this,' he called out. 'Then I thought we could take the mutt for a walk and grab a bite somewhere. Is that all right?'

'Sure,' she said. 'Whatever you want.'

Three hours later. They sat together in a Lebanese cafe on the Edgware Road. The same one they had visited on their second meeting when he had laughed as she teased him about his fondness for illegal substances. She was teasing him this time too but there was no laughter and the mood was very different.

They were in an alcove full of cushions and reclining sofas, surrounded by Arab men sharing houka pipes while Middle Eastern music played in the background. They were sharing one too. The effect was supposed to be mellowing but not on her. The hit of tobacco combined with the alcohol she had drunk and the emotions that churned within her created a far more dangerous effect.

'If all goes to plan,' she told him, 'my film could be made this time next year.'

'That would be an achievement.'

'And what will you have achieved in that time, I wonder? Apart from your annual quota of drug busts.'

'Give it a rest.'

'Don't be so sensitive.'

'I'm not.'

'Poor little Jacky. Have I hurt your feelings?'

'Don't call me that. It makes me sound like a kid.'

'You are a kid but I don't mind; I find it endearing. For now, anyway.'

He was holding the pipe. She took it from him and inhaled, filling her lungs with smoke scented with roses while watching men take sly glances at her. She was the only woman in the room but even if she hadn't been she could still have attracted their attention. It was so easy. Men were idiots. Full of sound and fury signifying nothing. None of them would ever be able to hurt her. She was far too clever for that. Or so she had once believed.

Jack looked tense. She knew she should stop taunting him but was unable to do so.

'What are you thinking about?' she asked.

'Things I've got to do.'

'Isn't that my line?'

'What are you suggesting? That I don't do anything.'

'What's the matter with you? You're not being very good company. Maybe I should talk to someone else.'

He reclaimed the pipe. 'Maybe you should.'

The need to torment him increased. 'Who do you suggest?'

'That's up to you.'

'What about him?' She gestured to a well-dressed man of about forty whose wrists and fingers were decorated with expensive looking jewellery. 'He looks successful.'

'Since when has money turned you on?'

'What's wrong with being successful?'

'Nothing.'

'Then why sound threatened?'

'I don't.'

She took the pipe back. 'Is that a fact?'

'And you accuse me of trying to play the psychiatrist.'

'Scared I'll get too close to the truth?' Breathing out smoke she caught the man's eye. He smiled at her. She smiled back. Slowly. Deliberately.

'Don't lead him on.'

'Who says I am?'

A snort.

'Are you jealous?'

273

'Do you want me to be?'

'Don't flatter yourself.'

'Maybe I should leave you to it.'

'That's right. Run away. Why break the habit of a lifetime?'

'What do you know about my life?'

'That it's one big act of escape.'

'And yours isn't?'

'I'm making something of mine. You'll never make anything of yours. How can you when you're too frightened of failure to even try.'

'And that's the difference between us. I'm frightened of failure. You're frightened of everything.'

'Bullshit. Nothing scares me.'

'Then why is your whole personality an act?'

She turned towards him. 'What do you mean?'

'What I say. All the confidence and poise is just armour to stop people seeing the real person beneath it, and the sad thing is, that person is someone I could care about if you weren't so terrified of letting me see her.'

They stared at each other. Unexpectedly a look of pity came into his eyes. It left her feeling exposed and defenceless. As pathetic as the person he wanted her to believe she was. And she couldn't bear that.

'I'll tell you what's sad. That your dad went to his grave ashamed to call you his son.'

The pity vanished. 'That's crap.'

'Face facts, Jack. He left your brother the responsibility of administering his estate and what did he

274

leave you? Half a dozen pop singles. The sort of thing you'd leave a child.'

'You don't know what you're talking about.'

'So why did he pick your brother and not you? Because he knew which one was man enough to get on with it rather than sit around in a drug-induced haze wallowing in self pity. He thought you were a loser and the really sad thing is that now he's dead you'll never be able to prove him wrong.'

Flinging down the pipe he rose to his feet.

'That's right, Jacky. Run away like the coward you are. You say I can't face the truth about myself but when it comes to self delusion I'm not even in your league.'

He marched out of the cafe. She remained where she was, her heart pounding. The man with the jewellery gave her another smile. She tried to smile back but felt suddenly sick. So she followed Jack out.

He was marching towards the boat. She called his name. He ignored her. Calling out again she ran towards him. He turned, his eyes blazing. 'Fuck off!'

'Don't walk away from me!'

'Leave me alone. Go back to your new friend and find some tender spot to stick the knife into.'

'I don't care about him. This is about us.'

'There is no us. Not now. Go back. Flirt with him. Sleep with him. Do whatever you want. You have my full permission.'

'I don't need your permission. Who the hell do you think you are? My father?'

For a moment the anger remained. As hot and cruel as her own. Then it faded and the pity was back.

'No,' he said softly. '*I* don't think that.'

'What's that supposed to mean?'

'Don't you know?'

'What?'

'Just how frightened you are.'

'And you're a pathetic loser. No wonder Ali decided to look for someone better. Any girl you'll ever meet will deserve better than you!'

A taxi was approaching. She flagged it down. He caught hold of her arm. Pulling herself free she jumped in, slamming the door behind her.

Four o'clock on Saturday morning. She sat in her flat, chain smoking. The ashtray was overflowing. Her mouth felt as raw as if it had been scrubbed with sandpaper.

A tear rolled down her cheek. Angrily she wiped it away. She was not going to cry over him. The only emotion he deserved was contempt. She tried to summon the feeling but when it came the only person it attached itself to was herself.

Outside she could hear raised voices. People shouting drunkenly at each other in the car park below. The sound frightened her. Suddenly everything seemed to frighten her just as it had once frightened a girl who had waited in vain for her father to return.

She knew she was in danger. That she had to act. Do

something to protect the personality she had created for herself before it crumbled and was lost to her for ever.

So she decided to go back to the place where the act of creation had taken place.

Home.

Lunchtime. She sat in her mother's kitchen, eating the meal her mother had prepared.

'I'm sorry it's not much,' her mother said. 'There wasn't time to get stuff in.'

'It's fine. I should have given you more notice.' She gestured to the new decorations. 'They look smart.'

'Karen helped me choose.'

'Well, she's good at that sort of thing.' She sipped her tea and realized her words sounded like a dig. 'As are you.'

'Thanks.'

She picked at her food. A bacon and mushroom omelette. One of her favourite childhood dishes. Her mother always cooked them when she came home. Her appetite was non-existent but she ate anyway, trying to act as if everything was fine. Not wanting to have to deal with questions.

Her mother was watching her anxiously. She gazed back, remembering the pretty young woman whose approval had once seemed the most important thing in the world. Though still pretty there was now something transparent about her. Hollow. As if all the life had been drained away leaving an empty shell instead of a real person. Someone she could smash into pieces with a single blow of her hand.

She put down her fork. Her mother's look of anxiety increased. 'Is it not good?'

'It's lovely. I had a stomach bug last week and it's affected my appetite.'

'Have you been to the doctor?'

'No. Have you? Aunty Karen said you've been getting headaches.'

'They're not that bad.'

'You should still go. It's best to get these things checked out.'

Her mother began to talk about the builders, changing the subject perhaps because she considered it unimportant.

Or perhaps because she was scared.

'How's your room?' her mother asked.

'Fine.'

'People tell me to redecorate but I say it wouldn't be right. It's your room, not mine.'

'It's your house.'

'But it's your home. It always will be no matter how long you stay away.'

She lit a cigarette, fighting against the need to defend herself. 'My life is busy. You know how it is.'

'No, not really.'

Biting her tongue she breathed smoke into the air.

'I'm not getting at you. I'm just saying . . .'

'What?' Her tone was sharp.

'That I miss you.'

'Why? It's not like we've ever been friends.'

'But you're still my daughter. And because . . .'

Silence. Through the kitchen door she could see the mantelpiece where her mother's ornaments had stood until the rage had driven her to destroy them all.

Don't tell me you love me. Tell me anything but don't tell me that.

'And because your uncle's gone. I miss him too. I know I don't have the right. Not like Karen does. But it still hurts that he's not here.'

They stared at each other across the table. Again she was struck by how fragile her mother looked. An unexpected emotion rose up in her. Protectiveness.

'I do too. He was a good uncle just as he was a good brother. Don't beat yourself up about missing him, Mum. You have every right.'

Her mother smiled. The first one she had seen since arriving. 'Thanks.'

She continued to smoke.

'Do you miss your father?'

'No.'

'I do. Even after all these years.'

'You shouldn't. All he gave you was heartache.'

'Not just heartache.'

'What else?'

'You.'

She knew her mother was reaching out to her. The

feeling of protectiveness remained. As strange as snow on a warm summer's day.

'I'm proud of you, Chrissie. What you've done with your life. The person you've become. And what's more I know that if your father were here he'd tell you the same.'

The talk of her father made her uncomfortable. She tried to joke the discomfort away. 'Assuming he were sober enough to speak.'

'He wouldn't need to be sober to feel proud.'

'But he would need to be alive.'

'He *is* alive. I'd feel it if he were dead. As would you. Even more strongly I expect. You're a part of him after all.'

A lump came into her throat. Her mother continued to stare at her. Feeling exposed she looked away, back towards the mantelpiece.

And with the view came a memory of the day she had broken the first ornament.

'Look at yourself, Tina. Just look at yourself! Stupid, ugly and useless. That's all you are and all you'll ever be. No wonder your father left you. No wonder he couldn't wait to get away and leave you behind!'

The protectiveness vanished, devoured by a sudden blast of hate. 'Isn't it a bit late for this daughter of the year speech? I may have wanted to hear it once but I don't now. Least of all from you.'

Her mother went to wash the dishes, seeking refuge in action. Chrissie remained where she was, watching a weak, helpless woman who had hung all her hopes on a man only to see him grind them into the ground. A pathetic fool who tried to mask her fear of dying without having the brains to see that the life she clung to wasn't worthy of the name. It was just an existence. That was all she had. All anyone had who looked to others to make their dreams come true.

But that will never happen to me. I'm stronger than that. I'll never end up like her.

Oh God, whatever happens don't let me end up like her.

Two hours later. She escaped the chill of her mother's house for the warmth of Aunty Karen's.

Sue, two months pregnant, complained about morning sickness. 'The most inaccurate expression known to man. For the last few weeks I've been throwing up on an hourly basis.'

'Isn't that a sign of carrying the Antichrist?'

'Probably. Barry's mother's always telling me what a devil he was as a baby. Looks like she meant it literally.'

Aunty Karen appeared with cakes and biscuits. 'I'm not very hungry,' Chrissie said quickly.

'Nonsense. You've lost weight. You need feeding up.'

'Too much partying,' added Sue. 'So what's the eligible Mr Gallen really like?'

'Nice.'

'He can't be that nice if he likes you.'

'Oh, ha ha. Isn't it time for you to throw up again?'

'Not for ten minutes yet. Come on. Tell us more.'

'He's a good dancer. We went to that club in King's Cross.'

'He must be keen if he's willing to go to that dump.'

She laughed. Aunty Karen handed round slices of cake. Sue took a bite then grimaced. 'I don't think this is a good idea, Mum.'

'Try and eat some, even so. You must keep your strength up.' Aunty Karen shook her head. 'It's all that male hormone. I went through the same grief with your brother.'

'Mum's sure it's going to be a boy.'

'Is that what you'd like?'

'I don't care as long as it's healthy. That's what Barry says too.'

Barry was Sue's partner: a mechanic who worked at a garage on the outskirts of town. A dull but decent man who would make a reliable husband and father, just as Uncle Neil had.

'Are you two planning to tie the knot before the happy event?' she asked.

'Maybe, but if we do it'll be at a registry office. I told Rachel that last time she and Adam were down and guess what she had the nerve to say? That it's not a proper wedding unless it's in a church with about four million of your nearest and dearest in attendance. How you owe it to everyone to let them share your big day.'

'I dread to think how much her parents are going to

owe when it's done,' added Aunty Karen. 'They're not exactly rolling in it.'

'I told her that Barry and I are meant to be together and we don't need some huge ceremony to prove it.'

Feelings of protectiveness rose up in her just as they had with her mother. This time she didn't try to push them away. 'How *do* you know that? I mean for sure.'

'It was when I told him I was pregnant. He started crying and said it was the best thing that had ever happened to him and that he wanted to spend the rest of his life with me and our baby.' Sue smiled wistfully. 'That's when I knew it was what I wanted too.'

An image came into her head of Jack saying the same thing to her. Of him crying as he said it. Of her crying too. But that would never happen. Not after what she had said: that was the closest she would ever come to seeing him cry.

She pushed the cake around her plate. 'It must be wonderful to feel like that.'

On looking up she saw Aunty Karen staring at her. Quickly she looked away.

An hour passed. After an enjoyable bitching session about Rachel, Sue went home to Barry.

'So what's really going on?' asked Aunty Karen when they were alone.

'Nothing.'

'It's Jack, isn't it? That's what you're upset about.'

'I'm not upset.'

'And I'm not a fool. I know that's why you're here.'

She shook her head.

'Have it your own way. Can you help me with those plates?'

'He's not that special.'

'Neither was your uncle. Except to me. That's the point, Chrissie. It's not who they are, it's how they make you feel. How does he make you feel?'

'Confused.'

'And how do you make him feel?'

She thought back to the previous evening. 'Angry. I said things I shouldn't.'

'We can all say cruel things when our feelings are at stake or are you going to tell me that yours aren't?'

She didn't answer.

'I wish I could meet him.'

She summoned his photograph on her mobile. Aunty Karen studied it, saying nothing.

'Well?'

'He looks kind. Decent.' A pause. 'And that's not all.'

'What do you mean?'

'Don't you know?'

'That he looks like Dad? Yes, I know. How stupid is that?'

'It's not stupid. People say that when we look for a partner what we're really looking for is someone to right the wrongs of our parents. Perfect versions of them if you like.'

'No one's perfect, though, are they?'

'But it doesn't stop us looking.'

'I wasn't looking.'

'But you found him anyway. I can see why you'd be drawn to him. It's not just the similarities to your father, it's the differences. I see them in his face too. It's softer, gentler. He looks more . . .'

'What?'

'Controllable?'

The word hung in the air like a cloud. She stared down at her hands and saw they were shaking.

'Have you told him you love him?'

'No.'

'Why not?'

'Because I'm scared.'

'Oh Tina . . .'

'I'm not Tina. Tina's gone.'

'That's right. You're not that frightened little girl anymore. You're a beautiful young woman who can do anything she wants including dealing with this situation no matter how frightening it seems.'

'I hate myself for being like this. Do you know who I see when I look in the mirror? Mum. Everything I've always hated. That frightens me worst of all.'

'But you're not your mother. You're stronger than her. Strong enough to cope if you tell him you love him and he doesn't feel the same. That's what she could never accept with your father, but Jack's not your father and you can.'

'You think he doesn't love me?'

'How can I know? But one thing I'm sure of is that you need to tell him. You owe it to yourself. I hope with all my heart that he feels the same, but if he doesn't I also know you're strong enough not to let it destroy you the way it did your mother.'

'I don't feel strong. I feel weak.'

'It takes strength to admit weakness. Rejection is the hardest thing in the world to deal with but you're strong enough to risk it. I know it and in your heart you know it too.'

She swallowed. Her throat was dry. Aunty Karen reached out and squeezed her hand. She squeezed back.

'Thanks for trusting me, Chrissie. I won't tell anyone.'

'Do you promise?'

'Cross my heart and hope to die.'

'Don't say that. You're my real mother. I could cope with losing anyone but you.'

'Even Jack?'

'Even him. I know who I am. Whatever happens he's not going to destroy me. You can be sure of that.'

Sunday morning. She walked by the water, revisiting childhood haunts. The old playground was still there, looking as shabby as ever. Teenagers sat on swings, smoking cigarettes with a mixture of sheepishness and defiance while listening to music blaring from a stereo. She watched them, marvelling at how defenceless they looked and wondering if the people who had stopped to watch her and her friends had thought the same.

She ended up on the bench at the end of the harbour wall staring out across the mud flats at the marooned boats that scattered its surface. She searched for Uncle Neil's old dinghy but couldn't see it. Sue and Barry owned it now. They had offered to take her sailing but she had had enough of boats. Though the morning was warm a wind was blowing, bringing with it the returning tide and the smell of salt and oil.

She wondered what Jack was doing. Was he still upset about their argument? Was he missing her as badly as she missed him? She shut her eyes, trying to picture him but when she did so it was her father's face she saw.

Time passed. Her supply of cigarettes exhausted she walked into town to buy some more. The high street was unchanged. The same shops. The same people, a few of whom recognized her and smiled. A museum of her life, only it had never been her life, it had been someone else's. A person she had banished and who could never be allowed to return.

She entered the supermarket, passing the CD and computer games section. Teenagers studied the new releases, just as she and her friends had once done, while a woman stood with a girl of about seven who kept pointing to one of the games. As she stared at the woman she recognized her childhood nemesis: Philippa Hanson.

It had been years since she had seen her. Philippa had left school at sixteen and was now living on the fringes of town, bringing up a child after the father had walked out. There was little trace of the lovely blonde girl who had boasted of taking the modelling world by storm. Philippa looked tired, and older than twenty-five. She remembered Philippa's taunts over her own father's absence and felt a quiet satisfaction at how things had worked out.

The child was small and dark with none of her mother's prettiness. She kept pointing to the game and Philippa kept shaking her head saying it was too expensive. A couple of boys pushed past them, banging into the child who began to cry. Philippa crouched down to offer comfort, her wan features suddenly made beautiful by the light of unconditional love.

The sense of satisfaction vanished. Quickly she moved away.

Ten minutes later. Philippa Hanson stood at the bus stop, holding her daughter Cindy's hand, worrying, as she always seemed to be, about how to make ends meet. Though she worked six days a week there was never enough money to cover all the bills. If it hadn't been for the occasional handout from her parents she wouldn't have been able to manage at all.

A bus approached. She strained her eyes, trying to read its number before realizing that it wasn't hers. She gave Cindy's hand a squeeze. 'Never mind. Not much longer now.'

A woman walked towards her. Tall, beautiful and stylishly dressed. The sort that made her feel drab and threadbare. 'Hello, Philippa,' said the woman. 'Remember me?'

For a moment she didn't. Then recognition came. 'Hello,' she said, feeling suddenly exposed.

Cindy tugged at her hand. 'Who's she, mum?'

'My name's Chrissie. Your mum and I were at school together. What's your name?'

'Cindy.'

Chrissie held out a plastic bag. 'I've got a present for you.'

'What is it?'

'Look and see.'

Cindy opened the bag, pulled out the computer game she had wanted and let out a whoop of delight.

'You don't mind, do you?' Chrissie asked.

Philippa did, but didn't have the heart to spoil Cindy's pleasure. Shaking her head she turned to her daughter. 'What do you say?'

'Thank you.'

'My pleasure.'

Two little girls called to Cindy who went to say hello.

'It must be nice,' she said when they were alone. 'Being able to throw your money around like that.'

'You think I did it to make you feel bad?'

'Didn't you?'

'Get over yourself. This isn't about you, it's about her.'

'Why should you care about her?'

'Because I know what it's like when your dad does a disappearing act and I wouldn't wish that on any child.'

'Even mine?'

'Even yours.'

Another bus approached. Still not hers. 'You're doing well from what I hear,' she said. 'Quite the jet-setter by all accounts.'

'My aunt has a tendency to exaggerate.'

'Not your aunt. I heard it from your mother.'

'My mother?'

'Yes. She's really proud of you and who can blame her? Havelock Comp is hardly known for its success stories. You're the exception whereas I'm the rule.'

They stared at each other. Philippa remembered the frightened girl whom she had once victimized and wondered how the strong, confident woman before her could have ever been that person. 'How did you do it?' she asked.

'Do what?'

'Change. Become who you are.'

'Because I had to. Change or die. No choice at all when you think about it.'

'I envy you.'

'Do you think my life is perfect?'

'It's more perfect than mine.'

'So you'd swap, would you? Trade everything you have to be me?'

She looked at Cindy showing off her new game. 'No. Not everything.'

'Didn't think so.'

They continued to stare at each other. Suddenly Chrissie smiled. 'She looks like a great kid. You must be proud of her.'

'I am.'

'Do you ever hear from her father?'

'Not any more. Last thing I heard he was in Manchester but that was over a year ago.'

'Do you miss him?'

'Sometimes.'

'Don't. It's just pain you don't need. And, more importantly, don't let her miss him either. She doesn't need him. Anyone can see how much you love her and that's all any kid needs. To know that they're loved.'

Philippa felt a warmth in the pit of her stomach.

'Cindy. It's a nice name. Was that . . .'

'Yes, after Cindy Crawford. The star I was going to outshine.'

'Perhaps Cindy will do it instead.'

She shook her head. 'Not much chance of that.'

'Why not? Look at me. The success story whom no one believed could do anything. I had to do it on my own but she doesn't.' A pause. 'Promise me something.'

'What?'

'That you'll tell her that. That she can be special;

that if others put her down then they're just fools; that she can be whoever she wants to be if she just believes it enough.'

She nodded. 'I promise.'

'Take care of her. And of yourself too.'

'I will.'

'Goodbye, Philippa.'

'Goodbye, Chrissie.'

Chrissie walked away. Philippa watched her go, the feeling of warmth still there.

Cindy trotted back towards her. 'Why did that lady give me this game?'

'Because you're special.'

'Why?'

'Because you're mine. You're the most special person in the world to me and you always will be.' She reached out and tweaked Cindy's nose. 'Always.'

At last their bus arrived. Hand in hand they climbed aboard.

Four o'clock that afternoon. Chrissie stood by the window in her mother's living room, staring out at the waiting taxi.

Her mother appeared behind her. 'I could have driven you to the station. You didn't need to get a cab.'

'I didn't want to put you out.'

'You wouldn't have been.'

'Well it's done now.' As she braced herself for the farewell she was again struck by how fragile her mother looked. The realization upset her. She tried to push the feeling away but it clung to her like a leech.

'Do something for me, Mum. See the doctor. If you don't want to go on your own then take Aunty Karen and when you've seen him call and let me know what he says.'

Her mother didn't answer.

'Please. For me.'

'All right. For you.'

She leant forward and kissed her mother's cheek. The gesture felt stilted, like an unfamiliar scene at drama school, but when she stood back she saw her mother smile and was glad she had done it.

Seven o'clock that evening. She walked along the canal path just as she had two evenings previously, only this time she was preparing to expose herself to another human being in a way she had never done before. Laying herself open to rejection, pain and heartache and all the things she had spent her life fighting against.

But she could do it. He could hurt her but he could not destroy her. She was too strong for that, just as Aunty Karen had said.

Her phone was in her hand. He had not responded to her calls. Perhaps he was busy. Perhaps he was avoiding her. Part of her wanted to wait but if it was going to be done then it had to be done quickly. Confronted. Faced. Dealt with.

In the distance she could see the boat. He emerged

from the cabin door looking as scruffy as ever. Her heart turned over and her strength drained away. For a moment she wanted to turn and run. But he was smiling; his trademark grin spread across his face. When she saw it she knew it was going to be all right. That there was no need to be afraid.

Then a girl followed him out. Tall and slim with a pleasantly pretty face and pale red hair.

Ali.

She felt as if she was going to be sick.

Jack said something. Ali began to laugh; her face shining with happiness. The two of them kissed. The feeling of nausea increased. Crouching down behind a bush she continued to watch.

Bullseye bounced out after Ali, straining on his lead. The three of them made their way along the path in the opposite direction. Jack put her arm around Ali who pressed against him; the two of them locking together like parts of a whole. A perfect fit. A perfect couple to whom her appearance would be as welcome as a disease.

She remained where she was while pain turned her insides to fire.

Five minutes later she entered the cabin.

He had left the door unlocked. He was always lax about security. She had told him to be more careful or risk losing something that really mattered to him. As he was about to find out.

She reached under the sofa for the Kinks singles. The ones his father had left him. The possessions he valued above all others. Snatching up the first one, ready to tear it's cover to pieces, she saw that it was 'Waterloo Sunset': the song her father had sung to her on Uncle Neil's dinghy all those years ago. The soundtrack to her most precious memories that her father had then destroyed, just as she was about to destroy Jack's.

And at that moment she knew she couldn't do it. That it wasn't right. That whatever he deserved he didn't deserve that.

But the pain wouldn't go away. It stripped through her defences like acid, leaving her feeling as wretched as the day when she had sobbed on the bathroom floor after her mother had told her that she wished she had never been born.

Her phone began to ring. She snatched it up, needing the comfort of another voice. Who it belonged to didn't matter as long as it was friendly.

'Hi, Chrissie,' said Alexander.

Two hours later. Alexander walked into his living room with two mugs of coffee.

Chrissie sat on the sofa in front of a coffee table covered in empty mugs. 'I'm surprised you still have some clean ones,' she told him.

'There's loads left.' Through the window he could see it was growing dark. After switching on the lights he sat beside her.

'I'm sorry about this, Alec.'

'Don't be. I'm glad you felt you could tell me.'

She smiled but it was a poor effort.

'Cry if you want. I don't mind.'

'I wouldn't give him the satisfaction.'

'But he's not here to see.'

'I still won't.' She sipped her coffee. He fought an urge to put an arm around her. For the first time since they had met he felt needed. It was a good feeling.

'I suppose I shouldn't blame him,' she said. 'He was upset after all.'

'That's no excuse.'

'It's my fault, really. I shouldn't have gone to see him but I thought it was fairer to tell him to his face. I've always believed that. That if you're telling someone you don't care about them then you should do it to their face.' A hollow laugh. 'More fool me.'

'Trying to do the right thing doesn't make you a fool.'

'And then he comes out with all that stuff. Saying it was my fault Dad left us. How he couldn't wait to get away and leave me behind. How could he say that?'

'Because he's a jerk. Only a jerk could think that, let alone say it. You were only a little child. How could it possibly be your fault?'

She didn't seem to be listening. 'Because it wasn't my fault. I've always known that. It had nothing to do with me. Nothing at all.'

'He still shouldn't have said it.'

'He just cares about me. I wish I felt the same way but I don't. I guess it's true what they say. You can't control who you fall in love with. Not that it matters any more.' She swallowed. 'One thing I'm sure of is that I'll never hear from him again.'

At last the tears came. She wiped at them with her hand, almost slapping at her face as if punishing herself. He watched her, wondering if she was telling him the truth. Whether in fact Jack had been the one to call time on whatever it was that had existed between them.

But it didn't matter. At that moment the only thing that mattered was that she was there with him.

He noticed her lips moving. 'What are you saying?' he asked gently.

'I'm not this person. I'm not her.'

'Her?'

'Me. That's what I meant. I'm not like this. I'm not this weak.'

'You're not being weak. You're just being you.'

'Who am I?'

'Someone special.'

'Special?'

'Yes.' He hesitated, then decided to speak. 'To me.'

'Why?'

'Because it's true what they say. You can't help who you fall in love with.'

She turned towards him. He searched her face for pleasure but saw only fear. The look confused him. She had nothing to fear, not from him.

'You shouldn't love me.'

'Why not?'

'Because you don't know me.'

'I know enough.'

'If people care about me I hurt them.'

'You didn't mean to hurt Jack.'

'This isn't about him. This is about you.' Again she touched his arm. 'I care about you, Alec, but you mustn't love me because I know myself and I *will* hurt you. I may not want to but I won't be able to stop myself.'

The tears returned. This time she let them fall. He put his arm around her waiting for a rebuttal that never came.

'You can't scare me off. You talk as if you're a bad person but you're not. I've seen you with your friends. How you try and protect them and give them some of your strength. That's what drew me to you in the first place. Your strength. That and what lies beneath it.'

'And what is that?'

'You.'

She moved closer to him. 'Do me a favour,' she whispered.

'Anything.'

'Just hold me.'

He did so while she clung to him, sobbing into his shoulder like a child, while outside the last of the light faded from the sky.

*

Early the next morning. Chrissie sat by the window in Alexander's living room staring out at antique shops, cafes and mansion blocks full of apartments that would leave a purchaser with little change from a couple of million. The area was like an exclusive club to which Essex girls need not apply. But it was hers for the taking. Alexander would see to that. Her entry ticket to a brave new, rich new world.

From the corridor she heard movement. He must have woken and realized she was gone from the bed they had shared. That was all they had done. Just lain together. She felt bad at having lied to him about Jack but pride had made her do it. She wore it like a cloak in the hope it would protect her from the pain.

But it was still there. As raw as a wound that nothing could heal.

Except the rage.

She could feel it building inside her. The dragon shrugging off the last cobwebs of sleep and whispering its blandishments in breaths of fire.

I can make it better, Chrissie. I can make you feel strong again. I can do anything you want me to. All you have to do is ask.

Alexander appeared, wrapped in a dressing gown. 'Sorry I woke you,' she said.

'You didn't.'

'You look tired. Why not go back to bed.'

'I'm fine.' A pause. 'Would you rather be on your own?'

'No. Company would be good.'

He sat beside her, putting his arm around her shoulder. It felt nice. No more than that but it was a start. He loved her and the knowledge made her feel that she could put the hurt behind her and move on. That was what she had to do. She was not her mother; she would not be destroyed by love.

But the dragon kept whispering, its words like balm. As she listened she remembered something Aunty Karen had told her, when they were sitting on the bench at the end of the harbour path on the day it had driven her to attack her mother.

For your own sake, Tina, let the anger go. Don't keep hold of it. Don't let it grow because it'll only turn round and destroy you if you do.

But Tina was gone and the rage would not destroy her. She had controlled it in the past. She could control it now.

She offered Alexander a cigarette. Though he didn't smoke he took one anyway, clearly wanting to be as companionable as possible. She felt grateful for that.

'I'll have to go soon,' she told him. 'I've an early start.'

'Will I see you tonight?'

'No. I'm off to Norfolk. I'll be there most of the week.'

He nodded.

'Come up and see me if you want. I'd like that.'

His face lit up, giving off warmth like a tiny sun. She

stared at him and thought, I can make this work. I can put this behind me and move on.

They sat in silence, staring down at the street. A man walked along it leading a dog that looked like Bullseye. Again she felt the pain. And the rage.

He began to talk about his visit. She stroked her stomach, focusing on his words, trying to drown out the rumblings of the wild beast within.

Part 3

Domination

London: October 2004

Early evening at the police station, six days into the investigation. Nigel Bullen threw caution to the wind and lit a cigarette, willing to brave his wife's wrath just to satisfy his cravings. Besides, he needed one. He was looking at another late night.

'I don't understand what you're saying,' he said to psychiatrist Clive Lovell.

'Lucky you.'

'But love isn't complicated, it's an emotion we all experience. If it's really such a minefield then why aren't we all paying a fortune to pour out our feelings on your couch?'

'Because you're looking at it as an abstract feeling and it's not. Love isn't just an emotion; it's a surrender. The ultimate surrender of power. If you love someone you give them the power to hurt you more than anyone else can. You love your wife, you must know what I'm talking about.'

Nigel took another drag on his cigarette. 'I will when I get home. My eardrums are going to take a real pounding.'

'You're making light of it.'

'No, I just want to understand. None of this case makes sense to me. I can't get my head around it.'

'It's as I said, love is never an abstract emotion. There are all sorts of other feelings tied up around it. Need. Dependence. Guilt. Anger. Hate. For most of us that doesn't have to be a problem. We can express our feelings. Argue. Shout. Reveal what we're feeling inside without fearing rejection or abandonment for doing so. Secure in the knowledge that we'll still be loved and won't lose the most important person in our life through being honest. Take your wife: when you argue with her do you worry she'll leave you because of it?'

'Of course not. We row all the time, it's healthy, isn't it?'

'Exactly. It *is* healthy. I wish all relationships could be like that but they're not. For some people the fear of losing a loved one is so all consuming that it stops them ever being able to express their more negative feelings towards that person. But those feelings don't just go away. Instead they remain in the system like poison, growing stronger and stronger as time goes by.' A sigh. 'Until eventually . . .'

'What?'

'We end up with a case as awful as this . . .'

London: August 2004

Extract from 'Wicked Whispers': *Daily Mail*,
Tuesday 24th August
*'PSSSST! Which eligible bachelor boyfriend of
one of our top blue blood models was spotted
taking leave of a mystery redhead outside his flat
early yesterday morning?'*

Wednesday lunchtime. Karen shared a meal with her sister-in-law.

Liz put down her fork. 'I wish you hadn't told her.'

'She's your daughter. She has a right to know.'

'Why? It's not as if she'd care.'

'If she didn't care then why would she make you promise to see the doctor?'

'It's just seems like a lot of fuss.'

'Well it's not. Have you booked an appointment yet?'

307

Liz reached for her cigarettes.

'Have you?'

'No.'

'Then do it.'

'You will come with me, won't you?'

'Of course. Now phone the surgery.'

'All right.'

Karen heard a key in the lock. An excited looking Sue burst into the room. 'You've got to see this!'

'See what?'

Sue held out a celebrity gossip magazine. Momentarily Karen felt irritated at the interruption, knowing it would give Liz yet another excuse not to call her doctor.

Then she saw the article and all thought of doctors went out of her head.

Through Other Eyes: a Victorian Ghost Story, was in its fourth week of shooting.

Most of the scenes were being filmed in a mansion outside Norwich. Chrissie sat in the drawing room watching lighting men set up equipment while sharing a cigarette with Jeremy the assistant director and Wayne, the stand-in for leading man, Duncan Grant.

'What was this morning's row about?' she asked Jeremy.

'The usual. Francis wants it shot one way and Duncan another.'

She nodded. Duncan had been a little known actor when he had signed for the role, but in the intervening period another film he had appeared in had become a hit in the States and the sudden success had had a disastrous effect on his ego.

'It's a shame,' said Wayne. 'A friend of mine worked with him a year ago and said he was a nice bloke. It's scary what a whiff of fame can do.'

She blew smoke into the air. 'He needs to get over himself.'

'Do you want to tell him that?'

'I will if he gives Bob any more grief. He doesn't need it.'

'But Francis does,' interjected Jeremy. 'Seeing him wound up is my only pleasure.'

Elly, the continuity girl joined them looking harassed. 'Can I scrounge a smoke?'

'Sure.' She offered her packet. 'Who's rattled your cage?'

'The bloody house owners. I told them we'd have to move things around. At first they were fine about it, and so they should be when you think how much we're paying them to use this dump, but now they keep turning up to check everything. The woman's just gone ape because she can't find a vase. I said she didn't need to worry as no one was going to nick it and then she got upset and accused me of saying she had no taste.'

She laughed. The lighting men continued to run cables through the room. One of them said something to the other, speaking with a slight West Country accent that made her think of Jack. She wondered what he was doing then reminded herself that it didn't matter.

There was one other person in the room. Jane, a young actress playing a minor role sat by the window dressed in Victorian costume, skimming through a magazine while sending and receiving texts. One came in that made her smile. From her boyfriend, perhaps. Someone she loved and was loved by in return.

Chrissie pictured Ali in her coffee shop, texting Jack and receiving his replies; her face lighting up like Jane's. The image stuck in her brain like a parasite.

Jane continued to skim through the magazine. Suddenly her eyes widened. 'Chrissie, this is about you!'

'What are you talking about?'

Jane handed her the magazine. She saw a photograph of herself with Alexander; the two of them kissing outside his flat. A wave of shock swept over her. Momentarily she felt exposed. Naked.

'Is Alec calling time on Evelyne?' asked the title. 'It would appear so,' continued the narrative, 'now that he's often in the company of film director Christina Ryan . . .'

'Blimey,' exclaimed Wayne. 'You're a dark horse.'

'And since when have you been a director?' asked Jeremy.

She continued to read. Reference was made to the

evening at the dance club. The shock intensified. 'How do they know about that?'

'Well it's a big venue,' Elly told her, 'and he's quite recognizable. Evelyne looks sick.' There was a photograph of her looking wistful at some fashion show. No doubt it had been taken weeks ago, but it made the point.

'Marriage wrecker,' teased Wayne.

'Am I hell. They're not a couple.'

'But you are judging by that photo.'

'Don't you kiss your male friends?'

'Not if I don't want to get my head kicked in.'

'Yes,' said Elly, 'but when I do they don't look at me the way he's looking at you.'

'What way?'

'Love. It's written all over his face. You lucky cow. He's gorgeous.'

'And loaded,' added Wayne. 'His grandmother left him three hundred mill.'

She shook her head. 'It wasn't that much.'

'So how much was it?'

'I don't know. I've never asked to see his bank statements.'

'Well do,' Wayne told her. 'And for God's sake don't sign a pre-nup.'

More laughter. She tried to join in but felt indignant. 'Bloody cheek! Spying on us like that.'

'Well what do you expect? He's famous and so is Evelyne and so will you be if you shack up with him. Are you an item?'

'He'd like us to be.'

'And you *wouldn't*? Are you nuts? If he asked me out I'd bite his hand off.'

'A friend of mine met him,' said Jane. 'At a party in New York. She said he was really nice. Not weird at all.'

'Why would he be weird?'

'Well he's a Gallen, isn't he? The whole family's weird.'

'Not weird,' Jeremy corrected her. 'Eccentric. The way we'd all be if we could afford to indulge every whim.'

'Didn't one of his uncles kill himself?'

'I thought it was an accidental OD. That's what the papers said.'

'Maybe it was hushed up. Rich families are good at hiding scandals. What do you think, Chrissie? What does lover boy say about it?'

'I don't know. It's hardly the sort of question you ask on a first date.'

'The American media is fascinated by them. They're like the Hiltons over there. If they get wind of this you could end up in *People* magazine.'

'Oh, wow. My cup runneth over.'

'Don't knock it,' Wayne told her. 'Duncan hasn't managed that yet. Can I go and show him this? Let him know he's not the only superstar on the block.'

The lighting men came to see what the fuss was about. 'Blimey,' said the one with the West Country accent. 'We should be training these lights on you. You take a good photo.'

'Absolutely,' agreed Elly. 'You look great.'

It was true. In her embarrassment she had failed to notice. She imagined people she knew seeing it. Talking about her. Envying her.

Jack seeing it. Realizing what he had lost. Wanting her back. Much good it would do him.

The laughter continued. At last she felt able to join in.

That evening she sat with Bob and the others in the bar of a Norwich hotel. Yet again Alexander was the sole topic of conversation. An elderly actor called Roger Brookes told her that he had once met Alexander's grandmother. 'Years ago at some charity do.'

'What was she like?'

'Someone who knew her own mind. A formidable lady.'

'Sounds like someone else we know,' joked Wayne.

Roger began to tell a funny story about working with Charles Bronson. As she listened she noticed Bob staring at her quizzically.

'What?' she asked him.

'And where does this development leave Jack?'

'That's all over.'

'If you say so.'

'Ever tried minding your own business?'

'No. Life would be far too boring. Besides, I happen to care about you.'

'Then be pleased something exciting is happening in my life.'

'Of course I'm pleased. It must be lovely to have so rich a boyfriend.'

His words stung. 'You think I'm seeing Alec because of his money?'

'No, but I think you're seeing him because you hope he's going to make you feel better and that's still the wrong reason.'

'I don't need to feel better.'

'So what's Jack doing now?'

'Who cares?'

'You do. I've been asking around about Alec. Some people I know have met him; they say what a genuinely nice guy he is. And they also say that underneath the handsome exterior he seems vulnerable. Not surprising really when you consider his upbringing.'

'People make too big a deal about upbringing. Shit happens and you deal with it.'

'Or not.'

'Meaning?'

'Don't hurt him just because you've been hurt.'

'I don't get hurt. I told you that.'

'And I told you you're not as tough as you think you are. I know what love looks like and I saw it in your face when you talked about Jack. What's more I still do.'

Feeling exposed she downed the rest of her wine.

'Go easy,' he said.

'What are you? My boss or my mother?'

'Both in a manner of speaking. I think of you as a surrogate daughter. That's what comes of working for a middle-aged queer.'

'Oh, please. You don't look a day over forty-nine.'

'Ouch. I'm only forty-three.'

'And I'm sixteen.'

'Absolutely. God, the lighting is good in here.'

They both laughed. Briefly the mood eased.

'I want you to be happy, Chrissie, but getting involved with a guy you don't care about to forget one that you do isn't the right way.'

'It's a start.'

'But it's the finish that worries me.'

'I haven't promised Alec anything. He knows the score.'

'And if he doesn't?'

'He's old enough to take care of himself.'

Her mobile rang: Aunty Karen, no doubt wanting to discuss the article. She cut off the call, not feeling up to more questions. Her heart was racing. Part of her still hoped it would be Jack. But that would change in time.

'You're not this cold, Chrissie.'

'Who are you to say? One thing you're not is my father. I cut him out of my life and I can cut Jack out too. You just walk away and never look back.'

'Do you really think it's that easy?'

A man walked past them in the bar; tall, heavy set

and with a strong physical presence. But not as strong as her father's had been.

'Why not? It was for him.'

'But . . .'

'You don't need to worry. No one's going to get hurt. I know how to look after myself emotionally and if Alec's any sort of man the same will be true of him.'

Then, after refilling her glass, she joined in the general conversation.

The following afternoon she stood outside the mansion with Elly and the caterers.

An open top sports car made its way up the drive. 'Nice car,' said a caterer. 'Whose is it?'

'No idea,' she said, then recognized Alexander at the wheel. Momentarily she felt foolish. Then glad. A gold-digger would have known the exact make and value of his car.

He climbed out and hugged her. 'I've really missed you. Have you missed me?'

'Of course.' Gently she released herself. 'Come and meet everyone.'

She led him inside, Elly bouncing beside them like an excited fly. Her other friends were in the drawing room. They all gathered round Alexander like moths to the flame. 'I'm really pleased to meet you,' he told Bob. 'Chrissie's always saying what a great boss you are.'

'And Alec's gullible enough to believe it,' she added with a smile.

Bob introduced his partner, Malcolm, who was also visiting the set. 'You're a photographer, aren't you?' Alexander asked.

Malcolm nodded, clearly delighted that Alexander should know that.

'I'd love to see your work. Chrissie says it's wonderful.'

'Alec's grandmother was friendly with Cecil Beaton,' Chrissie explained.

Malcolm looked sheepish. 'Well I'm hardly in his league.'

'Except when it comes to bitchiness,' she said teasingly.

Bob asked Alexander about his journey. While answering he mentioned that he loved driving. Everyone nodded. She did too then realized that she should have known that. Another reminder of just how little she really did know him.

She introduced Jane. Alexander claimed to recognize her from a television play. Jane looked embarrassed. 'That was a terrible piece.'

'But you were still very good in it.'

Jane looked delighted, just as Malcolm had done. Chrissie was struck by the irony of the situation. All of them trying to please someone who was himself so eager to please.

'Are they filming?' she asked. 'Alec wants to see the master in action.'

'Only if it's no problem,' added Alexander quickly.

'It won't be.' She led him upstairs, the others following like an entourage. Francis was in the master bedroom rehearsing a scene between Duncan Grant and the actress playing his mother. He always made his actors act out their scenes half a dozen times before shooting. Bob was always complaining about the time it took, reminding him that they had a budget to stick to, but Francis insisted that this was how a true professional should always work.

They gathered in the doorway. The lighting men began to stare at Alexander. Francis, registering their distraction, glared at them and quickly they focused on the job in hand.

Duncan registered it too. On the next rehearsal there was less swagger in his acting; his self satisfaction deflated by the realization that he was not the only celebrity in the room.

They continued to rehearse. On the third run through Duncan regained his old swagger. Too much so for Francis's liking. 'You're supposed to be upset, not walking round like you've just won an Oscar. Tone it down.'

Duncan flushed. Chrissie heard Wayne snigger behind her and fought an urge to do so herself. Francis frowned at them. Quietly they all slipped away.

Two hours later. She sat in Alexander's car being driven back to London. The roof was still down and wind buffeted her face. She stared up at the vast Norfolk sky. 'I love it here. The space gives you room to think.'

'That's what my grandmother always said.'

'She liked Norfolk, did she?'

'We used to live here.'

'I thought you grew up in London.'

'No. My grandfather was from Norfolk originally. We lived here until I was fifteen.'

'Why did you leave?

'Most of my grandmother's friends were in London. Once my grandfather died she began to feel lonely.'

'So where did you live?'

'Amberton. A village near the north coast.'

'Can we go and see it?'

'Not today. There are roadworks and the advice is to give the area a wide berth.'

Half an hour later they sat in a Suffolk pub having a drink in an empty bar. She showed him the magazine article. He looked embarrassed though not surprised. 'I got a phone message from Evelyne this afternoon demanding that I call. Now I know why she sounded angry.'

'Well, to the uninformed reader it does look like you're giving her the elbow.'

He sighed.

'But you're not so what does it matter?'

'It makes her look bad.'

'No it doesn't. People break up all the time. Besides, it's media exposure which is what she lives for. If anything she should be grateful.'

'Do you want to be the one to tell her that?'

319

'Sure. Putting self important people in their place is my speciality.'

'So where's my place?'

'Under my thumb. Where else?'

He laughed. Not as heartily as Jack would have done but then he wasn't Jack. Not that it mattered.

'I meant us. Are we a couple?'

'Of course. Why else would everyone be so excited about meeting you? You're dating the eminent film director, Chrissie Ryan, and that's something to be proud of. After years of obscurity you've achieved the fame you've always craved.'

'I noticed the film director thing.'

'So did Jeremy. He told me I should wind Francis up by inviting him to my next master class.'

'I can see you as a director.'

'Think I'd look good bellowing orders through a megaphone?'

He nodded. She imagined Jack telling her that with her foghorn voice a megaphone would not be necessary.

'Why don't we stop off in Havelock on the way back?' he suggested.

'Why? It's a dump.'

'But it's where you're from.'

She shook her head.

'Why not? I'd love to meet your mother.'

'It's not much notice.'

'Surely she'd be pleased to see you.'

'You know my mother, do you?'

'No, but I'd like to. She's your closest relative, after all.'

She stared into her drink, imagining parading him in front of her relatives; her mother trying to impress while Aunty Karen waited for a chance to bombard her with questions she didn't want to answer.

'Not today. It really is too short notice. Tell you what. I'll call my cousin Adam and fix up dinner with him and his fiancée. How would you like that?'

'Very much.'

'Then I'll call.'

He went to the gents. She summoned Jack's picture on her mobile. He had never asked to meet her family. The only one of her boyfriends not to do so. The only one she had ever wanted to take home.

Had he met Ali's parents? What impression had he made? Had they despised him for his lack of direction or made allowances because he was the one for their daughter.

Pain swept over her. That and anger at her inability to control it. She tried to delete the image but as with all the other attempts, found that she couldn't.

Alexander reappeared. 'Did you speak to him?'

'No. His number was engaged. I'll try later.'

'You look worried.'

'Just wondering how Bob's coping without me. People push him around when I'm not there.'

'I could drive you back if you like.'

'It would take hours.'

'It doesn't matter. I don't want you to worry.'

She stared at him. His eyes were full of concern, the eyes of a man who only wanted to make her happy.

'What did I do?' she asked. 'To deserve someone as nice as you?'

'I could ask the same question.'

'I'm not that special.'

'You are to me.'

'Don't take me back, Bob will survive. Besides, I'd rather be with you.'

His face lit up. She felt guilty. He was so easy to deceive.

But one day it would be true. She wanted it to be true. She really did.

Together they left the pub.

Saturday evening. She sat in The Ivy with Alexander, Adam and Rachel.

It was the second time she had eaten there. Her previous visit had been with Bob and a German film producer. Bob had had to call in a lot of favours to secure a table but all Alexander had had to do was phone and say his name. He had also insisted on paying: a kind gesture that had backfired as Adam and Rachel had taken for ever to order, clearly trying to avoid the more expensive dishes for fear of looking like freeloaders.

'Are you sure you want fishcakes?' she asked Adam.

'Yes.'

'My friend told me they're a speciality of the house,' explained Rachel.

She nodded, having no idea if it was true. She had suggested the venue because Rachel loved star spotting. Not that much star spotting was actually taking place. Rachel was far too busy staring at Alexander.

'So when's the big day?' Alexander asked Adam.

'Next June,' Adam told him. She waited for Rachel's monologue on bridesmaids' dresses but it never came. Clearly Rachel was under strict instructions to keep the wedding talk to a minimum. One of the blessings of having a boyfriend Adam was eager to impress.

And impress was what he was trying to do, describing his job as if he were running the company rather than toiling a hundred rungs down the ladder. 'Let me top you up, Mr Trump,' she said as she refilled his glass.

Rachel took a bite of her fishcake. 'How is the seating plan?' Chrissie asked mischeviously. 'Is it finalized yet?'

'Yes.' Rachel swallowed her mouthful and prepared to take another, clearly wanting to give a longer answer but knowing she couldn't. Alexander, who had been briefed on Rachel's wedding obsession, caught Chrissie's eye and gave her a smile.

'Tell us about the catering arrangements,' she continued.

'It's rather boring.'

'Surely not.'

Adam kicked her under the table. Again Alexander caught her eye. This time there was a trace of disapproval behind the smile. Had Jack been sitting in his place the two of them would have been winding Rachel up mercilessly. But then, Adam would never have wasted time trying to impress Jack. Besides, Jack would never want to come somewhere as expensive as The Ivy. The closest he ever came to making an impression was offering to buy a round.

Loser. Stupid loser. I am so well rid of you.

Adam continued to exaggerate his achievements, describing a recent project as if it were of global significance. She scanned the nearby tables for famous faces. A designer, two actors and a politician. There had been a bigger turnout when she had come with Bob.

They finished their main course. A waiter cleared their plates. Another brought dessert menus. Alexander saw someone he knew on a nearby table and went to say hello.

'Cut the Master of the Universe act,' she told Adam when they were alone. 'You don't need to try and impress him.'

'I'm not.'

'Yeah, right.' She lit a cigarette. Yet another waiter appeared with an ashtray. 'Look, Ad, Alec doesn't care how successful you are. All he cares about is that you like him.'

'Do you think he likes us?' asked Rachel.

'Yes, so do me a favour and relax. If you want an

expensive dessert then have one and if you want to talk about the wedding or star spot then do it. Alec isn't going to mind.'

'He's not how I thought he'd be.'

'How did you think he'd be?'

'Stuck up.'

She shook her head. 'He's just a regular bloke.'

'Who just happens to have countless millions in the bank,' said Adam.

'And who just happens to be crazy about you,' added Rachel.

'Why do you say that?'

'Because I've got eyes. I see the way he looks at you.'

'No, Rach,' Adam corrected her. 'That's just a squint.'

They laughed. She poured herself more wine. 'You don't usually drink so much,' observed Adam.

'So what? It's a happy occasion. That's what we English do on happy occasions, isn't it? Drink ourselves into a stupor.'

'You don't seem happy.'

'How do I seem?'

'Distracted.'

'I'm very happy.'

'And who wouldn't be,' agreed Rachel, 'with a boyfriend like that? Gorgeous, nice and loaded. You lucky thing.'

'Ouch!' exclaimed Adam with mock indignation. Again they laughed.

She sipped her wine. 'Come on, Rach, how many celebs have you counted?'

'Six.'

'I've only managed four.' She pointed them out. 'Who are the other two?'

'Alec.'

'Oh, of course. And the other?'

Rachel smiled. 'Haven't you noticed people staring at you? Check out the table in the corner.'

She did. Two middle-aged women with stretched faces picked at their salads while glancing in her direction. She rolled her eyes at one of them and both quickly looked away.

'See? You're the girl who kicked Evelyne Cauldwell into touch. That makes you someone.'

She shook her head, feeling suddenly embarrassed. Then pleased.

Alexander returned. They placed their dessert orders. This time Adam and Rachel threw caution to the wind and chose expensive items. 'Alec's having a party next weekend,' she told them. 'Why don't you come?'

Adam looked awkwardly at Alexander. 'Well, if you wouldn't mind.'

'No, I'd love it. We both would.'

The discussion of work resumed, Adam keeping the muscle-flexing to a minimum. As Chrissie listened she felt eyes creep over her. It was a good feeling. Like an ego massage.

Rising to her feet she made her way to the ladies. The sense of being watched remained. That and the memory of a girl called Tina, alone in a darkened bedroom trying to walk like the models she envied so much. Models like Evelyne: people who were someone; who had only to move for everyone to turn and look.

Sometimes dreams did come true.

Early the next morning she called Aunty Karen from the living room of Alexander's flat. Alexander was still in bed and she hoped Aunty Karen would be too, allowing her to avoid the inevitable interrogation for a few more days.

But all in vain. The phone was answered on the fourth ring.

'Hi. It's me.'

'About time. Why haven't you called me?'

'I was in Norfolk.'

'You still could have called. Sue showed me the article. What's happened to Jack?'

'That's all over.'

'Why?'

'It just is.'

'Did you tell him how you feel?'

'No.'

'Why not?'

'Because.'

'Because what?'

'Because his ex-girlfriend got there first. Satisfied?'

Silence. She braced herself for the tidal wave of sympathy.

'So you're giving up without a fight?'

'Give up what? He's a loser.'

'Since when did inheriting a fortune make someone a winner?'

'Alec really cares about me.'

'And I'm sure you care about him too. The same way you cared about all the others I've met. People like Kev who trotted after you like lapdogs and bored you to death.'

'It'll be different with Alec.'

'So how does he make you feel?'

'I don't know . . .'

'You don't *know*?'

'Special. He makes me feel special.'

'Why? Because he's rich?'

'No!'

'Does he make you feel the way Jack did?'

She didn't answer. Inside her anger was building.

'Didn't think so.'

'You know how Jack *really* made me feel? Like Tina. Is that what you want?'

'I'm just saying . . .'

'Well don't. It's none of your business.'

'Of course it's my business. I'm your aunt.'

'No you're not. You were just my uncle's wife and now he's dead which makes you nothing so keep your fucking nose out.'

The phone went dead. She threw the receiver across the room, hitting a coffee mug on a nearby table which fell to smash on the floor. She waited for Alexander to appear but heard nothing. One of the benefits of such an enormous flat – sound had much further to travel.

Reclaiming the receiver she redialled Aunty Karen's number. It went straight to answerphone just as she had known it would.

'I didn't mean that. You know how much you mean to me. More than anyone . . .'

An image of Jack crept into her head. She pushed it away.

'. . . in the world. I know you care but I also know what's right for me and this *is* right. I'll call again soon. Please don't hate me. You're the last person I'd ever want to hurt.'

She made her way back to the bedroom. Alexander lay sleeping. After drawing the curtains she sat down on the bed and tickled his toes. Opening his eyes he smiled up at her. 'What time is it?'

'Half past eight. The day is already old.'

'I thought we were having a lie-in.'

'Not any more. Let's go for a walk.'

He stretched in the bed. 'If that's what you want.'

'It is.' She stroked the scar above his right eye. 'How did you get this?'

'Fighting a duel.'

'Is that right, Zorro?'

'No. I fell off a bike when I was a kid and cut myself on a table leg. How macho is that?'

'Very. So your grandmother let you ride your bike indoors, did she?'

'Not her. My father. It was in our New York apartment.'

'Which part of town?'

'Upper West Side. 72nd and Riverside. It had amazing views of the Hudson and a long corridor with wooden flooring where Dad taught me to ride my first bike.'

'Wouldn't it have been easier to teach you outside?'

'Not in a New York winter. We'd have frozen to death before I'd cycled five yards.'

She laughed. His expression became wistful. 'I remember the day it happened. Up until then I'd always ridden with stabilizers but Dad took them off and told me to try without. I remember the way the floorboards creaked and how vulnerable I felt – like I could fall at any minute, which of course I did. Dad ran towards me, hugged me and told me that everything was going to be all right.' A sigh. 'That's my only clear memory of him. Being comforted on the floor of our apartment after I'd fallen off my bike.'

She continued to stroke his scar. 'I've never told anyone that,' he said.

'Why not?'

'Because it's mine, I guess. My memory. The only one. I never had the chance to store any more. A few weeks later he was dead.'

'So why are you telling me?'

'Because I want you to know. I want you to know all about me. All the things that no one else does. Just like I want to know all about you.'

'You know everything already. I'm a bitch who looks great in Prada and kicks arse on the dance floor. That's all there is. No skeletons.'

'I don't believe that. You're not a bitch and everyone has skeletons.'

'What are you saying? That Mother Teresa was a secret crack whore?'

'Tell me about *your* dad.'

'I don't remember him.'

'You must remember something. However faint.'

'And you want me to tell you, do you? Something I've never told another living soul?'

He nodded.

'I broke one of your coffee mugs. Just now while I was on the phone. No one else in the world knows that. No one but you.'

She waited for laughter. Instead disappointment crept into his face. 'You can trust me. I won't tell anyone.'

'There's nothing to tell.'

'Did Jack ask you about your dad?'

'No. Not that it would have done him much good if he had. I wouldn't share my memories with a loser like him.'

'So you do have memories then.'

'My dad's in the past. He has nothing to do with my life.'

'Just like Jack doesn't. That's in the past too.' A pause. 'It is, isn't it?'

'Isn't it a bit early for twenty questions?'

'I just want to know about you, that's all.'

'My star sign is Aquarius. My shoe size is seven. My favourite city is Paris. My favourite singer is Joni Mitchell.' She tugged his hair. 'And the reason I'm here with you is that there's nowhere else in the world that I'd rather be.'

The disappointment faded. He rubbed his head against her hand, reminding her of the way Bullseye had responded to her touch. He was like a pet, just as Aunty Karen had said of all her other boyfriends. But she was not going to grow bored of his affection.

'Come on doggy,' she said teasingly. 'Time to put your collar on.'

Still smiling he headed for the shower.

That evening, as Alexander cooked supper, she wrote in her diary.

This morning we went to Kensington Park. I've never been there before. Amazing when you think I've lived in London for seven years. We saw Peter Pan's statue and Alec had someone take a picture of the two of us beside it. We look good together. Being six-one he can put his arm

*around me without looking stupid. Jack would
have to stand on a step to avoid looking like one
of the seven dwarves.*

On the way back to the flat we passed a
dress shop. There was an amazing backless
number in the window. Dark green. I said how
great it was and Alec told me to try it on. It
fitted perfectly and he bought it for me. £1000
on a dress! The shop assistant kept giving me
funny looks. She probably recognizes Alec and
thinks I'm a gold-digger. But I'm not, I didn't
ask him to buy it. He was the one who
insisted.

I wish Jack had seen me in it. I'd have blown
him away. Made him realize how out of his
league I am. Ali is his league. I'm not jealous
any more. They're welcome to each other.

Alec wants us to go to New York to meet his
cousins. It must be strange having no family in
this country. I'd really miss Aunty Karen if she
lived abroad. I still feel bad about this morning.
I wish I hadn't said what I did. God, I'm a bitch
sometimes.

But better that than a wimp. Like Ali. I bet
she's a wimp. I bet Jack wears the pants in that
relationship, only his would be full of holes and
covered in oil. Stupid loser. Aunty Karen doesn't
know what she's talking about. I'm not scared
of rejection. If I really wanted Jack he'd be mine

again in a second. I could eat Ali alive.
Especially in my new dress.

*Funny thing is that, now I've got it, I don't like
it so much. But I'll have to wear it. Alec will be
hurt otherwise and I don't want to hurt him. I
care about him in spite of what people like Bob
say. Bob's a wimp too. He'd get kicked all over the
film set if I wasn't there to carry him. Sometimes it
seems like I have to carry everyone.*

*Except Aunty Karen. And Jack. And Dad.
The only people I've ever really loved.*

*Maybe that's why. Because they didn't need
me to need them.*

*But I don't need anyone. Tina did, but I'm
not her, however close Jack came to convincing
me that I was. Stupid, useless prick. That's all he
is.*

*I still miss him though. All the time I think
about him. Wonder what he's doing. Hope he's
missing me too. Just a bit. That's all.*

That would be enough.

Late Monday evening. After finishing his shift in the
pub Jack returned to the boat.

The lights were on. From inside came the sound of
music and the smell of cooking. Ali stood by the stove
making risotto. He went to nibble the back of her neck.
Laughing, she pushed him away. 'You reek of beer.'

'Only a couple.'

334

'And crisps. You'd better be hungry.'

'Yes, Mum.'

'There's beer in the fridge. It should be cold by now.'

He took one out. She served the food. They ate on the sofa while watching Bullseye push the pan around the floor devouring leftovers. He told her that a friend had suggested visiting later in the week. 'I thought we'd take the boat out. Make the most of the weather before autumn really kicks in.'

'Good idea.'

'Can you get time off?'

'Are you saying you want me to come?'

'Of course. It wouldn't be the same without you.'

'Liar. The two of you will want to get stoned and brag about all the birds you've bedded. I'd only cramp your style.'

'We wouldn't do that.'

'This is me, remember.'

'I mean it.' He put his arm around her. She pressed herself against him while Bullseye climbed onto her knee. 'Want to share a joint?' he asked.

'Sure.'

He went to prepare one. A Joni Mitchell CD was playing. It made him think of Chrissie. He wondered what she was doing, whether she was OK. He hoped so.

'I saw something strange today,' Ali told him.

'What?'

She reached under the sofa for a magazine. 'One of

the customers left this behind. I was skimming through it and spotted this.'

He returned to the sofa. She pointed to a photograph of a young couple. He did a doubletake. 'Shit!'

'You know them?'

'That's Chrissie.'

'Chrissie? The one you . . .'

'Saw a few times. Yeah.' In the picture she looked happy. Only a couple of weeks since their parting and already he was old news. Momentarily he felt indignant.

'That explains it.'

'Explains what?'

'About a month ago she started coming to the cafe. She came in every day for at least a week and whenever I looked at her she was always staring at me. It freaked me out to be honest. I even spoke to Arno about it but then she stopped coming.'

He felt a lurch in his stomach.

'You told me it wasn't serious.'

'It wasn't. Just a bit of fun.'

'So she came to stare at me for fun, did she?'

'No.' He struggled for words. 'But I used to talk about you just like she used to talk about her old boyfriends. She wouldn't have been human if she hadn't been curious.'

'Staring at me every day for a week isn't being human. It's being obsessive.'

'Hardly.'

336

'So how much time did you spend checking out her ex's?'

He didn't answer.

'Exactly.'

'It's not obsessive.'

'It's spooky, Jack. She must have been mad about you.'

'Well maybe she was then but she's clearly not now, is she?'

Her expression became troubled. 'Were you mad about her?'

'No.'

'Then you should get your eyes tested. She's stunning.'

'Photos can be deceptive.'

'Not that deceptive. I've seen her in the flesh, remember.'

He stroked her arm. 'I'm sorry about that.'

'Are you sorry I'm here now and not her.'

'Absolutely not.'

'Honestly?'

'Hey, come on.' He kissed her nose. 'Of course.'

'How did you meet?'

'In the pub. We got chatting and ended up back here. Just a one night stand that sort of developed.'

'What night? Not the one when you missed my birthday party?'

Guilt swept over him. 'No,' he said quickly. 'I really was ill then.'

'Lucky you. It was a lousy party. The power went

off, we had to use candles and someone managed to set light to the curtains. Good thing I wasn't evicted!'

He laughed. She did too. It was a beautiful sound: warm and trusting. It made him feel protective. Made him want to be honest. About some things at least.

'You want to know what it was between us, at least as far as I was concerned. Ego. She had this strength about her. This presence. I was amazed that someone so focused would go for a bum like me. But when I got to know her I realized it was all an act and underneath it was a frightened kid who had no clue who she really was. The last time I saw her I told her that. We had a huge row and she ended it, but I'm glad she did and that's the truth.'

Again Ali looked at the picture. 'I guess she's moved on now.'

'It's only fair. I have, after all, and I'm glad of that too.'

Leaning forward she hugged him. He hugged her back, waiting for the old sense of being trapped. Only it never came. Instead there was just relief that she was back where she belonged. That and happiness because there was no need for it to ever change.

Unless she found out about the other lies. But there was no reason for her to do so.

Or so he told himself.

Wednesday evening. Back from another stint in Norfolk, Chrissie made her way towards Melanie's flat, responding to an SOS call she had received earlier in the day. 'I need to talk to you,' Melanie had told her before becoming guarded about her reasons. Hopefully she had dumped that idiot Rick.

It was still light when she reached Warwick Avenue tube. Although it was a longer journey, she walked past the canal. Not that she was hoping to catch a glimpse of Jack – she just fancied some air.

His boat was gone from its usual mooring. Perhaps he was taking Ali on a trip just as he had taken her. Not that it mattered, they were welcome to each other. Losers both.

An anxious-looking Melanie let her into the flat. 'Has Rick done something?' she demanded.

'No. We're fine.'

'Good.' She tried not to sound disappointed. 'So what's up?'

'I got a call at work today. Some woman asking about a book we're publishing at Christmas. At least that was what she asked about initially but then we started talking about the Book Awards. She said she'd been there and wasn't it great and what table had I been on and what were the people like and suddenly she's asking all these questions about you.'

For a moment she was baffled. Then came comprehension.

'A *journalist*? What did she want to know?'

'Just what you were like. How long we'd been friends. What you were into.' A pause. Melanie began to look uncomfortable.

'And?'

'Were you materialistic?'

'Am I a gold-digger in other words.'

'I didn't say anything. Well nothing bad. I told her you were a brilliant friend and the least materialistic person I know.' Another pause. 'Do you think that sounded defensive?'

'How do I know? I wasn't on the other end of the phone.'

'I'm really sorry. I should have twigged sooner.'

'It's all right, it's not your fault. Did she ask what we thought of Evelyne?'

'Yes, but I was getting suspicious so I said she was really nice and even more attractive than in her photos. Was that OK?'

'Perfect. Well done.'

'Thanks. I didn't know how well I could lie under pressure.'

She laughed. Melanie did the same. Then something occurred to her.

'How many other people has this woman called?'

'I don't know. I asked around at work but nobody else got a call. At least that's what they said.'

'Well, I suppose you're the obvious one. I was your guest after all.'

'Do you think she's tried to call your family?'

'She hasn't called my aunt. I would have heard otherwise. Anyway, Aunty Karen wouldn't have said anything bad. She's quite sussed.'

'What about your mum?'

'Oh Christ . . .'

'Do you want to call her and find out?'

Nodding, she pulled out her mobile. Her mother answered on the third ring. 'Chrissie! What a nice surprise. I'm—'

'Have you had any calls from people asking questions about me?'

'No. Why?'

'Some journalist phoned a friend of mine. It's because I'm seeing Alexander Gallen.'

'I know.' A sigh. 'Karen told me.'

She wasn't in the mood for a guilt trip. 'Look, if anyone calls then do me a favour and tell them I'm not a gold-digger.'

Her mother's tone became hurt. 'Of course. What do you take me for?'

'Just be careful.' A pause. 'Have you been to the doctor yet?'

'No. I've been busy. But I am going to.'

'When?'

'Soon.'

'Now.'

'You make it sound so easy.'

'It is. Just pick up the phone and make an appointment. What's difficult about that?'

'Nothing, I suppose.'

'Then stop being feeble and do it.'

Again the hurt. 'OK.'

'I've got to go. Call me when you've seen him.'

She put down the phone. Suddenly Melanie smiled. 'It's quite exciting, isn't it?'

'That's one way of putting it.'

'Oh come on, it *is* exciting. For me anyway; I've never had a famous friend before.'

'I'm not famous.'

'Yes you are. I was in a newsagents today looking through magazines to see if there were any other pieces about you.'

'Were there?'

'No.'

'Oh,' she said, feeling an odd mixture of relief and disappointment.

'But I only had time to check a couple. Besides, there will be more if today is anything to go by.'

'Just as long as they don't say anything nasty.'

'I'm sure they won't but even if they do what does it matter? You're happy so let people think the worst if they want to. People close to you know the truth.'

Another nod.

'You are happy, aren't you?'

'Of course. Alec's a fantastic guy. I'd have to be completely stupid to want to be with someone else . . .'

Two hours later. She walked back towards the tube, again taking a roundabout route past the Wayfarer pub. Just for the exercise. That was all. Jack wouldn't be there anyway. Not that it mattered.

Someone called her name. Turning, she saw Jack's neighbour Stephen walking towards her with a younger man, both looking slightly inebriated.

'Hi, Chrissie. How are you?'

Aware he might report back to Jack she put on her brightest smile. 'Never better.

'This is my partner, Tim.'

Tim offered his hand. 'It's nice to meet you at last.'

At last?

'How's Jack?' asked Stephen. 'We saw his boat was gone when we got back.'

'Have you been on a trip?'

'Up to Birmingham to see my family. We were away for three weeks.'

So they didn't know what had happened. As far as they were concerned she and Jack were still an item. The realization pleased her, made her feel in control.

'We're going to have a nightcap,' Stephen told her. 'Want to join us?'

'Sure.'

The pub was virtually empty. She sipped mineral water while her companions drank beer. 'So how was your trip to Oxfordshire?' asked Tim.

'We only made it as far as Marlowe.'

'That's a shame. Still, there's always another time.'

'Not for Jack and me. We split up after we got back.'

Both Stephen and Tim looked uncomfortable. 'I'm sorry,' said Stephen.

'Don't be. There's nothing like a week in a confined

space to realize how incompatible you are. Besides, we're both seeing other people now which only goes to show how totally devastated we both were.'

The discomfort became relief. 'That's great,' Stephen told her.

'It is. My new boyfriend's wonderful, I'm really happy.' Momentarily she wondered if she sounded over emphatic but both looked convinced.

'Who's Jack seeing?' asked Tim.

'His ex-girlfriend. The one who works in a coffee bar.'

'Ali? They're back together again?' Stephen beamed. 'That's brilliant.'

The words stung. 'Is it?'

'Yes. They were great together.'

'In what way?'

'She understood him. Accepted him for who he was. The few previous girlfriends we've met always wanted to change him. Ali seemed happy to just let him be who he was. I think that's why he cared about her so much.'

Jealousy surged through her. She swallowed it down. 'I'm glad they're back together. He used to talk about her all the time. Saying how great she was. Good thing I'm not the jealous type, otherwise I'd have hated her guts.'

'You'd like her if you met her.'

'Perhaps I will soon. Alec, my new guy, is into boats. I'll have to ask Jack if he can take the two of us down river.'

'So Alec's not the jealous type either?'

'God, no. Besides, what does he have to be jealous of? Jack and I were just a bit of fun. Ships that pass in the night if you'll forgive the nautical terminology.'

They both laughed. The sense of control returned.

Stephen bought another round. More pints for him and Tim. Another mineral water for her. 'I'm really happy for Jack,' she said on his return. 'He deserves someone nice. When he used to talk about the two of you I always got the sense he was envious. That he wanted to have something as special with someone as the relationship you have with each other.'

Stephen smiled at Tim. 'We do knock along pretty well together.'

'How did you meet?'

'At a pumping out station on the river near Coventry,' explained Tim. 'Steve cruised in to pick up some diesel but picked me up instead.' A grin. 'How romantic is that?'

'Romantic enough. You're lucky. You radiate happiness. If Jack and Ali's relationship is anything like yours then they'll be a very fortunate couple.' She sipped her drink. 'One thing always puzzled me though. Why they split up in the first place. I asked Jack about it once and he said something about Ali deserving better. It surprised me as he's hardly the insecure type, though when feelings are involved I guess we can all be paranoid.'

'As I know from experience,' Stephen told her.

'I have a close friend called Bill,' elaborated Tim. 'In the early days Steve was sure there was something going on between us. But there wasn't,' he added hastily.

Again Stephen smiled at Tim. 'You don't have to convince me, Bill's a great guy. All Tim's friends are great.'

'As are Jack's,' Chrissie added. 'Judging by the two of you.'

Both looked flattered. Just as she had intended.

'I know Ali really liked you. Jack was always talking about that too.'

More smiles.

'Did he like her friends?'

'Sure,' said Tim with a laugh. 'Though not as much as he liked her sister.'

'Oh, come on,' Stephen told him. 'That was just a one off and anyway . . .'

Suddenly he stopped. His eyes widened. Just as Tim's widened.

Jack slept with her sister. That's why he said he deserved better. The bastard slept with her sister.

Her companions were looking uncomfortable. Quickly she tried to put them at ease. 'He never got to meet any of my friends. Or my family. Mind you, when it comes to the latter category he had a lucky escape. My mother can bore for England.'

They both laughed a little too enthusiastically. Relief

that she had not picked up on the inadvertent bombshell.

And Ali doesn't know. She can't know. Otherwise why would they look so panicked?

She began to tell a story about her mother, continuing to allay their fears while trying to collect her thoughts.

Ten minutes later, she stood in front of the mirror in the ladies room staring at her reflection, listening to the words the dragon whispered into her brain.

You've found it, Chrissie. The means to hurt him. To make him pay. Because he has to pay. He's hurt you and if you let him get away with it then you're no better than Tina. As stupid, ugly and useless as her.

Her eyes were shining. Dark and savage, like those of an animal. She stared into them and felt afraid. Because she didn't want to hurt him. All she wanted was to put the pain behind her. Make a new life with Alexander. Forgive and forget.

But you can't, Chrissie. To forgive is to be weak. To be the person your father abandoned and everyone despised. Listen to me. I'm what makes you strong. Without me you're nothing. Nothing at all.

'Go to hell,' she whispered to the air.

It's true, Chrissie. Or is it Tina? Sometimes I can't tell the difference any more.

She marched from the room, slamming the door behind her as if trying to leave the dragon confined.

*

Midnight. Alexander sat in his living room watching a news programme.

He heard a key in the lock. Chrissie came to sit beside him. 'Is Mel OK?' he asked.

'Sure. If still being with that jerk Rick could be considered OK.'

'What did she want to see you about?'

'Some journalist called asking questions about me. It freaked her out.'

'Has it freaked you out?'

'A bit.'

'I'm sorry.'

'Why?'

'It's because of me that they're calling.'

'Don't be.' She gestured to the television. 'What are you watching?'

'Nothing. Turn it off if you like. Do you want coffee?'

She shook her head.

'You said you'd be back earlier. I was worried about you.'

'There's no need; I can look after myself. I've been doing it long enough.'

'But you don't need to any more. You've got me now. I want to look after you.'

'Like I said, there's no need.'

'It's not because there's a need. It's because I care.'

She didn't answer. He put his arm around her, kissing her cheek. She kissed him back half heartedly.

Increasingly he was noticing that she seemed preoccupied when they were together. As if her mind was somewhere else. With someone else?

'So how was your evening?' she asked.

'Incomplete.'

'Why?'

'Because you weren't here.'

'So was mine.'

'Good.'

She made a face at him. 'You want me to be miserable?'

'Only when you're apart from me.' He stroked her hair, as thick and beautiful as his grandmother's had once been. 'You hate Rick, don't you?'

'Of course. Mel deserves so much better. She deserves someone like . . .'

Jack? Is that who you're thinking of? Would you rather he was here instead of me?

'You. Only that's not going to happen. You're spoken for.'

He continued to stroke her hair. 'Did you see anyone else?' he asked casually.

'I ran into some friends of Jack's and had a drink with them. I didn't want to but it would have been rude to say no.'

'How is Jack?'

'Back together with his ex. Poor cow. Wait until he gets all obsessive about her.'

'Just like he did about you.'

'But that's in the past now.'

Is it? Is it really?

'I'm looking forward to your party,' she told him.

'Do you think it'll be a success?'

'How could it not be? Rick can't make it and all my other friends are under strict instructions not to blow their noses on the curtains.'

'What about wiping their fingers on the carpets?'

'Let's not run before we can walk.'

He laughed. She did too. He loved her laugh. He loved her. Totally. So much that sometimes it frightened him. The sense of dependence. The surrender of power to one who could exploit it however they saw fit.

But she would never exploit it. Causing pain was not in her nature. Or so he wanted to believe.

'Do you know what would really make me complete?' she asked.

'What?'

'Strong and black with no sugar. If the offer's still there.'

'Of course it is.'

Again she kissed his cheek. He went to make her coffee.

Thursday morning. Chrissie sat at her desk, checking through the post that had accumulated during her time in Norfolk.

Amongst the usual assortment of bills, submissions

and invitations she noticed one handwritten envelope addressed to herself and marked personal. Opening it up she found a single piece of paper with a message written in the same hand:

> *Congratulations on being Alexander Gallen's new flame. Aren't you the lucky one? But don't get too complacent. Believe me, there are a lot of envious women out there.*
> *Take Marion Evans. I'd bet she'd give every breath in her body to be in your shoes.*

A coldness swept over her. As if someone had walked over her grave.

What did it mean? Who was Marion Evans and what did she have to do with Alexander?

She picked up the phone, ready to call him. Then put it down again. She didn't want him to know she felt insecure. She would never let any man see that.

Her computer had internet access. She entered Alexander's name into the search engine. Once the results were in she cross-referenced them with the name Marion Evans but found no matches.

She picked up the envelope. The postmark said Swindon. She entered Marion Evans into the search engine then cross-referenced the results against Swindon. No matches were found. She tried again, cross-referencing New York then London but still nothing.

One final option occurred to her. Amberton. Alexander's childhood home in Norfolk. At last a single result was displayed. A newspaper article about a group of retired women who had become regional champions in a pub quiz league. She printed it off and read it. There was a photograph of Marion: a sweet-faced pensioner leaning on a cane. Just the sort of femme fatale who might steal Alexander's heart for ever.

It was just spite. Someone trying to cause trouble. Much good it had done them.

She decided to keep the note and article as a reminder not to be stupid.

Saturday. The evening of the party.

Alexander's grandmother's house was a huge, four storey villa in a sidestreet off Kensington Church Street. The weather was mild for early September and people spilled out of the main living room into the walled garden at the back. As well as providing a lavish buffet Alexander had also hired caterers who glided from guest to guest offering snacks and replenishing glasses.

It was a good turnout. Seventy people at least. All her friends had come as well as Adam and Sue with Rachel and Barry. Alexander's friends were there too as well as almost everyone from his office. She moved through the crowds, checking on her guests while watching Alexander do the same. He was an excellent host: letting everyone know that he was pleased to see them. Tara commented on it as they smoked in the garden. 'He makes everyone feel welcome. It's a great quality and this is a great party. Are any celebs coming?'

'Sadly not. We invited Madonna but it clashed with her Kaballah meeting.'

'What about Jack? Is he coming?'

'No.'

'Kabbalah too?'

'Naturally. It's ancient history, isn't it?'

'Are you OK about that?'

'Of course. Isn't it obvious?'

'How would I know? I've hardly seen you in the last two weeks.' A hurt note crept into Tara's voice. 'In case you'd forgotten we're supposed to share a flat.'

'We do. It's just kind of got intense with Alec and I've had to be in Norfolk too and . . . well, you know how it is.'

'Are you going to move out?'

'Wasn't planning to. I need a refuge when Alec and I fight.'

'Why would you fight? Anyone can see he's crazy about you.'

'So now all we need is to find someone for you. Alec's got some nice friends. Maybe one of them could be your Mr Right.'

Alexander appeared beside them. 'We need to find Tara a decent bloke,' she told him, 'but you're taken, remember.'

353

'That goes without saying. How do you think it's going?'

'Brilliantly,' said Tara.

'And made all the better because you're here,' Alexander replied. 'Why don't the three of us get together soon. You could come and see the flat.'

Tara's face lit up. Chrissie felt pleased.

'Graham and Gail are here,' he told her. 'Will you come and meet them?'

'Thanks for making Tara feel special,' she said as they moved back into the house.

'Anything for you.'

'So if I asked you to talk weddings with Rachel for the rest of the evening you'd do it.'

'If that's what you wanted.'

She laughed. His expression remained serious. He really would do it. He would do anything to make her happy.

Graham and Gail were both pale and plump and looked more like brother and sister than husband and wife. 'It's lovely to meet you,' said Graham. 'Alec's told us so much about you.'

'That sounds ominous.'

'Not at all,' said Gail. 'It was good stuff.'

'That's even worse.'

They laughed. The doorbell rang and Alexander went to greet new arrivals. 'I gather you've known Alec longer than anyone,' Chrissie said to Graham.

He nodded. 'Since we were nine.'

'Did you like boarding school?'

'Hated it. As did Alec. I think we kept each other sane.'

'Pity you're not still there, then perhaps Alec wouldn't be such a nutter now.'

Gail frowned. 'What do you mean?'

'Nothing. Just joking.'

'Of course. Sorry.' Gail flushed slightly.

Chrissie sipped her drink. 'You live on the river, don't you?'

'Yes, in Bermondsey.'

'I love the water. I used to live on the Essex coast so I guess it's in my blood.'

'So you're an Essex girl then?' observed Graham.

'Yes, and I've heard all the jokes.'

'You think that's bad. I come from a village called Little Sodbury. People have a field day with a name like that.'

Suddenly time went into reverse. She was back in the Wayfarer having an almost identical conversation with Jack.

An ache ran through her. 'I can imagine.'

Silence. She continued to sip her drink, aware of both of them studying her, making her feel as if she was being evaluated, which she undoubtedly was. They were Alexander's closest friends after all. But still their scrutiny made her feel uncomfortable.

'Are you enjoying the party?' asked Gail.

'Very much. As are all my friends. But then, we'd

be happy anywhere with free champagne.' She laughed then worried that her comment had sounded like something a gold-digger would say. 'Alec's a great host,' she continued. 'He knows how to make everyone feel special but I'm sure you don't need me to tell you that.'

'No,' said Gail. 'You don't.'

Was that a dig?

No of course not. She's just agreeing with you. Don't be so paranoid.

Someone called Graham's name. He moved to another group.

'How long have you been married?' she asked Gail.

'Just over a year.'

She risked another joke. 'How are you enjoying domestic slavery?'

'Loving it. Graham's a fantastic guy. I'm very lucky.'

'I feel the same about Alec.'

'I'm glad to hear it. You look wonderful by the way. That dress really suits you.'

'Thanks. That's what Alec said.'

'Did he buy it for you?'

'Yes. We were out walking and saw it in a shop window. He told me to try it on then insisted on buying it.'

Gail nodded.

She doesn't believe me. She thinks I made him buy it.

'I tried to talk him out of it but you know how persuasive he can be.'

Another nod. The eyes continued to study her.

Don't you judge me. Don't you fucking dare.

The need to charm vanished. 'But then you know all about his generosity. I gather you'd have lost your house if he hadn't kept up the mortgage payments. Thank God for friends with deep pockets, eh?'

Gail flinched. Chrissie lit a cigarette. 'Better go and check on my friends. Lovely to meet you. We must talk again later.'

Then she turned and walked away.

Ten minutes later she stood in the garden with Sue and her partner Barry. 'This is an amazing place,' Sue told her.

'And this is amazing booze,' said Barry, downing more champagne.

'Don't rub it in,' said Sue, staring wistfully at her orange juice.

'Mother-to-be,' said Barry affectionately, putting his arm around her. He was wearing a battered jacket and faded jeans and looked scruffy compared to the other guests. Just as Jack would have done had he been there.

Barry went to talk to Adam. 'How many bedrooms are there?' asked Sue.

'I don't know. Let's go and count them.'

'Shouldn't we ask Alec first. It's his house.'

'Why? He won't mind.'

'You're very sure of him.'

'Shouldn't I be?'

'You haven't known him that long.'

'Long enough to know how he feels about me. Are you up for it?'

'Definitely.'

They moved through the drawing room, out into the hall and up the stairs. The first floor was an assortment of reception rooms and bedrooms, all beautifully furnished but devoid of human touches. The second floor was the same. She tried to guess which room had been Alexander's but was unable to do so. The whole place was more like a luxury hotel than a home. All style with no heart. Elegant but cold.

Only one room stood out. A bedroom on the second floor with windows looking out onto the street below. At its centre was an antique four-poster bed. By the window was a large dressing table with a huge mirror. On a mantelpiece was a row of framed photographs, all seemingly of the same person. Alexander's mother.

Above the mantelpiece was a full length painting of a handsome, elderly woman who stared down at them with cool, appraising eyes.

'Who's that?' asked Sue.

'Alec's grandmother,' she replied, studying the face that had nothing in it to suggest beauty yet conveyed its illusion so effortlessly.

She remembered the Cecil Beaton portrait in Alexander's flat. The woman in it had radiated confidence and strength. Though the painter had captured both qualities in the portrait he had captured others too. Harshness. Severity.

An image crept unbidden into her brain. The picture of Marion Evans in the newspaper article. The two women resembled each other so closely they could have been sisters. Only Marion was the anaemic version. Softer. Warmer. Weaker.

The door opened. Alexander entered. 'What are you doing in here?' he demanded angrily. She had never seen him angry before. It made her feel uncharacteristically vulnerable.

'Just looking,' she told him.

'This is my grandmother's room. You've got no business in here.'

'We were just looking.'

'Don't be angry with Chrissie,' said Sue quickly. 'I asked her to show me around.'

The anger vanished. 'I'm sorry. I didn't mean to snap.'

Her sense of self returned. 'I should think not. What did you think we were going to do? Steal something?'

'I'm sorry,' he said again.

'It's Sue you should apologize to.'

'Of course.' He turned to Sue. 'Forgive me.'

Silence. Alexander looked anxious, Sue embarrassed. Chrissie tried to ease the tension with a joke. 'Actually you were right to be worried. I've already had to stop Sue pocketing a couple of paperweights.'

'You did not!' said Sue indignantly. Then laughed.

Alexander did the same, anxiety fading from his face as quickly as the anger had done. 'If you like,' he said 'I could show you both the rest of the house.'

'Shouldn't you get back to your guests?'

'No, they'll be OK for a few minutes.' He grinned at Sue. 'Will that be enough time for you to properly case the joint?'

'Definitely. I need a new washer drier. Do you have one I could fit into my bag?'

'I'm sure we can find one.' He moved behind Chrissie, wrapping his arms around her. 'Sorry I was a jerk,' he whispered.

'You're forgiven,' she whispered back.

He hugged her tightly. Sue, clearly touched, beamed at her. She beamed back, feeling the warmth of his breath on the back of her neck. Feeling loved. Feeling needed.

And, for the first time, smothered.

But only because it was stuffy in the room.

She gestured to the photographs on the mantelpiece. 'Why aren't there any of you?'

'My grandmother didn't like pictures of me. She said they didn't do me justice.'

'So she thought you were hot stuff. Well that figures. Love is blind, after all.'

'Chrissie takes a great photo,' announced Sue. 'Particularly when she's got a bag over her head.'

Alexander continued to hug her. 'Even with a bag over her head she'd still look perfect to me.'

Again Sue beamed. Chrissie felt Alexander's hold on her tightening and remembered times when Jack had held her. How his grip had felt as strong as Alexander's did now. But never like a vice.

Again she felt needed. Again she felt smothered.

Over her head she could see the dressing table mirror. Her face was reflected in it. For a moment her eyes looked as hard and cold as those of the woman in the portrait.

A trick of the light, perhaps.

Gently she released herself from his grip. 'Come on. Much as I'd like to it's not fair to keep you all to myself.'

His face lit up. She stared into it and told herself that she was happy.

Together the three of them made their way downstairs.

Two hours later and the party was winding down. The few remaining guests were gathered in the garden. Gail stood talking to a pretty, blonde girl called Mel who claimed to be Chrissie's best friend. 'I'm responsible for her meeting Alec,' Mel explained. 'I took her to the Book Awards where Alec and Evelyne ended up on our table.'

'So what did you think of Evelyne?'

Mel's eyes became wary.

'It's all right. You can be honest. For what it's worth, Graham and I couldn't stand her.'

'Neither could I. She spent the whole evening looking superior. I found her quite intimidating, actually.'

'But Chrissie didn't?'

'Are you kidding? Chrissie isn't intimidated by anyone.'

Gail looked over at the striking young woman sitting with Alexander, surrounded by people who seemed to be hanging on her every word. 'I can imagine that.'

Mel moved away. Gail remained where she was, watching Chrissie.

Graham appeared beside her. 'Well?'

'I don't like her. She's too confident.'

'Since when was confidence a crime?'

'It's not just that. It's the way she talked about Alec. That joke about him being a nutter. Do you think she knows about the breakdown?'

'He's never told us it was a breakdown. A virus. That's what he said.'

'Bad enough for him to miss a term of school?'

'Why not?'

'And when he comes back they've moved to London. It just seems . . .'

'What?'

'That they were running away from something.'

He rolled his eyes.

'I'm serious. Whenever I mention it he changes the subject. You know how good he is at that. It's like . . . I don't know. He's ashamed.'

'You read too much into things.'

'And you never knew Laura.'

'Who?'

'A girl I was at school with. She had a breakdown. We were told she had a virus but I found out the truth because her mother confided in mine. Then the family moved away and years later, when I met Laura at a party, she pretended that it never happened. That it was nothing. The way Alec does when he talks about that missing term.'

'I'm sure Chrissie didn't mean anything. I was the one who started the joke, she was just following my lead.'

'Chrissie isn't the sort of girl anyone can lead.'

'You're not giving her a chance.'

'So I shouldn't trust my instincts?'

'Provided they're unbiased.'

'You think I'm jealous?'

'A little. Have you ever seen Alec look so happy? For the last year you've been the most important woman in his life. Now you're not and that's got to hurt.'

She shook her head.

'Maybe just a little?'

'Perhaps. Alec's like a brother. It makes me protective.'

'Overprotective, even?'

'I just wanted to like her and I didn't. I can't say why. I just didn't.'

'You think she's a gold-digger?'

She watched Chrissie talk to a cousin and her partner; a shabby looking pair who seemed out of place in such glamorous surroundings. But Chrissie didn't seem to care. She was smiling at both of them, her eyes warm and affectionate.

'No,' she said softly. 'I don't think that.'

'So stop worrying. I'm thirsty. Want another drink?'

'Sure.'

He moved away. Her eyes shifted to Alexander. He had his arm around Chrissie, gazing at her as she talked to her relatives. His eyes were shining. Love poured out of them. Suddenly he leaned forward and kissed Chrissie's cheek. Chrissie kissed him back. Lightly on the nose. A tender, if slightly dismissive gesture. Gracious. Indulgent.

Tolerant.

Graham returned with their drinks. She continued to watch. Her unease remained.

Wednesday. Just as she had the previous week Mel was spending her lunchtime in a newsagent near the office scanning the gossip magazines.

This time there were two articles about Chrissie and Alexander. Though neither mentioned the party, both mentioned Alexander's visit to Norfolk, This time Chrissie was described as being the film's sole producer. She imagined Chrissie's delight and smiled.

There were pictures of Evelyne too with a new beau. Some male model with bland but perfect features.

According to Evelyne she had been the one to call time on her relationship with Alexander. There was also a subtle dig at Chrissie. 'We met her at an awards ceremony,' Evelyne announced. 'I was impressed by her: she's very sure of herself. The sort of person who knows what she wants and goes after it.' A backhanded compliment if ever there was one. The suggestion of gold-digging was too obvious to ignore.

Mel hoped Chrissie would ignore it. See it for the pathetic spite it was. Yet instinct told her Evelyne would soon be eating her words.

Buying three copies of each magazine she rushed back to show her colleagues.

Friday night. Back from Norfolk, Chrissie walked along the South Bank.

She was heading for the Queen Elizabeth Hall. An avant garde Czech dance troupe were doing a one-off performance and Alexander had booked tickets. 'I've been scanning *Time Out*,' he had told her on the phone, 'and it sounds just the sort of thing you'd enjoy.'

'But would *you* enjoy it?' she had asked him.

'Of course. Besides, as long as we're together I don't care what we do.'

The evening was cool: autumn finally starting to take hold. Her mobile buzzed in her pocket. No doubt it was Alexander, wanting to check on her progress. He had wanted to meet her train but she had told him it wasn't necessary. That they would be together soon enough. He had sounded ready to burst with excitement. She had been excited too. Or at least she had wanted to be.

The phone kept ringing. The sound was like an angry wasp; it made her feel hounded. In the distance she could see the NFT where, two months earlier, she had watched the Garbo film with Tara. Outside it people milled around long tables covered with second hand books. Approaching one of the tables she noticed a biography of Vivien Leigh. Picking it up she looked at the photographs in its centre while her phone continued to ring.

'Shouldn't you answer that?' said a voice.

'What's it to you?'

A laugh. 'Sorry. I should have known better than to ask.'

Looking up she saw Jack.

He was just as he always was. Scruffy. Unshaven. Impish. Perfect.

Her heart turned over. For a moment she thought her legs might collapse.

He smiled. She forced her lips upwards. Her face seemed made of lead.

'How are you?' he asked.

'I'm great. Really great.'

'I saw a picture of you and Alexander Gallen in a mag. You looked good together.'

'Thanks.'

'He looks like a nice bloke.'

'He is. I'm lucky to have met him.'

'I'm glad.' His smile remained and she knew he meant it. The realization stung like a flesh wound.

'And how is Ali? I gather you two are back together.'

'She's fine.' He glanced at his watch. 'I'm meeting her in a few minutes.' He gestured to the NFT. 'We're going to see a film.'

'Which one?'

'*The Phantom of the Opera.* The silent version. I remember you telling me how good it was supposed to be.'

And that we could see it together. Only you don't want to remember that.

'What about you?' he asked. 'Why are you here?'

'I'm meeting Alec. We're seeing a dance recital.'

'Not off to a star-studded party then?'

'No, that's tomorrow night. Some art exhibition. Invitation only.'

'Quite the jetsetter. Well, hey, I always knew you were out of my league.'

'No I wasn't.'

His smile became strained. Again he looked at his watch. 'I'd better go. Ali's asked me to buy the tickets and she'll kill me if it's sold out. I'm glad life is good. Take care, yeah?'

'Thanks. You too.'

He walked away. She remained where she was, reliving the moment all those years ago when she had thought she had seen her father. Watching him walk away. Feeling, just as she did now, that a wicked fairy had turned her body to stone.

Tears came to her eyes while her phone continued to ring.

Five minutes later she reached the Hall.

Alexander had arranged to meet her in the foyer. She saw him standing by the ticket office. Not feeling ready to face him she sought refuge in the ladies where she checked her reflection in the mirror. Her mascara was smudged. She looked a wreck. Just one brief meeting and all her strength had turned to dust.

What is wrong with you? What the hell are you doing? Giving a man power over you. Letting Tina win. You're better than this. If you want this to end then you know what you have to do. Who you have to be. The person I taught you how to be.

'Who's Tina?'

She turned. A woman nearby was staring at her.

'What?'

'You're talking to yourself.'

'No I'm not.'

The woman continued to stare. Turning back to the mirror she repaired the damage to her face.

'I was worried about you,' Alexander told her when she joined him. 'I tried to call.'

'Sorry, my phone was in my bag. Am I late?'

'No. There's still ten minutes to curtain up.'

The auditorium was packed. Their seats were at the centre. The best view in the house just as he had promised. Once they were settled he put his arm around her. 'I've missed you like mad. Have you missed me?'

'Of course. You don't need to ask.' She noticed a young woman in the row in front whispering to her companion before both turned to stare.

They've recognized Alec. They know who he is. Who we are. And they envy me.

She waited for the rush of jubilation. Of triumph and power. Only it never came. Pain continued to eat away at her insides, like acid dripping onto her heart.

Alexander was smiling at her: his face full of the warmth that once she had longed to see in her mother's. She tried to project the same emotion back while a single thought flashed inside her brain.

Why can't you make this pain go away?

The lights dimmed and the show began. Dancers moved like shadows, more like beings of air than of flesh and blood. One in particular caught her eye. A dark haired young man at the front of the stage, jerking like a puppet on elastic strings.

Alexander's arm tightened around her. She stared at the man, imagining that he was Jack. That he was a puppet dancing on flaming coals, wanting to escape but unable to do so, controlled by strings that only she could pull.

Saturday night. A private art showing at converted cellars in Bermondsey.

The event was packed. The artist had undergone crucifixion in the Philippines and created a series of paintings to reflect the experience. Though all were powerful, the most arresting piece was a video of the crucifixion itself played on a continual loop to a soundtrack of electronic music. Such had been the level of media coverage that the event was invitation only and journalists mingled with the guests, all studying the work and each other.

She stood with Alexander watching the film, wearing a new dress that he had bought her that morning. Again he had been the one to insist on buying it. All she had done was express an interest.

The film reached its conclusion. The artist, suspended on the cross slumped forward in a faint. A gasp went up from all those watching, most of whom then looked away as if disturbed by the image. She did the same and noticed a beautiful blonde young woman standing with a dark and equally beautiful young man and staring intensely at her. Evelyne.

She nudged Alexander. Evelyne and her companion approached. Leaving the screening area they went to meet them.

'Hello, Alec,' said Evelyne coolly. 'I didn't expect to see you here.'

'It's a lovely surprise. How are you?'

'Very well.' Evelyne gestured to her companion. 'This is Liam by the way.'

'Nice to meet you,' said Liam, offering his hand. His voice was flat and weak and diminished the impact of his appearance, like a silent film star undone by the coming of sound.

'And this is Chrissie,' said Alexander. 'Though you two have already met.'

Evelyne's eyes flicked over her dismissively. 'Have we?'

'At the Book Awards,' Chrissie told her.

'Oh, of course. You're making a low budget film aren't you? The one that's . . . what's the word? Psychological.' The tone was as dismissive as the eyes which focused on the dress she was wearing. 'Though I expect the budget's not so small any more.'

Alexander's hand stroked her back like an adult soothing a child. The gesture annoyed her. She was not a child and she had never needed anyone's protection.

'You're right there,' she replied. 'But that still won't make it any easier to follow.'

'No doubt I'll be able to decide for myself when I come to your big West End premiere.'

'You'll come? How wonderful. Saffron Ellis has already agreed to provide the star quality but we can still use as many pretty faces as we can get.'

The eyes became slits. 'Lovely dress by the way. I never realized film production could be so lucrative.'

'Alec bought it.' She rested her head on his shoulder. 'He's so good to me.'

'I'm sure you've more than *earned* your place in his affections.'

'Well, it wasn't hard. All it took was the brains to see him as something more than a PR opportunity.'

Gripping her arm Alexander steered her away. Looking back she saw Evelyne staring daggers at her. Raising her glass she blew a kiss.

'Don't.'

'Why not? She deserves it. If she'd looked any further down her nose at me she'd have gone cross-eyed.'

'You still shouldn't.'

'Because she's someone and I'm not? Sorry. How stupid of me to forget my place.'

'Why are you so angry?'

'After the way she behaved I have a right.'

'It's not just her. You've been like this since last night. What is it? Did something happen at work to upset you?'

'No.'

'Then is it me? Is it something I've done?'

'Oh, for Christ's sake!'

His eyes widened. She sensed people nearby falling silent. 'Don't shout,' he told her. 'People are staring.'

'So? Welcome to my world. That's what people like me have to do to get attention when we don't have money and a famous name to do the work for us.'

He swallowed. Hurt flooded his face. Momentarily she felt bad. Then she noticed Evelyne grinning and the feeling vanished.

'I can't help being who I am.' he said.

'Neither can I so do me a favour, OK?'

'OK.'

'Remember that not every feeling and mood I have is about you.'

The hurt returned. He looked younger suddenly. Vulnerable. Weak. She tried to summon shame but felt only contempt.

'I'm going to circulate,' she said before walking away and leaving him to stand alone.

Five minutes later she was back in the video area. The artist was lying on the cross, shuddering as nails were hammered into his hands. She watched but didn't see, her attention focused on the film running on a screen behind her eyes. The one that showed Jack lying on the cross, grimacing in agony as she drove the nails home.

Half an hour later. Alexander searched for Chrissie.

He found her in a quiet alcove leaning against the wall, deep in conversation with a man of about thirty. The man was leaning towards her, his body language signalling desire, which a laughing and clearly drunk Chrissie was doing nothing to discourage.

Anger rose up in him. He pushed it down. It was a dangerous emotion; one that poisoned everything it touched.

He cleared his throat. Chrissie turned. 'Hi Alec. This is Kieron.'

'Hello, Kieron. Chrissie, there's someone I'd like you to meet.'

She made no move towards him. 'Kieron's a journalist. He's been talking to Evelyne. Seems she's still insisting that she was the one who finished with you.'

'What does that matter?'

'Because it's not true.'

He didn't answer.

'Or maybe it is. Perhaps I've just caught you on the rebound.'

'I can't imagine any man needing to be on the rebound to want to be with you,' Kieron told her.

She stroked Kieron's cheek with her finger. 'Is that right?'

'Absolutely.'

'Then hold that thought. I may not be spoken for for much longer.'

'You're not a rebound. Evelyne never broke up with me. I'm with you because I love you. You know that, don't you?'

A softness came into her face. 'Yes, I know it. Poor Alec.'

'He's hardly that,' said Kieron archly.

'Yes he is. If people love me I hurt them. That's my talent. That's who I am.'

'I wouldn't mind being hurt by you.'

'Yes you would. You just don't know it yet.' Leaning forward she kissed Kieron, biting down on his lower lip, making him wince.

'Come on Alec,' she said suddenly. 'Let's meet these friends of yours.'

'Chrissie . . .'

She moved out of the alcove, covering his mouth with her finger. 'I'm here, aren't I? I'm with you. Isn't that enough?'

As they walked away he looked back. Kieron was watching Chrissie, his eyes hungry with desire. Like those of a predator stalking its prey.

The anger returned, this time laced with fear.

Three hours later. Back at his flat he made coffee for Chrissie and himself.

She was sitting on the sofa in the living room, smoking and staring into space. He wanted to touch her but her body language did not invite intimacy. Music wafted from the CD speakers while outside people laughed loudly on the street below.

'I'm sorry,' she said eventually. 'For tonight, for acting like a bitch. Blame it on the drink. It always brings out the worst in me.'

He nodded, wanting to believe it *was* just the drink yet sensing otherwise.

'Evelyne was a bitch too,' he told her.

'But you wanted me to back down in front of her. Only I never back down. I learned the hard way that if someone attacks you then you have to fight back. You never show weakness. If you show weakness you lose everything.'

'You won't lose me.'

Silence.

'Will I lose you?'

'Who to? Kieron? He's a creep. I was only talking to him because I was pissed off with you and Evelyne.' A sigh. 'Thanks.'

'For what?'

'For backing me up. For not letting her win.'

'It's not a competition.'

'Yes it is. Win or die. I learned that the hard way too. Never let anyone get the better of you. Fight every step of the way.' Bitterness crept into her voice. 'Thanks, Dad. I owe you for that.'

'It wasn't your fault that he left.'

'How do you know that?'

'Because I know you.'

'You didn't know her. She's the one he walked out on and I'm glad because it made me strong. Made me change into someone no one would ever want to leave. Only it didn't work. People still leave. They still walk away and never look back.'

Jack? Is that who you're talking about? Is that what this is really about?

'Stupid, ugly and useless. That's what my mother used to call me. Maybe she was right. Maybe everything else is just window dressing. You can't hide who you are.'

'You don't need to hide it from me. I love you.'

'I know you do. Poor Alec.' Softly she began to sing. 'I beg your pardon. I never promised you a rose garden.' As he listened a memory crept into his head.

Standing by the window in the house in Amberton watching his grandmother lovingly tending the flowers in her garden before creeping out later and uprooting them all.

'Do you want to end it?' she asked.

He swallowed. His throat suddenly dry.

'Do you?'

'No.'

'No. You just want to make me happy. You're a good person.'

Another memory. Of returning to this same flat from the hospital after watching his grandmother die of an unexpected heart attack. Of walking through its rooms feeling totally, utterly alone. Feeling that whatever stabilizers had existed in his life had been yanked away and that any minute he could topple and fall with no one there who cared enough to help him rise again.

'I don't want to end it. I love you, Chrissie. Who do I have if I don't have you?'

'Your cousins.'

'I don't matter to them. We hardly know each other. If I died tomorrow the only thing they'd care about is what would happen to my money.'

'What about Graham? You said he was like a brother.'

'But he has Gail. I don't matter to him any more. Not like I matter to you.'

Silence. He waited for a denial but none came. But no agreement either.

'Chrissie . . .'

'I'm sorry if I upset you tonight. I didn't mean to. Don't take any notice of me, Alec. Tomorrow I'll be myself again. I'll be the person my dad taught me to be.'

At last she moved towards him, allowing him to pull her close.

Yet still the sense of distance remained.

That night Chrissie dreamed she was back at the South Bank.

It seemed the whole of London was walking by the water. She pushed through the crowds, searching for Jack but seeing her father standing by the wall, holding a little girl who was sitting on it, laughing and pointing to the boats that slid past in the water. *Persephone* was one of them. Jack stood by the tiller with Ali, the two of them holding hands, oblivious to everything except each other.

She edged closer to her father. The girl he was holding looked like Tina yet was nothing like her at all. This Tina was confident and fearless – a child any parent would be proud of. A child no one could ever leave.

She touched her father's arm, breathing in the smell of him. He turned towards her, his eyes blank. 'I don't know you,' he said. 'You're nothing to me.'

'I was once.'

'No you weren't. I was just killing time.' He kissed the child's head. 'I have what I want now. She is everything to me. Nothing in this world could make me leave her, not even for a day.'

He turned back towards the water. Again she touched him. Saw him flinch. Saw a knife in her hand, its surface red with blood.

When she woke the room was in darkness. Sitting up in bed she lit a cigarette, blowing smoke into the air, watching it dance before her like the ghost of a murdered child. Beside her Alexander moved restlessly in his sleep, disturbed perhaps by dreams of his own. Turning over, he draped his arm around her. She pushed it away, feeling his need and despising it. The cigarette glowed in the darkness. She wanted to grind it out against his chest. Drive it into his skin like the nails in the crucifixion. Instead she drove it into her own hand. It hurt but not enough to take the pain away. Only the rage could do that.

The window was open. She heard women's voices in the street below and imagined them stopping and pointing. 'That's Chrissie Ryan up there. The one who kicked Evelyne Cauldwell into touch. The one who's someone. The one with the perfect life. The one we all wish we could be.'

Only they wouldn't. Not if they knew. Not if they really knew.

She felt adrift. Lost. Frightened. Of what she could do to others.

Of what she could do to herself.

*

Tuesday lunchtime. Karen sat at home reading an article in a tabloid newspaper.

Its heading was 'From Duckling to Swan: The Metamorphosis of Gallen's Girl'. It described a plain, timid, working-class girl who had turned herself into a beauty and gone on to have a successful career and win the heart of one of the most eligible men in the country. Its tone was admiring. Holding Chrissie up as an example of how drive and willpower could get you whatever or whomever you wanted. She thought of the hatchet jobs she had read in the past and felt a sense of relief. It could have been so much worse.

Yet still it upset her.

How would Chrissie feel, seeing Tina lain bare for all the world to gawp at? She wouldn't like it, that was for sure. She wouldn't like it at all.

Later she made her way to the shops, watching everyone she passed. Suspicious of all of them. Feeling as if she were surrounded by spies.

As Karen did her shopping Chrissie read the article herself.

She was on set again. The shoot was only days from completion and a celebratory atmosphere surrounded her. Already there was a feeling that the film was a winner that could boost the careers of all involved.

But she didn't care about that.

'She was so quiet,' said one former classmate who had chosen to remain nameless. 'She never spoke at

380

all. Most of the time we forgot she was there. Even the teachers did. That was how little impression she made.'

Who had said these things? Who had betrayed her? Who had told these lies?

Elly the continuity girl came to join her. 'Did you know that piece was running?'

She shook her head.

'I read it this morning. It's quite good actually. I guess you've got Evelyne to thank for that. A friend of mine's a journalist and he says that he and his colleagues think she's a stuck up bitch. That's why they want to write nice things about you. It rubs her nose in it.'

'Are you fucking kidding?'

Elly jumped.

'This isn't nice. It's shit. I was never like that. I was never her.'

'Her?'

'This weakling they're talking about. Does that sound like me? I bet most of the people they've spoken to have never even met me.'

Elly pointed to a class photograph. 'But that's you, isn't it? The one on the end.'

'No,' she said before she could stop herself.

'Yes it is. Anyway, what's the big deal? So, you were shy at school. What's wrong with that? I was too. Loads of people were.'

'You don't get it, do you?'

'Get what? You're going out with a celebrity who, it

seems, dumped another celebrity to be with you. There's bound to be media interest. You just have to deal with it.'

'Or dump him.'

'Are you nuts? If I was in your shoes the papers could write the nastiest stuff in the world and I wouldn't care.'

'You would if it was lies.'

'It's tomorrow's chip paper. Who's going to remember what it says? And anyway, what do you think the papers will say if you dump him?'

'Who cares?'

'You should. There'll still be media interest only it might not be so complimentary. People might say you were just using him to get publicity for yourself and the film.' A pause. 'Or that he dumped you.'

'They wouldn't say that.'

'They might. And even if they don't the public perception of Alec is of a decent guy who, in spite of all his money, has had some tough breaks. If you're seen to hurt him then people will think you're a bitch.'

She shook her head, feeling suddenly trapped.

'Look, Chrissie, you're bound to feel freaked out but don't do anything stupid because of it. You don't really want to dump Alec, do you? You care about him, don't you?'

She didn't answer.

'Don't you?'

'Of course.'

'Then keep remembering that. I've got to check the layout for the new scene. Talk later, OK?'

'OK.'

Elly left. Chrissie remained where she was, staring at the photograph of ten-year-old Tina, standing at the back of the class trying not to be noticed. Trying not to exist.

Picking up her cigarette she drove the butt into Tina's face, burning it away.

That evening she sat in the pub with Elly, Bob, and all her other friends from the set, just as they always did. The same as any other evening.

Only now it would never be the same again.

She acted as if everything was fine. As if she didn't have a care in the world, yet all the time she was studying them, searching for changes in their behaviour.

Because they knew about Tina. The secret she had always tried to keep hidden. The person she had thought was buried for ever.

Wayne the stand-in was telling funny stories about Duncan. She laughed along with the rest of them while watching their faces, waiting for looks of pity. Of surprise. Of contempt.

Bob was beside her. As Wayne continued to talk he touched her arm. 'Are you OK?'

'Why wouldn't I be?'

'That thing in the paper. Elly said it freaked you out.'

'Naturally. It's all lies. People who never knew me making up stuff just to see their words in print.'

He nodded.

'I mean, can you see me just blending into the background. Being that pathetic victim they were talking about? I was never like that.'

Another nod.

'Don't you believe me?'

'Of course, Ballsy.' His tone was warm though she sensed a lack of conviction in his use of her nickname.

Or was that paranoia?

She tried to focus on Wayne's stories but her head ached and she felt claustrophobic so she sought sanctuary in the ladies, locking herself in a cubicle, needing space to think.

Two minutes passed. The door opened. She heard footsteps, then the sound of taps running. That and two voices.

'She's not so stunning in the flesh. She looks better in photos.'

'Fantastic figure though. Looks like she'd be great in bed.'

'Do you think that's why Alexander Gallen's with her?'

'Probably. Who'd want to date a model? They're so thin. It must be like shagging a broom. No normal guy wants to do that.'

'How long do you think they'll last?'

'Not long. With his money he could have anyone he wants. She looks sexy, but hard. Not classy. He could do better.'

'Like you for example.'

'Naturally. One look at me and she'd be history. How long do *you* think they'll last?'

'A couple of months.'

'I'll give it two weeks.'

More laughter. She felt as if she were back at school, hiding from bullies gathered in packs ready to tear her to shreds. Rage surged through her like fire. Opening the cubicle door she walked out. Two pretty girls barely out of their teens stood checking their make-up in the mirror. She began to do the same while they watched her with dropped jaws.

'You're right,' she said coolly. 'I *am* great in bed.'

Both turned crimson.

'And smart too. Far too smart to badmouth some-one sitting three feet away.'

'I'm sorry . . .' began the one who had boasted about taking Alexander away from her.

'Why? I'm sure Alec would be putty in your hands. I'll bring him here one night so you can meet him. A word of advice though, don't undo so many buttons on your blouse. For someone who knows all about being classy it's a pretty basic mistake to make.'

Both turned and left. She remained where she was, imagining similar conversations taking place in wash-rooms across the country. Of people taking bets on how long she and Alexander would last.

Of how long she would last.

Because even if she were the one to end it people like that would never believe it.

She stared at her reflection but didn't see it. A timid ten-year-old stared back at her.

The sense of being trapped increased.

Later, in her hotel room, she phoned Aunty Karen.

'Are you still angry with me?' she asked.

'Of course not. I miss you and I want to see you. I could come up next week. Whenever's convenient for you.'

'Anytime. You don't need an appointment.'

'Your mother's going to the doctor on Saturday.'

'Tell her I'll be thinking of her.'

'Why not tell her yourself?'

She didn't answer.

'It wasn't her that talked to the papers.'

'Then who did?'

'I don't know.'

'If I find out I'll make them sorry.'

'Why? Tina's gone. She's never coming back. That piece was about a ghost.'

'I don't believe in ghosts. Once you're dead you stay buried.'

'Does Jack stay buried?'

'Yes. He's nothing to me any more. I know you don't believe me but it's true. Let me know when you're coming; it'll be good to see you.'

The call finished she summoned Jack's picture onto the screen, imagining him reading the article and discovering Tina for the first time. Only there would be no discovery. He knew Tina already. She had let him glimpse her when they had been together. When she had loved him. When he had made her weak.

And she hated him for that. Almost as much as she hated Tina.

She lit a cigarette. Again she thought of driving nails into his flesh. Of making him sorry. Of making him scream. Punish him for leaving her, just like her father had.

The tears came. She let them fall, alone in her hotel room where no one could see.

Saturday afternoon. She walked through Little Venice with Alexander.

They had had lunch at Mel's. Just the three of them. Rick was away on yet another business trip. Mel had talked about the article, expressing surprise at its content. Chrissie had laughed it away, dismissing it as lies while sensing Alexander watching her, worrying, perhaps, that she blamed him for it. Which she did.

His sports car was parked in a side street. As he unlocked the doors she checked her purse. 'I need more cigarettes.'

'We can get them in Kensington.'

'I want them now. There's a place nearby.'

'Where?'

'What does it matter? You don't need to come. We're not joined at the hip.'

'I'm sorry for the article.'

'You didn't write it.'

'But it's because of me that it was written. I know it upset you.'

'It didn't upset me. Come or stay here. It's up to you.'

She moved away. He followed, like a dog pulled by an invisible lead. She slowed her pace, feeling hounded. Feeling trapped.

Nearby was a small parade of shops and cafes. She bought her cigarettes from a newsagent on the corner. Outside she stopped to light one while he hovered beside her, shifting from one foot to another, clearly sensing her irritation and uncertain what to do about it. She wished he would grow angry. Shout. Only that wasn't his style. Dogs, like leopards, could never change their spots.

Suddenly she heard a familiar laugh. Turning she saw Jack. He was with Ali: the two of them arm in arm and heading in her direction. The sight of them made her feel sick.

He saw her too. For a moment he look alarmed. Then he smiled. She smiled back, wanting to walk away but unable to do so. Like a junkie desperate for any sort of fix.

'Hi, Jack,' she called out. 'How are you?'

'I'm fine.' The two of them approached. 'And you?'

'Never better. We've just had lunch with a friend who lives here. This is my boyfriend Alec by the way.'

Alexander offered his hand. 'And you must be Ali,' she said, offering her own. 'It's so nice to meet you.'

'Likewise,' said Ali. The handshake was limp. Her sense of strength returned.

'What are you two up to?' she asked.

'Just going for a coffee. The gas is off on the boat.'

'Not again. That was always happening when I used to visit.'

Ali nodded, her expression wary.

'That's what we're doing too,' she announced. 'Why don't we join you?'

'I thought we were going home,' said Alexander.

'Why? We've nothing planned, have we?'

'No, I guess not.'

'Good. How about Carlitto's? You like their pastries, don't you, Jack?' She rolled her eyes at Ali. 'You know what a bottomless pit his stomach is.'

'Sure.'

'Then that's decided.' Smiling, she led the way.

Nick Hooper, paparazzi photographer, sat at one of the outside tables at Carlitto's, finishing his capuccino. A famous Hollywood star, currently making nightly appearances in a West End play and, it was rumoured, equally frequent appearances in his co-star's bed, was staying in the area and enjoying an unexpected and reputedly fraught visit from his wife. The two of them were regular visitors to Carlitto's but Nick's hopes that they would appear that afternoon appeared to be in vain.

As he prepared to leave he noticed two young couples

enter the cafe. He recognized Alexander Gallen, together with his new girlfriend, the film producer Chrissie something. Though their story was not as newsworthy, he remembered a conversation he had had with a journalist friend called Kieron the previous night. 'I met them at an art show,' Kieron had told him. 'I had a long talk with her and she was definitely up for it but then he turned up and she went all cold.' Nick, aware that Kieron considered himself God's gift to women had nodded and kept his scepticism to himself.

'It's an odd relationship,' Kieron had also said. 'He's the one with the money and connections. You'd think he'd have all the power but it's like she's got him on a string. She must be an amazing lay.'

'Not that you'll ever know.'

'I wouldn't want to. She's a bit full on for me.'

It had been rubbish, obviously. Just Kieron's ego trying to protect itself.

But in spite of that Nick decided to stick around.

Five minutes later. Chrissie sat next to Alexander, facing Jack and Ali. A waitress took their order. She tried to tempt Jack into having a pastry but he declined. 'That's a first,' she remarked to Ali. 'You must be a star in the kitchen.'

'She certainly is,' agreed Jack. 'Her beans on toast are the best in town.'

Ali looked embarrassed. 'I can cook more than that.'

'I know. You're a great cook.' He squeezed her shoulder.

Chrissie stubbed out her cigarette. 'So where's the love of your life?'

Ali looked startled. 'What do you mean?'

'Bullseye. No woman could ever compete with that mutt, no matter how good she is with a frying pan.'

'He's back on the boat.'

'Well at least it's moored. Has Jack told you about Bullseye nearly drowning when we went down the Thames. Not that it was Jack's fault. He was otherwise engaged at the time.'

'Otherwise engaged?'

'Below deck, leaving me to steer. Why? What did you think I meant?'

'Nothing.'

'Probably trying to fix the gas.' She laughed. 'Some things never change.'

'How's your film?' Jack asked.

'Great. We finished shooting yesterday. Next weekend we're having a wrap party here in town. Our American investors want to sample Swinging London nightlife.'

'It's a great film,' added Alexander. 'It's going to be a big hit.'

His enthusiasm annoyed her. 'How would you know? You haven't seen it.'

'Well, from what you've said. Everyone seems to be really excited about it.'

'Film people have to be excited. So much rides on each production, at least for those of us who don't have trust funds to fall back on.'

He blinked, his colour rose slightly. 'I'm just teasing,' she told him before turning back to Jack. 'It should be a good party. Why don't you two come?'

'We can't,' said Ali.

'Why not? It's not going to be exclusive. You wouldn't feel out of place.'

'It's not that.'

'Then what?'

Apart from the fact that you feel threatened by me. It's written all over your face.

'We'll be in Winchester,' Jack explained. 'I'm meeting Ali's parents for the first time.' He grinned. 'So wish me luck.'

'You don't need luck,' Ali told him. 'Just be yourself and they'll love you.'

Chrissie nodded. 'Just don't light a spliff in front of them. That never goes down well.'

Jack's hand was on the table. Ali covered it with her own. Chrissie repressed an urge to ram a fork through it.

Their coffees arrived. She lit another cigarette. 'Tell me,' she asked Ali, 'do you have a big family . . .'

Jack poured sugar into his coffee. Ali nudged his arm. 'Taste it first.'

'Why? I like it sweet.'

'Greedy!' She tweaked his nose. An uncharacteristically proprietorial gesture. Chrissie was clearly making her uncomfortable. He wished they were somewhere else.

'Do you?' Chrissie asked Ali.

'What?'

'Have a big family?'

'Not big. One sister.'

'You're lucky. I always wanted a sister. I think that's always the way with only children.' Chrissie turned to Alexander. 'Did you want a brother when you were growing up?'

Alexander nodded. 'Though at least I've got Graham. He's like a brother.'

'Well you've certainly been like one to him. How many people have friends who'd pay the mortgage if they fell behind?'

Ali looked impressed. 'That was good of you.'

'It was nothing,' said Alexander quickly.

'Don't get embarrassed,' Chrissie told him. 'It *was* good of you. Especially as you'll never see a penny back.'

'That's not important,' Alexander replied. His voice sounded tight. Jack sensed that he and Ali weren't the only ones who wanted to be somewhere else.

'Of course it's not.' Chrissie stroked Alexander's hair. 'You're a generous guy. Too generous sometimes. Good thing I'm here to stop people taking advantage of you.'

'Graham's not taking advantage of me.'

'Did I say that?' Her fingers tightened in his hair, pulling his head towards her and kissing him on the lips. 'Don't be so touchy,' she said softly. 'There's no need.' He kissed her back. Warmth flooded his face. He was obviously in love with her. As dazzled by her as if she were the midday sun.

Poor guy.

Chrissie turned back to Ali. 'Are you close to your sister?'

'Quite.'

'Thought so. Sisters are always close. Not like brothers who are competitive. Sisters share more. Make-up. Secrets.'

Ali nodded. 'Though they can be competitive too.'

'That's true. Particularly over boyfriends.' Chrissie gave Alexander's hair another tug. 'Good thing I've got no sisters to steal you away from me.'

Jack felt a lurch in his stomach.

'No one could steal me from you,' Alexander replied.

Again she kissed him. 'What's your sister's name?' she asked Ali.

'Debbie.'

'That's a nice name. Do you like it Alec?'

'Yes.'

'More than mine?'

'No.'

'Good. That's how it should be. Just as Jack shouldn't

394

like the name Debbie more than Ali. That's right, isn't it, Jack? You don't prefer Debbie to Ali do you?'

Again Jack felt a lurch. Only this time it was far stronger.

She knows. Jesus Christ, she knows!

She turned towards him, her eyes as hard as stone. '*Do* you?'

'No. Nowhere near.'

'I'm glad to hear it.'

Though his coffee was steaming he began to gulp it down. Eager to finish and escape.

Ali sipped her hot chocolate and watched Jack swallow his coffee. He seemed in a hurry to finish it. Perhaps he was as eager to leave as she was. She hoped so.

A drop of dark liquid fell onto her blouse. She wiped it away with a paper napkin. 'Can't take me anywhere,' she said with a laugh.

'Don't worry,' Alexander told her. 'We all do it.'

'Well Jack certainly does,' said Chrissie with a smile. 'When we were out together I used to want to tie a bib around his neck.'

Jack continued to slurp his coffee. Ali felt protective. 'He's not that messy.'

'I'm only teasing him. You know I'm only teasing, don't you, Jack?'

He nodded.

'See. No need to take offence.'

'I wasn't. I was just . . .' Ali stopped, uncertain of

what to say. Not wanting to look stupid or gauche. Chrissie continued to smile; the beautiful green eyes focused totally upon her making her feel like an exhibit under a microscope just as she had all those times when Chrissie had come to the cafe. Self-conscious. Exposed.

Threatened.

It wasn't just the intensity of the gaze. It was Chrissie herself. The aura she projected. Strength. Purpose. Force of will. Someone who knew how to get what she wanted.

Does she still want Jack?

Ali smiled back, feeling drab and dreary. Extinguished completely by someone whose light burned so much brighter than her own. A drop of cream slid down her mug. She wiped it away while beside her the slurping continued. Jack's shoulders were hunched. She sensed his discomfort. Again she hoped it was due to embarrassment. And not desire.

Does he still want her? Is that why he's uncomfortable?

Chrissie offered her cigarettes around. Ali declined, as did Jack. Alexander too until Chrissie pressed him. 'Come on, what gentleman lets a lady smoke alone.' The description struck Ali as apt. There was something of the gentleman about Alexander. He was very handsome. More conventionally good-looking than Chrissie but with none of her magnetism. In an argument she imagined Chrissie eating him alive.

Jack finished his coffee and glanced at his watch. 'We must go. I need to fix the gas.' A waitress walked by and he asked for the bill. Again Ali felt self-conscious. 'Do you two want anything else?'

Chrissie shook her head. Making the decision, just as she had expected.

The bill arrived. Ali reached for her purse. 'How much is it?'

'Don't worry. Alec'll get this.' Chrissie turned to Alexander. 'You don't mind, do you? After all, we did crash their party.' Her tone was firm. Less a request than a command.

Alexander took out his wallet, produced a credit card and handed the tray back to the waitress.

'Thank you,' Ali said. 'It's very kind.'

'My pleasure,' he replied with a smile.

Chrissie turned away, her eyes wandering over the other patrons while fiddling with a lock of her hair. Her fingers were strong. Ali watched them move, imagining them caressing Jack. Feeling suddenly jealous.

Alexander watched them too. Hesitantly he stroked one. Chrissie, preoccupied, pushed him away as if dispelling a pesky insect. For a split second his smile faded. A look of intense hostility came into his face. Raw. Savage. Momentarily Ali felt chilled.

Then it was gone. The smile returned.

He hates her. He loves her but he also hates her.
Really hates her.

She shivered.

Jack caught her eye. 'OK?'

'OK,' she told him, forcing on a smile of her own.

The waitress returned with the credit card slip. Alexander signed it, adding a generous tip while aware of Chrissie staring into space. On the other side of the table Jack draped his arm around Ali, giving her cheek an affectionate peck. Feeling like a voyeur he tried to mask the fact that he was watching.

While sensing that Chrissie, in spite of her apparent nonchalance, was watching too.

Because she cared about him in spite of her denials. And she still does.

He didn't want to believe it yet every instinct he possessed told him it was true. That what he had only suspected was cold, hard fact.

Again the feeling of being unbalanced. Of being alone. The feeling he hated above all others. The one Chrissie alone could make disappear. But only if she chose to stay.

Jack caught his eye and gave him a grin. He grinned back feeling hate surge through him so hot he thought he might combust.

This is your fault. We'd be happy if it wasn't for you.

Everything would be perfect if you didn't exist.

He tried to push the feeling down into the secret place inside himself where all dark things were buried. The place with no air where they could be left to wither and die. Only they didn't. They lived on. Feeding on each other to grow strong again.

Too strong?

He thought of the back bedroom in Amberton. Pictured a door he thought had been locked for ever. The image frightened him yet drew him like a siren's song, luring him back inside to rediscover what was stored there.

He turned away, catching his reflection in the glass at the front of the shop. His expression was calm. Tranquil. Giving no clue to the turmoil within.

Nick Hooper watched the two young couples rise from their table. Rising from his own he moved to the corner of the street, his camera in his hand.

They emerged from the restaurant and said their farewells. A simple scene with nothing in it to make it newsworthy yet some instinct told him to record the moment. He took some shots then moved away, heading towards the West End and whatever new stories the evening might deliver.

Two hours later. The gas now fixed Ali made coffee while Bullseye bounced around her feet, begging for treats.

Jack sat on the sofa, smoking a cigarette, staring into space. She went to join him. 'Why didn't you accept one of Chrissie's? You could have saved yourself 20p.'

'I'm not that hard up.'

'Every penny counts.' She laughed. 'God, I sound like my mother.'

'Do you think she'll like me?'

'Of course. They both will.'

'Just be myself, eh?'

'Yes. That'll be enough for them. It is for me.'

He smiled but didn't answer.

'Is it for you?'

'What do you mean?'

'Me. Am I enough for you?'

'You know you are.'

'Even after seeing her again?'

'Because of that. Not that I needed convincing.'

'What did you think of Alec?'

'Nice.'

'I thought he was unhappy.'

'He will be if he stays with her.'

'Why?'

'Because she's damaged. That makes her dangerous.'

To us? Is that what you mean? Is she a threat to us?

She needed reassurance yet didn't want to ask for it. Not wanting to appear clingy. Knowing he was a free spirit. Someone who never wanted to be tied down. Hating the silence she sought to end it. 'She was wrong about sisters, they're not always close. I haven't heard from Debbie for weeks.'

'Have you tried to call?'

'No.'

'There we are. You're both just busy.'

'Have you spoken to your brother?'

'Why would I? I don't need him telling me what a loser I am.'

'You're not a loser, Jack. That's the last thing you are.'

'My dad thought I was. He never said it but I knew he felt it. My brother gets his estate to administer and my mother to take care of and what do I get? Just some records. That shows what he really thought about me.'

'That's not true.'

'How can you say that? You never knew him.'

'But I feel like I do. You talk about him all the time. The things you did together; the amount of times you sat up all night talking. He thought the world of you.'

'But not as much as he did of my brother.'

'Have you ever thought that maybe he gave your brother the responsibility to try and make him feel as special as he made you feel. And as special as you made him feel?'

He shook his head. 'You don't really think that.'

'Yes I do. Your dad was proud of you, Jack. So you didn't go to college and end up with some high powered job but who cares about that? You are who you are. You never pretend to be someone you're not and that takes strength. I know it and your dad did too.'

'I know something,' he said softly. 'About my dad.'

'What?'

'That he would have loved you. Almost as much as I do.'

She felt a lift in her heart. 'You've never said that before.'

'But I'm saying it now. I love you, Ali, and I don't want to lose you.'

The warmth in his voice evaporated her fears. Leaning forward she hugged him. 'You're not going to. Not ever. I promise you that.'

He didn't answer. Just hugged her back. Tightly. As if his life depended on it.

As Jack and Ali sat together on the boat Chrissie wrote in her diary.

It's hours since I saw him but I can still smell him. It's not the same smell Dad had. It's softer. Sweeter. I can taste it in my mouth. It's like when you're a kid and you've eaten chocolate and keep a bit on your tongue to remind you of how good it was.

Only it wasn't good. It hurt. Seeing them together. Watching her touch him the way I used to. Loving him the way I used to.

The way I still do.

I hate him. I want him to suffer. I want to hurt him like he's hurt me. But had he turned to me at that table and asked me to go away with him for ever I would have done it. I want him that much. I need him that much.

Just like Tina needed her father.

I don't know who I am any more. I look in the mirror and see a fake. Someone who's not as tough as she thinks she is. Just as Bob tried to warn me. I feel scared. The only thing that makes me feel safe is the rage.

But that scares me too. Of what it could do. Of what it could make me do.

Twenty minutes later. Alexander prepared supper in the kitchen. Yet another attempt to make up for the article.

Chrissie appeared in the doorway. 'What were you doing?' he asked.

'Writing my diary.'

'About Jack?'

'And if I was?'

'Nothing. Just asking.'

'Are you threatened by him?'

'Should I be?'

'I told you what happened between us. It was all on his side. Don't you believe me?'

No

'Yes.'

'But still you're threatened. I can see it in your eyes.' She walked towards him, tracing their outline with her finger. 'What are you, Alec? A man or a mouse?'

'I want to be what you need me to be.'

'And what is that?'

403

Desperation swept over him. 'You tell me.'

A softness came into her face. It looked like pity. 'Don't ask me that.'

'Why not?'

'Because you might not like the answer.'

'Tell me anyway.'

'I don't need anything. That's my answer. Need is weak. Don't you understand that?'

He nodded.

'But still you feel it for me. I guess that answers my question.'

'Chrissie . . .'

'I'm going to call Aunty Karen. Fix a time for her visit.' She gestured towards the cooker. 'That smells lovely. You spoil me. I don't deserve you.'

She walked away. He watched her go, feeling dizzy with the multitude of emotions that swept over him. Love. Anger. Need. Hate. Fear.

She closed the door behind her, while in his head he saw another door open.

Monday morning. Jack phoned Chrissie.

'This is a surprise,' she told him. Only it wasn't, she had expected him to call.

'I need to talk to you.'

'Then talk.'

'Face to face.'

'I'm busy. I could probably manage a coffee at the end of the week.'

'No. Today. It must be today.'

'Why must it? Because it's what you want? Sorry, Jack. You can't just click your fingers and expect me to come running. Those days are over.'

'Please, Chrissie.' He sounded frantic. She felt glad. Or at least she wanted to.

'Where are you?' she asked.

'On the boat.'

'And Ali? Is she at work?'

'Yes.'

'Then I'll come now.'

She put down the phone and reached for her bag.

Lunchtime. Alexander let himself into the flat. Though he knew it would be empty he still called out Chrissie's name. Needing to check. To be sure.

But there was no answer. No sound at all except for the pounding of his heart.

He made his way towards their bedroom, preparing to do what had to be done. As he reached the door he hesitated.

Don't do this. What's seen cannot be unseen. What's known cannot be unknown.

But he had to know. So he did it anyway.

Chrissie reached the boat. Jack sat in the bow smoking a cigarette and looking anxious. 'I thought you weren't coming,' he told her.

'Why not? I said I would. What's so urgent that it couldn't wait?'

He didn't answer. Just beckoned her inside. Bullseye ran towards her, barking a greeting. She noticed a new cotton apron hanging on a peg. As soft and feminine as the one she had burned. The cabin was tidy. Flowers stood in a vase on the side next to a photograph of a smiling middle-aged couple. Chick lit novels and pop CDs covered other surfaces. Ali's influence was everywhere.

Sitting down she lit a cigarette. 'Why am I here?'

'What is it that you think you know?'

'It's too early in the day to be cryptic.'

'You know what I mean.'

'So you're a mindreader, are you? Or is that just another dope-induced hallucination? I need an ashtray by the way.'

He brought her one. Bullseye climbed onto the sofa and tried to lick her face. She imagined him doing the same to Ali and pushed him roughly away.

'Don't,' Jack told her.

'Why not? He's only a dog. All I have to do is pat him on the head and he'll love me. That's the great thing about animals. They're so much easier to please than people.'

'Maybe you should get one then.'

'What's that supposed to mean?'

'They're also easier to control. An animal won't ever leave you the way a person might.'

'People don't leave me. Not if I don't want them to. Anyway, what does that have to do with my being here?'

'You know why you're here.'

'Still playing the mindreader. It's getting boring.' Stubbing out her cigarette she rose to her feet.

'That stuff about Ali's sister. What did you mean by that?'

'Just an observation. Ali's your girlfriend. It wouldn't be very chivalrous to prefer her sister.'

'I don't.'

'Not now. But what about before. When it happened?'

'What happened?'

'When you slept with her. Because you did, didn't you? Tim let it slip.' She shook her head. 'That was stupid, Jack. Telling other people. Something like that is always best kept to yourself.'

He stared at her, his face rigid with tension. Again she tried to feel pleased; to feel strong. To feel nothing for him but contempt.

'How could you do that to her?'

'It only happened once.'

'Who cares how many times it happened?'

'It was a mistake.'

'Down to dope again, was it? Still playing the kid, Jack. Isn't it time to grow up and take responsibility for your actions.'

'That's up to me, isn't it?'

'I think Ali should know what sort of person she's involved with.'

'Why? What does it matter to you? You're with Alec now. A nice guy who's clearly crazy about you. I made a mistake but that's all it was. If Ali finds out she'll only be hurt. I don't want to do that, why should you?'

'Because she stole from me!'

It came out as a scream. He jumped. A frightened Bullseye slunk away.

'You were mine and then she came along and took you and I hate her for that.'

'I wasn't yours. You ended it with me.'

'And it didn't take you long to move on, did it? I saw you together that Sunday night. I came to see you and found you already back with her. The two of you kissing and hugging. Acting like I didn't even exist!'

'You ended it, not me. It was you.'

'And do you know why? Because I was scared.'

'Why were you scared?'

'Because I love you. That's why.'

He stared at her. She reached for her cigarette and realized her hand was shaking.

'That's what I was coming to tell you that Sunday. When I saw you with her.'

'This is crazy.'

'It's the truth.'

'Is it hell!'

It was her turn to jump.

408

'You don't love me. You can't love anyone. You don't know how.'

The words felt like a blow. 'That's not true.'

'Yes it is. Loving someone means giving them power over you and that's the one thing you can't do. You have to be in control at all times. That's the only way you feel safe.'

'It's not true!'

'Then why haven't you had any real relationships?'

'I have! What was Kev? What was Angus?'

'You don't have relationships. You have campaigns. It's not about love it's about conquest. If you meet a guy you like you hammer him into submission. Turn him into a doormat who can never hurt you, and the really sad thing is that when the war is over you despise him for letting you win. You turn men into eunuchs then discard them for having no balls.'

'You don't know what you're talking about.'

'Don't I? You were the one who was going on about Ali knowing the truth about me. Well this is the truth about you.' He began to laugh. 'And it hurts, doesn't it?'

'Don't you dare laugh at me!'

'Why not? I bet you laughed at them. You didn't care that you'd hurt them.'

'Well why should I? If they were real men they wouldn't have let me. It's not my fault they're weak!'

'But it's not their fault they're not your father!'

409

They stared at each other. He was breathing hard. So was she.

'Because that's what this is about. What it's always been about. You pretend not to remember him when really he dominates your whole life! If you control a man then he can't leave you the way your father did. You're the one that leaves, damaging their lives in the process just like your father damaged yours.'

'Well what if it is? They all deserve it. Men!' She spat the word out. 'They're all bastards who think they can walk away whenever they want and never worry about the pain they leave behind. If I hurt them then they got what they deserved. I'm only doing to them what they want to do to others.'

'You think I'm like that?'

'Of course you are; you're a man. That's what you're going to do to Ali because she's too fucking weak to stop you!'

'You're wrong. I love Ali. She's never tried to control me the way you did.'

'I didn't try to control you.'

'You suffocated me. It was like you were whittling away at me all the time. Trying to make me feel worthless and grateful. Trying to neuter me like you did the others so I'd never leave you. So you could be the one that did the leaving.'

She shook her head. 'It was different with you.'

'Only because I got wise to you. If I hadn't it would have been the same old story just as it will be with Alec and all the others who come after him. You don't know how to be happy, Chrissie. You have no clue at all.'

'I would have been happy with you.'

'No you wouldn't. In the end you'd have hated me like you hate the rest of them.'

Silence. Pity came into his eyes, just as it had on that final night outside the houka bar. 'You should talk to someone. You really should.'

'I don't need a shrink!'

'Don't you? Are you really happy being like this? Seeing every guy you meet as a threat. Someone you've got to emasculate so he can't hurt you the way your father did.'

'Are you comparing yourself with him?'

'No. *I'm* not the one doing that.'

'You're nothing compared to him. He was more of a man than all the rest of you put together. You're just pale imitations.'

'But that's not our fault.'

'Then whose is it? Who can I blame because I can't blame him. He's not here, is he? He went away where I can't find him and tell him.' She swallowed. A lump came into her throat. 'And I need to tell him. I need to tell him . . .'

'What, Chrissie? What do you need to tell him?'

She shook her head, suddenly unable to speak.

'Tell me. What is it that you need to tell him?'

'That I still love him.' It came out as a wail. 'That I still love him and I want him back. It doesn't have to be

411

for ever. Five minutes would be enough if he'd just tell me that he's sorry for what he did. That he's never forgotten me. That I mattered. That I wasn't nothing. That's all I need and then maybe I can stop hurting and get some peace.'

He was still staring; the pity remained in his eyes. She saw herself reflected in them. Only it wasn't her: it was Tina. The frightened child praying for her father to come and hold her and make her feel safe again. The person she still was. And always would be.

Emotion overwhelmed her. Collapsing onto the sofa she began to sob.

Jack remained where he was, watching.

She was curled into a ball, releasing howls of pain from a place so deep inside herself that she had probably never realized it existed. It hurt to watch her yet it felt good too, knowing he had helped her reach a catharsis.

Crouching down he put his arms around her, pulling her towards him. 'It's OK,' he whispered. 'Let it out. Take as long as you need.'

She pressed herself against him, her tears soaking his shirt while Bullseye crept back into the room and hovered anxiously nearby.

'You've got to make peace with him, Chrissie. Let him go. He did a terrible thing to you but that doesn't make him a terrible person. From what you've told me about him it's obvious he loved you and what's more, I'm sure he still does. He wouldn't want you to be unhappy, least of all because of him.'

He heard her swallow. 'Then why isn't he here to tell me?'

'I don't know. But I do know that hurting other people isn't going to make you hurt any less. The only way you can do that is to forgive him. Then maybe you really can find the peace you're looking for.'

She didn't answer. Just continued to cling to him.

'It's like with Ali. You don't really want to hurt her. It won't bring him back or make you feel any better. It'll just cause her heartache and you, more than anyone, should know that there's already more than enough of that in the world.'

He felt her stiffen. She pulled away from him. 'Ali?'

'I just meant . . .'

'That's who you're worried about. Not me. Her. You used my father against me. You used the worst thing that's ever happened to me just to protect her.'

'Look, I didn't . . .'

She rose to her feet, staring down at him. It was like the day when she had wept on the boat, taken refuge in the cabin and then emerged coated in a layer of steel. Only this time it wasn't steel. It was ice.

'And you're going to be sorry for that. *Really* sorry.'

Turning she walked out, ignoring Bullseye who ran after her. Leaving the cabin and slamming the door behind her. From the window he watched her leave the canal path, walk out onto the street and flag down a passing cab.

And suddenly he knew where she was going.

Reaching for his mobile he dialled Ali's number but received only the message service. He tried the coffee bar only to hear the engaged tone. A scream of frustration escaped him, causing Bullseye to flee for a second time.

Half an hour later. Ali walked across Ludgate Circus towards the coffee bar.

She was feeling happy. In her hand was a bag full of Kinks CDs to replace the ones Jack had had stolen. They had cost a fortune but it didn't matter. The look on Jack's face would be worth all the money in the world.

Her mobile was in her pocket. She pulled it out, preparing to phone him. But before she could switch it on she saw something that banished her good mood completely.

Chrissie stood outside the coffee bar, looking expectant.

She slowed, feeling threatened just as she had the previous afternoon. Wanting to run and hide.

But it was too late. Chrissie strode towards her, moving like a goddess, radiating confidence with every step.

'Hi,' she said cheerfully, trying to act confident herself. 'How are you?'

'Fine.' Chrissie gestured to the bag. 'Get anything nice.'

'Just some records.'

'For you?'

'No. Jack.'

'Let me guess. Kinks?'

'Yes. To replace the ones—'

'That were stolen.'

She nodded.

'Did you keep the receipt?'

'No. Jack's not going to want to change them.'

'But you might when you hear what I've got to tell you.'

The sense of threat intensified. 'Tell me what?'

'About Debbie.'

'My sister?'

'That's right. The one you share things with. More than you realize as it turns out.'

'What do you mean?'

'Jack, of course.'

She felt dizzy. The pavement seemed to shift beneath her feet. Looking around her she noticed a young woman standing nearby, gazing into a shop window, seemingly preoccupied but still close enough to hear their conversation. The sense of being watched helped her focus again.

'You don't believe me? Well, who can blame you. I wouldn't want to either but it *is* true. Ask Stephen and Tim if you don't believe me. Or, better still, ask

Jack. He'll probably deny it but look into his eyes and you'll know it's true.'

She swallowed.

'I'm sorry. I know it must hurt but you seem like a nice person and I thought you should know the truth. I can tell how much you care about Jack. I cared about him too until I wised up to what a prick he was.'

The dizziness returned. She wanted to scream. To sink to her knees and howl there on the street with all the world to see. But that was what Chrissie wanted too. And from somewhere inside herself she found the strength to keep her dignity.

'Thank you for telling me but I knew already. Jack told me some time ago. It hurt but I forgave him. He's a good man and I love him just like you still do. I feel sorry for Alec: he seems like a nice bloke and all you're doing is using him. But you shouldn't take him for granted because deep down I think he knows it too.'

Then she walked away, into the shop, keeping her back ramrod straight. Arno, her boss, called out to her from behind the counter. Ignoring him she made her way to the ladies, finding an empty cubicle and closing the door behind her.

Only then did she begin to cry.

Three o'clock. Paparazzi Nick Hooper sat in the Streatham flat he shared with his girlfriend Paula, planning his evening's activities.

His mobile rang. It was Paula sounding excited. 'Guess who I've just seen?'

'Who?'

'You know you saw Alexander Gallen with his new girlfriend. The redhead.'

'Yes. Chrissie Ryan.'

'I was in Ludgate Circus and saw her talking with some other girl. I managed to earwig their conversation . . .'

He listened to what she told him. 'What did this other girl look like?'

'Like Chrissie. Pretty but not as attractive.'

'Shit. Thanks, babe. See you later, yeah?'

He put down the phone then switched on his laptop where he stored his photos. He kept them all, regardless of whether he could sell them. One day's trash just might turn out to be another day's treasure.

He found the ones of Chrissie and Alexander taken the previous afternoon, saying goodbye to their friends in Maida Vale. Enlarging them he studied them one by one.

And found gold.

Jack tried the coffee bar again.

Arno answered on the third ring. 'Hi, it's Jack. I need to talk to Ali.'

'You can't, Jack. I'm sorry. She's gone. Told me she had to leave town and didn't know when she'd be back.'

He felt sick. 'Where has she gone?'

'I don't know. I hope she's all right. She looked like she'd been crying. I—'

Cutting Arno off he put down the phone. Then, just as Chrissie had done earlier, he collapsed onto the sofa and buried his head in his hands.

Half past ten. Chrissie let herself into Alexander's flat.

Her head was spinning. She had spent most of the evening drinking in a bar. Not that it had cost her anything. A succession of men had paid for her, all of them trying to charm her into bed while she had toyed with them like the slobbering dogs they were. Only using them the way they would use her given half the chance.

Alexander appeared from the living room, his face white with worry. 'Where the hell have you been?'

'What's it to you?'

'Tara's just left. We'd invited her round for the evening.'

'So? I forgot.'

'How could you forget? She's your friend!'

'She'll get over it.'

'She was almost in tears. She already feels like you've dropped her and tonight will have just confirmed that.'

'And if she does feel that then whose fault is that? You're the one who wants all my attention. You're the one who can't bear for us to be apart.'

'So where were you all this time?'

'Oh give me a break . . .'

'I tried to call you at work but they said you'd gone out mid-morning and never come back. I was worried sick. Don't you understand that?'

'Whatever.' She tried to push past him, needing another drink.

He grabbed her arm. 'Chrissie—'

'Take your fucking hands off me!'

He released her, his cheeks colouring as if they had been slapped.

'You're so needy. You drone on about what I need and how you want to take care of me and it's a complete joke! You're the neediest person I've ever met! No wonder your grandmother didn't want any pictures of you in her bedroom. Who'd want to be reminded of someone as pathetic as you?'

His colour rose. 'Leave my grandmother out of it.'

'Why? Have I hit a nerve? Is that what she thought of you? I bet it was. I bet she despised you: her spineless grandson and heir. It's a pity she's dead. If she were alive she and I could have a great time comparing notes on just how pathetic you are!'

'You don't know what you're talking about.'

'Yes I do. I can see it in your face. You're a man after all and there isn't a man alive smart enough to fool me.'

'Why are you doing this?'

'Why are you letting me?'

'We shouldn't be fighting. We need each other. We've

both lost people that mattered to us when we needed them most. We both know what that's like.'

'Perhaps, but the difference between us is that I didn't kill any of mine!'

'You shut your mouth, you fucking bitch!'

Rage flooded his face. As savage and raw as her own. Suddenly he looked poised to attack her. Momentarily she felt afraid. Afraid but excited. Wanting him to strike her. Needing him to take control.

Because I'm not in control of myself. Not any more.

They stared at each other. Again she laughed. 'Come on then. Hit me. Show me you're not a eunuch. Show me you've still got some balls.'

For a moment the rage remained. His expression was murderous. More like that of an animal than a human being.

And then it was gone. His face went blank. He pushed past her, heading for the door.

'Don't walk away from me! Don't you dare!'

Ignoring her he left the flat. Alone, she slapped her own face, as if administering the punishment he was unable to do.

Four hours later. Alexander re-entered the flat. It was in darkness. Silent too. Clearly Chrissie was in bed. Stepping softly so as not to disturb her he went into the bathroom, and stood in front of the mirror, studying his reflection. His expression was tranquil, as calm as the surface of a pond on a still summer's day. No trace of the violent currents that lurked beneath the surface.

Only there were no such currents. Not any more.

His hair was a mess. He had been driving for hours; the wind pounding his face like a fist, hammering the darker emotions out of his head. He smoothed it down, remembering how, when he was a child, his grandmother would chastise him for leaving it uncombed. How he would often come down to breakfast in the house in Amberton only to be sent back upstairs to comb it properly. Back to the bathroom with the cool white walls and huge antique bath. The one next to the back bedroom where the bad things were hidden.

The room had always frightened him, just as it had frightened his grandmother. It had been a secret they had never discussed. One that in the end she had taken to her grave to haunt any dreams she had there. But there was no need to be frightened. The door was still secure. The darkness still contained within.

'Don't be scared,' he whispered to his reflection. 'Everything will be all right. She didn't mean the things she said. She loves you, really. I know she does. Tomorrow she'll be sorry for what she said. I know that too.'

He entered the bedroom. Chrissie lay on her side, restless in her sleep. Haunted by dreams perhaps. Gently he stroked her cheek, watching over her just as, in childhood, he had so often done with his grandmother. There, when she had been at her most helpless, he had felt the most tenderness. All his secret fears soothed by the belief that, in spite of everything, he was still loved and needed.

Chrissie moved in her sleep. He bent down, kissing her softly, breathing in deeply, trying to suck in her pain and make it his own.

In her dream she was on the boat with Jack. They were making love or rather she was making love to him, straddling him like a horse, pinning him to the bed with all her strength. Outside it was stormy. Rain battered the window. She could see Alexander looking through it, watching them both, his eyes full of silent reproach. Like a dog abandoned by the owner it trusted and left to fend for itself.

Jack tried to rise up. She pushed him down, leaning over him, burying her face in his chest and biting into the skin. Looking up again she saw Alexander had gone. In his place was a policeman with a camera, snapping pictures, calling for others to come and look.

Her mouth felt wet. She licked her lips and tasted blood. Looking down again she saw that Jack was gone. In his place lay her father, his skin cold and white except for the hole in his chest where she had torn out his heart.

When she woke she saw Alexander staring down at her. 'Where did you go?' she whispered.

'I was driving. That's all. What were you dreaming?'

'I don't remember. It's gone.'

He nodded.

'I'm sorry. I didn't mean what I said.'

'Nothing was said. It's gone just like your dream. Do you want me to go? Sleep in the spare room?'

She didn't answer. Again she saw her father lying cold and white beneath her. Gone for ever. Never able to return and tell her he was sorry. Reaching up she pulled Alexander down to her, needing to feel the warmth of his skin. Needing not to feel alone.

'No. Stay. Help keep the dreams away.'

They made love, tenderly at first, then with increasing passion. She lay beneath him, clawing at his back, feeling him thrust into her, imagining his cock was a spear that could kill the dragon that grew ever stronger within.

Interview between Simon Cooper and Catherine Butler. Oxfordshire. May 2006.

The living room was small but welcoming, full of light and colour and photographs of happy, smiling faces. The ambience was one of warmth and security. A house that truly felt like a home.

Simon stared at his hostess. A middle-aged woman with a kind face that showed signs of strain. Understandable in light of the previous eighteen months. Had his own mother been through a similar experience no doubt she would have shown similar signs herself.

'Thank you for agreeing to see me,' he said.

'I'm glad you wanted to come. I've read the articles you've written. They were never sensational. Unlike others, I always sensed you were trying to get to know the real people.'

'I think it's essential. If you really want to understand a case you have to understand the people behind the headlines.'

'And now you're planning to write a book. Do you think you might have missed the boat? There have been two published already.'

'But they were just cut and paste jobs. Cash-in-quick exercises with no substance. I want what I write to have depth.'

'So do I.'

'I'll need to tape our conversation. Are you happy with that?'

'Yes. I trust you.'

He switched on his tape machine. 'How old was Alexander when you first met him?'

'Nine. He and Graham started at boarding school together. They became friends pretty much from the first day but it wasn't until the second term that I met him. He came to stay with us for a weekend. To be honest I wasn't keen. I knew who he was. Heir to God knows how many Gallen millions and whose home was a Norfolk mansion.' Catherine gestured to the room they sat in. 'I couldn't imagine someone

*like that wanting to come and stay somewhere
like this, but Graham begged me so of course I
said yes.'*

'And how was the weekend?'

'Delightful. Alec was delightful. He had the
most beautiful manners of any boy I'd ever met.
He was so polite. So grateful for everything my
husband and I did for him.'

'What did you do for him?'

'Very little. Made him meals. Took him and
Gray to the cinema and for pizzas and all the
junk food they never got at school.' A wry
laugh. 'Pretended not to hear when they played
soldiers upstairs in Gray's bedroom when they
were supposed to be asleep. I just wanted him to
feel at home.'

'Did he talk about his own home much?'

'Not the first time. I remember him talking
about New York. He still had a faint American
accent back then. He told us about the things he
did with his cousins on the rare occasions he
visited them there. I always got the impression
that he missed America and wished he could
have stayed there, but of course he never said
that. He was too polite.'

'Did he talk about his parents?'

'His father, yes. All the time. He still missed
him. But never about his mother. If she came up
in conversation he'd skate around the subject

then talk about something else. That's another thing I remember. Even at that age he was good at avoiding subjects he didn't want to discuss. Mind you, when it came to his mother I could understand it, particularly when you think how she died. That's a heavy burden for any child to bear.'

'Do you think he felt guilty?'

'Yes, I think so. But, as I said, he never talked about it.'

'And what of his grandparents? What did he say about them?'

'Very little about his grandfather though perhaps that was understandable too. They only lived together for a year. He sounded like a nice man and it always seemed so sad for a child as young as that to have lost so many people.'

'Though he still had his grandmother. What did he say about her?'

'He loved her very much, that was clear, and was terrified of losing her too. Once we watched some television play in which a woman died and that night Alec had a nightmare about his grandmother dying. The woman in the play had reminded him of her.' A sigh. 'Poor Alec. Normally he was so cheerful. That was the only time I ever saw him cry.

'And he wanted her to approve of him. Even when she wasn't there he wanted her approval. I

remember one night we had a dinner party and when I came down the next morning I found that Alec had got up early and done all the washing up. I remember giving him a hug and him asking me if, when his grandmother phoned, I'd tell her that he'd done it. That he was making an effort and being good.'

'How often did you meet her?'

'Not often. She rarely went to school functions. Just the odd prize-giving. And at the end of term she'd send a car to take him back to Norfolk. She never came herself. At the time I assumed it was because she found the drive tiring.'

'What were your impressions of her?'

'Cold. That's the word that comes to mind. She projected great strength but little warmth, not even for Alec. She was never affectionate with him. Whenever I'd see Gray I'd hug him so hard his bones would rattle.' Another wry laugh. 'Gray hated it and would tell me to stop embarrassing him, though being a mother I took not a blind bit of notice. But Alec's grandmother was always so controlled with him. They used to shake hands when they met. I could sense Alec wanting more but she never gave it.'

'Not in public but what about in private?'

'You know the answer to that already.'

'But not your view. At the time at least.'

'When Alec talked about his home life he made it sound happy and that was what struck me. It was too happy. Like a child's fantasy of the perfect home. Something he'd read in a book rather than experienced for himself. There was one time in particular . . .' She stopped. Tears came to her eyes.

'Would you like to break?'

'No. I'm sorry. It's just . . . I cared about him very much. This isn't easy for me.'

'I understand. Please take your time.'

'He would have been about eleven and was helping me with the washing up. He was always trying to help. I think he liked feeling needed. I was telling him about a game I'd played with my mother and brother when I was a girl, and he said that he played the same game with his grandmother. He began to describe a particular incident and I realized that he was actually describing an incident with Gray and me. At the time I put it down to confusion. We can all jumble memories. But now I think it was wishful thinking. Wishing Gray's life was his own.'

'You know what happened when he was fifteen. At the time did you realize how serious it was?'

'No. I thought he'd been ill, just as Gray did. That was what we were told. It was only Gail who thought there was more to it.'

'If you'd known the truth would it have changed anything?'

'My feelings towards him? I don't know. I would have been shocked but I hope I would have been able to understand. Just like his grandmother did. That was something I did notice. On the few occasions I met her afterwards her behaviour towards him was warmer. Kinder. As if she were trying to make amends.'

'Do you think that made any difference to him?'

'Superficially, perhaps. But not really. The wound was too deep by then. So much poison had been poured into it that it could never truly heal.'

'Which leads us to Chrissie. Did you ever meet her?'

'No. Gray and Gail did. He liked her, she didn't. At the time Gray put it down to jealousy. Gail was possessive of Alec. Not in a bad way you understand, just overprotective.'

'With reason when it came to Chrissie.'

'I don't think so. In spite of everything that was said at the time I don't think she was to blame. At least not directly. If Alec hadn't met her who's to say he wouldn't have had the same experience with someone else. He was drawn to Chrissie because she reminded him of his

*grandmother. What is it they say? That when we
look for a partner we're really looking for a
perfect version of our parents. His grandmother
was the one person above all whose love he'd
always needed and the tragedy was that
someone else like that in his life was the very last
thing he needed.'*

Silence. Again she looked close to tears.

'Do you want to stop?' he asked again.

*'No. I want to talk about it. It just hurts. He
was such a sweet child with so much love to give
had he only been allowed to. If fate had dealt
him a kinder hand he'd probably be happily
settled with children of his own and none of this
would have happened.'*

'Do you really believe that?'

Her eyes became troubled.

'Do you?'

'I want to believe . . .'

Tuesday evening. Chrissie stood in Alexander's kitchen,
cooking supper. This time it was her who felt the need
to make a peace offering.

She checked her watch. Ten-to-seven. Alexander
was celebrating a work colleague's birthday in a
Westminster pub. She wondered if Jack had gone to
work or stayed home to nurse his grief. Earlier that
day she had phoned the cafe to be told that Ali no
longer worked there. Quit to go no one knew where.

Good riddance too. She tried to feel happy but couldn't. In shattering that relationship she had also destroyed all chance of restablishing the only one she wanted for herself.

A half-empty wine bottle stood on the counter. She was drinking more and more as if trying to drown the emotions that churned inside her. It helped her feel grounded. Stable. In control. Feelings that had once been second nature but now seemed as elusive as shadows.

Leaving the food she went to the bedroom. Her cigarettes were in her bag. She pulled them out but could not find her lighter. She must have left it in the office though there was a spare in the lower drawer of her bedside table. The place where she kept her diary.

She opened the drawer. Her diary was buried under a pile of magazines. The top one had a picture of Colin Farrell on the cover, smiling up at her like Jack's younger, better looking brother.

Or at least he had the last time she had looked. But not this time. The magazine, though still in place was the wrong way round.

For a moment she was baffled. Then she understood. Alexander had read her diary.

She felt sick. Betrayed. Violated. As if all her innermost thoughts had been exposed to public view. Just as Tina had been exposed. Alexander had done that to her and now, every time he asked her about Jack she would have to look into his eyes and see that he knew she was lying. That she was the needy one. That when it came to love she was just as weak as him.

And he was going to be sorry for that.

Pulling out the diary, sitting crouched on the floor she began to write.

Jack called today. He's finished with Ali. He said that seeing me with Alec made him realize what a huge mistake he's made. That I'm the one he really loves. When he told me I felt so happy that I wanted to scream.

He wanted to see me but I put him off. I'll make him suffer the way he's made me. But not for long. I won't be able to hold out. I want to feel his arms around me. To feel him inside me. To be with a man again instead of a spineless cripple. Someone I can respect. Not someone I just tolerate like I'd tolerate a stray dog . . .

The pen flowed across the page. She poured out her venom while, like the rage inside her, the forgotten meal boiled and burned in the kitchen.

'I'm sorry about supper,' she told Alexander as she lay in bed, watching him undress.

'It doesn't matter. It was lovely anyway.'

'I was writing my diary and lost track of time.' A quick laugh. 'You know what girls are like with their diaries.' She waited for him to ask what she had written but he didn't. No doubt he would check for himself when the opportunity arose. As if to confirm this his eyes darted towards the bedside table, the gesture so quick that had she not been looking for it she would not have noticed it at all.

And she noticed something else too. There were scratches on his back. The result of the previous night's passion. She hadn't realised she had been so aggressive.

But he deserved it. He deserved everything he got.

They made love that night too: the act as intense as before. As he reached his climax she whispered Jack's name. Too softly for the word to be clear, but clear enough for a doubt to be raised.

He collapsed on top of her, gasping. She bit down on her lip to muffle the laughter that bubbled inside her like a suppurating wound.

The following evening Karen sat with Chrissie and Alexander in a tapas bar off Kensington High Street. The place was crowded. Mostly young people in groups, eating, drinking and talking more loudly that was necessary. As was Chrissie.

She was on her third Marguerita, knocking them back with uncharacteristic relish while radiating a restless energy. Like a wild animal confined in an invisible cage.

'Go easy,' Karen said, trying not to sound parental.

'Sorry, Mum.'

'Talking of your mother, she's heard back from the doctor. Her headaches were just eye strain. Poor thing. She'd been imagining something terrible like a brain tumour when all she needs is a pair of glasses.'

'That's good news,' Alexander told her.

'Yes, isn't it?' agreed Chrissie. She held up her glass. 'Hurrah for Mum.'

'Chrissie!'

'What? I'm pleased. Can't you tell? Alec can. He can read me like a book which is how it should be. We love each other after all. People in love should always know each other better than anyone else.'

Alexander smiled. A small, nervous gesture. As Karen watched him she remembered her only meeting with Kevin. Again it had been in a London restaurant. Kevin had gone out of his way to be charming, clearly wanting her to like him while Chrissie had done little more than go through the motions, saying the right words but with no feeling behind them. Radiating the boredom that signalled the relationship's imminent doom.

Once more she saw the boredom. But she saw more besides. Frustration. Anger. Hate.

And Alexander saw it too. Though his expression gave no suggestion of it still she sensed that he did.

'What are you doing with him?' she asked Chrissie when he went to the gents.

'Being young and in love. What does it look like?'

'You don't love him. You don't even like him. You're just using him to try and feel better about yourself.'

Chrissie reached for her cigarettes.

'Little Chrissie Ryan from humble Havelock being fawned over by one of the richest men in the country. It's quite an ego boost.'

'At least I've achieved something. I'm not nothing anymore. I'm someone.'

'You were never nothing and what makes you think you're someone now? The only reason people are interested in you is because of who you're sleeping with and because of who he supposedly stopped sleeping with to climb into your bed. Alec and Evelyne are the so-called somebodies in this situation. Yours is just reflected glory and that's no glory at all.'

'You don't know what you're talking about.'

'Yes I do. I'm the one who *really* knows you. I remember a girl everyone still called Tina vowing to me that one day she was going to be famous. I always believed it too. I just never thought she'd stoop to prostitution to achieve it.'

Chrissie's eyes widened, looking suddenly like the child she had once been. 'How can you say that to me?'

'Because you need to hear it. Everything about this relationship feels wrong and you have to end it before you get in too deep.'

'I'm already in too deep.'

'No you're not. You don't love him. You're not going to be hurt.'

'But he will. People will think I'm a bitch.'

'Since when have you cared what people think?'

'Since I met Jack.'

The two of them stared at each other.

'The last time I saw him he said that all I want to do to men is hurt them. If I break up with Alec then he'll be hurt and Jack will have been right and I can't have that. Not after everything he said. Not after that.'

Chrissie swallowed. Again she looked younger. Frightened. Lost. Karen's sense of alarm increased.

'What else did he say?'

'That when it comes to men everything I do is about Dad. That I hurt them because I can't hurt him.'

Silence. Karen wanted to say that it was rubbish. Only she couldn't.

'Chrissie, this whole thing with Alec feels . . . I don't know. Unhealthy. Please end it. For me if not for yourself. Because . . .'

'What?'

'Because I'm scared something really bad is going to happen if you don't.'

Alexander returned. Chrissie forced on a smile. 'We were about to send out a search party.' Her tone was warmer than it had been.

Alexander sat down again. 'Would you like anything else?' he asked Karen.

'No, thanks.'

'Then let's get the bill.'

She took out her purse. 'Put it away,' Chrissie told

her. 'This is our treat and we're also paying for your taxi to Adam's.'

'There's no need.'

'Yes there is. I *am* glad about Mum. Give her my love and tell her Alec and I will visit soon and take her out to celebrate.' Chrissie turned to Alexander. 'That's OK, isn't it?'

'Of course. If that's what you want then that's what we'll do.'

Another silence. Chrissie rested her head on Alexander's shoulder. The gesture was easy and fluid. Like that of a trained actress. One determined to play out her role no matter how unrewarding it might be. Both smiled at Karen. She smiled back, feeling an ache behind her eyes like the start of a headache brought on by an impending storm.

Friday. The lunchtime shift finished, Jack returned to the boat with Bullseye.

As he climbed into the bow he heard music playing inside. Fearful of being burgled he charged inside and found Ali sitting on the sofa waiting for him.

Bullseye leapt onto the sofa to lick her face. She looked as if she had lost weight. Guilt overwhelmed him. It made him defensive. 'Here for your stuff?' he asked curtly.

'That and an explanation.'

'There is no explanation. I did it.'

'I deserve more than that.'

'Just as you deserve better than me.'

'Cut the self pity. It doesn't suit you.'

'What does it matter? I did it. I'm a prick and for what it's worth I'm sorry. I'll leave you to it. You don't want me around.' He turned to go.

'Please Jack. I need to know.'

'Did you talk to Debbie?'

'Yes. She said it was all just a drunken mistake. That it didn't mean anything.'

He turned back. 'She's telling the truth.'

'I want to believe her. I love my sister. I don't want to lose her.'

'Then don't. I was the one who instigated it. I'm the one to blame. Not her.'

She shook her head.

'Don't you believe me?'

'Don't you understand?'

'What?'

'That I don't want to lose you either.'

A lump came into his throat. He tried to swallow it down only it wouldn't go. He sat down beside her. 'Do you really want to know why?'

'Yes.'

'Because it was a way to hurt you.'

'Why? What did I do?'

'Made me feel trapped.'

She looked bewildered. 'How? I knew you needed your space. That you needed to feel free. That's why I always tried to act like being with you was just fun. To

438

not let you see that in reality it was the best thing that had ever happened to me.' She gave a frustrated sigh. 'And Christ that was hard. You've no idea how hard.'

'And that was why. You understood me like no girl I'd ever met before. They all wanted to tie me down but you didn't. You let me be myself and that scared me. It scared me something rotten.'

'Why?'

The lump was back. Bigger than before.

'Why, Jack?'

'There's a saying. If you want a bird to stay in your hand then keep it open. Never close it. If you keep it open the bird will always come back. That's how it was with you. You never tried to cage me and because of that I knew that I'd always want to come back. And I was scared of that. My whole life has been one long act of running away and I knew that I'd never be able to run from you.' He exhaled, trying to keep the tremor out of his voice. 'That's why I did it. Knowing I'd done something so bad and feeling so guilty about it made it easier to push you away. To put distance between us. Make you into just another ex rather than someone . . .'

'Someone?'

'That I wanted to share my life with.'

He waited for a response but none came.

'You mustn't blame Debbie. I initiated it and when it was over she cried because she felt so bad. Please don't lose your sister because of me. I'm not worth it.'

'I told you, self pity doesn't suit you.'

'It's not self pity. It's the truth. Do you know where I was on the night of your birthday party? In bed with Chrissie. That was the evening I met her. I guess I was looking for an excuse not to come. I was worried about how I'd feel when I saw you and Chrissie seemed safe. Someone who wanted sex with no strings. All fun and no emotion. Someone who was never going to want to tie me down because she was too scared of being tied down herself.' He gave a hollow laugh. 'And the irony was that she wanted to control me more than any girl I've ever met.'

'But you liked her. You felt something for her.'

'I was flattered by her, that's all. I know you feel threatened but you shouldn't. The one good thing about being with her was that it made me realise how much I wanted to be with you.'

Another silence. He listened to the music. A lesser known Kinks track. 'Is this your CD?' he asked.

'Yes. That and the others.' She gestured to a pile on the table. 'I bought them for you the day Chrissie told me about you and Debbie.'

The guilt became unbearable. 'I'm so sorry, really I . . .'

'Do you want them? Because if you do then you should know they come with a condition.'

'And what's that?'

'That I come too.'

He burst into tears.

She put her arm around him wiping his eyes and staring into his face. 'I love you,' she whispered. 'And I forgive you.'

'Are you sure?'

'Yes. I want to share my life with you too. I have done since the first day we met. I was just too scared to tell you.'

'You don't need to be scared. You're the best thing that's ever happened to me. Don't be frightened of keeping your hand open. I'll never feel caged when I'm with you.'

They kissed each other while Bullseye bounced around them like an excited child wanting attention from parents who only had eyes for each other.

Saturday night. The wrap party for *Through Other Eyes*.

It was being held in a private members club in Soho. Three floors, each with bars full of cast and crew members hugging each other and making promises to stay in touch that would go largely unhonoured, while those who had come as guests stood around looking awkward, as if at a reunion for a school they had never attended.

Chrissie stood on the top floor by the window looking down on the street below, watching gay couples head into Old Compton Street and tourists search for restaurants and theatres while listening to Elly the continuity girl talk about an ex-boyfriend who had invited her to New York to see if they could rekindle their relationship. 'I can't wait,' Elly told her. 'I was gutted when he broke up with me.'

'So now he clicks his fingers and you jump. Be careful. He's probably just looking to get laid.'

Elly looked indignant. 'It's not like that.'

'He's a man, isn't he? They're all like that given half the chance.'

Indignation turned to hurt. She felt guilty. 'Hey, don't take any notice of me. Recently a girl I know found out that her boyfriend had been sleeping with her sister. It's jaded my perspective.'

'Poor cow. What did she do?'

'Dumped him on the spot. Just what the prick deserved.' She tried to keep the bitterness out of her voice. 'You're right to go. It could be good. I hope it is.'

'The only problem now is what to do about the cottage.'

'What cottage?'

'My parents own one in Suffolk. They're in Spain and I was supposed to be checking on it next weekend but I can't as I'm flying out tomorrow night. You don't know anybody who fancies a trip do you?'

She looked across the room to where Alexander stood talking to a group of people, charming them all just like the perfect boyfriend he was.

'I could do with getting away. Where is it exactly?'

Elly jotted down the address, explaining that a set of keys were hidden under a brick by the back porch.

Alexander kept looking over as did the others he was with: Bob and Malcolm. Graham and Gail. Feeling pulled by an invisible string she made her way over.

'Great party,' Graham told her.

'Thanks. I'm glad you could come.'

He smiled. Gail did too. Once again she felt as if she were being judged. A waiter walked past with champagne on a tray. She seized a glass and downed it, needing, as she so often did, to dull her senses with alcohol.

'Alec's been telling me that he's planning to invest in the twins project,' Bob told her.

'Naturally,' Alexander added. 'If Chrissie believes in it then it must be good.' As he spoke he put his arm around her. She fought an urge to pull away.

Bob beamed. 'Well that would be great, wouldn't it, Chrissie?'

She nodded. Gail continued to stare at her. Looking for distraction she scanned the room and noticed an inebriated Francis Chester talking animatedly to a handsome young waiter. 'Looks like someone's pulled,' she announced. Francis heard and looked over. 'Don't worry,' she called out. 'We won't tell your wife.'

The waiter moved away. Scowling, Francis did the same. From downstairs came the sound of cheering. Most of the other people in the bar went to see what was going on.

'That was mean,' Bob told her.

'Why? Everyone knows he swings both ways.

Besides, I'm just having a laugh. It's a party, isn't it? That's why people come to parties to have a good time.' She noticed Melanie entering the room and felt pleased. Then Rick entered too and her mood evaporated.

The two of them approached. She introduced them around. 'I didn't think you were coming,' she told Rick.

'The deal I was working on fell through.'

'Oh well, big businesses' loss is our gain.'

'Sorry we're late,' said Mel. 'We got waylaid. You know that pub I took you to once? The Wayfarer? We were in there last night and Rick left his car keys behind. We popped in to pick them up and found a party going on. Do you remember the barman? Jack? Well he and his girlfriend have just got engaged. Loads of people from the boats were there and they insisted we stayed for a celebratory drink.'

The ground shifted beneath her feet. She thought she might collapse. Alexander's arm tightened around her.

'Are you OK?' asked Graham.

She nodded, suddenly unable to speak.

'You've gone pale.'

She found her voice. 'Too much to drink, that's all.'

'Then maybe it's time to stop,' suggested Bob.

'His girlfriend seemed really nice,' continued an oblivious Mel. 'Jack had written this poem about how he felt about her. He read it out and she cried.'

'Though not as much as Mel,' added Rick. 'Soppy thing that she is.'

Others laughed good naturedly. Chrissie wanted to run but there was nowhere to go. Inside her the dragon began to stir.

Mel looked embarrassed. 'Well it was lovely.'

'What sort of things did he say?' asked Gail.

'That she was the best thing that had ever happened to him. How being with her made him feel complete. That she could trust him with her heart because no matter what happened between them he'd never want to leave.'

Chrissie's stomach heaved. She thought she might vomit. Alexander's grip felt like a vice. She turned towards him. His eyes were full of emotions only she could read. Concern. Pity. Pleasure. Triumph.

Because he knew it all. He had read it in her diary. Including the words she had written to make him jealous. The words he now knew were pathetic lies.

The dragon rose, its wings unfurling.

'I'd better not write you any poems,' Rick told Mel. 'You'd only drown us all.'

More laughter. The wings were moving. Catching the currents of the air. And suddenly taking flight.

'I'm sure you're right,' she said. 'Only if you wrote what you *really* thought about Mel they wouldn't be tears of joy we'd drown in.'

Everyone stared at her. 'What do you mean?' Mel asked.

'He doesn't care about you. Just your parents' money. That's why he's hit on all your friends including me. He's a piece of crap only you're too infatuated to see it.'

Mel paled. The others looked shocked. 'Chrissie—' Bob began.

'What? I'm only telling her the truth and it is the truth, isn't it, Rick?'

He glared at her. 'You stupid cow!'

'Hardly stupid. After all I turned you down. Mind you, that doesn't take brains. You'd have to be blind not to see what a nasty piece of work you really are.'

Mel burst into tears. Rick tried to put his arm around her but she pushed him away.

'Poor Rick. Guess you can kiss the money goodbye now. But never mind, I'm sure you'll soon find some other gullible rich girl to con.'

'Well you'd know all about conning the rich,' said Gail suddenly.

'You think I'm conning Alec? Well you'd know all about that, wouldn't you? What have I got to show for our time together except a couple of dresses? Doesn't compare to months of mortgage payments, does it?'

'That's enough!' shouted Alexander.

'Really? What are you going to do, Alec? Hit me? I doubt it. That's not your style. You'd prefer to creep off and read my diary. God, when it comes to being spineless they really broke the mould with you, didn't they?'

Gail threw a drink in her face.

She raised her arm, ready to strike, only to be pulled

away by Bob and Malcolm. Mel was still crying. Gail glared at her. She glared back, while Alexander stood between them like a rabbit caught in the headlights of an oncoming juggernaut, looking weak, frightened and everything she despised. Her need to lash out intensified.

'Who are you going to choose, Alec? Her or me? Because you can't have us both. Not anymore.'

'Stop this!' demanded Bob.

'Why? It's how it is. Her and Graham or me.'

'You can't do this to him!' shouted Gail.

'He shouldn't let me! What sort of man lets people treat him like this? Come on, Alec. Show us all what sort of man you really are.'

'A better one than you deserve,' Gail told her.

'Is that true, Alec? Do you think you deserve better than me?'

Alexander was staring at her. His eyes were pleading. *Hit me Alec. For Christ's sake, take control. I need someone to take control.*

'Fine. I'm leaving. Have a good life.' She marched towards the door.

'I choose you.'

She stopped, turned back. 'Do you mean that?'

He nodded.

'Then let's go.'

'You're an evil bitch,' Gail told her.

'Better evil than weak. Good luck with the mortgage. You're going to need it.'

She walked down the stairs, ignoring the crowd who had gathered to listen in the corridor, not bothering to wait for Alexander. A part of her hoping that he wouldn't follow.

But he did. Running behind her like a puppy fearful of being abandoned.

They walked out into the night. His car was parked in a side street nearby. She reached it first, waiting as he unlocked the doors before pulling one open.

'Not you,' he said. 'Get a cab.'

'Screw that.'

He reached into his wallet and pulled out a handful of notes. 'Here's the money. Just get one. Believe me, it's better if I'm not around you at the moment.'

She stared into his face. For a moment she saw the same rage she had seen the last time they had fought.

And then, as before, it was gone. As, suddenly was her own.

'Go back and tell them you choose them. Gail's right. You deserve better than me.'

'It's too late. It'll never be the same between them and me now. You've seen to that.' His words were harsh but his voice was neutral. Devoid of all emotion.

Then he climbed into the car and drove away.

Two hours later. Back at the flat she wrote her diary.

I have to let Jack go just as I have to let Dad go.
I know it's the only thing to do.

But I can't. I hate him but I still love him. In spite of everything I still do.

Ali's the one I really hate. It's all her fault. If she weren't around he'd still be mine. I wish she was dead. I wish someone would kill her so he could be mine again. Just as he was once. Only this time I'd never let him go. I'd be whatever or whoever he wants me to be. Even Tina. I'd do whatever he asked just as long as he promised never to leave me.

Just like he promised her.

Later she woke from sleep to hear movement in the bedroom. Alexander was undressing in the dark. She didn't tell him to put on the light, not wanting him to know she was awake.

He climbed into bed beside her. His body smelled of the outside air. No doubt he had been driving, just as he had the last time. He whispered her name; she didn't answer. He moved closer, hugging her in the dark while she lay as unresponsive as a statue.

Time passed. She remained motionless, feeling his arms around her like shackles while staring up at the ceiling, imagining that it was sinking down to smother her. The room was like a prison. One of her own making but from which she now knew that she had to escape.

Monday morning. Half past nine. She let herself into Alexander's flat.

He was at work. She had pretended to go too, then waited in a nearby coffee shop until the coast was clear. There would only have been a scene if she had told him what she was planning and after the events of Saturday night and the unspoken reproach of the following day that was something she just couldn't face.

Moving quickly she packed a bag, taking enough to last a couple of days. She was going to Suffolk, seizing the chance to clear her head, put herself together again and decide what to do.

It was only when driving out of London in a hire car that she realized she had left her diary back at the flat. She considered returning for it but the traffic was heavy and it would only take more time. Besides, it wasn't as if the contents needed to be kept hidden from Alexander. Not when he knew them all anyway.

The traffic began to ease. Gunning the accelerator she continued on her way.

Noon. Alexander stood at the window of his Whitehall office, staring down at the street below, watching civil servants jostle with tourists clutching cameras making their way towards the Houses of Parliament. His mobile was in his hand. Graham's number was on the screen. All he had to do was press the call button.

But he couldn't. What could he say to Graham? After Saturday night how could he ever look his best friend in the eye again.

Hatred for Chrissie surged through him. He tried to

fight against it, tried to push it down inside himself to the secret place where bad feelings went to die. Only it didn't. It continued to eat away at him like a maggot feeding on his insides.

There was a knock on his door. A colleague put his head around it. 'Hi Alec. We're . . . are you OK?'

'What do you mean?'

'You look sick.'

'I'm fine. Just drank too much last night. What is it?'

'We're going to the pub for some lunch. Want to come?'

The hatred grew stronger. So strong it threatened to burst his head in two.

Suppress it. You must. What other choice do you have?

'Sure,' he said.

Interview between Simon Cooper and Annabel Rice: Amberton, Norfolk, May 2006.
A beautiful Georgian country house. Simon checked his question list while aware of his companion staring at him. A handsome elderly woman, as elegant as her home. 'Is it on?' she asked, gesturing to his tape recorder.

'Yes.'

'Then let's begin.' Her tone was brisk and businesslike. He wondered if it masked discomfort at breaking the commandment of never speaking ill of the dead.

'You were friends with Alexander's grandmother, Madelaine.'

'Not friends. Acquaintances. We mixed in the same circles. An easy thing to do in a place as small as this. But no, not friends. I could never be friends with a woman like that.'

'Like what?'

'You know that already.'

'Yes. But I'd still like to hear it from you. What were your perceptions of her?'

'Controlling. In everything she did she had to be in control. The way insecure people so often have to be.'

'Why was she insecure?'

'Who can say? Her background probably played it's part. Her father was the steel baron, Joseph Gallen, as you know and I don't think she ever saw much of him or her mother. He was too busy building up his empire and she was too busy playing the social butterfly. Privileged but isolated. That was the impression I always had of Madelaine's early life.'

'What sort of mother was Madelaine herself?'

'The sort who is her own worst enemy. She wanted a child more than anything. For years she tried but suffered a succession of miscarriages so when Alexander's mother Vivian was finally born she became the centre of Madelaine's world. I'm sure that's true of many

*women who've been through similar experiences
but Madelaine didn't know how to love
someone and let them be. She had to control
them. Only then could she feel secure.*

*'It wasn't a problem with Vivian's father. He
was a weak man, happy to be led by his wife.
But Vivian was different. She was strong willed
and though she grew up here in Norfolk she
escaped to New York as soon as she was
eighteen and never came back.'*

'And then she died.'

*'Yes. And then she died. Madelaine was
devastated but in her grief showed no interest in
Alexander whatsoever. In fact on the few
occasions when she talked to me about him her
tone was almost hostile. Her husband used to
keep in contact but she made no effort to do so
herself.'*

*'So why did do you think she had him to live
with her after his father died? Surely there were
other relatives he could have gone to?'*

*'Because by that time her husband was ill. A
terminal heart condition. I suspect Madelaine
was frightened of being alone and thought
Alexander would be protection against that. I
remember when he arrived in Norfolk. Poor
little boy: sent across the ocean to live with
people he barely knew. He had this bewildered
look about him. That and a desperate need for*

affection. His grandfather gave it to him but then he died too.'

'And what was Madelaine like with him?'

'Cruel. She used to talk about his mother all the time, and though she never said it directly she never let him forget that it was his fault that her daughter was dead. That he had taken Vivian from her and that . . .' A pause. '. . . and that he had to make it up to her.'

'Only he couldn't.'

'That's right. He couldn't.' A sigh. 'The awful thing was that there was clearly a part of her that wanted to love him. There were times when she'd be affectionate with him and then in the blink of an eye it would stop and she'd push him away. Can you imagine what that must be like for a child? Never knowing where you stand. It must have been like living in a house of cards that could just collapse about you at any moment.

'And he was a lovely little boy. The sort you wanted to pick up and hug. But not Madelaine. She just wanted to control him. To make sure he'd never leave her.' A shudder. 'Some of the things she did to him . . .'

'Like the roses?'

'Yes.'

'Tell me about that.'

'You know that story already.'

'I'd still like to hear it from you.'

'Madelaine was a keen gardener. She'd spend hours tending her flowers. One day Alexander uprooted a whole load of her roses. I think she'd been particularly hard on him and he was trying to express his anger against her. Of course Madelaine was furious and to teach him a lesson she refused to speak to him. For two months afterwards good morning and good night were the only words he heard from her. Can you imagine what that must have been like for a child of eight? It must have driven him half frantic but it certainly achieved its goal. From that day on he was good as gold.' A bitter laugh. 'Control restored.'

'But he must have still felt angry. He must have hated her.'

'But after a lesson like that he'd never dare express it. What with all the loss he'd already experienced he couldn't risk losing her too. From that moment on his anger had to be kept hidden no matter what she did to him. But it still existed. Deep down inside him. Feelings that strong can never die no matter how hard we try to kill them.' Another sigh. 'As we both well know . . .'

Monday afternoon. After arriving at the cottage Chrissie phoned Alexander.

It was on the coast, at the end of a track with no other houses to be seen. A path led down to a stony beach and the cold grey expanse of the North Sea. Gazing across it she saw dark clouds building on the horizon and guessed there would be a storm before nightfall.

He sounded anxious. 'I tried to call you at work. They said you hadn't been in all day.'

'I've decided I need to get away for a few days.'

'Where?'

'Just somewhere.'

'It's Jack, isn't it? The engagement. You're upset about that.'

She wanted to deny it but couldn't. Not when he had read the diary.

'You deserve better than him. Someone who loves you. Someone like . . .'

'You?'

'Yes. I'd do anything to make you happy. Why isn't that enough?'

'Because it's not. I'm sorry, Alec. I don't want to hurt you. Please believe that.'

'What is it that you do want?'

'You've read my diary. You know what would make me happy and it's not you. I wish it was but it's not.'

'We should go away. We could go to New York. My cousins have contacts: the name Gallen opens even more doors there than it does here. They could get you into TV, anything you wanted. We could start again, just the two of us. We could be happy away from him. I know we could.'

'I can't do that, Alec. I can't run away. I have too much pride for that.'

'But . . .'

'Nothing. That's how it is. I'll call you when I get back. We can talk properly then. See if we can stay friends. I'd like that. I hope . . .'

The line went dead.

She put down the phone and looked out to sea. The clouds continued to build. In the distance she heard the first rumble of thunder.

Ten o'clock that night. Alexander sat in his flat, alone except for a bottle of brandy and the constant screaming of his thoughts.

It was over with Chrissie. That was what she had tried to tell him. But it couldn't be, not when he loved her. Not when he needed her. He had lost too many people. He could not risk losing her too.

And I do love her. The hate isn't real. It doesn't exist. It can never exist. Because if it does . . .

He knew what he had to do. Persuade Jack to go away. Give him enough money to start again somewhere else. He would pay a fortune if necessary. Whatever it took to make him leave. Once Jack was gone Chrissie would forget him: he would make her forget him. He would be whatever she needed. He would see her through the pain and at the end she would love him for it and there would be no need to hate. Everything would be safe and there would be no reason to ever be afraid.

Reaching for his jacket he made for the door.

Ali sat in *Persephone*, writing a letter to her sister. That afternoon the two of them had spoken on the phone for over an hour and Debbie had expressed genuine delight at news of her engagement. She was glad of that. She loved her sister and life was too short to waste on grudges. Better to make peace and move on.

In the distance she could hear music and laughter. The people moored on the far end berth were having a party and everyone had been invited. Jack was still there with Bullseye but she had left early, wanting to write her letter.

The boat began to rock. Jack was returning. He knocked on the cabin door.

'It's not locked,' she called out.

The door opened, Alexander Gallen entered.

Startled, she rose to her feet.

He looked agitated, his body radiating nervous energy like electric waves. 'Where's Jack?' he demanded. His words were slurred, as if he had been drinking.

'He's not here.'

'Why not?'

'He's at a party. I'll get him.'

He remained where he was, blocking the door. 'He should be here.'

'Why? What is this about?'

'You know what it's about. Chrissie and him.'

'There *is* no Chrissie and him. That's in the past. Jack and I are engaged.'

'And Chrissie's gone.'

'Gone? Gone where?'

'I don't know!'

The tension went from his body. He sank down onto the sofa, looking suddenly as defenceless as a child. Her sense of alarm faded, replaced by pity. She sat down beside him, the cabin rocking as another boat slid past in the water outside.

'What happened?' she asked.

'I don't know. It doesn't make sense. I did what she asked. I've stopped seeing Graham and Gail. Why isn't that enough?'

She remembered their conversation in the coffee bar. 'Graham? The one who's like a brother to you? She asked you to give him up?'

'Yes.'

She put her arm around him and realized he was trembling. Her sense of pity increased. What Chrissie was doing was cruel. Evil.

And he needed to see that.

'Why did you do it, Alec? Did you think it would make Chrissie love you because it won't. She doesn't love you. She can't love anyone. That's what Jack told

459

me and he's right. What sort of person asks someone they're supposed to love to give up someone else they care about. That's a terrible thing to do.'

He didn't answer. The trembling increased.

'Alec, listen to me. You have to let her go. You'll never make her happy. No matter what you do it will never be enough. Can't you see that?'

Silence.

'You *do* see it, don't you?'

'Yes.'

'You're a lovely guy. You deserve someone who loves you for the person you are. Not someone who just views you as emotional punch bag.'

'You're right. I can't go through that. Not again.'

She was confused. 'Again?'

'With her. Whatever I did for her it was never enough. I tried and tried but it was never enough.'

'With whom? Alec, who are you talking about?'

Rising to his feet he began to pace up and down the cabin. She sat and watched him. Only she didn't feel that she was watching him anymore. Suddenly it was like watching someone else entirely.

And as she watched she remembered something else of their meeting in the coffee bar. The moment when she had seen his guard drop: when the light of love had faded, just for a second, to reveal the darkness that lay behind it.

She began to feel afraid.

'For years and years I tried and it was never enough.

All my life and it was never enough! And I hated her for that. Oh God did I fucking hate her for that!'

She began to rise. 'I should get Jack. You should talk to him. You should—'

'Sit down!'

She shrank back onto the sofa.

'And now it's the same story with Chrissie. All I've ever done is try and make that fucking bitch happy but does she ever stop to think about that? Oh no. It's always about what *she* wants. What *she* needs. Well what about me!'

He turned towards her. She stared into his eyes. His pupils were widening, becoming as big as mirrors in which she could see herself reflected. Only it wasn't herself she saw but Chrissie. For the first time she realized how physically alike they were.

Fear became terror. She wanted to scream. She opened her mouth but no sound came out; her vocal chords paralyzed while he just kept talking on and on in a voice that was almost like a scream itself.

'And I hate her too. I want to make her sorry for treating me like this. I want to make her wish she'd never been born . . .'

And that was something he knew all about. From the age of six he had spent his whole life being told that he should never have been born.

As on a warm summer day in Norfolk. When he was fifteen.

It was lunchtime. His own meal finished he remained at the dining table while his grandmother finished her coffee. She was wearing her favourite pale green dress and looked very beautiful. Far more so than Graham's mother even though his grandmother was twenty years older.

He wanted to feel happy. The last few days had been good ones. She had been more affectionate than she had in months. The previous afternoon she had taken him to Norwich to buy a new sports jacket for school, discarding one after another because they didn't do him justice. As they had left the shop he had kissed her cheek and told her that he loved her and she had squeezed his arm and looked pleased.

But she didn't look it now, she looked distracted. Her eyes kept wandering over to the table by the window where the pictures of his mother stood. He watched her, feeling disorientated and helpless. Wondering what he had done to make her angry. Wanting to make her dark mood disappear but not knowing how.

Anxiety made him fidget. She frowned at him. 'Are you bored?'

'No.'

'Is it too much to expect you to sit with me?'

'I like sitting with you. You know I do.'

She lit a cigarette. He fetched her an ashtray then sat down again and continued to watch her.

'Why are you staring at me?'

'Because you look nice. That dress really suits you.'

'Not as much as it would have suited your mother. She looked wonderful in green. People always said it was her colour.'

He nodded.

'She was so beautiful. People always said that too. Too good for your father. When I look at you I see nothing of her. Only him.'

'That's not my fault. I can't help the way I look.'

'No. Nothing's ever your fault is it? Someone else is always to blame.' *She sighed.* 'I can see you're bored. I expect you'd rather be with that friend of yours. Graham. Don't you spend enough time with him already? All term and then half the holidays too. Sometimes I think you'd be happy if you never saw me again.'

'That's not true. I really miss you when we're not together.'

'But still you're going to his next week. Leaving me alone again.'

'You're not alone. You have your friends.'

'It's not the same as having you. Who can I count on in this world apart from you?'

'*You can always count on me. You know you can.*'

'*Even though I hardly see you.*'

'*I never asked to go to boarding school. It was your decision.*'

'*So maybe you should leave then. Go to a local school.*'

'*But I like my school.*'

She stared at him, her eyes reproachful. They made him feel guilty.

'*I won't go to Graham's next week. I'll tell him I'm ill.*'

'*Lie in other words.*'

'*Only to make you happy.*'

She looked back at the pictures. She didn't need to speak. He knew what she was thinking. Underneath the table he clenched his fist so tight the nails dug into his skin.

'*What do you want me to do? Just tell me and I'll do it.*'

'*Leave me to finish my coffee in peace. That's what I want you to do.*'

He walked towards the door. On reaching it he turned back. She remained where she was, sipping from her cup, radiating a quiet triumph. Knowing that he would cancel his trip to Graham's, stay in Norfolk to make her happy. Only it wouldn't. At least not for long. Nothing he ever tried worked for long.

He made his way upstairs. From the bathroom came the sound of hammering. Brian Evans, a local plumber was fitting a new bath. He entered his bedroom, staring at a poster for a rock festival he and Graham had planned to attend that summer. An exciting experience that now only Graham would be able to enjoy. Feeling trapped he walked back into the corridor, wandering aimlessly, ending up in the back bedroom with views of the woods behind the house. As he stared out at them a sense of helplessness overwhelmed him. Whatever he did would always be wrong in her eyes. The only way he could truly make her happy was to turn back time and obliterate himself entirely. Resurrect his mother for her. Give her back that which he had taken.

Make her happy by destroying himself.

Anger swept over him, so intense he felt as if he could explode. But he could never express it. No matter what she did he could never risk doing that.

He heard footsteps behind him. Marion Evans, Brian's wife, entered the room. She was a tall, thin, middle-aged woman who worked for his grandmother as a cleaner. She frowned when she saw him. 'You shouldn't be in here. I've only just dusted it.'

He didn't answer. Feeling hounded. Needing to be alone with his emotions.

'It's a lovely afternoon. You should be outside enjoying the sunshine, not skulking around in here.'

'I'm not skulking. Go away and leave me alone.'

'There's no need to be rude. I'm just saying . . .'

'What? That everything I do is wrong. You don't need to tell me, I know it already.'

'I'm not saying that at all. What's the matter with you?'

He stared at her. She was still frowning just as his grandmother so often did. She looked like his grandmother. He had never realized how much before.

'What is it, Alec? What's the matter with you?'

His vision blurred. Suddenly it was as if his grandmother was standing before him. Only this time he was not afraid to show her how he really felt.

'It would have been better if I'd never been born. Is that what you think?'

'No, of course not. Alec . . .'

'But it's what she thinks. She won't come right out and say it but I know it all the same. I can see it in her eyes every time she looks at me.'

The frown faded, replaced by alarm. The

sight excited him; made him want to hurt her.
Make her pay. Make someone pay.

'All I ever do is try and make her happy. It's all
I've ever done my whole life and all she can do is
look at me and wish that I was dead. Fucking
bitch! It's always about her. What she wants. How
she feels. What she needs. Well what about me?
Who gives a fuck about me!'

She opened her mouth. He punched her in the
face, knocking her to the ground. She cried out
and tried to crawl away but he was too fast.
Jumping on top of her, pounding her face with
his fists before taking her throat in his hands.
From somewhere far away he heard a voice.
Brian Evans was trying to pull him off but he
kept clinging onto her neck, trying to choke the
life out of her just as he had so often felt that it
was being squeezed out of him.

He felt a blow to the head. Brian had kicked
him, gashing his forehead so badly that a small
scar would always remain. Releasing his grip he
fell to the floor, watching Marion writhe beside
him, choking for breath.

His grandmother stood in the doorway, her
eyes wide and fearful. He stared into them
feeling the rage fade away, replaced by horror at
the enormity of what he had done.

The police had never been called. His
grandmother had seen to that; offering the

Evans's whatever had been necessary to protect him and the Gallen name. It took some doing but in the end Marion had agreed to tell the world she had fallen down the stairs in return for enough money to ensure that she and her husband never had to work again.

Shortly afterwards he and his grandmother had moved from Norfolk to London. He had missed a term of school, spending it in a private clinic run by a psychiatrist who was also a family friend. For hour after hour he had sat listening to the psychiatrist speak of suppressed rage and displaced aggression, crying and expressing regret while telling himself that it was all just a bad dream. A moment of madness that, like all the bad feelings he had ever had, could be kept buried in a place so deep and dark inside himself that it could never be retrieved.

Especially when there was no reason for it to ever happen again.

He punched Ali in the face, knocking her onto the floor.

She cried out, trying to back away. Trying to escape. He grabbed her hair; as thick and beautiful as Chrissie's, feeling clumps of it tear out of her scalp.

'Alec! Why are you doing this to me? I'm not her!'

He stared down into her face; her eyes full of the fear

he wanted to see in Chrissie's. Just once. For her to know that he was not nothing. That he was someone. That he had the right to exist.

'But you're in the room,' he told her. Then hit her again.

Chrissie sat by the window of the cottage, watching lightning flash across the sea.

The water was alive; a great turbulent beast ready to swallow any boatmen foolish enough to venture onto its surface. She imagined Jack sailing *Persephone* across it. Of waves washing him overboard while she stood by the shore watching him drown. But when the scene played in her head it was her father that she saw with herself swimming towards him, willing, in spite of everything, to give her life for his.

Because he was the one she really wanted. The only one she had ever wanted. Just as Jack had told her the last time she had seen him. The time she had said that she hated him and then set about trying to ruin his life. But he hadn't deserved it. It wasn't his fault. He was just a man after all, and no man could compete with an ideal.

And she wanted him to know that. Picking up her mobile she typed him a text.

'I love you. I'm sorry for what's happened. Please forgive me.'

For a moment she hesitated. Then she pressed send. The message gone she switched off her phone, remaining by the window, watching the storm rage so fiercely it threatened to split the sky.

Jack made his way along the canal path towards *Persephone*.

He was walking slowly, aware that in spite of his promises to Ali he was seriously drunk. Not that it mattered. She would just give him an exasperated look, a cup of coffee and a hug. That was what he was looking forward to. That hug. The one that told him that she loved him no matter what. Just as he loved her.

Bullseye bounced around him, clearly eager to see his mistress. 'I'm going in first,' he said forcefully. 'She's not wasting her hugs on a mutt like you.' Bullseye nudged his leg as if in protest, knocking him over. Laughing, he climbed back to his feet.

And saw Alexander emerge from *Persephone*'s bow.

His good humour vanished. Why was Alexander there? Was Chrissie there too?

What was going on?

He called out Alexander's name but received no acknowlegment. Instead Alexander hurried up the path, through the gate and out onto the road.

Bullseye broke into a run, jumping into *Persephone*'s bow and vanishing into the cabin. For a moment Jack froze, feeling suddenly afraid. Then he continued on. Climbing into the bow and entering the cabin. Then, for the second time, he froze.

It was in disarray. His possessions scattered everywhere while Ali lay motionless in the middle of them, her eyes open but unseeing. Her face and neck were battered and bloody and handfuls of her hair lay scattered around her head.

At first he just stood and stared. Feeling his head pound as his brain struggled to process the sight before him while Bullseye crouched whimpering at his feet. Slowly he backed away, out into the bow, closing the cabin door behind him.

His mobile buzzed in his pocket, signalling receipt of a text. He told himself that it would be from Ali, taunting him for believing what was only a particularly nasty practical joke.

But it wasn't from her. It was from Chrissie.

A pleasure boat passed by, causing *Persephone* to rock. People in dinner jackets stood on deck, drinking champagne and waving to the people they passed. A middle-aged couple raised their glasses to him.

Leaning forward he vomited into the water.

Half an hour later Alexander sat in the living room of his flat.

He was trembling, just as he had on the boat, but fear not rage consumed him. Shutting his eyes he pretended that it was all a dream and that soon he would wake and find himself safe in bed. But when he opened them again the scene remained unchanged and the dream continued.

His phone was in his hand. He dialled Chrissie's number, needing to hear her voice. To hear her tell him what to do. For her to save him. Just as his grandmother had.

Because she *had* to save him. In killing Ali he had only been trying to make her happy.

Or so he told himself. It didn't seem so bad when he told himself that. But the phone rang and rang unanswered.

There was noise in the street. The sound of cars pulling up outside the mansion block. Forcing himself to his feet he went to the window and saw two police cars in the street below.

This isn't happening. It can't happen. Everything will be all right. Just like it was last time.

Again he tried Chrissie's number. Again there was no answer.

Suddenly there was the sound of hammering on the door.

At first he remained where he was. Too terrified to move. Wanting to hide, but knowing there was nowhere to go. He was trapped in a nightmare of his own making from which there would never be any escape.

But it was Chrissie's nightmare too. He would see to that. He had given her his love and she had repaid him by abandoning him when he needed her most.

And she would be sorry for that.

Slowly, like a sleepwalker he made his way towards the door.

Tuesday lunchtime. At the police station Nigel Bullen stared at Alexander Gallen's face smiling out at him from the cover of the *Evening Standard*.

Tony Webb approached carrying cups of coffee. 'Have you seen this?' Nigel asked.

A nod. 'So much for keeping it under wraps. The press'll be all over us now.'

'Well it's hardly surprising. The golden Gallen boy labelled a murderer.'

'Almost a double one. That's what I was coming to tell you. We've just had an anonymous tip-off that apparently he's done this before. When he was a teenager he attacked a woman called Marion Evans. Would have killed her if her husband hadn't pulled him off.'

Nigel frowned. 'Is there any record of that?'

'No. Apparently the Evans's were paid a fortune to keep quiet. According to the source Mr Evans is dead now. Marion's still alive but in poor health. Chances are she's only got a couple of years at most.'

'So she might want to make a clean breast of it?'

'It's worth looking into. A crime's a crime, however long ago it was committed.'

Nigel sipped his coffee. 'What about Chrissie? What do you think about that?'

'Gallen insists that he did it for her. That it was what she wanted. That she said as much to him the last time they spoke.'

'Still no idea where she is?'

'No. All we know is that she's gone away.' A harsh

laugh. 'And may not come back now the shit's hit the fan.'

'Do you think she could be guilty?'

'Jack Randall's sure of it. Says she was dangerous and more than capable of trying to bring something like this about. He says her text proves it.'

'But he's grieving. His fiancée's dead. He's looking for people to blame.'

'What about the diary? Gallen keeps talking about that. Saying it's all in there. We've got the warrant for his flat. Shall I send a team to get it.'

Nigel hesitated. 'If it says what it's supposed to then she'd hardly have left it lying around, would she?'

'Why not? She didn't know Gallen would be spotted. If Randall hadn't come back when he did . . .'

'Excuse me sir.'

Nigel turned. A female officer stood beside him, holding a celebrity gossip magazine. 'I think you should see this. It went on sale this morning.'

He took the magazine. 'Is the Honeymoon over for Alec and Chrissie?' asked the headline. Two photographs accompanied the article. Alexander, Chrissie, Jack Randall and Ali Baker stood outside a cafe taking leave of each other. In the first Chrissie stared at Jack, desire clearly visible in her face.

But it was the second that held him. Chrissie was now looking at Ali; her beautiful green eyes deep pools of hostility. So raw he could almost feel the heat radiating out of them.

Savage. Brutal. Murderous.

'Jesus!' exclaimed Tony Webb who was looking at it himself.

Nigel reached his decision. 'Search the flat. I want that diary and anything else you can find . . .'

Wednesday afternoon. Chrissie drove back to London.

She felt calm. The break had done her good. With the cottage being so isolated and having bought food on the journey up she had managed to spend the time entirely alone. She hadn't even read a paper or watched the news. Though the flat had a television she had found a collection of old films on video and spent hours watching those instead.

But much of her time had been spent outside, walking along the deserted beach, staring out to sea, thinking about the future and what she wanted from it.

She had to stop hurting people. Alexander first amongst them. He was a good man who deserved someone who loved him in a way she never could. Only by leaving him would he have the chance to find them. When it was done they might manage to stay friends. She hoped so.

But most of all she had to let her father go. To make peace with his abandonment and move on with her life. Perhaps a psychiatrist would be a good start, just as Jack had suggested. Whatever it took she would do it. It wouldn't be easy but she was going to try.

She entered Kensington High Street, heading to

Alexander's flat to collect the rest of her possessions before returning to Islington. As she drove she switched on her mobile for the first time since sending the text to Jack. The phone began to ring; her message service announcing that she had twenty-three messages. The number surprised her. She assumed most would be from a frantic Alexander and prepared to listen to the first one.

Then she put the phone down.

To her left was an *Evening Standard* billboard. 'Hunt Continues for Gallen Girl,' read the headline. She felt startled. Had something happened to Isabella Neve or one of Alexander's other cousins?

She turned into Alexander's street. His mansion block was twenty yards away. A policeman stood outside it talking to a group of people brandishing cameras. She stopped. Instinct screamed for her to turn and drive away.

But it was too late. Someone saw her, called out her name. Within seconds her car was surrounded by people taking pictures or pressing their faces up against the glass. She shrank down in her seat, fighting an urge to scream.

The policeman opened the car door and leant inside. 'What's going on?' she demanded. 'Has something happened to Alec?'

He stared at her with cool, appraising eyes. 'Christina Ryan, I am arresting you in connection with the murder of Alison Baker. You are not obliged . . .'

His voice faded, drummed out by the pounding of her heart while distorted faces pressed against the glass like a pack of demons ready to drag her down to hell.

Wednesday evening. Nigel Bullen entered the interview room with Tony Webb.

It was spartan: white walls, a harsh overhead light and a table with recording equipment. Nigel had always found it a depressing place. 'Like a cell in a loony bin with the padding taken out,' he had once observed to a colleague. Now, as he considered the darkness of the story unfolding before him the comparison seemed chillingly apt.

The suspect and a lawyer sat behind the table. They had been whispering to each other but now fell silent. A sign of guilt, perhaps, though Nigel had been in his profession long enough to know that simply being in the presence of a policeman could make even the most innocent of people feel they had something to hide. It was just one of the pitfalls of the job.

But it *was* his job. And he meant to do it.

Five minutes later and the interview was underway. 'It wasn't like that,' Chrissie said for the third time. 'I swear it wasn't.'

'Wasn't it? That's how it looks to me and that's how it'll look to a jury. You see that, don't you?'

Silence. Chrissie stared at the ground, looking pale, frightened and suddenly much younger. More like a child than an adult. The way suspects so often did when confronted with the enormity of what faced them. For a moment Nigel felt sympathy. Then he remembered the details of the case and the feeling vanished as quickly as it had come.

'Let's start again. Go right back to the beginning. And remember, I want to know everything . . .'

Florida. Three weeks later. Burke Heller looked about his bar.

It was a shabby place. One of half a dozen bars in a nowhere town on the Atlantic coast. Few people visited more than once but still it had its regulars. Losers, mostly. Burned out wrecks who came to watch the sea and drown their regrets in beer. Like the man who sat in the corner, nursing an empty glass and staring at a newspaper. The big man with grey hair and the air of a prizefighter who had taken one too many punches to the head.

'Want another?' Burke called out.

The man continued to stare at the paper. Curious, Burke made his way over.

'What's so interesting?'

The man didn't answer, just kept staring. A picture of Alexander Gallen was on the cover. The case had been all over the news for weeks, the media salivating over this terrible scandal that had rocked one of the country's most prominent families. The previous evening Burke and his wife Carolyn had watched Isabella Neve talking about it on some chat show, insisting angrily that her cousin was being framed while Carolyn had shaken her head and said that Isabella was only angry because none of her exploits had ever generated the same number of headlines.

But then, none of Isabella's exploits compared to beating a girl to death.

There was another picture beside that of Alexander. One of a beautiful red-haired girl with striking green eyes. Chrissie Ryan. Alexander's girlfriend, whom, it was suggested, had been the mastermind behind the crime.

'Another beer?' Burke asked again.

Still the man didn't answer. Just kept staring at the paper.

And Burke saw that he was crying.

'Hey? What's up with you?'

The man pointed to Chrissie's picture.

'You know her or something?'

'Yes.'

'No shit! How come?'

No answer. The man just kept staring.

'Think she's guilty?'

'No. Tina wouldn't do that. She's a good girl. She wouldn't hurt anyone.'

'Tina? Who's Tina?'

'Her.' Again the man pointed to the picture. 'My daughter . . .'

Epilogue

Havelock, December 2004

Christmas Eve. Chrissie sits at the desk by the window of her childhood bedroom staring down at the street below. Though the night is cold the window is open to clear the smoke from the endless chain of cigarettes she is smoking.

The street is empty. The night air is tinged with the scent of the sea. As she breathes it in she wishes she could board a boat and sail away to a distant shore. Find a safe refuge where no one knows her.

Not like England. Everyone knows her here.

The case is proving a sensation. In the build-up to Alexander's trial the press has been speculating endlessly on the lurid facts soon to be revealed, particularly now Marion Evans has agreed to testify. For months journalists from the UK, America and other countries have hounded her every step. Firing questions. Wanting to know more. Wanting the truth.

Because she hasn't told it. Not as far as her involvement is concerned. That is the public perception. One that, no matter how hard she protests her innocence, she cannot shift.

In the weeks following Ali's murder she was grilled relentlessly by the police. A search of Alexander's flat had revealed her diary, the note about Marion Evans and the press article taken from the Internet. Police officers put it to her that she had known about Alexander's capacity for violence and used it to her own ends. Messed with his head, using her tongue and her diary as her tools, driving him to distraction until finally he was willing to take her rival's life. 'He was putty in your hands,' one officer told her. 'We've heard that from everyone who knew you both. He would have done anything to make you happy. Even kill.'

She had denied everything. Sworn it was all coincidence. That she hadn't wanted him to kill anyone. Again and again she had sworn it while they had sat on the other side of the table staring at her with cold eyes that told her more clearly than words of their unshakeable belief in her guilt.

But in the end they had to let her go. The Crown Prosecution Service decided there was insufficient chance of conviction to send her for trial. That the evidence against her was too circumstantial to guarantee a finding of guilt beyond any reasonable doubt.

Unlike Alexander. With him the case was always

clear. He is the guilty one. She the so-called innocent party. In the eyes of the law at least.

Though not in the eyes of the world. The photograph of her with Ali has seen to that. Like the infamous mug shot of Myra Hindley it is an image that has defined her in the public consciousness and from which she may never escape.

Others too have been eager to condemn her. Jack, Gail and Graham, Rick, who has told reporters about her own capacity for violence and how she had boasted of her power over Alexander. The Gallen clan, too, have attacked her in print, using their wealth and power to smear her reputation in an attempt to protect one of their own. None of it is sufficient to bring her to court but more than sufficient to damn her outside of it.

For though Alexander has the lead role in the forthcoming trial she will be its true star. The one with whom people across the world have become fascinated. The girl from nowhere who walked into the life of one of England's wealthiest men and destroyed it utterly in a matter of weeks. As she waits to hear whether she will be called as a witness she knows that even if she does not attend she will still be the dominant presence in the courtroom. Alexander's legal team will see to that: casting him as a victim, driven by his grandmother's abuse to attack Marion Evans, and by her own abuse to attack Ali. They will try to redirect as much blame as possible towards her. She will be as much on trial as him, though without the right to defend herself.

She is trying to brave it out. Keep her head high, carry on as normal and convince the doubters she has nothing to hide. But her fight is wearing thin. Everywhere she goes she sees people studying her. Judging her. Like the film star she always dreamed of being she is constantly on public view, and like many such stars she has discovered that the only way to avoid the once-craved attention is to vanish from view entirely. When the trial is over that is what she will do. Take the money that publishers and film companies are already offering for her story and seek sanctuary abroad while people forget the controversy that once raged around her.

But will they forget? Is she doomed to spend her whole life being the girl in the Gallen case. The girl of whom much was suspected but nothing proved. Will she end up like a latter-day Greta Garbo, a solitary figure pounding the streets trying to escape from an image that time has set in stone.

Her cigarette burns out. She draws another from the packet, turning the cheap disposable lighter over in her hand, remembering the day she first used it. The day when, after seventeen long years, she had finally been reunited with her father . . .

It had been a grey November afternoon. He had sat in her Islington flat, drinking coffee while trying to make her understand why he had done what he had done.

'It wasn't you I was leaving, you must believe that. It was that place. I felt I was suffocating there.'

'I know. I read your note. *I've tried but it's no good. I'm suffocating here and I can't stay. I'm sorry.* After all this time I can still quote it by heart.'

A weak smile. 'You always did have a good memory.'

'It doesn't take a good memory to remember fifteen words.'

He lit a cigarette, taking refuge in action. She watched his hand shake. His body was bloated, his face puffy and his skin florid. In spite of the clean clothes she could smell alcohol seeping through the pores of his skin.

'Why didn't you take me with you?'

'How could I? You were just a kid. I didn't know where I was going. I didn't have any plans. What sort of life would that have been for you?' His voice, though ragged, still had the faintest Irish lilt.

'You could have asked me. You could have given me the choice.'

'It wouldn't have been right. You had your life in Havelock.'

'You *were* my life. My Dad. The one person who could always make me feel safe. The one I thought loved me more than anyone. I'd have followed you to Hell itself if only you'd given me the choice.'

Tears came into his eyes. 'I did love you.'

'But still you left and never came back. What sort of love is that?'

485

He wiped his eyes, his hand continuing to shake. She wanted to cry herself: it wasn't just the sight of him but the sight of what he had become. There was no trace of the physical presence that had once filled any room he entered. His whole aura was one of defeat. He was just a pitiful, washed-up wreck. A pale copy of what he had once been.

'At least you had your mother.'

'Did I?'

'She loved you.'

'She hated me. All she ever did was blame me for your loss. She told me it was my fault you'd gone. That you were ashamed of me. That I'd driven you away. I tried to make her love me but I never could. You were the one she wanted. I was just the baggage you left behind.'

Again he wiped his eyes. 'I'm so—'

'Don't.'

'What?'

'Tell me you're sorry. It's too late.' Bitterness rose to the surface. 'It's seventeen years too late!'

'But I *am* sorry.'

'Then why didn't you tell me before? Why did you have to wait so long? Just a letter or a call. That was all I wanted. Something to let me know you hadn't forgotten me.' She swallowed, fighting her emotions. 'Do you know what is was like, day after day, month after month, praying for you to come back while not even knowing if you were still alive.'

'I've never forgotten you and I've never stopped loving you. There hasn't been a day gone by that I haven't thought about you. Wondered how you were. What you were doing.'

She shook her head.

'It's true.'

'But it doesn't help. Not from you. I need to hear it from him.'

'Him?'

'My dad. The one I remember. The one I used to lie awake at night and cry for. The one next to whom no man I've ever met has been able to hold a candle.'

A look of real pain came into his face. 'Tina—'

'Tina's dead. You killed her when you left. And you're dead too. For years I waited for my dad but you're not the man I waited for. I don't know you at all.'

His tears resumed. She watched him; her own need to cry suddenly gone, replaced by anger that he had not returned sooner to show her that the man she had dreamed of no longer existed. That he had never truly existed except inside her own head. For if he had the nightmare she was living through might never have come about.

Or so she wanted to believe.

'We don't know each other anymore, Dad. We're strangers.'

'We don't have to be. We could start again. I want us to start again.'

487

'But I don't. You should leave. Looking at you now just makes me hate myself and I have enough reason to do that already.'

Later, when he had gone she found the lighter he had left behind. Though wanting to throw it out a small part of her that was still Tina had kept it instead.

The street is quiet now. She continues to stare down at it but does not see it. In her head is an image of a fourteen-year-old girl sitting in the same room writing in her diary of how one day she will be famous and that everyone will know her name. Of how newspapers will write stories about her and everyone who has ever despised her will boast that they once knew *the* Christina Ryan.

Of how her father will read about her and come and tell her he is sorry, only to be laughed at and sent on his way.

Of how there will be other men to love her. Men like Alexander who will kill if necessary, just to stay in her life.

Of how it will happen. Of how she will make it happen.

Whatever it takes.

All she ever wanted. A dream come true.